Eileen Alder 6/13
good read. thanks

August 2012
Reham u ney
Very enjoyable

The WIDOW of LARKSPUR INN

Alice W Carter
Sept 21, 2012
Very enjoyable
Very!

Visit *www.lawanablackwell.com*

LAWANA BLACKWELL

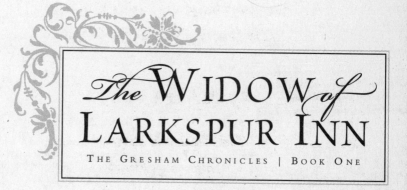

The WIDOW of
LARKSPUR INN

THE GRESHAM CHRONICLES | BOOK ONE

BETHANYHOUSE
Minneapolis, Minnesota

The Widow of Larkspur Inn
Copyright © 1998
Lawana Blackwell

Cover design by Jennifer Parker

Published by Bethany House Publishers
11400 Hampshire Avenue South
Bloomington, Minnesota 55438

Bethany House Publishers is a division of
Baker Publishing Group, Grand Rapids, Michigan.

Printed in the United States of America

ISBN   978-0-7642-0267-4

The Library of Congress has cataloged the original edition as follows:

Blackwell, Lawana, 1952-
    The widow of Larkspur Inn / by Lawana Blackwell.
        p.   cm.
    ISBN 1-55661-947-2 (pbk.)
    I. Title. II. Series: Blackwell, Lawana, 1952-   Gresham chronicles ; bk. 1.
PS3552.L3429W53   1997

                                                                    97-33858
                                                                    CIP

This book is lovingly dedicated
to my mother,
Polly Chandler,
who taught me how to be a lady.

LAWANA BLACKWELL has eleven published novels to her credit including the bestselling GRESHAM CHRONICLES series. She and her husband have three grown sons and live in Baton Rouge, Louisiana.

*London
March 1, 1869*

*How many miles to Nottinghamshire?
Sixty, seventy, eighty-four.
Will I be there by candle light?
Just if your legs be long and tight.*

Julia Hollis stopped reading and looked down at the child asleep in her arms. The combination of rocking chair and *Tales of My Mother Goose* had proved too formidable an opponent for a five-year-old's nightmares. Grace's heart-shaped face was now the epitome of peaceful slumber; her lashes resting gently against her cheeks, her lips parted slightly, and her breathing steady.

Give her sweet dreams for the rest of the night, Lord, Julia prayed silently. She did not begrudge being roused from her bed by a frantic nanny. If only her own nightmares could be chased away so easily.

From her left side came the whisper of felt slippers against the carpet. Julia turned her head to look at Frances, whose gaunt figure was swathed in a flannel wrapper, her brown hair wrapped in curling papers.

"It's time to put her back to bed now, missus."

Recognizing the injury in the nanny's tone, Julia knew that it was because Grace had refused to be pacified until she came. *What was I to do? Refuse my own child?* Nevertheless, she would attempt to make it up to Frances by asking Jensen to extend her next half-day off to a full day.

"I believe I'd like to hold her a bit longer," Julia whispered back. "Did she wake the others?"

"I just looked in on Miss Aleda—she's fast asleep. And there

7

wasn't a peep from young master Philip's room."

"I'm glad. They're just starting to sleep well themselves. And they resume lessons with Mr. Hunter tomorrow."

"And that's why the child needs to be back in her own bed. If you coddle her too much, she'll repeat the same behavior again and again."

Julia was beginning to feel a faint irritation. True, Frances had been with them since Philip was born, and responsible nannies were supposed to be difficult to find . . . but she was, after all, the children's mother and the mistress of the house. *And it's high time Frances became aware of that*, she told herself.

But then worry set in, squelching any rebellious thoughts. If she made Frances angry, she might possibly be cross with the children tomorrow. They certainly didn't need that, not after having lost their father three weeks ago. *It's probably better to compromise this time.* Giving the nanny her most nonoffensive smile, she said, "You're right, of course. But I know I shan't be able to sleep until I'm positive she won't wake again. Why don't you go on back to bed, and I'll be sure to tuck her in very soon."

"Well . . . I suppose it won't hurt," Frances said after covering a yawn. "But just this once, missus. I cannot abide a spoiled child."

"Yes . . . thank you."

"I'll go straighten the bedclothes. You be sure and tuck them around her shoulders so she won't catch a chill."

"I will."

After Frances had padded back into the night nursery, Julia leaned her head against the back of the chair and resumed rocking. The warmth of Grace's body against her shoulder and the sound of her faint snoring were comforting. She closed her eyes and her grip upon the book in her lap loosened.

If all the world were apple pie,
And all the sea were ink,
And all the trees were bread and cheese,
What should we have to drink?

"Mrs. Hollis?"

Images of inky black sea water dissolved at the sound of her name, but it took Julia a few seconds to realize that the voice had not been part of a dream. She turned to peer over her left shoulder. Jensen, the butler, stood framed by the doorway leading into the corridor. He was a man of about sixty and carried himself erect with a restrained dignity that would befit any palace guard. He was just as restrained with his facial expressions as with his bearing. In the fourteen years that she'd known him, Julia couldn't recall ever having seen him smile.

"Yes, Jensen?"

"My apologies for disturbing madam at this late hour, but there is a caller downstairs. A Mr. Deems."

"Deems?" Julia's neck began to feel the strain, so she asked Jensen to come around close to the rocking chair so she could see him without waking Grace. "What time is it?"

"Eleven, Mrs. Hollis," he answered, stepping into the night nursery.

It was then obvious that the butler had dressed in haste, for two of the buttons to his black tailcoat were misfastened, and at the crown of his head a loose strand of iron-gray hair bobbed comically. But Julia would not even think of laughing aloud.

"I informed the gentleman that the household was asleep, but he insists the matter cannot wait until morning."

"I don't recall ever hearing that name .... Deems." A tinge of some nebulous fear pierced the fog that had occupied her mind these past three weeks. Surely no good could come from a stranger's visit at this late hour. "Did he explain what the matter was?"

"Mr. Deems refused to say, madam. Only that he had been acquainted with Dr. Hollis."

At the mention of her husband's name, the now familiar lump welled up in the back of Julia's throat. One minute Dr. Philip Hollis, a brilliant surgeon at Saint Thomas's Hospital, was examining a patient, and the next, he suffered a massive heart attack and became the object of medical attention himself. But to no avail. Swallowing, she thought, *Why did it have to happen, Philip?*

She bent her neck to kiss the top of Grace's soft head. The dark curls smelled of lavender soap. *A man with a wife and three children is supposed to take care of himself. What are we to do without you?*

"Mrs. Hollis?" Jensen's voice broke into her thoughts. "If I may be so bold, I most strongly suggest a meeting with the gentleman."

Forcing herself to keep her scattered thoughts focused upon the situation at hand, Julia answered, "But if Mr. Deems is .... if he *was* acquainted with Dr. Hollis, surely he's aware that the household is in mourning."

9

If not, then the black crepe hanging from the windows should have served notice. And mourning or not, eleven o'clock in the evening was not the proper time to be making calls. Irritation replaced the apprehension that had come over her just a moment ago. To the butler she said, "Please relay my apologies but ask him to come back some other time. I'm just not up to speaking with anyone at this hour."

Instead of leaving, Jensen took another step forward and cleared his throat. "Mrs. Hollis, I must report that Mr. Deems threatens to go straight to the authorities if madam refuses to see him."

"The authorities?" Completely baffled, Julia shook her head. "But for what reason?"

The butler's brown eyes shifted evasively from hers, but not quickly enough to hide the knowledge in them. "It would not do to have Dr. Hollis's name besmeared publicly. . . ."

"My husband was beyond reproach, so how could anyone besmear his name?"

"As I stated, madam, the gentleman did not say."

But you know, don't you, Jensen? Julia thought. *And it's something you can't take care of yourself this time, isn't it?*

How humiliated he must feel, being forced to solicit her help. For fourteen years now, ever since she'd come to Philip's London home as a seventeen-year-old bride, the butler had treated her with little more than the politeness required of his station. It was as if he resented the fact that a baronet's daughter fresh out of finishing school was now mistress of the house over which he'd enjoyed almost total rule.

"Oh, he's probably a bit jealous," Philip once consoled when she broached the subject. "He practically raised me at Uncle George's, and I confess I've allowed him to take over far too many responsibilities here."

It had not occurred to Julia during those early years that it was Philip's duty to establish her as the mistress of the house and demand that she be given due respect. Unfortunately, some of the older servants had absorbed Jensen's attitude over the years, to the point that there were times when Julia felt like a guest—and one that must cause the least amount of trouble possible—in her own house. *Thank God for Fiona,* Julia thought. What would she have done without her?

"Mrs. Hollis?" There was clear impatience on the butler's face now.

"Oh, I'm . . ." *Sorry*, she had started to say. "Please, Jensen," she said, her eyes staring directly into his. "You must tell me what you know."

After a hesitation, he replied, "I would assume that Dr. Hollis owed him some money, madam."

"My husband never mentioned owing money to anyone." Of course, it was not the sort of thing Philip would have discussed with her, but the luxuries he'd provided for the family—the well-appointed, four-story Park Lane townhouse, fashionable clothing, and a battery of servants—were proof of a more than adequate income. "Is this Mr. Deems a banker?"

"He did not introduce himself as such. Mr. Deems has most likely made private terms with Dr. Hollis." Jensen flung a scathing look back toward the center of the floor, as if he could see the visitor downstairs through layers of carpets and wood. "And he would not be the first to appear at the door with a promissory note in hand."

"I don't understand."

Another pause, and then, "Dr. Hollis occasionally indulged in . . . gaming, madam."

"Gaming?" A brief, ludicrous picture of Philip swinging a croquet mallet flitted across her mind until Jensen's words sunk in. "You mean gambling?"

The butler nodded, then looked down at the still-sleeping Grace. For a second his face actually softened. "Shall I assist madam in carrying the child to her bed?"

———

They walked in silence down the staircase. On her way through the hall, Julia caught sight of herself in a mahogany-framed wall mirror. Her auburn hair hung wildly down to her waist like a horse's mane, gray shadows lurked under her green eyes, and her dressing gown was wrinkled from the heat of Grace's relaxed body. *We look like a pair of pantomimists*, Julia thought grimly, for Jensen looked little better in his hastily donned clothes. But her steps did not slacken. Anyone with the cheek to come calling at this time of night—and with such dubious intent—deserved to be greeted in such a manner.

An anxious-looking man rose from one of the incidental chairs when Julia, flanked by Jensen, walked into the vestibule. Mr. Deems appeared only slightly younger than Julia herself, tall and beardless and impeccably dressed in a well-cut gray frock coat and black trousers. On the entrance table a silk top hat reflected the lamplight with a lustrous sheen, and a pair of kid gloves, the color of rich caramel, lay neatly beside it.

"Mrs. Hollis, forgive me for intruding upon you at a time like this," he began, his eyes darting to Julia's black dressing gown.

Julia noticed a fleshiness about the patrician lines of the man's face, a faint coloring under the eyes that hinted of late nights and fast living. This was not the sort of person with whom her husband usually associated. *Philip, gambling!* she told herself. *Impossible!* She did not invite the visitor to resume his seat but stood some six feet away and said, "May I inquire as to the nature of your call, Mr. Deems? I am sure you're aware of the lateness of the hour."

A slight twitching of one clean-shaven cheek accompanied his answer. "It's a matter of fifteen pounds, Mrs. Hollis. I've a note-of-hand signed by Dr. Hollis himself."

Julia knew nothing of such things, having never seen a note-of-hand in her life. When Mr. Deems dug a slip of paper out of his waistcoat pocket and stepped across the Brussels carpet to give it over to her, she handed it to Jensen. The butler removed a pince-nez from his own pocket and squinted down at the paper.

"It is legitimate, madam," was his grave reply. "It's Dr. Hollis's signature."

When would Philip have had time to gamble? Julia asked herself. *He practically lived at the hospital.*

Mr. Deems fidgeted with his silk cravat. "I won it at Crockfords over a month ago, Mrs. Hollis. When I found out what happened, I waited as long as possible to come here, but now I'm in a bit of a tight spot myself. . . ."

You mean there's a card game waiting, Julia thought. As the man's voice droned on, she wished with every fiber of her being to creep back upstairs, bury herself in her sheets, and pretend that this visitor had never appeared upon her doorstep. But that was a luxury she could not afford at present. Acknowledging the man's apology with a nod, she said in a flat voice, "If my husband signed it, then we shall have to pay it."

She suddenly recalled what Jensen had told her upstairs, something she'd been too stunned to absorb right away. *He wouldn't be the first caller to show up at the door with a promissory note.*

"Please wait here," Julia told Mr. Deems, not inviting him to resume his seat again. She turned to Jensen again and motioned for him to accompany her out of the vestibule and through the open doorway of the hall. When they were alone, she asked in a low voice, "Where does . . . where *did* my husband keep money for such matters?"

"Why, on his person, madam," the butler replied uneasily.

"And how did you handle these debts when Dr. Hollis was away from home?"

Jensen cleared his throat. "A locked drawer in his study usually contained several quid."

Why wasn't I aware of that? Julia thought. *Has my head been up in the clouds for the past fourteen years?* "Are you saying that there is no more money in the desk?"

"There is none left at present, madam." And obviously, it was this circumstance that forced Jensen to make her aware of the situation. "But there are bank cheques. I suggest madam consider drafting—"

"Isn't there any money in the house at all?" In her present state of mind, she didn't care to admit to the butler that she had never drafted a cheque in all of her life.

Jensen shook his head. "Only the household funds, madam."

"And where are they kept?"

"In my office." Raising his chin, the butler assumed his usual authoritative posture. "But those are strictly for the purchase of provisions, and the servants' wages."

Don't allow him to bully you about this too! She realized then that she must be the very picture of insecurity, for she was nervously twisting the gold and amethyst wedding ring on her finger. Forcing her hands to her sides and her own chin a little higher, she asked, "Are there fifteen pounds?"

Indignation flitted across Jensen's expression. No doubt he resented being questioned like a scullery maid who'd broken a saucer. "I would assume so, madam. But as I made mention, those are strictly—"

"Jensen," she cut in.

He looked stunned that she would dare interrupt him but nonetheless managed a tight-lipped "Yes, madam?"

Anger, at Mr. Deems for his dreadful note-of-hand, at Jensen for his subtle intimidation of her for fourteen years, and even at Philip for his secrets, fueled an assertiveness Julia had never before possessed. "I would like you to pay Mr. Deems what he's owed."

After a brief but sullen hesitation, he replied, "Yes, Mrs. Hollis."

"Thank you," Julia said, then turned on her heel and left the room without stepping back into the vestibule to bid Mr. Deems good evening. *You'll have to replace the money from the household funds*, she told herself on her way up the grand staircase to her boudoir. After a rift with his late Uncle George's solicitor, Philip had never trusted solicitors, preferring to take care of their financial matters himself whenever possible. *I'll have to learn to use one of the bank cheques Jensen mentioned.*

A spot above her right eyebrow began to throb, and she massaged it with her fingers. Not only had she never drafted a cheque, but she had never seen the inside of a bank. The funeral had been blessedly taken care of by Saint Thomas's, since Philip was the hospital's major surgeon, and thus she had been spared having to think about money until now.

But just the idea of leaving the house for any reason drained her strength to the extent that lifting one foot above the other to climb the stairs required an extra effort. *I'm not up to any of this yet*, she thought. *But I suppose I'll have to go in the morning.* Or better yet, she would muster up the nerve to ask Jensen to attend to that errand.

In her bed two hours later, Julia discovered again that weariness was no guarantee of slumber. Images of other callers bearing notes-of-hand haunted her. *Mr. Deems has to have been the last*, she reasoned, plumping her pillow for the fourth time. Philip had been gone for three weeks now. Surely anyone else he owed money to would have presented himself by now.

A picture of the crumbling, vermin-infested tenements in Saint Giles drifted inexplicably into her mind. Every Christmas and Easter she made visits with the Ladies' Home Charity Society, bearing food, blankets, and medicines. Had *all* of the poor creatures who resided there been born into poverty, she wondered? Or was it possible that some had been blessed with wealth, only to mismanage it?

Could that happen to us? Immediately she pushed the thought away. *Philip loved his family. He would have made certain that we were well provided for.*

*F*iona O'Shea, one of the upstairs maids, woke Julia with a tray the next morning. "Good mornin' to you, ma'am," the maid spoke in her lilting Irish brogue. A capable, calming presence, she was the only servant Julia had been responsible for hiring. She looked much younger than her twenty-five years, with wide violet-colored eyes set in a delicate-looking oval face and sable black hair pinned up into her lace cap.

Julia opened one eye and groaned, "It can't be morning already."

"Ah, but I'm afraid it is." Setting the tray on the bedside table, Fiona went to the closest window and pulled the heavy velvet drapes apart. "See? The sun has been up for quite a while."

Julia sat up on her pillows, shielding her eyes with her hand from the sunlight slanting in through her open curtains. "I shouldn't have slept so long," she said, assuming that the hour must be at least noon. When a glance at the scroll clock on the chimneypiece revealed half past nine, she yawned and considered easing back into the covers. Sleep, no matter how fitful, was preferable to dragging through the day with a heart that had turned to stone in the pit of her chest.

If I lie in bed long enough, perhaps the pain will go away. But remembering that her children needed her, she asked if they'd already breakfasted.

"Aye, ma'am. They're startin' their lessons now." Fiona looked up from tucking Julia's napkin under her chin to give her a smile. The violet eyes betrayed concern, though. "I heard you were up late last night. Would you be wantin' some more sleep? I can come back a bit later."

Though the idea was tempting, Julia shook her head. "I've spent too much time in bed lately."

"Some food will give you strength." Fiona stepped back and lifted

15

a silver cover to reveal a slightly misshapen egg dish with bacon, toast, and marmalade. "Mrs. Capshaw tried her hand at some of those French omelets. We had them in the servants' hall—they're quite tasty."

"Yes." Picking up a fork from the tray across her lap, Julia manufactured a look of interest in the food in front of her. She knew the maid would grieve if she didn't eat at least some of her breakfast. If it weren't for Fiona's coaxing, Julia supposed she wouldn't even have the strength to get out of bed by now, with the little appetite she'd had since Philip's death. *I don't know how I could have gotten through all of this without her*, Julia thought.

Seven years ago an eighteen-year-old immigrant from Kilkenny, looking days past her last meal, had shown up at the kitchen door. Julia happened to be out on the terrace with little Philip when the cook coldly informed the girl that there were no positions available. The look of utter despair that came across the young face when the door slammed behind her so moved Julia that she found herself asking her husband to hire the girl.

Never had Julia been given cause to regret her impulsive behavior. Once Fiona was shown her responsibilities, she gave her wholehearted attention to the tasks at hand, while even attending evening school for servants at the nearby Wesleyan chapel. Much more than that, Fiona was a friendly presence in the house who didn't intimidate her, as did the butler and other servants, or condescend to her, as did the wives of her husband's associates.

After Julia had managed to force down half of the omelet, some toast, and tea, Fiona picked up the tray and set it atop the bedside table. "Would you like to pick out a gown?" she asked on her way to a cherrywood armoire against the wall.

"Pick out a gown?" Julia let out a sharp bleak laugh. "One black gown is as good as another, don't you think?"

"I just thought you would feel better if—"

The anger Julia had felt last night came bubbling up to the surface again. "I've discovered that my husband had secrets he did not care to share with me, Fiona. And you believe choosing my own gown will make me feel better?"

"I'm sorry, missus," Fiona said in a quiet voice.

Julia immediately felt ashamed. She had never spoken so sharply to any of the servants, and now here she was mistreating the one who had served her with unquestioning loyalty these past seven years.

Dear God, help me. I'm turning into such a shrew! Tears welled into her eyes, blurring the image on the other side of the room. "Forgive me," Julia whispered. "I was caught unawares by something last night."

"There is nothing to forgive," Fiona answered, then moved to the chest of drawers and took out a handkerchief. She came over to the bed and pressed it into Julia's hand. "Is there anything I can do to help, missus?"

Julia wiped her cheeks. She longed to tell Fiona what she had learned about her husband, but the pain was so fresh that she could not bear to have it brought out in the open again. "The strain of these past three weeks has me overreacting to everything," she said finally. "Tomorrow has to be better."

"Aye, it will at that, ma'am. God takes care of His own."

The calm assurance in the maid's voice caused Julia to muster a weak smile. How she envied Fiona's unwavering faith in God! "I needed to be reminded of that. You're such a blessing to me, Fiona."

"Me, bless you?" she replied, her violet eyes widening. "I don't see how. *You're* the one who saved me from the workhouse."

"I could always talk with you." And with Philip having been away so much, her friendship with Fiona meant all the more. *He was at the hospital*, Julia insisted to herself. As the major surgeon, he must have faced tremendous pressures. And though she didn't approve of gambling, perhaps an occasional game of cards had been what her husband had needed in order to relax.

He could have relaxed with his wife and children, a voice spoke in her thoughts, bitter as quinine, but she forced it away and moved her legs from under the coverlet and over the side of the bed. "I suppose I should choose a gown after all."

Fiona beamed back at her. "That's the spirit, ma'am."

After Julia had washed up and Fiona had helped her into a gown of black bombazine with tiny jet buttons and a modest bustle, Julia sat down at the dressing table—not because she had any interest in her appearance, but because it wouldn't be good for the children's morale to have their mother looking disheveled. Standing behind her, Fiona picked up a boar's-hair brush and set to work immediately. The feel of the brush pulling through her hair was soothing, and as a chignon began to take shape at the nape of her neck, Julia had the idle thought that any stranger looking in at the two of them would assume that *she* was the one from Ireland.

17

While Fiona's hair was a shiny ebony, Julia's was the color of burnished copper. And while Fiona's complexion was clear, save a small strawberry birthmark over one eyebrow, a baker's dozen of small freckles dotted Julia's cheeks and nose. Fiona had even remarked once that a number of her Irish relatives had the same coloring as Julia, down to the emerald green eyes.

The remark had surprised her, for Fiona was tight-lipped about her life back in Kilkenny. Julia had waited, wondering if the maid would reveal more about her family, but the topic was carried no further. All she knew was that Fiona had five sisters and exchanged letters every summer with one by the name of Breanna.

Julia respected Fiona too much to pry into her past. But it did strike her as curious that such a pretty young woman seemed to have no interest in finding a husband. Apparently others had wondered as well. Julia once overheard Alice, the head parlormaid, declare, "Fiona must be daft," because she showed no interest in any of the male servants who contended for the honor of sitting near her Sunday mornings in the servants' galley at Saint James'.

Perhaps it's good sense that keeps her from marrying, Julia told herself as Fiona clasped a tortoise-shell comb above her chignon. She immediately regretted the cynical thought. *You loved Philip.* She would have married him without hesitation had she that choice to make all over again. Thinking otherwise was to wish her children had never been born, a notion too terrible to contemplate.

The faint sound of a doorbell drifted up from downstairs, directing her thoughts to practical matters. No doubt the butcher's or greengrocer's cart waited outside while supplies were being delivered through the kitchen door. *The household funds,* Julia thought. *I should ask Jensen about the bank cheques right away.*

As she started down the stairs to find the butler—she had never once mustered the courage to ring for him—Julia realized she was beginning to feel just a bit more optimistic about the future. Assuming responsibility for the finances seemed a staggering task, but surely it was one she could learn. And it would be good to have a project with which to occupy her mind, especially since the children would be spending weekdays with their tutor again.

The butler met her at the foot of the stairs. "Good morning, Jensen," Julia said. She opened her mouth to ask about the bank cheques but closed it when she noticed his gray expression.

"Madam has callers in the drawing room," he said in a somber tone.

Julia felt a sudden tightening in her chest. "Not another like Mr. Deems . . ."

"No, madam. These gentlemen are from the Bank of London."

————

Staring across at Messrs. Forbes and Waldegrave from the Louis XV velvet sofa, Julia could almost feel pity for the two bank officers. Their faces wore the pained expressions of men more comfortable with balance sheets and profit-and-loss statements than with the grim task before them.

"H-how . . ." She swallowed against the raw ache at the back of her throat and began again. "How long before we have to leave the house?"

Mr. Waldegrave, the younger of the two, studied the fingers he had laced together over one knee. He was a thin man, with a bulbous nose that seemed at odds with the sharp angle of his jaws. His hair was slicked back with a thick sheen of pomade that had filled the room with the odor of apples upon his entrance. "The new owner has agreed to allow ten days, Mrs. Hollis."

"Ten days?" Julia gasped.

"The bank was fortunate in that a buyer expressed interest in the house so soon." His voice sounded tinny, as if echoing through a tunnel, yet the words were as devastating to Julia as if he'd roared them.

Julia swallowed again. *God help us!* She had never felt at home in this house, with its bric-a-brac infested rooms, pompous wallpapers, and furniture crafted more for decoration than comfort. But now she looked at it through the eyes of her children. It was the only home they had ever known, so she had to fight this for their sake. "I can't believe you would foreclose on a widow and her children less than a month after her husband has died."

The men exchanged uneasy glances, and this time it was Mr. Forbes who spoke. He wore bushy side-whiskers and had the faded complexion of someone who has spent the better of his fifty-plus years indoors. "Surely your husband . . ." He paused and cleared his throat. "Surely Dr. Hollis made you aware that we served warning of impending foreclosure over a year ago? A financial institution simply cannot afford to carry overdue debts on the books that long. We do regret being forced to take this course of—"

"Please." Julia held up a hand and braced herself against a fresh onslaught of tears. "No more apologies. And no, he did not tell me."

When she could find her voice again, she asked if there would be any money left after the foreclosure. The weight in her chest grew heavier when Mr. Forbes glanced down at his ledger and shook his head. "Your husband's debts were immense, Mrs. Hollis. Even after the furnishings are auctioned, we predict we will barely come out on evens."

"You're going to take *everything*?"

"You may keep your clothing, of course, and any strictly personal items. All jewelry must be surrendered to the bank for auction." He cleared his throat twice. "Mr. Waldegrave and I are required to collect your jewelry this morning."

"My wedding ring as well?" she asked, fingering the setting she had worn on her left hand for fourteen years.

"I'm afraid so, Mrs. Hollis."

Suddenly Julia grasped the reason why her jewelry had to be surrendered immediately, and it filled her with shame. Because Philip had acted less than honorably in paying his debts, did the bankers suppose she was cut from the same cloth? *Perhaps I would have held some back*, she thought. How long *would* the string of pearls or her mother's diamond brooch feed the children? *Why are we being punished for what he did?*

"Then take it now, please." Twisting her wedding ring from her finger, she held it out toward Mr. Waldegrave. "I will ask my butler to get the rest of it from the safe before you leave."

The younger banker blushed but got to his feet and took the ring. *Think about something else*, Julia commanded herself. To the bankers she asked, "What about the servants? Are they to be displaced as well?"

"Actually, the buyer has expressed a desire to keep them on. He has just retired from government service in India, you see, and currently resides at the Wellington Arms. Two grandchildren are to reside here as well, so even the nanny may continue her position."

Mr. Waldegrave nodded. "And the buyer has generously agreed to take on the wages of your servants and any provisions you will need for the next ten days, provided you agree to vacate the premises when the time is up. He wishes to avoid having it spread about town that he forced a widow and children out into the street."

The current of words was moving too swiftly for Julia. Her eyes met those of the older banker. "My children were *born* in this house, Mr. Forbes. Is there no other way?"

"I'm afraid not, Mrs. Hollis," he replied with a grim voice. "We shall assist you in contacting your family, if you wish. Surely they would be willing to take in you and your children."

"My parents were in their later years when I was born. They are deceased now, as well as the uncle who raised my husband. We had no siblings, so there are no family of whom to speak."

As Julia said those words, she thought of how she'd give anything in the world to have her mother and father seated on each side of her right now. Just their very presence would give her the strength she so desperately needed. *Mother . . . Papa . . . are you watching from heaven? You worried about my marrying Philip so young, but I was too headstrong to listen. I thought you were too old to understand what it meant to be so much in love.*

She had been only sixteen when she was introduced to thirty-four-year-old Philip at a garden party at the home of one of her school friends. How flattered she was when such a handsome, charming older man appeared to hang on her every word. And the fact that he was a surgeon intrigued her, for here was a man who saved lives in the course of his daily activities. *How could I have guessed that the gem was so badly flawed?*

She realized then that Mr. Waldegrave had been speaking and caught the rest of ". . . no shame in asking for assistance from your church. Mayfair is a wealthy parish."

"No," Julia said adamantly. "We can't live the rest of our lives on charity baskets." Besides, the children had adored their father, no matter how little time he'd found to spend with them. To ask for assistance from the church would be to admit publicly what he had done, thus condemning the children to live with the knowledge and the stigma of having a father who failed to provide for them.

Mr. Forbes' face settled into lines of profound sadness. "Mrs. Hollis," he began, lifting his hands helplessly from the ledger book on his lap, "Mr. Waldegrave and I have wives and children. We take no pleasure in this action."

There was genuine sympathy in his voice, and the resentment Julia felt toward the gentleman started to crumble at the edges. After all, it wasn't *their* doing that put her and the children in this predicament.

"I'm aware of that, Mr. Forbes," she told him as calmly as possible, pressing her hands together tightly so that the two men wouldn't notice how they trembled. *You have to think now! What are you going to do for your children?*

"Haven't you any means of support?" asked Mr. Waldegrave. "A trust from your family, perhaps?"

"I turned over a sizable inheritance to my husband immediately upon receiving it ten years ago," she answered, then couldn't stop herself from adding in an acid tone, "as would any dutiful wife."

Mr. Forbes looked through his ledger again. "You know . . . there is something here you may wish to consider."

The faint hope in his voice caused Julia to lift her chin. "There is?"

Mr. Waldegrave seemed just as surprised, for he raised an eyebrow at his partner.

"The old inn that Dr. Hollis attempted to sell. Where was it located?"

Nodding recognition, Mr. Waldegrave replied, "Shropshire. Gresham is the name of the village."

The name sounded familiar to Julia, but she couldn't place it at the moment.

"Your husband's uncle, a George Hollis, came into possession of a piece of property there shortly before his death. He'd inherited it from a distant cousin, Ethan Banning."

She did recall Philip mentioning something about some property—most likely to Jensen within her hearing, for he would not have discussed such matters with her. "There was an old coaching inn in the Banning side of my husband's family, but I believe it has been out of business for some years."

"Eight years, to be exact." Mr. Forbes gave her an ironic smile. "And that is fortunate for you, Mrs. Hollis, or the bank would likely be seizing it now as well. But truthfully, the property is useless to us. We informed Dr. Hollis of that fact two years ago when he offered it as payment for some of his debts."

"You see," he went on, crossing his knees, "the railways have cut the lifelines of hundreds of coaching inns. It was the Severn Valley Railroad that affected the two in Gresham when it bypassed the village by some twelve miles. We researched the *Larkspur*—that is the name of the inn—when your husband made the offer to us. It would be futile to open it up for business again, because the inn that is still functioning there, the *Bow and Fiddle*, is barely making a go of it."

Julia let out a relieved breath, the tenements of Saint Giles fading

22

from her mind. "You mean . . . we can live there?"

"It belongs to you, so you may do with it as you like. I don't suppose your husband sold it privately, or he would have used some of the money to prevent foreclosure."

"We're aware that you have no solicitor, Mrs. Hollis," the older gentleman said. "Therefore I'm not certain if all the necessary papers have been filed. But we will be happy to have one of our bank solicitors look into that for you. I must caution you not to expect a palace, though. The inn has been shuttered up for eight years."

A frightening thought occurred to Julia and threatened the feeble hope that had just been presented to her. "But how will we live? I have no skills beyond needlepoint." *That, and hostessing the occasional dinner party*, she thought with bitter self-recrimination. She looked down at her slender hands, of which she'd always been so proud. A lifetime of pampered living and applications of imported cremes had kept them soft and white. Now their fragile beauty seemed to mock her. *I've never had to answer my own door, brush my own hair, or brew a pot of tea.*

She realized that Mr. Waldegrave was speaking, giving answer to her question. "Gresham has several dairy farms, Mrs. Hollis, and a thriving cheese factory. The railway hasn't hurt those businesses at all. I'm certain you'll have no trouble hiring on."

"Hiring on?" she echoed, staring down again at her useless hands. Who would hire someone who'd never worked a day in her life?

Mr. Forbes must have sensed the panic in Julia's thoughts, for he leaned forward and added gently, "They won't expect you to know what to do on your first day, Mrs. Hollis. They'll train you."

"Yes," Julia whispered. "Of course."

"No doubt your son could find a position as well," Mr. Waldegrave said, avoiding her eyes.

She took in a sharp breath. "He's only thirteen, Mr. Waldegrave."

"It is not rare for children to have to help their families. I myself was apprenticed at the age of twelve."

Never! she thought, while a more desperate side of her argued, *Would you have him starve instead? How much can one woman earn at a cheese factory?*

A wave of nausea swept through Julia, bringing a clammy chill to her skin. Closing her eyes, she folded her arms tightly to her chest and waited for it to pass. *Just let me die right here and now.*

"Mrs. Hollis?"

She opened her eyes and gave Mr. Forbes, who was staring at her with brow furrowed, a somber nod. And since there seemed to be no point in belaboring the situation any further, she pushed herself to her feet and reached for the bell cord with trembling fingers. "Thank you for your concern and advice, gentlemen. We will comply with the new owner's wishes."

The men got to their feet as well, looking guiltily relieved that the visit was over and they could return to their stoical duties on Threadneedle Street. When the butler entered the room, Julia said, "Will you please show these gentlemen to the jewel safe, Jensen?"

There was a hesitation so fractional that only someone who had lived in the same house with Jensen would have caught it. "Yes, Mrs. Hollis," he replied.

Mr. Forbes frowned miserably. "Mrs. Hollis, I wish there were some other way. . . ."

"Apparently there isn't, Mr. Forbes," Julia told him. "At least we seem to have a place to live."

When they were gone, she walked unsteadily down the hallway to Philip's study. She could picture him seated in the leather chair behind his desk. His medical books stood neatly arranged upon shelves lining one wall, and it struck Julia to wonder if they would be auctioned with the rest of the household furnishings. *I hope someone burns them!* she thought, bitterness rising like bile in her throat. *Why didn't you tell me about the debts, Philip? Did you think that the problem would just go away? Were you afraid we wouldn't love you anymore?*

"That's why it hurts so much," she half-sobbed, reaching out to touch the onyx paperweight on her husband's desk. Philip had professed to love his family. Had these blows come from a stranger or enemy, they would have been far less devastating to the heart. Perhaps he *had* loved them. A lump welled up in her throat. *But not as much as he loved gambling.*

She had to leave this room at once, for recriminations were a luxury she could ill afford at the moment. From the corridor Julia turned to give the study one last look before the door clicked shut. She knew she would never open it again.

As she walked back up the corridor she paused at the foot of the staircase, seized by an almost overwhelming desire to run upstairs and take her children in her arms. If she could only hold them tightly enough, as a mother hen tucks her brood under her wings, surely no ill could befall them. She fought against the compulsion. She had to appear strong for their sakes, and never in her life had she felt so weak. Returning to the drawing room, she paced the carpet like a prisoner in solitary confinement.

They've been through so much already, she thought. *How can I tell them that they're living in a house that is no longer theirs? That everything familiar to them is about to be taken away?*

Impossible! The weight of it all threatened to crush her, and she flung herself into a chair and began to weep against one of the padded arms. "God, where are you?" she whimpered.

*S*ometime later Julia heard the drawing room door open over the sound of her own moaning. She opened one swollen eye and blinked away the haze of tears. It was Jensen, regarding her curiously.

"Would madam care for my pocket handkerchief?" he asked from a respectful distance.

She lifted a hand to show him a crumpled scarf she'd pulled from the top of the chair.

"Shall I ring for a maid to accompany madam to her room?"

"No," she rasped through a raw throat.

"Some tea, then?" There was a strange helplessness in his voice now, as if he weren't quite sure if he should leave or stay.

"No. Thank you."

"Very well then, madam," he said. After watching her for another few seconds, he turned slowly to leave.

"Wait, please." Julia eased herself to sit up straight in the chair, wiped her eyes, and blew her nose again. "I should talk some things over with you. Do you mind?"

With an "as you wish, Mrs. Hollis," he inclined his head toward her, his expression once again unreadable.

"I suppose you're aware that the children and I will have to leave this house."

He did not deny that he'd listened at the door. Philip had often joked about it, declaring that spying was the reason Jensen knew more about the goings-on in this house than anyone else. "Yes, Mrs. Hollis."

"Do the other servants know about. . . ?"

Mercifully, he answered her question before she had to finish it.

"Dr. Hollis was careful to conceal his . . . recreational activities from everyone in the house."

You mean, from everyone but you, Julia thought, barely able to stand the sight of the butler now. But she could not manage the house without him, so she swallowed her resentment and said, "The new owner is going to send over enough money to keep the house going for ten days. But is there enough money left in the household account now for our train and coaching fare to Shropshire?" She thought about Mr. Deems and wished she'd not been so hasty in handing over the fifteen pounds. No doubt it was wasted in a card game last night.

"One would presume more than enough, Mrs. Hollis. There are twelve pounds left, plus some odd shillings. But I shall send for a railway timetable to be certain."

How can he stay so composed, Julia wondered, *when this turn of events affects his life as well?* While Jensen had never pretended anything but veiled hostility toward her, surely he had some misgivings about serving a new employer. He simply stood there awaiting further orders, his face its usual austere mask.

"I don't wish to interrupt the children's lessons, but I should tell them as soon as they're finished," she said, rising to her feet. "Before word travels around the house. And if the servants ask why we are leaving, I would appreciate your not mentioning my husband's debts. They'll know soon enough after we're gone."

Jensen nodded again. "That would seem appropriate, madam."

He held the door for her to leave the room, and she could feel his eyes upon her back as she walked toward the staircase. *No doubt he's gloating inside over his victory,* Julia thought. *Perhaps he'll even dance a little jig when we're gone.* By the time she reached the bottom step, she could stand it no longer. She turned, and sure enough, he was still watching her from the open doorway.

"I know you've never cared for me from the beginning, Jensen," she said in a voice remarkably clear, considering her frame of mind. "Although I don't understand why you should begrudge a seventeen-year-old girl for becoming mistress of the house. I never interfered with your authority—never."

He simply stared at her for several long seconds. When he finally seemed to be opening his mouth to reply, Julia did not allow him the opportunity to speak. "I'm not finished," she said flatly. She had kept certain matters inside for too long now and needed to give them vent. "But no matter what grievance you have against me, I can't imagine anyone being so callused as to have no pity for the children. They've just lost their father, and now their home. Will it make you happy to think of them living in poverty, Jensen?"

She went on up the staircase, aware that she'd given him more cause to dislike her, but caring not one whit. In the nursery corridor she pressed her forehead against the closed door of the schoolroom. She could hear eleven-year-old Aleda's muffled voice reciting the months of the year in French to her tutor.

"Forgive me for my bitterness and doubts, Lord," she prayed under her breath. "But I'm so afraid."

Having lived all her life under the provision and guidance of her parents and then her husband, Julia had never needed to depend upon God totally. Now she was learning a lesson in how weak her faith really was.

A thought came into her mind then, something she supposed she'd heard in church. No matter how weak our faith, God's Word still stands true. *And it says you're the Father to the fatherless. Please show me how to provide for your children.*

"Are we poor now?" thirteen-year-old Philip asked that afternoon as Julia and her children sat together in the day nursery's window seat. Like his mother and Aleda, he had hair that became burnished copper in the sunlight shining through the glass. The cobalt-blue eyes were inherited from his father.

Julia put her hand upon the boy's shoulder. He was only a few inches shorter than her own five feet four now. Though the knowledge of her husband's irresponsibility hurt more than any sickness she'd ever experienced, and their sudden plunge into poverty frightened her immensely, she managed to keep her tone of voice as encouraging as possible. "We won't have servants or many belongings as nice as we have now. But you're never poor if you have family and a place to call your own. And this *Larkspur Inn* belongs to all of us, from the ridge pole to the cellar."

"I don't see why we can't bring my piano," Aleda said from Philip's other side. "When the Simmons moved in next door, they shipped all their furniture from their old house in Yorkshire."

"I've explained that," Julia told her patiently. She couldn't fault the eleven-year-old for despairing of giving up her music. Aleda had a natural flair for the keyboard and had taken lessons for the past five years. "Perhaps one of our new neighbors will have a piano and allow you to play occasionally."

"Will there be other children?" asked Grace at Julia's left. Grace was the only one of the children to inherit their father's curly, chestnut brown hair, though like her older sister, she had Julia's emerald green eyes.

"I'm sure Gresham is full of children. And you'll be able to go to school there. You'll have many nice friends."

Aleda wrinkled her freckled nose. "I don't think I'll like going to school with country children. They seem rather dull to me."

"Why, you've never met any," Julia admonished lightly. "I'm sure they're no different from city children."

"And schools have competitions, and recesses when you can go outside and play," Philip told his sister.

Julia felt a pain knot up inside of her at the forced optimism in his voice. He was trying so hard to be the man of the family now, helping to encourage his sisters. How could she for even a second have considered allowing him to quit school to take on a job? *We'll take in washing, plant a garden . . . anything to keep him from giving up his education.*

"But why can't you sell that old house so we can stay in London?" Aleda pressed.

"Because it would be almost impossible to sell." Julia gave the children a brief explanation of the coaching inn business decline, as told to her by the bankers. "But just because no one else wants it doesn't mean it won't make a lovely home. And think of all the room we'll have to potter about." Aleda's shoulders sagged, and Julia knew she was thinking of the neighborhood friends she would be leaving.

"It's too bad your jewelry is gone," the girl finally sighed. "You could have sold it like Charmagne Courtland did when the Duke of Torbay tried to take her land. Then we could stay here."

"Charmagne Courtland?" Julia frowned. One of the nanny's duties was to read to the children at bedtime, but reading had never been Frances's favorite activity—unless it was a serialized story from a magazine. "Has Frances been reading magazines to you again?"

"Well, sometimes," the girl admitted, lowering her green eyes. "She says the storybooks are too boring. You won't scold her, will you? She won't allow us sweets when she's angry."

"I'm only going to speak to her about it."

"Will Frances come with us?" Grace asked.

"Why, no, dear," Julia said patiently. "We won't have any servants."

29

"Then who's going to tuck us in?" Genuine worry crossed the child's heart-shaped face, which saddened Julia more than any of the children's other reactions to her news. Did Grace actually believe her own mother incapable of providing the nurturing that heretofore had been dispensed by a hired servant? *But Frances made it clear I was in the way,* she rationalized yet felt no better.

What kind of mother allows a servant to dictate how much time she may spend with her own children? she asked herself, already knowing the answer. *A childish, silly one!*

Reminding herself that her self-accusations could be saved for a sleepless night, Julia touched Grace's cheek. "I'm going to be tucking you in from now on. All of you."

"You, Mother? And read to us?"

"Every night, Grace." The smile that lit the little face made her feel better. Yet Julia couldn't bring herself to tell the children they would be spending most of their waking hours on their own in that unfamiliar house while their mother worked long hours in the cheese factory or on a dairy farm. First, she had to allow them time to adjust to the idea of leaving home.

A shrill, distant whistle sounded through the window glass. Julia and her children turned to peer over their shoulders at the terrace below. Two of the neighborhood boys were squinting up at them, and their jaws dropped at the sight of Julia.

"They've come here for the past three days," Aleda sniffed indignantly. "They want Philip for cricket."

Julia's eyes went to Philip, who was directing a negative shake of the head to the boys through the glass. "Would you like to play?"

An eagerness lit up his eyes for a fraction of a second, but then he shook his head again. "It wouldn't be right. Not yet, anyway."

Touching her son's shoulder, Julia said, "You've all shown great respect for your father's memory. But if he were here right now, he would tell you that it's time to start seeing your friends again."

"Are you sure, Mother?"

"I'm sure. As much as he loved you, he wouldn't want you to spend the rest of your lives grieving over him."

When the children were gone—Philip to his cricket match at Hyde Park, and the girls, under Frances's watchful eye, scouting for friends with whom to play dolls—Julia rested her head against the window frame and closed her eyes. What she'd just told the children about their father came back to her.

30

It's true, she thought. Anger and hurt had caused her to doubt it earlier, but Philip had loved his children. As much as he was able, that is, for his capacity for loving was obviously not as great as it should have been. *How did that happen?* Even though he'd been orphaned as an infant, Philip's late Uncle George and Aunt Winnifred had provided a loving home, had even doted upon him. In fact, his upbringing had been similar to hers, with every need and almost every want provided for. His becoming a surgeon had not been out of a necessity to earn a living, but because the science of medicine had always fascinated him.

She wondered now. Had the lack of any real hardship undermined Philip's character, as it had so obviously stunted her own spiritual growth? Was he unable to love deeply because he had never experienced a loss?

And were the children on their way to becoming just as handicapped? The notion was too taxing for her weary mind to comprehend fully, but it occurred to Julia to wonder if God were forcing them out of their soft lives to save them.

———

"But I don't *care* about keeping my position here," Fiona insisted one week later after packing one of Julia's skirts into a gaping leather trunk. "I've no family but you and the children, ma'am. Please allow me to come with you."

Julia folded another pair of wool winter stockings and set them down into the trunk. She had never helped pack before but figured it was past time she learned how to perform some of the chores that had always been done for her. "How can you say that, when you've family all over Ireland?" Fiona's violet eyes darkened, making Julia wish she could snatch back her words.

"Aye, they're family. But I can't *see* them or talk with them. And none have treated me as kindly as you have."

It would be wonderful having her with us, Julia thought as she leaned down to pull open another drawer from her walnut Empire-style chest of drawers. The argument had gone on for the good part of an hour now, with neither side giving quarter. *I wouldn't worry so much about the children with Fiona there to care for them while I'm away at work.*

But she didn't want to be selfish. Philip's selfishness had all but ruined her life and the children's. How could she ask someone she cared so much about to suffer the hardships that would be forced upon them? To consign herself to a future that promised to be bleak, at best? Straightening, she turned to face the maid again.

"Fiona, there is something you should know."

"Yes, missus?"

The hateful words swelled and stuck in her throat. Only sheer will allowed her to give them vent. "The children and I aren't moving away just because we wish to live in the country. We have no other place to go. My husband gambled away his fortune and left us in debt."

The maid gave a solemn nod. "I'm aware of the debts. I didn't realize the cause, though. I'm so sorry."

"How did you know about the debts?"

"Your wedding ring," Fiona explained. "After those gentlemen from the bank left last week, you no longer wore it. And when Alice asked Mr. Jensen if you'd be taking the silver cutlery with you to Gresham or crating it with the rest of the household goods, he told her that there would be no crating of anything."

"The silver is to be auctioned . . . with everything else," Julia said bleakly but dry-eyed. She wondered if her tear ducts had simply worn themselves out during the past four weeks. "It was a wedding gift from my parents."

"Is there no other way?"

"None that I can see." She drew in a long breath. "Oh, well. It's foolish to grieve over cutlery, isn't it? Especially when I've some very real concerns about keeping the children fed."

"And that's why I should be with you," Fiona said. "I can help."

"But I don't see how I could pay your wages."

"I don't care about wages. You saved me from starving. Won't you allow me to return the kindness?" As Julia fumbled for an answer, the maid said, "I'm a grown woman, ma'am. Old enough to choose my own lot in life, just as I did by coming to England seven years ago. And this is the path I wish to take."

"Excuse me, missus." Betsy, one of the downstairs maids, stood just inside the doorway. The sight of the calling card on the silver tray in her hand caused Julia's pulse to quicken.

Please not another creditor, she prayed silently before answering, "Yes, Betsy?"

"It's Mrs. Pankhurst downstairs for you."

Mrs. Pankhurst? Why would the chairwoman of the Saint Thomas's Women's Auxiliary be calling, when she'd already made a perfunctory condolence call two weeks ago? Especially considering that Mrs. Pankhurst had never acted overly warm toward her? "Did she say why she's here?"

"No, missus," the maid shrugged.

Julia had been reared to consider hospitality one of the most important virtues, but the thought of sitting through a social call seemed absurd after all that had happened lately. Small talk did not mix well with worries about her children going hungry. "Please tell her I'm not free at the moment."

"Yes'm."

The maid was already turning when Julia added, "And please be sure to offer my regrets."

When the door was closed again, Fiona gave Julia a concerned look. "Don't you think you should see her, ma'am? She may be offering to help you."

"I've told no one but you about the state of our finances," Julia answered with a shake of her head. "No doubt she wants me to provide decorations for some fund-raising fete."

"With you in mourning?" Fiona's voice was skeptical. "How could it hurt to hear her out?"

"I just don't want . . ." Reluctantly, though, Julia stopped to ask herself *Are you going to allow your pride to get in the way of your children's well-being?* With a sigh, she handed the chemise in her hand over to Fiona. "Very well."

She quickly walked over to open the door. "Betsy?"

Footsteps could be heard upon the stairs, and then the maid reappeared in the doorway. While her posture was attentive, her eyes betrayed some annoyance at being called back. "Yes, missus?"

"I suppose I can see Mrs. Pankhurst after all. Would you send for some tea?"

After Betsy was gone, Julia turned back to the Irish maid. "Are you quite sure you want to do this, Fiona? You won't know a soul in Gresham."

Fiona smiled. "Why, I'll know four people straightaway, missus. And dear to my heart they are, too."

Tears welled again in Julia's eyes. *Lord, you knew how much I needed a friend.* "Then, we would be happy to have you with us."

———

As footsteps faded on the other side of the door, Fiona O'Shea bent down over the trunk and began taking out the items of clothing that her mistress had packed. She smiled weakly at the folds in all the wrong places, straightened out each article, and replaced them. *Perhaps I should have shown her the right way,* she thought. But with all that was troubling Mrs. Hollis, it seemed cruel to burden her with a reminder of her helplessness.

And word was all about the house that she would be seeking work at a *cheese* factory! Fiona's lips tightened at the recollection of how Frances had smirked at the news. It had taken her years to figure out why some of the servants felt such scorn toward Mrs. Hollis, even though she'd never raised her voice to any of them. Mr. Jensen clearly regarded her with little affection, and since he ruled the house, there were some who would do anything to curry his favor.

"Even bite the hand that feeds them," Fiona muttered. Because they'd figured out long ago that the hand would never strike back.

Fiona sighed and crossed the sleeves over the front of a black silk blouse before refolding the whole garment. Mrs. Hollis would last perhaps two days at a factory—not because she was unwilling to work, but because she'd never been forced to develop the strength required for grinding physical labor. *And that's why I must come along.* While she had never taken on anything besides domestic chores, she was used to staying on her feet from sunup to sundown. Mrs. Hollis would have to learn to keep house, but at least it would require less stamina than factory work. And she would be able to spend some time with the children—so precious were they, and so much in need of their mother!

But the main reason Fiona was determined to follow the Hollises to the end of the earth, if need be, was that they had been kind to her, the missus and children. After eighteen years of mistreatment, it had been a wondrous thing to be treated as a person with feelings and needs. She did not take any of that for granted. They would have food on their table if she had to work her fingers to the bone. *And You'll help me, won't You, Lord?* she prayed while brushing the wrinkles from a poplin skirt. *Because You love them even more than I do.*

*A*nd when I heard you were leaving London, I said to myself, 'Irvetta, it's your Christian duty to do what you can to help those good people!' " Mrs. Pankhurst said from the sofa after a sip of her tea. Inclined toward overplumpness, the woman managed to restrain her generous bosom within rigid stays that pushed so much flesh up under her chin that her neck seemed short to the point of deformity. Rings bedecked every pink finger, and a gown of chartreuse taffeta billowed about her like a frothy cloud.

"I do appreciate your concern," Julia told her. After all, it *was* thoughtful of Mrs. Pankhurst to go to the trouble of paying another visit. She was not surprised that news had spread about her family's impending relocation to Gresham. Fortunately, few people were aware of the tragic events that had forced such a move. "I'm sure it has been the prayers of people like you that have helped us through the past month."

"Ah . . . yes." Mrs. Pankhurst drained her cup and set it down upon the tea table. She then scooped up another iced cake and bit into it appreciatively. When it was gone, leaving a smear of icing on her upper lip as evidence, she gave Julia a sympathetic blink of her little eyes. "You *have* been in my prayers, Mrs. Hollis. Constantly, in fact, you and your two precious little ones."

"Three," Julia reminded her tactfully.

"Oh, dear me, yes! How could I leave out little Gladys!"

Grace, Julia thought. She stole a glance at the grandfather clock against the wall.

"In fact, I've wracked my brains to find something I could do for you, Mrs. Hollis." The woman's mouth stretched into a broad smile. "And the answer came as I was having my breakfast this morning!"

"Something you could do for me . . ." Julia was slightly wary now. "Just keep us in your prayers, Mrs. Pankhurst."

"Oh, you can be sure of that. But let me tell you my idea." Mrs. Pankhurst licked her lips and pressed her fingertips together eagerly. "No doubt you're aware that my daughter, Coralie, is engaged to be married this summer. You're at the very top of our invitation list, by the way, but I suppose with your living elsewhere . . ."

Managing another smile, Julia stole a second glance at the clock. In another forty-five minutes, the children and their tutor would be taking their noon recess. The mid-March day was so unseasonably pleasant that she had asked Mrs. Capshaw to send lunch out to the terrace, where she planned to join them. Small luxuries like that would likely become nonexistent in the future.

"Coralie's fiancé—he's the second cousin of an earl, by the way—hails from Bristol, and of course, Coralie will live with him there."

"I see." Julia didn't see, actually, why this information would have propelled Mrs. Pankhurst over to her drawing room this morning, but she maintained a pleasant expression.

"Naturally, we would love for Coralie to have a beautiful trousseau so that her new husband's family will recognize that she comes from quality. But you can imagine how expensive everything is . . . the wedding *and* trousseau." Giving an exaggerated roll of the eyes, Mrs. Pankhurst added, "And here we are with five more daughters at home! It's staggering, when you consider the expense . . ."

The children have never been anywhere but London and Brighton, Julia thought. She found that she could keep up her end of the conversation simply by keeping her eyes focused on Mrs. Pankhurst's face and nodding every few seconds. *Oh, Father, please don't let them be too homesick.*

". . . and how nice it is that you've managed to keep your waist so trim after three children. Why, you and Coralie appear to be the same size."

Julia nodded again. *We won't have room in our trunks for all of their toys. But the children will need some reminders of their lives here. Perhaps we could pack a small satchel with their favorite keepsakes.*

". . . likely you'll be wearing black for at least a year, won't you? By the time you start wearing colors again, the styles will have changed. What a shame to waste such lovely gowns!"

Surely there will be enough lawn for a vegetable garden. I wonder when it's the proper time to plant seeds?

". . . and ordinarily, I wouldn't *dream* of buying used clothing," Mrs. Pankhurst said, wrinkling her pert little nose. "But with Coralie living in Bristol, no one would be the wiser."

Those last words caught Julia's attention. She cocked her head, not sure that she had heard correctly. "I beg your pardon?"

"It's a way to help both of us . . . don't you see?"

Realization sunk in. "You're offering to buy my clothes?"

Mrs. Pankhurst gave her a shrewd smile. "Not at the price *you* gave for them, of course. After all, they aren't new. And with Coralie being somewhat shorter than you . . . there is the cost of altering the skirts to be considered. But I'm sure you could use every little extra bit now, couldn't you?"

Suddenly Julia recalled being introduced to a cousin of Mrs. Pankhurst's at a hospital auxiliary dinner party last year. *His name was Waldegrave—and Mrs. Pankhurst mentioned that also being her maiden name.*

She knew now with dreadful certainty that Mrs. Pankhurst and the bank officer Mr. Waldegrave were related. In all likelihood, the woman sitting before her had known of Philip's debts before she herself had been informed! Struck speechless, Julia could only stare at the woman, who had obviously not noticed her shock and was going on about the exorbitant price of hiring a skilled alterations seamstress.

The door from the hallway opened before Julia could find her tongue. Jensen walked into the room carrying a wool wrap and snapped to attention at the side of the sofa. "Here is your wrap, Mrs. Pankhurst."

Mrs. Pankhurst was startled into silence for a fraction of a second, then lifted her chin. "Oh, but I wasn't leaving."

"Oh, but you were," the butler insisted, his expression benign.

"You misunderstand, I'm sure."

"On the contrary, madam. I understand everything."

Her cheeks flushing crimson now, Mrs. Pankhurst raked Jensen with a withering look before leveling her eyes at Julia. "I say, Mrs. Hollis, do you allow your servants to treat your guests so rudely?"

Staring up at Jensen with her mouth agape, Julia could only mumble, "Apparently so."

The older woman heaved herself up to her feet and snatched the wrap from Jensen's hand. "Well, I've never heard such cheek!"

"I shall be happy to show you to the door, madam," the butler offered, unruffled.

"When pigs fly, you will!" Mrs. Pankhurst's skirts made a hissing sound as she stalked to the drawing room door. There, she wheeled around and stabbed the air with a plump finger. "Everyone said that Dr. Hollis was foolish to marry such a child, Julia Hollis, but *I* was willing to give you the benefit of the doubt. Now I can see it was only the *beginning* of his road to ruin!"

She grabbed hold of the doorknob and seemed poised to slam it, but then turned again to direct a parting gibe.

"And those cakes were practically tasteless, by the way!"

The door thundered shut, rattling teacups against their saucers. Her face burning from the insults Mrs. Pankhurst had flung at her, Julia stared at the silent butler for one long moment. "Thank you, Jensen," she said when her heart had finally stopped pounding against her ribcage.

He acknowledged her gratitude with a nod. "Is madam all right?"

Julia glanced back at the closed door, and a shudder caught her. "I'm fine. I think. But she was quite odious, wasn't she?"

"Quite so, madam."

"I suppose I should have accepted her offer to buy my gowns, though. Every little bit *would* help."

Jensen shook his head. "There are legions of used clothing shops on Petticoat Lane if madam wishes to sell some garments, and she would no doubt fetch a better price than what Mrs. Pankhurst would offer. But it shouldn't be necessary."

"What do you mean?"

"May I speak plainly, Mrs. Hollis?"

"Of course," Julia answered, still not quite sure what to make of this new side of Jensen she was seeing. Motioning toward the nearest adjacent chair, she said, "Please . . . have a seat."

The butler stared at her as if she'd asked him to perform a ballet upon the tea table. "That would not be proper, madam."

"And was it proper for you to dismiss Mrs. Pankhurst?" Julia couldn't resist asking with an innocent lift of her brows.

Jensen's face flushed, but nevertheless he lowered himself gingerly onto the edge of the chair cushion, as if it were a bed of nails. Clearing his throat, he said, "I am quite fond of reading periodicals, Mrs. Hollis. And I have noticed an interesting trend of late."

He stretched out to hand her a folded piece of paper from his right coat pocket. "From the February issue of *The New Monthly Magazine*," he explained as she opened up the paper.

Julia's eyes quickly scanned the printed page—it looked to be a continuation of an article having to do with bird-watching on the Isle of Saint Agnes.

"The top right corner," Jensen said before Julia could raise a question.

She looked—it was an advertisement listing all of the amenities of a particular lodging house at Weymouth Beach. "That's very nice," Julia told him, lowering the page. "But why are you showing it to me?"

"I often see advertisements such as this. But they're almost exclusively for the tourist cities, such as Weymouth and Brighton, and then, primarily seasonal rentals. Why doesn't madam consider turning her coaching inn into a lodging house?"

"A lodging house?" Julia shook her head. "But from what I've been told, Gresham is a dairying village—not a tourist city by any stretch of the imagination."

"Exactly. I've been to Weymouth, Mrs. Hollis, on holiday with my brother's family. And while it was a pleasant diversion, I would not care to take up permanent residence in such a transient atmosphere."

The idea of staid, somber Jensen splashing in the waves flitted across Julia's imagination, and she found herself struggling to keep back a smile. Jensen seemed to read her mind, for he lifted his chin a fraction.

"I do not care for sand in my shoes and clothing, Mrs. Hollis. I allowed the younger ones to take on the beach."

Suitably chastened, Julia nodded.

"One would have to compose the advertisements with *permanent* lodgers in mind," the butler continued, as if no break in the flow of conversation had occurred.

"But who would want to take up permanent residence at a lodging house? Oh, I know there are hundreds in London, but in a dairy village?"

"People of advanced age, Mrs. Hollis, for the most part. Those weary of living in congested, noisy cities, but who do not care to take on the responsibilities of a house and servants in the country. Those who are loathe to be dependent upon their families but are too well off for the almshouses. As one ages, one is willing to pay a premium for peace. And Gresham is a pleasant place, Mrs. Hollis. Green and quaint."

"You mean . . . you've been there?"

"I have." His expression became grim. "I served as Dr. Hollis's valet when he visited there two years ago. Madam was in Brighton with the children."

"But he said he had surgeries to perform. Why did he go to Gresham?"

Taking a deep breath, the butler explained that his master had wanted to inspect the *Larkspur Inn* before offering it as payment for some of his debts. "He was concerned that the bankers would take advantage of his desperation and decline to offer the full value of the inn. As it turned out, the bank declined any interest whatsoever."

And so he sent us off on holiday beforehand so I wouldn't find out about his debts, Julia thought. What a wretched secret life her husband had led! But she reminded herself abruptly that, with her family's future at stake, this was not the time to brood over Philip's painful betrayal.

"This coaching inn," she asked Jensen, "what kind of shape is it in?"

"It is structurally sound, in spite of its two-hundred years. Ethan Banning added water closets and lavatories to each floor only a year before his passing away. There are cupboards of linens and cookery too . . . almost everything needed to set up housekeeping."

Julia mulled over Jensen's suggestion. To be able to stay at home with the children would be the most wonderful blessing imaginable. But what did she know about managing a lodging house . . . or any other business? She had never even managed her own household.

"It sounds so . . . risky," she finally said, "and with the children's livelihood at stake, I don't know if I dare."

"And what would madam be risking?" Jensen pressed. "The price of some advertisements? You already own the building and furnishings. Put them to good use."

"But I've never tried to manage a business before."

"No one was ever *born* having managed a business, Mrs. Hollis. Madam could learn."

I could learn, she echoed silently, but then remembered the dismal reality of their poverty. She shook her head and told him in a flat voice, "I shall have to find a position as soon as possible, Jensen, or we'll starve. Fiona will be with us, but she cannot possibly transform the inn into a lodging house by herself. Not with it having sat idle for eight years."

Without a word, Jensen shifted to his right so that he could take something from his left pocket. He stood briefly to give her another paper, then resumed his chair. "Another advertisement?" Julia asked as she unfolded the paper, but then stared at a bank cheque written for one hundred pounds. She looked at the neatly scripted signature at the bottom—*Lawford Jensen*—and thought, absurdly, considering the circumstances, *I never even considered that he had any other name but "Jensen."*

"I cannot accept this," she said, holding the cheque out toward him. "But you'll never know how much it means to me that you would offer it."

As he sat there before her, the butler's features settled into their usual calm. "Then consider it a loan, Mrs. Hollis. It was a legacy bequeathed to me by Mr. George Hollis, Dr. Hollis's uncle—I was his butler for some years before Dr. Hollis moved into this house. I would suggest madam use it to bring the six guest chambers up to a standard that lodgers of means will expect. Wallpapering and such. And when madam's establishment has been operating profitably for some time, I will look forward to being repaid."

She didn't know what to think. As casual as Jensen was about the money, it was likely his security for the years when he could no longer perform his duties. What if she failed? But then the children's faces came to her mind. *You can't even think about failure,* she told herself. To Jensen, she said, "You're *that* certain I can do this?"

"I am, Mrs. Hollis."

"And people will want to live there?"

"I would not be investing a hundred pounds if I did not think so."

For the first time in at least a decade, Julia found herself smiling at the butler. And for the first time ever, he smiled back. "Why are you doing this for me?" she asked.

Jensen's brown eyes took on a suspicious liquid sheen. He focused them at something just over her shoulder for a second, then back at her. "I was aware that Dr. Hollis was throwing away money at the card tables, Mrs. Hollis. But *never* did I imagine that things would come to this. He commanded such imposing wages from the hospital."

"What happened wasn't your fault, Jensen."

"But perhaps if I had warned you . . ."

Now the smile that Julia gave him was a bleak one. "I would have approached my husband about it, yes, and he would have assured me that you were overreacting." She could picture them together now, Philip's taking her chin gently between his fingers and joking about what a worrier his butler was. In the end, they both would have laughed, and then Philip would have changed the subject to some humorous observation he'd made about one of the administrators at Saint Thomas's.

"And I would have believed him," she added.

The butler let out a long sigh. "Thank you for being so generous with your assurances, Mrs. Hollis—however ill-deserved on my part." His face then took on a cautious expression. "If I may be so bold to add, madam, I do not believe Dr. Hollis intended to inflict such hardship on his family. He was as beguiled by the cards as the drunkard is by his gin. That was his great weakness."

"I know that now," Julia sighed. "And mine was blindly trusting that all was as it should be." She looked down at the cheque in her hand again. "Jensen . . . if this is because you feel you have to atone for anything—"

The butler held up a hand. "I have a tendency to be judgmental where people are concerned, Mrs. Hollis. You were correct in pointing out that I've wronged you from the beginning. Perhaps it is atonement I am seeking, but it feels . . . well, rewarding, to do this for you and the children."

"Truly . . . I don't know what to say."

"It is not required of you to say anything, Mrs. Hollis. Just put it to good use. And if I may make another suggestion . . . post the advertisements as soon as possible. Newspapers in the cities would provide the most immediate publication. I can procure a list from the reading library if madam so desires."

With a nod toward the clock, Jensen made an abrupt change of subject. "Is it not time for the children's lunch recess?"

"Yes," Julia said, rising from her chair. The butler immediately got to his feet as well. But instead of leaving the room, Julia took two steps over to Jensen and put her arms around him. He stood there, rigid as a gatepost during the embrace, but when she took a step backward, he looked pleased.

"You have given me and my children new hope for the future, Jensen," Julia told him. "From the bottom of my heart, I thank you."

"Not at all, madam."

"And if you would *ever* care to move to Gresham, you've a place to live. Always."

"Very kind of you." The butler's eyes took on a sheen again just before he turned toward the door. "I should make certain the collier delivered the correct order."

Julia smiled at his retreating back. "Yes, you should do that."

*J*ulia turned her head to take another look out of the hired coach's window on her right side. The passing north Shropshire farmland was blanketed by a morning haze, broken occasionally by a dense hedgerow or black-and-white half-timbered farm building. A pleasant odor of damp earth permeated the air. Over the hum of wheels and dull thuds of horses' hooves against the macadamized road surface, she thought she could hear a faint lowing of cattle, no doubt heading from a barn into the fields.

She settled back into her seat and looked around at her fellow passengers. They could have made the journey from London in one day, but Jensen had advised against it.

"It would be best to arrive in Gresham in the morning," he'd said. "You will need several hours to ready the house for sleeping. Besides, the children will require rest after seven hours on the train."

Since leaving the inn at Shrewsbury this morning, the children and Fiona had lapsed into a contemplative silence, no doubt wondering about the life that lay ahead. Julia breathed another prayer of thanks for the way her children seemed to accept moving to a new home. Only Aleda had shed some tears as the day drew closer, but even she began to show some interest as she helped Frances pack her things.

Now Julia's petition to God was that He would make her capable of running the *Larkspur Inn*. The ambitious plan Jensen had given her would take a great deal of confidence, something of which she found herself woefully lacking. *But you know how to make people feel at home,* an inner voice comforted. *Surely that's more important than any business experience.*

"Why, I do believe I see a hill in the distance," Fiona said, staring out of the window on the left side. "Could even be a mountain."

"We must be nearing Gresham." An anxious chill ran through

Julia at the thought. "That has to be the Anwyl you're seeing."

"The Anwyl, ma'am?"

Julia leaned over Grace, who was seated between them, and peered through the window herself. In the northwest rose a stout brownish green hill of some five hundred feet. "From an old Celtic word for 'beloved' . . . according to Jensen. The cheese factory uses its picture as a trademark."

"Of course! *Anwyl Mountain Savory Cheeses.* Why, Mrs. Capshaw wouldn't tolerate any other brand in her kitchen."

"Do you think we'll be allowed to hike it?" Philip, seated across from Fiona, asked his mother after taking a look himself. The boy wore a splint and bandage on his left finger, souvenirs from his latest cricket match. "I've never hiked before."

"I don't see why we shouldn't," Julia answered, relieved to hear some excitement in his voice. "Wouldn't it make a lovely picnic?"

Grace nodded absently from beside her, though it was obvious she hadn't paid attention. In her lap she held a tin bucket with *Cooper's Snowy-white Lard* stenciled on the side. The girl had snatched a sparrow from the jaws of the neighbor's cat—but not soon enough to prevent damage to its wing, which Jensen had splinted for her. Settled on a nest of soft grass, the bird would let out a tentative *peep* every so often, causing its rescuer to lean down and coo reassuring words.

"He's just worried," Grace said to the others, her small face wearing its usual somber expression. "He's never been away from his home before."

Next to Philip on the rear-facing seat, Aleda stopped brushing the hair of her porcelain doll long enough to inform Grace that birds didn't care where they lived, as long as there was food nearby. "He likely doesn't even know the difference between one town and another."

Grace ignored her sister and lowered her face back to the top of the pail. "You'll be at your new home soon," she cooed down at the bird. "And just you wait and see how nice it is."

Turning back to peer from her own window, Julia caught sight of a red sandstone church tower off to the northeast. It rose above a group of dwellings as if they were its brood, and the sight of it brought her a measure of comfort.

Living in the country will be good for us, she reminded herself. *It's just going to take some getting used to.* The trick was to not allow the things she had loved about London—Hyde Park, omnibuses, Grosvenor Square, coffeehouses, the National Gallery, operas, Charing Cross—to occupy any space in her mind. One couldn't plan for the future while clinging to the past. And hadn't Jensen impressed upon her that a country village would be better than London for raising children?

True, Gresham would not offer the same cultural and educational opportunities of the city, but she could plainly see that neither was its air tainted with black fog from thousands of coal chimneys. Nor, by Jensen's account, was the water from the River Bryce, which ran east to west through the north part of the village, evil-smelling and choleric from raw sewage like the Thames. *And the children will have the security of knowing that their surroundings will stay the same.* Not like London, where streets were constantly being dug up for continued expansion of the underground railway system.

The wheels left the macadamized road surface and took on the cobbled stones of a lane, causing the coach to give a slight lurch and Grace to cradle the tin more tightly in her arms. Dainty shops and pleasant little cottages lined each side of the shady lane, flecked with broken sunlight filtered through the trees that stretched out their branches overhead. From Julia's window a huge half-timbered house came into view. She held her breath hopefully, but let it out again when a signboard displaying the words *Bow and Fiddle* caught her eye.

She knew from Jensen that this was the village's other unfortunate coaching inn that at least had managed to keep its kitchen fires going because dairymen, farmers, and factory workers still needed a place to trade stories over clay pipes.

They passed more cottages and shops, and then the horses slowed almost to a stop at an intersecting lane. On the far left sat a two-story building, facing the east. Julia leaned closer to the opposite window. She did not need to even glance at the old wooden signboard that hung askew on a post outside the gate, for the desolation of the place told her that it was the *Larkspur Inn.* Moss and ivy swarmed over weathered red sandstone walls and shuttered windows, and the garden behind the low stone wall was choked with weeds. Early blooming flowers that had obviously reseeded themselves added splashes of color as they valiantly struggled to survive in the melee, but it would take more than a few flowers to dispel the gloom that hovered over the house and gardens.

Well, I was warned, she thought dully but couldn't tell if her sudden nausea was brought on by the long coach ride or by the thought that her family's future security lay inside those neglected walls.

The coach turned west and rolled another thirty yards before turning right into a gravel carriage drive. In the crook of the L-shaped inn was a large flagstone courtyard, fringed by stables, a coach house, gardening cottage and potting shed, and overgrown areas that had likely been a bowling green and kitchen garden. Once the five passengers were helped to the ground, the coachman began withdrawing luggage from the boot. Meanwhile, the three children stared at the back of the inn with expressions of stunned disbelief.

"I warned you it would need some sprucing up," Julia said, biting her lip.

"Well, it's certainly got the fireplaces, hasn't it?" With typical optimism, Fiona pointed up at the six chimneys rising above the slate roof. "We'll always be warm and cozy."

"But it's such an ugly house, Mother," Grace said. She held a hand over the top of her lard tin, as if to shield the sparrow from such a sight.

It is at that, Julia thought. *But it's a far cry from the tenements of Saint Giles.* She reached down to scoop her youngest daughter, tin and all, into her arms. Pressing the soft cheek to her own, she turned her face toward the house again. "But it's all ours, my sweet Grace. And we'll make it pretty."

She felt a touch at her arm and turned to see Philip staring at her. "When are the lodgers coming?"

Julia reached up to tousle his auburn hair. "Our advertisements should be published in a week or so." Following Jensen's advice, she had sent the advertisements to newspapers in the major cities instead of to monthly periodicals, so that they would be printed sooner and receive more exposure. "We'll find out after that." *It can work,* she reassured herself, refusing to give ground to the negative thoughts that loomed in the back of her mind. *God gave us the idea through Jensen—and He'll help us make it work.*

She set Grace back on her feet, turned to the coachman, and dug his fee out of her beaded reticule. As she tipped the man an extra florin to bring the trunks and bags inside, she heard a voice as raspy as dry leaves drift over from across the lane.

"So . . . ye've come to live in the *Larkspur,* have ye?"

The group turned, and Julia sent a wave to two white-haired women seated in front of a thatched-roof cottage. She had heard of lace spinners, had even seen them used as subjects of paintings, but had never before actually seen any in person. In the centuries-old custom, the women sat in the sunlight with lap cushions, pins, patterns, and reels of thread to weave their delicate laces.

"Yes, we have," Julia answered genially.

"We're Iris and Jewel Worthy, dear." This came from a voice as soothing as the first had been grating. "Jewel was a Perkins before she married my brother Silas."

"I moved in with my sister-in-law after my husband passed away," the one named Jewel explained. Her nimble fingers never slowed down from winding threads around the pins sticking from her pillow. "Folk have called us the Worthy sisters for years, even though we ain't blood related. And ye are. . . ?"

"Julia Hollis." A wagon bearing a man wearing the fustian work clothes of a laborer passed between them, slowing so the driver could cast a curious stare at the group standing in the carriage drive. Julia offered a smile, but the man gave a quick nod in return and directed his attention back to his team. When the lace spinners were in sight again, Julia made quick introductions of her children and Fiona, then sent the Worthy sisters another wave. "It's a pleasure to make your acquaintance. We should go inside now."

"Ye aren't going to sleep in there tonight, are you?" the raspy voice queried.

Julia turned. "I beg your pardon?"

"Nothing, dear," Iris answered with a sharp look at her sister. "But do pop over later when you've time. There is something you'll want to know."

Jewel's white head bobbed in agreement. "Come *alone*, mind you."

"What did she mean by that?" Aleda asked, clutching Julia's sleeve with one hand and her doll with another as the group walked across the courtyard, shaded by a sentinel oak with wide-reaching branches. The driver brought up the rear, shouldering a heavy trunk.

"I'm sure it's nothing, dear." They passed cast-iron benches mottled with algae before arriving at a solid oak door. A wrought-iron bell pull was fastened to its frame, worn smooth by generations of hands that tugged at it. Julia fished the ring of keys, two candles with tin holders, and matches from her satchel and said to the children, "Now remember, it's been closed up for eight years."

"Will there be mice?" Still at her side, Aleda asked the question

47

in a low voice so as not to alarm Grace.

"I wouldn't imagine," Julia answered, at the same time sending up a quick, *Please, Lord, no mice!* She tried one key and then another. "There should be no food inside to attract them. We should probably get a cat later, though."

"A cat?" It was Grace, the animal lover, who perked up at this. "Can it be a mother cat, so she'll have kittens? And black, please, with a white face and paws."

"Just as soon have the mice, if it was me," grunted the overburdened coachman from the rear. "Will ye open that door, or are we to stand out here all—"

"This is the right one." The rusty hinges squeaked and the door stood wide open. Julia was encouraged to hear no scurrying sounds as she peered inside. A corridor stretched out before them, mustysmelling and murky black beyond the light coming in from the doorway.

Julia lit her candle and stepped inside. Now that the corridor was illuminated, Julia could see that it was actually a very short one, emptying into another longer corridor running the long part of the "L" of the house. It looked no less forbidding, however, for cobwebs hung as thick as bed curtains in some spots. Aleda came up behind her and gripped at her sleeve again. "Please, Mother, let's leave now," she whimpered.

"It's going to be just fine, Aleda," Julia answered, wiping a string of cobweb from her cheek as she took another step forward.

"Would you like me to lead the way, ma'am?" asked Fiona, her candle now glowing.

The idea was enormously tempting, but Julia turned down her offer. What message would be sent to the children if she were to cower behind Fiona? She turned to the right and walked cautiously down the corridor, passing two closed doors at either side of her before pausing at the arched open doorway to a central hall. Julia took a step through the doorway and gasped when something crunched beneath her foot. Behind her, Aleda let out a squeal.

"What is it, ma'am?" Fiona asked from the rear.

"I don't know." Julia lowered her candle, and discovering something resembling dried leaves scattered over the stone floor, she scooped up a crumbling handful. "How odd. Why would anyone strew leaves all over the floor?"

Fiona stepped past the children and into the room, then bent to take up some leaves. Her circle of amber candlelight then illuminated her smile. "They're likely meadowsweet—perhaps some lavender as well. To keep away mice and moths."

Thank you, Lord, Julia prayed, silently blessing whoever had had the foresight to take such precautions. Holding the candle above her head, she could make out a high rafted ceiling and cavernous stone fireplace. Sheets covered with dust draped every piece of furniture, many showed signs of rot where the years of neglect had taken their toll. Combined with the cobwebs, they gave the room a decidedly ethereal atmosphere.

The children came into the room in a huddle. Julia turned to reassure them that the room would look quite different when cleaned and was disheartened to see that the anxious expressions upon their faces had deteriorated into something resembling terror. *Perhaps we should stay at the Bow and Fiddle for a couple of days until the place is more presentable,* she thought.

They had sufficient money to do so. Besides the hundred pounds lent to her by Jensen and the six quid still left from the original household money, she had an extra thirty-five pounds from selling several gowns to a shop on Petticoat Lane. Some were of Parisian design and worth five times what she received for them, but she'd been too grateful for the extra money to feel any loss. In fact, she would have culled out even more of her wardrobe had not Fiona persuaded her to keep some colorful gowns for when her year of mourning was up. "You won't be wearing black forever," the maid had argued. "And your lodgers will expect their landlady to look cheery and presentable."

But I've no idea how much it's going to cost to refurbish the house, Julia thought, mentally counting the money again. How could she know, until all the rooms had been examined and cleaned? And her children's futures lay in making the *Larkspur Inn* presentable to lodgers who were accustomed to quality.

The driver grunted from beneath the trunk. "Where d'ye want this?"

This is our home. We have to stay. Julia shot a questioning glance to Fiona. But where indeed should the luggage go? She wasn't even sure which bedrooms they would choose for their own yet.

"How about in here?" Fiona suggested. "We can always move everything later."

"Yes, that's fine," Julia said to the coachman. "But why don't you rest before unloading the others?"

49

"Want t'make Shrewsbury before lunch," the driver replied. When he was gone, accompanied by Philip to hold the door for him when he returned with another load, and while Fiona went to look for the lantern room, Grace pointed to a sheet-covered form in a familiar shape. "Look, Aleda!" she exclaimed. "That looks like a piano. You'll be able to play for us."

"I'm not touching anything in *this* house . . . ever," her sister sniffed.

Julia squelched the sharp words that rose in her throat. *She just needs time to get used to the idea.* Mercifully, a few minutes later the doorway they had walked through earlier became brighter and brighter, until Fiona appeared carrying two paraffin lamps. "I found a lantern room just inside the courtyard door," she said, placing one on each side of the chimneypiece. "Candles, paraffin, and gallons of oil. We'll have enough light for months to come. And I'll bring more lanterns in here when we've uncovered the tables. A little light always makes a room more hospitable."

This fact lifted Julia's spirits, but the girls still huddled close to her with dazed expressions. *Give them something to do*, she thought when Philip had returned and the coachman was gone. *It'll keep their minds occupied*. And today was as good a day as any for the children to understand that the days of having servants attending their every need were over.

"Look, children, I've a little chore for you," she said.

"Chore, Mother?" Philip said, but the puzzlement was across all three faces. Julia sighed inwardly, recalling the two times she'd explained to the children that their help would be vital to making the *Larkspur* a success. It still obviously hadn't sunk in, for now all three sets of eyes had drifted over to Fiona.

Aleda was the only one with enough bluntness to voice what they were all thinking. "But why can't Fiona do it?" There was no animosity in her voice, just the incomprehension of a child who'd taken it for granted all her life that children amused themselves and servants did the work.

"Because Fiona can't do it all. And she and I need to see how the other rooms are laid out." Moving over to a sofa-shaped form, Julia took up a corner of the sheet and snatched it aside. A cloud of dust overwhelmed her nostrils and brought on a fit of sneezing.

"It's better to fold the sheets aside, ma'am," Fiona said tactfully as Julia wiped her eyes with her handkerchief. The maid demonstrated, lifting a corner of the cloth and making a series of folds until a Georgian tea table with cabriole legs was uncovered. "We should go through the sheets later to see if any are worth salvaging. The others we can cut up for cleaning rags."

"See?" Julia said with forced cheeriness after blowing her nose. "The rooms won't look so frightening when the furniture is uncovered. You can busy yourselves with that while Fiona and I decide where we're to sleep."

Aleda's face fell again. "It'll take years and years to clean this old house. Why don't you hire more servants now?"

"And why don't *you* stop complaining!" Julia snapped, her nerves strained to the limit. Immediately regretting her burst of temper, she walked over to put an arm around Aleda's young shoulders. The girl buried her face in Julia's side.

"Yes, in time we will," she said softly. "But it's never going to be like it was in London. We're going to have to learn to do some things for ourselves."

"I *hate* this place! I want to go back *home*!" Aleda said amidst muffled sobs.

"I know you do," Julia murmured as she smoothed the girl's auburn hair and allowed her to cry while the others looked on with long faces. Close to dissolving herself, she thought, *If you could have looked ahead to the future, Philip, and seen the tears of your daughter ... would you have thrown our future away so recklessly?* "But I give you my word, we're going to make a home out of this place."

When Julia had calmed Aleda somewhat, she and Fiona got the children started on the task of uncovering the furniture. But no matter how carefully they folded the sheets aside, dust scattered into the air. It was Philip who came up with the idea of taking handkerchiefs from the luggage and tying them around their faces highwayman style.

The ground floor consisted of two main corridors. Along the corridor running west to east and forming the long part of the "L" were the scullery, kitchen, and a sizable dining room ending at the main hall. Facing those rooms from across the same corridor were the pantry, a back staircase, the short courtyard corridor they had entered the house through, the cook's and housekeeper's chambers, water closet and lavatory, and a main staircase that ended at the hall again.

Another corridor ran north to south from the hall. Julia was following Fiona down it when the front bell clanged. Automatically

51

Fiona turned in her tracks, but Julia switched the lamp she was carrying to her other hand and touched the maid's arm. "It's about time I learned how to answer my own door."

Crunching dried leaves with her feet, Julia hurried back into the hall, where the children were staring with uncertain expressions at the front door. Like herself, they'd been raised to take for granted that servants answered doors without exception. *We've a lot of habits to unlearn,* she thought on her way past them. "It's all right, children," she assured them, picking up her reticule from the exposed tea table and taking out her keys. She tried three keys on the chain before one unlocked the front door, but she finally swung it open to find four people standing upon the stoop.

"Good day, madam," said an elderly gentleman with fresh pink cheeks and clear blue eyes. He switched the cane in his right hand to his left and lifted a bowler hat from his balding head. "I'm Vicar Wilson, and this is my daughter, Henrietta, our housemaid, Dora, and our gardener, Luke. We've come to offer our assistance to Gresham's newest residents."

"But we've barely just arrived," Julia said after a second of stunned silence. "How did you know. . . ?"

"News travels fast in a small village, madam."

The daughter, a sturdily built middle-aged woman with brown sausage curls peeking from her bonnet, nodded down at the basket in her arms. "And we brought you some lunch."

"Firewood too," said the gardener, doffing a billycock cap.

Julia could see part of a small gardening wagon behind him, heaped with split logs.

"The nights and mornin's still got a nip in 'em. And if ye don't mind me lookin' out back for a ladder, I'll see to opening those shutters." A gap between his front teeth caused "shutters" to come out with a faint whistle.

Dora, a young woman in apron and lace cap, simply gave a quick bob. Julia put a hand up to her cheek and tried to imagine Reverend Douglass, her former rector at Mayfair, condescending to helping someone with housework. Or even herself doing the same just weeks ago.

"Why, I don't know what to say," she finally told them.

" 'Come in' will do very nicely," the vicar said, smiling.

As it turned out, Vicar Wilson was very familiar with the layout of the *Larkspur*, having been a close friend of Ethan Banning, its previous owner. The vicar was kind enough to take up a lantern and offer a tour.

"That would be wonderful," Julia told him, and even the children managed some enthusiasm this time. They left from the hall again, along the corridor that Julia and Fiona had started to explore. This passage had rooms only on the south side—the first was a small library, then a storage room. Three bedrooms were next.

"These are the family quarters," the vicar explained.

"Downstairs?" Philip asked.

The old gentleman smiled. "In the coaching inn business, the proprietor has to keep a sharp eye on the goings-on of the establishment."

There were six bedchambers upstairs that would hopefully lodge people instead of spiders one day, a linen room, storage room, water closet and bath, and a sitting room. In the attic were also six bedchambers—smaller because of the slope of the house—but surprisingly well insulated and each with a fireplace and garret window. Julia opened one door and gasped at finding another water closet. She had expected those on the two other floors that Jensen had mentioned, but even her house in London hadn't provided such an amenity in the servants' quarters.

"Ethan Banning was a thoughtful man," the reverend said with an amused little smile. "When the water closets were added, he decided that the servants should have one as well."

"It makes sense to me." Julia smiled back at him.

Hours later, when the foursome were on their way back to the vicarage with a promise to return the next day, Julia put aside her dusting cloth long enough to wander down the family corridor with an appreciative eye. At Julia's insistence, Fiona was assigned to the housekeeper's quarters, which would hopefully be cleaned by tomorrow evening.

"Just until we've time to ready the maids' rooms in the loft," Fiona had finally relented. "You'll need this chamber when you can hire on a housekeeper."

Julia had smiled at Fiona's statement, made totally without guile, and hoped the time would indeed come when she could afford to pay a housekeeper's wages—and she already had a certain young Irishwoman in mind for the position.

She ran her fingertips lightly along the inside cobwalls of the family corridor. They felt slightly damp from the scrubbing she and Dora had given them earlier. The vicar's maid had had to teach her how to use a broom on cobwebs, and then how to clean one section of the wall at a time before moving on. Such a deceptively simple-looking chore had caused Julia's back to ache and arms to feel leaden, but she was so determined not to draw attention to her lack of skills that she'd pushed herself on. And learned something with the effort. How startling it was to discover the sense of satisfaction that could be experienced while wringing out a cloth in a bucket of warm sudsy water!

So much had been accomplished today. Even the vicar, hindered as he was by rheumatism, and Philip by his sprained finger, did what they could to sweep away some of the neglect of the past eight years. Beds were made in the children's rooms, cobwebs swept away, and wood fires now snapped in the fireplaces, warding off the evening chill. Best of all, unshuttered windows gave vent to the remaining evening sunlight.

Julia stopped in the doorway of the girls' room, where Aleda and Grace had helped Fiona unpack their trunk. A pinkish conch shell, gathered by Aleda at Brighton Beach, sat on a dresser top alongside her delft blue music box, a framed photograph of both girls seated atop a pony, and Grace's book of fairy tales. Two dolls shared a small crib on the floor near Grace's side of the bed, next to the sparrow's lard tin.

She was so glad that she'd allowed the children to pack some treasures from their old rooms, even though luggage space had been tight. The abrupt change in their lives was softened by these familiar reminders. *It's closer to looking like a home,* she thought.

True, there was still much work left to do. She and Fiona would be sleeping on divans in the hall until their rooms could be cleaned. Most rooms on the ground floor, including the kitchen, still needed serious attention. The upstairs floor and attic hadn't even been touched, and with the children starting school on Monday, their help would be unavailable for the better part of the weekdays.

But we're here, and not out on some London street. What had Saint Paul written in the Scriptures? *In whatever state I am in, I have learned to be content.* So that meant if contentment did not come naturally, it could be learned.

Julia went to the window at the end of the family corridor and stared out of the freshly scrubbed glass. The sun stood poised to dip behind the brown mass of Anwyl. Its downward way was marked by clouds of every sunset color—flame, purple, pink, violet, and all the tints of gold. *I am not happy, Lord,* she prayed silently. Philip's death and then the discovery of his betrayal were wounds she felt so deeply in her soul that she wondered if she would ever know joy again. *But with Your help, I will learn how to be content.*

*T*he Worthy sisters had retired to their cottage by the time Julia walked across the dark lane after the family had suppered on the remaining roast beef sandwiches from Henrietta Wilson's generous basket. She was weary to the bone and had yet to take a bath, having removed only the worst of the grime from herself. But the two elderly women were her nearest neighbors, and she wanted to start out on good terms with them.

Two good-sized windows set in the sisters' wattle-and-daub structure were separated by a sturdy oak door. Illuminated from inside as they were now, and with top frames obscured by overhanging thatching from the roof, the windows resembled inquiring eyes set under a mop of amber-colored hair. Since darkness had forced the sisters to vacate their posts, the house looked as if it had taken up the responsibility of watching the goings-on at the crossroads.

"Come in, Mrs. Hollis," the sister named Iris said, answering Julia's soft knock at the door. "We were just about to have a cup of hot chocolate. It has become a habit of ours after supper. Will you have some with us?"

"I'd be delighted," replied Julia, "but only if you're sure you have enough." After receiving an answer in the affirmative, Julia stepped inside. The two-room cottage was simply but not shabbily furnished, with brightly colored rag rugs over a stone floor, baskets of lace in one corner, and a calendar from *The Churchman's Almanack* over the chimneypiece. A tallow candle flickered light on a plain table in the center of the room, where Jewel stood filling crockery mugs. There were three set out, so obviously the sisters had been expecting Julia's visit. She breathed a sigh of relief, for the temptation had been great to put off this little chore until tomorrow.

"We was beginnin' to wonder if ye'd forgotten," Jewel's raspy voice said in a slightly accusatory tone. Her wrinkled face looked like old parchment in the candlelight.

"Well, I'm here now." Julia smiled back at her, sinking thankfully into one of the rush-bottomed chairs that Iris offered. "I do apologize for making you wait."

"That's quite all right, dear." Iris, settled at the table now, patted her hand and gave her a sympathetic smile. "You're a lovely young woman, Mrs. Hollis. How long since your husband passed away?"

"Five weeks."

Even the outspoken Jewel seemed stricken at this. "Five weeks? How sad for you. And those poor children!"

Julia thanked them for their condolences and even answered their questions as to how Philip passed on, but then was forced to become a little outspoken herself. "I do appreciate your hospitality, but I shan't be able to stay for too long. I'd like to tuck the children into their beds."

"That's what we wished to speak with you about, dear," said Iris with a worried crease in her forehead. "Must you sleep in there tonight?"

"Ye could stay at the *Bow and Fiddle*," Jewel suggested. "The rent would be fair, since they've seldom any guests. And you can get good boiled beef and dumplings for sixpence."

Politely Julia asked, "But why would we stay somewhere else?"

Jewel's blunt reply was, "Because the *Larkspur Inn* may have a ghost livin' there, that's why."

Julia didn't intend to chuckle, but the bone-wearying activities of the day had weakened her resistance considerably. Still, it was just a small burst that sounded more like a cough, and she covered her mouth with her hand and apologized at once.

Jewel was not mollified, for her gray eyebrows almost met over her frown. "Won't be so funny when he puts a knife at yer throat one night, Mrs. Hollis. And with you bein' a widow, the protection of yer little 'uns is in your hands."

"Gently, Jewel," Iris admonished, then patted Julia's arm. "We're only concerned about you and the children, dear."

"It's not too late to go over to the *Bow and Fiddle* for the night," advised Jewel, nodding. "Then tomorrow, ye go over to the schoolyard and break off a bundle of elder twigs and ye make sure to put one in every room. Ghosts can't abide them."

"Ladies," Julia finally was compelled to say, "I appreciate your concern, but I must tell you that I don't believe in ghosts."

The two exchanged startled glances, and then Iris leaned forward. "Well, we didn't either, child . . . until Jake Pitt died."

In spite of herself, Julia had to ask. "Jake Pitt?"

They began to explain, one taking up when the other ran out of breath or paused for a sip of chocolate. It seemed that Jake Pitt had been an itinerant knife sharpener who made rounds from village to village, pushing a handcart with his foot-pedaled grindstone. "He came through Gresham thrice yearly," Jewel said. "He'd stop at every cottage and shop, and folk would bring out their knives and tools."

"Most itinerant traders are eager to chat," said Iris. "It's a lonely life, you can be sure. And most people are just as eager to hear from them, for they bring news of happenings in the surrounding villages."

Jewel nodded. "But Jake Pitt weren't that sort. You would ha' thought that words cost a quid apiece, so sparin' was he with them. And what a lively temper he had! Children used to gather round so they could watch the sparks fly when he worked, and he would just glare at 'em."

"And he stayed at the *Larkspur Inn*?"

"Stayed at the *Larkspur*?" Jewel echoed, as if she found the question absurd. "No, he surely didn't have the means to be staying at no inn. He slept under a canvas in the fields when weather allowed. In barns when it wouldn't."

"Then what does he have to do with—"

"I'm coming to that part, dearie. Well, he showed up in Gresham the winter of '56 . . . ." Jewel paused, chewing on her lip. "No, it were '57, because our niece Emmeline married Heath Adams that following spring."

"He was such a decent man," Iris sighed. "I can't fathom why Uncle Stone never cared for him."

"Never cared for Jake Pitt?" asked Julia, a little dazed.

"No, Heath Adams," Jewel replied. "It wasn't as if Emmeline had suitors knocking down her door, even if she was a comely woman. Emmeline had webbed fingers, you see. It weren't 'till she was thirty-five or thirty-six that Heath took her down to Shrewsbury for an operation to make 'em normal."

"You would have thought that would make Uncle Stone change his opinion," Iris said, clucking her tongue sadly. "Stubborn as a mule, he was."

Julia thought of her children across the lane, likely changing into nightclothes now with Fiona's assistance. Tonight, of all nights, she wanted to tuck them into their beds and hear their prayers. And her patience was being stretched to the limit. She cleared her throat and sent a meaningful look toward a long-case clock against the wall. It worked, for the sisters returned to the subject at hand.

"Anyhow, that January were a cold one, with snow on the ground," Jewel went on. "But Jake Pitt came through as always. Only this time, he looked all dotery. Ye could see his hands tremblin', even with wool gloves on. Well, Ethan Banning owned the *Larkspur Inn* and brought out some knives to be sharpened."

Julia now knew all about Ethan Banning. He had passed on eight years ago, leaving the inn to his cousin George Hollis, Philip's uncle, who then passed away himself three years later.

"It took some doing, but Mr. Banning insisted Jake stay at the *Larkspur* until he were well enough to move on. Fed the old man some warm broth with his own hand, he did."

Shaking her head, Iris said, "But poor old Jake became delirious and cursed Mr. Banning for not allowing him to die in peace. He didn't last the night. A chambermaid found him in his bed cold as stone the next morning."

Apparently the story was finished after this, for both women folded their arms and watched Julia's face expectantly.

"I see," she told them. "That's truly sad. But it's comforting to know that Mr. Pitt passed away in a warm bed and well cared for."

"But that's not all," Jewel said. "Our nephews, Merle and John, was hired by the joiner to help carry the coffin out of the *Larkspur*. Only, they was already out to the carriage drive when Merle stumbled on a stone, and the lid came awry. It were then they found they'd carried Jake's body out of the house backward."

"Backward?" asked Julia.

"The head first . . . before the feet." A noticeable shudder accompanied Iris's answer.

"I'm sorry . . . I don't understand."

Jewel's faded blue eyes widened in the parchmentlike face. "Ye don't? Why, Mrs. Hollis, everybody knows that a corpse has to be carried out of a house feet first."

"And if he's not?"

"He'll return to that very house to do mischief! And that's just what happened, because Mr. Banning died in his sleep three years

59

later. He were barely fifty years old, Mrs. Hollis, and fit as a plum pudding."

Iris sighed. "We tried to warn him to take precautions after Jake's funeral, but he just laughed. Said he didn't believe in ghosts . . . just like you."

"But we felt it were our duty to warn you. Old Jake's put a curse on the *Larkspur Inn*. Look what happened to that cousin Ethan Banning left it to."

"George Hollis," Julia said. "But my husband's uncle was killed in a railway accident five years ago. He never even lived in the *Larkspur* to my knowledge."

"And who did the inn pass on to after he died?"

"Why, my husband."

Again the two exchanged pointed glances. "So now that makes three owners of the *Larkspur* dying within eleven years of Jake Pitt's curse," Iris said in a somber tone. "And now the inn belongs to you."

An eerie silence descended, aided by the flickering of the tallow candle and the somber expressions of both Worthy sisters. Julia thought of the old knife sharpener, spewing curses with his dying breath, and a little shudder snaked down her back. *This is all coincidence,* she thought, then reminded herself, *You don't believe in ghosts.*

"I see," she said finally. "Well, thank you for the warning." Julia's appreciation was sincere, for she could tell that the sisters' motives were nothing less than honorable . . . even if their judgment was somewhat lacking. "I wish I could visit longer, but the children will need to go to bed."

Jewel's eyelids fluttered. "Ye aren't going to stay there *now,* are ye?"

"I'm afraid we must. But I'll bear all of this in mind, I assure you."

She got to her feet then, thanking the two for the chocolate and promising to have them over to tea as soon as the family had settled in.

Iris replied, "Tea would be lovely, dear, but as early in the afternoon as possible, please."

"We don't fancy the idea of having evening creep up on us in that house," Jewel added with a decided frown.

Julia opened her mouth, then realizing she had no ready reply, she closed it again and took her leave. The night sky was overcast, with few stars piercing the fog. As she crossed the lane, the *Larkspur* loomed ahead of her, vine-covered and mossy. She could understand how the Worthy sisters' imaginations could run amuck at seeing such a sight from their windows night after night. *When it's cleaned up and the garden is replanted, they'll forget about this ghost nonsense.*

———

The house seemed almost too quiet as Julia walked down the corridor to the family quarters. Ever since the day in the nursery when she'd broken the news about having to leave London, she had been tucking in the children herself. Frances had balked, of course, but Julia had insisted. She couldn't believe how unthinkingly she'd allowed a nanny to perform that important ritual. Having been raised the same way, it was simply something she had taken for granted. How tragic that it had taken her husband's death to show her where she had neglected her duties as a mother.

I don't care if the Larkspur becomes the most successful lodging house in England, she thought. *Never again will I hire someone else to rear my children.* The girls' room was the first to her left. Though light still edged from underneath the door, she was not reassured, for no sounds came from the other side. Had they fallen asleep with the lamp on? *Why didn't I come home sooner?*

She breathed a little sigh of relief upon opening the door to find two faces looking at her from the pillows in the bed they shared. "I was afraid you'd be asleep by the time I got back."

"It's going to be hours before I can sleep," Aleda intoned a martyred voice. "I wish I were back in my own bed."

"Then I'm going to say an extra prayer that you sleep soundly tonight," Julia said, sitting down on the side of the bed. "When we have lodgers, this house will seem much more like a home. In fact, I believe we'll all enjoy having lots of people about."

For the first time it struck Julia why the idea of operating a lodging house now seemed so attractive to her. *My children will have something resembling a large family.* With only one parent and no grandparents, that was important. She read from Grace's *Wonderful Stories for Children* by Hans Christian Anderson, listened to their prayers, kissed both foreheads, and walked down the corridor past her bedroom to the last door. *I'll only allow lodgers who don't mind having children about the place,* she decided as she gave the door a soft rap.

Philip was sitting up on his pillows, staring down intently at an open book in his lap. He'd arranged the treasure he had brought, a marble chessboard and set of ivory carved men, on top of a writing desk in the corner.

"I came to see if you'd like me to read to you, and here you are going ahead without me. What is it?" Julia asked, crossing the room to sit on the side of his bed.

The thirteen-year-old smiled and held up the book so that Julia could read *Lord Brownlea's Economic History of the British Empire* on the cover. "I found it in the library. Some of the words are difficult, but I'm learning so much." He gave a self-conscious little shrug. "I think."

The best surprise of that day had been the trunk of books in the shelf-lined library. Apparently the Bannings had been prodigious readers. "Economic history?" Julia leaned over to scan a sentence or two. "Why, that's a university text. Weren't there novels as well?"

"Yes," Philip answered. "But novels won't help you do well in school."

Julia took the book out of his hands and continued to page through it. "I wouldn't say that. Anyway, why are you concerned about doing well in school? Mr. Hunter was always impressed with your work."

Philip chewed on the tip of his bandaged finger and gave a casual shrug, but Julia caught the worry in his green eyes. "Is it because you'll be starting school Monday?" she asked.

After a moment, the boy admitted, "I've never even been inside a real schoolroom. I don't know what the other children will be learning. What if it's something I haven't been taught yet? What if they think I'm ignorant for not knowing it? What if they laugh at me?"

"There's a big difference between being ignorant and experiencing something you've not yet learned." Julia reached out to touch his freckled cheek. "No one will think you're ignorant."

He looked doubtful. "Are you sure of that?"

"Absolutely, positively sure. Besides, it may even be the other way around. You've probably learned some things from Mr. Hunter that they've not yet been taught."

Finally some hope came into Philip's expression. "I didn't even consider that."

Julia smiled. "I think people care more about whether you're kind to them than about how much you know. If you're friendly they're going to like you whether or not you've memorized Lord Brownlea's book."

Julia's bedroom, which was between the two rooms now occupied by her children, had been cleared of webs but not cleaned yet. After her bath she slipped into nightclothes, released her hair from its chignon, then walked up the corridor to the hall. Fiona had already prepared bedding upon two horsehair-stuffed sofas facing each other about ten feet apart. The room looked a little less forbidding with the furniture uncovered, floor swept, and immediate cobwebs vanquished. She knew that webs still clung to the high oaken beams beyond the light of the single candle upon the tea table, and that it would take a ladder and broom to clear them away. Leaving the candle burning for Fiona, Julia crawled under the covers, crossed her arms behind her head, and stared up at the blackness high overhead. She felt very small surrounded by such space and thought that it was a good thing she didn't believe in ghosts. *I would be sleeping between Grace and Aleda right now if I did.*

Fiona walked into the room from the lavatory. "Are the children comfortable in their rooms?" she asked, extinguishing the candle she carried.

"I believe so, except for Aleda."

"She'll come round, missus." The maid snuffed the candle on the tea table, plunging the room into darkness. There were rustling sounds as the maid settled herself into her covers. "Once she makes new friends."

"I hope so." Julia smiled in the darkness and told Fiona about the book Philip had been reading. "He's concerned about making a good impression on the other students."

"He's a good lad. I'm sure he will."

It was reassuring to have someone with whom to talk about the children. How could she have survived if Fiona hadn't insisted on coming along? Julia suddenly recalled the way the maid's face lit up this afternoon when Philip announced the discovery of the trunk of books in the library.

"Fiona?" she said.

"Yes, missus?"

"You know you're welcome to read any of those books you like."

There was another rustle of sheets and quilts. "I am?"

"But of course. Weren't you allowed to borrow from our library in London?"

After a hesitation, Fiona answered, "Mr. Jensen forbade it. But the Wesleyan chapel had a small subscription library for servants."

The news that her friend wasn't allowed access to her own library cut her to the quick—still worse was that she'd lived such a self-centered life that she'd never been aware of it. "Fiona . . . why didn't you ever tell me? I could have asked my husband to speak to Jensen about it."

"It's water under the bridge now, missus," the maid answered with no reproach in her voice. Changing the subject, she asked if Julia had enjoyed her visit with the lace spinners across the lane.

"It was quite interesting." Julia recounted her conversation with the Worthy sisters. To that, Fiona gave an audible sigh.

"I thought only we Irish believed in that sort of thing."

Julia automatically raised an eyebrow, though no one could see it. "Surely *you* don't believe. . . !"

"No, missus," Fiona answered. "But I did years ago, when I was a girl. I worked at a big old house, sleepin' alone in a drafty loft. Every time the wind howled or the roof creaked, I just knew it was some spirit intent upon doin' me harm. I got very little sleep in those days, you can be sure."

"Is that why you ran away?" Julia asked before thinking, then immediately added, "I'm sorry. I didn't mean to pry."

"That wasn't the reason I left," Fiona answered simply. "And when I learned how to pray, I stopped fearing the noises." A sheepish note crept into her voice. "*Most* of the time, that is."

Though the sofa was as comfortable as any bed and the quilts ample for warmth, Julia's sleep was fitful and besieged by dreams. They were not of itinerant knife sharpeners, however, but of her late husband. Philip was here in Gresham with them, taking charge, hiring servants, dazzling her and everyone in the village with his charm. And she slipped gratefully back into the role of a trusting, dutiful wife.

"It was all a mistake," he said, giving her his most beguiling smile. "Gambling? Debts? Foreclosure? Why, none of it ever happened."

"It never happened?"

"Never happened."

She sighed happily and rested her head upon his strong shoulder, safe within the circle of his arms. "I knew it, Philip. You love us too much."

"I love you too much."

The images were so real, as well as the feelings they evoked, that when she woke from the dream Julia buried her face in her pillow and wept silently for what might have been.

A sniffle interrupted Fiona's dream about clearing endless cobwebs. Mumbling to herself, she opened one eye and attempted to orient herself in the early morning dimness. *The inn,* she thought. She could see the sleeping form on the other sofa. Then she heard a second sniff.

"Missus?" she said, slipping from under the covers and kneeling on the floor in front of the sofa. The hall rugs had not been unrolled yet, and the flagstones sent chills up her knees.

Mrs. Hollis turned her face from the pillow and blinked. "Oh, Fiona, I'm sorry. Did I wake you?"

"That's all right," Fiona said, reaching to push back a strand of hair from her employer's wet cheek. "Bad dream?"

"No, actually a good dream." Mrs. Hollis gave her a feeble smile, but there was misery in the red-rimmed eyes. "A bad one would have been easier to take, I think."

"I understand."

"You do?"

Fiona nodded. "I do." Softly, as if tending a fretful child, she began stroking the auburn hair while humming a tune she remembered from a long time ago.

"Cold," Mrs. Hollis mumbled, her eyes closed again. "You need to go back to bed."

"I'm all right, missus. Now go to sleep." She waited until the breathing was steady again before slipping back under her own covers. *Lord, send her another husband one day,* she prayed. *A good man this time, one who'll understand how special it is to have a family.*

She wished she could make that same supplication for herself but couldn't. Not while her past in Ireland still dug its talons into her skin.

*T*he *Larkspur*'s kitchen was a huge room some thirty feet long and nearly as broad, with a fireplace capacious enough to roast an ox. Set in the middle of the stone-flagged floor was an oak table of a size sufficient to seat a dozen people. An open door at one end led to a scullery, where dishes were washed. Farther down the corridor were the pantry for the storage of dry foods and a larder for meats. Having rarely set foot in her own kitchen in London, Julia had little knowledge of the inner workings of a kitchen quarter. The rooms boasted every convenience a cook could desire, so Julia figured it would be an easy matter for her and Fiona to brew up some morning tea.

Half an hour later the sun had just crested the treetops of Gipsy Woods to the east when the courtyard doorbell clanged. Julia, searching cupboards for teacups, exchanged a curious glance with Fiona, who was still attempting to light the nickel-plated *Rumford* oil stove. "Surely it's not the vicar this early," Julia said. Waving away Fiona's offer to answer the door, Julia left the room and walked down the short corridor to the entrance. She paused a second to put a hand up to her hair. After several attempts to coil her hair into a chignon this morning, she'd simply fastened it with a comb at the base of her neck. The fringe on her forehead dangled over her eyebrows, but until they could light the stove, Fiona could not teach her how to heat the curling rod.

Oh, well, no one can expect a princess this time of the morning. She opened the door to find a young visitor on the doorstep. "Yes?" she said in a voice one uses with small children, but then flushed at her misconception, for the woman standing there was a dwarf.

"Happens all the time, dear," said the woman, smiling under a straw bonnet. The voice was that of a woman in her middle forties.

"Or it did, before folks got used to the sight of me. I'm Audrey Herrick. Squire Bartley's footman told me he spotted a family moving in here. Would you be looking to hire a cook?"

"Would you care to come in?" Julia said. "I'll offer you some tea when we've figured how to brew it."

"Oh, there's a trick to that stove," the woman said, hurrying on past her. Reaching the kitchen, she brushed Fiona aside after taking the matches from her hand. Less than two seconds later, a front burner was alight with flame.

"Thank you," Julia said, then introduced herself and Fiona to her visitor. "Neither of us has had any experience in the kitchen."

"Is that so? Cups are in the tall cupboard in the scullery, love. Cutlery in the second drawer. And there's a set of good Wedgewood in the dining room dresser. Blue Onion pattern it is . . . one of my favorites."

Julia's eyebrows raised. "Why, you've cooked here before."

"Aye, for twenty some odd years," the woman said, wiping her small hands upon her apron. "Started out in the scullery when I was fourteen." She motioned toward a dusty step stool beside one of the cupboards and winked. "Worked my way up . . . in more ways than one. Don't mean to sound prideful, but ask anyone about town—they'll tell you Audrey Herrick is the best cook in Gresham. Mr. Pool at the *Bow and Fiddle* is always asking me to work for him, but his missus has a proper temper and a habit of running off servants, so I don't want to put meself into that situation."

Soon the water was hot and the three sat at the worktable with steaming cups of tea. Audrey Herrick removed her straw bonnet and hung it on the corner of a neighboring chair. Her ginger hair was streaked with gray and drawn up in a topknot, but her lively brown eyes sparkled and laugh lines flanked the corners of her mouth. Julia asked if she was employed at present.

"We work for Squire Bartley up at the manor house, me and my Karl."

Julia had heard about the squire yesterday from Dora when they were busy scrubbing walls. Squire Bartley, from the manor house on the southeast side of Gresham, was founder and owner of *Anwyl Mountain Savory Cheeses*. "He keeps to himself as much as possible," the vicar's maid had told her tactfully.

"Karl is caretaker there. It's a decent living for both of us." Mrs. Herrick's voice sobered. "But truth be known, we were both happier here. And after growing up in the circus the way he did . . . well, this was the first real home he ever had."

Julia suspected that it was Karl Herrick who had strewn the meadowsweet in each room. When she asked Mrs. Herrick if it were so, the woman nodded. "He kept his old set of keys, figgering someone would come and ask for them one day. Karl didn't want pests ruining Mr. Banning's things, so he brought around a couple of bushel baskets every summer. He would've liked to have kept up the grounds if the squire didn't keep him so busy."

"That was terribly kind of him," Julia said. "Please do ask him to come visit some time so we can thank him."

"Oh, he didn't mind none." Mrs. Herrick dabbed at a tear. "Mr. Banning was a tender old soul, and it was Karl's way of remembering him."

Looking close to tears herself, Fiona asked, "And how does Squire Bartley treat you?"

The woman shrugged her shoulders. "The squire is a grouchy old blister, but at least he stays out of my kitchen. I suppose he can't help being a bear—he suffers from dyspepsia, and all his stomach can abide is gruel or porridge. A little broth and bread now and then if he's feelin' adventurous, but that's the limit. There ain't much joy in cooking miserable fare such as that."

"Why, then, did he hire the most skilled cook in Shropshire?" Julia asked the cook. "I would imagine any kitchen maid could conjure up such simple meals."

"Oh, Squire has to have the best of everything, Mrs. Hollis. You should see his flower garden . . . which you likely won't because he hardly ever entertains. He doesn't trust the gardeners, so he spends most of his days there himself, digging and pruning with his hopes set on ribbons at the flower shows."

"Surely he allows you to cook proper meals for his servants," Fiona said. "He can't expect everyone else to live upon gruel and broth."

"Coo! Depends upon your definition of the word 'proper.' The master reckons that since he can't stomach tasty meals, he'll not be footing the bill for his servants to live all high and mighty. And since he gets his cheeses for naught, he insists that I cook up as many cheese dishes as possible." Mrs. Herrick pointed a teaspoon in the air. "Scrambled eggs with cheese, cheese sandwiches, potato soup with cheese—how many rarebits do you think a body can take before it starts to sicken at the sight and smell of them?"

Sighing, Julia poured herself another cup of tea. "I would love to hire you, Mrs. Herrick. Fiona and I have so much work to do on the house that we can't be learning to cook at the same time. And the truth of the matter is that we're turning this into a lodging house. But as I've no idea how many people will respond to my advertisements, I can't ask you to leave a secure position for one with an uncertain future."

Even as she spoke those words, Julia felt guilty for them. *Where is your faith?* she asked herself. *Has God abandoned you yet?* But she could not ask someone else to take that leap, not when Jensen and Fiona had already done so. The pressure of being responsible for yet another person's investment of time or money would be too great to bear.

To her relief, Mrs. Herrick nodded understanding. "Well, I do appreciate your frankness, Mrs. Hollis," she said, pushing out her chair. "With a son at university, I can't go taking chances. But if you don't have a cook by the time you've taken on lodgers, please keep me in mind. And Karl, too, if you've a need for a caretaker."

She left then, with Fiona accompanying her down the lane as far as the bakery. Julia woke the children and helped them dress, so they would be ready for breakfast when Fiona returned. "You mean we're going to have to work *again* today?" Aleda groaned as Julia cleaned her face with a flannel but immediately followed her complaint with an apology before she could be lectured.

"I've two brothers and a sister in Clun, but no family in Gresham," Audrey Herrick told Fiona as the two walked up Market Lane. It was Fiona's first opportunity to see a bit of the village, and she found it as picturesque as the ones described in novels she'd read. It seemed that every cottage, from stone to brick to wattle-and-daub, boasted a garden in the stages of early spring.

"I moved here to get away from my family, if you want to know the truth," the cook continued. She rolled her eyes. "They couldn't bear the shame of having someone like me in the family."

"Someone like you?" Fiona's eyes widened. "You mean, your height?"

"Silly, ain't it?" The cook smiled up at Fiona without a trace of resentment in her brown eyes. "Thank God you can pick your friends, even if you can't pick your family."

They parted company at the bakery, a red brick building with sash windows and *Johnson's Baked Goods* etched on a sign hanging from a cast-iron post. A bell gave a cheery tinkle as Fiona opened the door. The inside was warm and yeasty, and an assortment of baked goods was displayed under a glass counter. Another customer, a middle-aged woman wearing a straw bonnet and gingham apron, gave Fiona a timid, curious smile as a man behind the counter wrapped her selections in paper. Fiona smiled back but did not speak. She was wearing her black-and-white uniform and lace cap, and she knew most people considered it beneath their dignity to hold social conversations with servants.

But the woman was either exceedingly friendly or exceedingly curious, for she finally said, "I've never seen you before. D'you work at the manor?"

The baker, heavyset with dark eyebrows that met over the nose, stopped wrapping pastries to listen in.

"No, ma'am. At the *Larkspur Inn*. We just arrived yesterday."

"Oh." The smile on the woman's face grew stiff and unnatural-looking, and she traded glances with the man behind the counter. She gave Fiona a curt nod before leaving the shop with her parcel tucked into her basket.

What did I say? Fiona wondered.

The baker was silent as he took Fiona's order. Minutes later, when he handed her the parcel of scotch eggs and raspberry tarts, he asked, "Anybody warn you?"

"Warn me?"

"You know." He jerked his head in the direction of the *Larkspur*. "Th' ghost."

Some of the tenseness in Fiona's shoulders drained, for she realized then that she had done nothing personally to offend the woman. "Yes, sir," she replied.

He leaned closer across the counter. "I'd be careful if I was you. Put a chip of coal in the toes of your shoes and put one under each side of your bed, and you shan't suffer harm."

"But I don't believe—"

"In each shoe, now. And don't forget you heard that from me."

"I won't forget," Fiona sighed. "Thank you."

"Audrey Herrick?" Vicar Wilson said to Julia later that morning as he cleaned lamp globes while she polished furniture in the hall. "Why, she's indeed the best cook in Gresham. Perhaps even the whole of Shropshire."

"She mentioned having a son away at school."

"Ah yes, Edward. Fine boy, he is. He's an undergraduate at Trinity College in Stafford." He seemed to read the question in Julia's mind, for he smiled and added, "I haven't seen Edward since Christmas past, but he was a strapping five feet nine inches then."

He went on to tell how the village went agog twenty years ago when Audrey went down to Shrewsbury with other servants to visit a traveling circus and came back engaged to be married to another dwarf . . . and a German one at that. Ethan Banning had been the only person willing to give a manual labor position to a former sideshow exhibit with a foreign accent, thus incurring the ridicule of almost everyone in the village. Karl turned out to be a diligent worker, however, and over time people accepted him into the fraternity of Gresham laborers.

"It was a good lesson for people around here to learn," the vicar said. "If you give someone a chance to prove himself, you'll almost always be pleasantly surprised. I think Karl was so grateful for the opportunity to leave the circus that he worked extra hard for Mr. Banning."

Julia closed the newly polished piano lid and said, "I'm glad Mr. Banning gave him that chance. Knowing he was so kind makes me feel better about living in the house he once owned."

"Oh, houses do seem to develop personalities, don't they?"

"Yes, they do." Julia thought about the house she'd left in London—Philip's house. From her first day it had seemed an aseptic, unwelcoming place . . . probably because the servants had treated her with such veiled contempt. A startling realization came to her—she felt more at home today, after just one night in the *Larkspur*, than she had felt for fourteen years on Park Lane!

The two worked on in a compatible silence until Julia voiced another thought to the vicar. "You know, I was warned of a ghost in this house."

"Indeed?" He sighed and shook his head. "I was afraid that would happen. Would that have come from the Worthy sisters?"

Julia winced. "They've told you, then?"

"Not directly. But Jake Pitt's name isn't an unfamiliar one in

71

Gresham. I thought to mention it to you yesterday, but I didn't want to spoil your first day here. Are you very upset?"

"Upset? Why, no. I just think it's a little silly to believe in ghosts."

"Well, I'm afraid it goes deeper than that. Some are convinced he walks the floors of this house. And they would consider you foolish for having moved in."

"You're serious?"

"It is unfortunate that people are so superstitious," Vicar Wilson sighed, "but I'm afraid it's that way in every small village. You should hear how many magical remedies for *warts* abound here—burying chicken feathers by the light of the moon and so on. I've preached sermons on the subject, but obviously with little effect."

He stopped to give her an apologetic smile. "I've gone and frightened you now, haven't I? Well, I wouldn't worry, Mrs. Hollis. Most folks will be too polite to mention Jake Pitt to you. And once it becomes obvious that no disasters have befallen you and your children, I'm sure they'll forget about him."

Julia felt somewhat relieved. "Should I tell my children?"

He thought this over for several seconds, then nodded. "They'll surely hear something about old Jake at school Monday. Forewarned is forearmed, as they say."

After a lunch of another batch of Henrietta Wilson's roast beef sandwiches, Vicar Wilson proposed that Julia and her family should have a grand tour of Gresham. "Surely you can take an hour away from work to learn about your new home, can't you?"

Julia wasn't sure if the excitement on her children's faces was because of an interest in Gresham, or because they would have an hour away from their cleaning chores. Either way, she had no recourse but to agree. Besides, she was curious about the village as well.

Since the vicar's trap wasn't large enough to hold everyone, Luke, who had been pulling vines and scraping moss from the outside walls, was dispatched to the iron foundry to borrow a wagon. The gardener was back half an hour later with a wagon and team of English blacks. He obviously had also taken some of that time to change his clothes and slick back his dark hair with water. Julia thought this a bit odd for just a wagon ride through the village . . . until she caught the glance he sent in Fiona's direction.

He's smitten with her, Julia thought, smiling to herself. *It would be wonderful if Fiona found a husband here.* It then occurred to Julia that if she could wish such a thing for Fiona, then she herself must not have soured completely toward marriage. *At least not for others,* she amended. She would certainly not be interested in placing her security and her children's in the hands of another man. What if he turned out to live a lie, just like Philip?

After gathering bonnets, shawls, and coats, for the late-March air still carried a nip, Luke helped everyone into the wagon. "Here you go, Miss O'Shea," he said to Fiona, though Henrietta and Julia stood closer to the wagon in the carriage drive. Julia exchanged an amused glance with the vicar's daughter while Luke managed to escort Fiona to the space directly behind the driver's box. No doubt he would have put her on the box beside him if the vicar's joints could have tolerated sitting in the back.

Fiona responded to this attention with politeness but did not return the flirtation, bringing back to Julia's mind the things she'd overheard from the other servants back in London. "She must have a sweetheart back in Ireland," Alice had once said.

But Julia wondered if there could be another reason for Fiona's coolness toward men. Just as Philip's actions had left her with no desire to ever marry again . . . had some past hurt affected Fiona's feelings about marriage? *Is that why she left Ireland with little more than the clothes upon her back?*

As the wagon started moving down the carriage drive, Julia sent a wave to the Worthy sisters across the lane and turned her thoughts toward her new home. Whatever had happened to any of them in the past, Gresham was their present and future. She would embrace the village as if her own ancestors had once walked the cobbled and dirt roads, and try to help Fiona do the same.

As Luke drove the team of horses at a leisurely pace, Vicar Wilson conducted the tour from beside him, turning often to point out this cottage or that quaint shop. Each cottage garden was a riot of color; early tulips, crimson, white, pink, bronze, and purple, vied with yellow daffodils and white narcissus. Polyanthus and the stiff crown imperials added their bit to the charming picture. Wild yellow jonquils and multicolored primroses grew in abundance along the lanes, attended by humming bees and flitting butterflies. Red stone farmhouses with mossy or thatched roofs could be seen nestled among the low hills in the north, where black-and-white Friesian cattle grazed.

Julia committed to memory every lane the vicar pointed out and soon began to understand the way Gresham was laid out. The village reposed tidy along the willow-lined River Bryce, with its village green, main roads, and businesses to the south of the river, the cheese factory and pastures to the north. Market Lane, upon which the *Larkspur* sat, was the only road that crossed the river. According to the vicar, the stone bridge had been widened twenty years ago to accommodate carrier wagons from the cheese factory.

Running east to west and intersecting Market Lane, Church Lane was the second oldest road in the village. Newer roads—but still decades old—included Walnut Tree Lane, Thatcher Lane, Short Lane, and Bartley Lane.

Every villager they passed raised a face to stare curiously, sometimes followed with a lift of the hand for the vicar. As the team pulled the wagon back up Church Lane on its way back to the inn, Julia looked to her right and caught sight of a half-dozen women gathered at the pump on the green. They looked up from their gossip and buckets to stare at the passing wagon. Some rested fists on their hips, resembling two-handled mugs. Julia risked sending them a smile and wave of the hand and was relieved when at least half returned the gesture. *This is going to be home one day. It may take some time, but it's going to happen.*

———

Trumbles, a stone building on the corner of Market and Thatcher Lanes across from the *Bow and Fiddle*, was like no shop Philip had ever seen. Multifarious as a bazaar, it boasted shelves from floor to ceiling with merchandise on display from tools to tooth powder, cloth to candy, teapots to timepieces. And to the left of the doorway was another counter with shelves divided in dozens of slots, for the shopkeeper also served as Gresham's postmaster. Philip saw no sign of a safe, though smaller print etched underneath *Trumbles* on the signboard in front had stated that banking could be done at the establishment as well. He reckoned that the curtained doorway behind the counter contained the safe. Or did the shopkeeper/postmaster/banker just store the money in a dresser? Perhaps people were more honest here than in the city, he told himself. *You couldn't get away with that in London.*

A tall man was stacking boxes of matches on a shelf behind the merchandise counter when Philip walked up to it. The man glanced over his shoulder, then became of average height as he stepped down from a short stool. Philip had a feeling that this was Mr. Trumble himself—the thinning blond hair, drooping walrus mustache, and round, friendly face seemed to match the name somehow.

"And what might I do for you today, young fellow?" the shopkeeper asked, smiling.

"Are you Mr. Trumble?"

"I am indeed. And who might you be?"

"Philip Hollis. We just moved into—"

"The *Larkspur*?"

"How did you know?"

Mr. Trumble tapped his temple with a finger. "It's what you call conductive reasoning, my young friend. A new family moves into the inn, and then the next day there's a new face in my shop."

"Don't you mean . . ." Philip started to say, then clamped his mouth shut before *deductive* could come out. Hadn't Mother just told him last night that people were more impressed with kindness than with knowledge? Producing his list, he said instead, "I mean, my mother would like these things, if you have them."

"Soap cakes, lamp mantles, iron . . ." the man mumbled, then looked up at Philip. "My, that's quite an order. Think you can pack all that, or should I send it round in the cart later?"

Philip drew himself up to his full height of five feet. "I can carry it."

"Now, that's the spirit, lad."

While Mr. Trumble filled the order, Philip looked at the shelves of merchandise in front of him. His eyes immediately fastened upon a wooden box on a lower shelf containing some familiar-looking round objects.

"Are those marbles?" he asked the next time Mr. Trumble looked up from the list.

"Yes, but they aren't for sale. I'm all out of the other kind, but I expect them in next week. You can look at those if you like."

"Yes, please. Thank you." The box was set before him, and Philip picked up one of the marbles. It was of clear glass, dark with age, and marred by a tiny chip on the surface. There were dozens like it—some chipped, and a handful with flawless surfaces. Still others appeared to be made of clay, but so hard that he couldn't make a dent with a fingernail.

"Came from the ruins atop the Anwyl," the proprietor said with his back to Philip. "I found a few when I was a boy like yourself and started savin' them."

"You mean they're Roman?"

"And older than you and me put together, with the vicar thrown in for good measure." Mr. Trumble gave him a sidelong look and added, "No disrepent intended, of course. The vicar's a good sort, he is."

Philip closed his fingers around one of the bits of glass and tried to imagine a toga-clad boy his own age playing with the very same marble. And now that boy was long dead, his bones turned to dust. Could he have imagined that centuries later a British boy would hold that very same marble in his hand? The thought gave him a deliciously morbid shiver, and he wondered who would be handling his chess set centuries from now.

"Like 'em, do you?" Mr. Trumble asked over the stack of goods he had gathered.

"I've never seen anything like them."

"Going to take 'em down to the British Museum and make a fortune one day." He bent down to tap his knee. "Only . . . this leg can't take the Anwyl no more. Got kicked by a horse ten years ago."

"I'm sorry," Philip said, wincing sympathetically.

"Oh, it doesn't pain me any. Just can't make the hill. But children bring 'em to me once in a while and trade 'em for sour balls."

"They trade these for *candy*?"

The mustache widened with a grin. "Candy's a rare treat for some of the little ones. And I tell 'em what I plan to do with the marbles, so there ain't any inception on my part. You should go search some out for yourself, if you're interested."

"You mean *anyone* can look for them?"

"Anyone without a lame leg, that is." Soon the shopkeeper had the order packed neatly in a soap box. Philip handed over the money his mother had given him, pocketed the change, and thanked the shopkeeper for allowing him to look at the marbles.

"Any time, Mr. Hollis. Are you *sure* you don't want me to send it on later?"

"No thank you," Philip grunted, hoisting the box in his arms.

Mr. Trumble came around the counter to open the door. "You tell your mother I put an extra cake of soap in there, on account of you bein' new customers. Compliments of *Trumbles*."

"Thank you," Philip said again.

As he trudged home with his load, he found himself wondering if the shopkeeper had any children. A twinge of envy passed through him at the thought. What must it be like to have a father who actually

76

seemed to have time to converse with children instead of giving them a pat on the head every so often? If only his father had been more like Mr. Trumble.

Father saved people's lives! he reminded himself, suddenly ashamed of his disloyalty. How many boys could make the same boast?

But he could also recall days at a time when his father did not come home until he and his sisters were asleep. Oh, he'd understood that there were many ailing people that Father had to help, but even on the brief times that they were together, it seemed that his father was distracted. By what, Philip had no idea, but he'd always felt a resentment toward the vague enemy that positioned itself between a father and his own children.

Perhaps it was this resentment that had kept him dry-eyed at the funeral, even as his mother and sisters wept. Or perhaps, he thought now, it was because he had spent years grieving the loss of his father. The grave was just another excuse for not being at home.

———

After hearing the children's prayers that night, Julia changed into a nightgown and went to the bedroom that was to be hers. She was grateful to see that Fiona had slipped inside earlier and turned down the covers. She felt so bone-weary that it was a relief not having even that small chore to tend to. Yet, she thought as she pulled the sheets about her shoulders, her weariness was different from the tortured lethargy that had gripped her for the past five weeks. Tonight, her limbs were simply worn out from physical labor, and they sank greedily into the feather mattress. Today her bedroom and Fiona's had both been cleaned and scrubbed, and the kitchen was now clear of cobwebs.

She offered up a quiet prayer, thanking God again for giving them a place to live and for His protection and guidance. As her thoughts began to melt into a dreamlike state, she recalled what the vicar had said regarding Karl Herrick and Ethan Banning. *If you give someone a chance to prove himself, you'll almost always be pleasantly surprised.* Was God now giving her a chance to prove herself? And would He be pleasantly surprised if she succeeded in making something worthy from the ruins that had become her life?

Not surprised, my child, a gentle voice beyond her thoughts seemed to say. *For I'm going to help you all the way.*

Saint Jude's lone bell broke solemnly through the chill morning air as Julia, the children, and Fiona exited through the front door of the *Larkspur*. It was Julia's first church attendance since her husband's funeral, and she wore a simply cut gown of obsidian black poplin with covered silk buttons. The children were dressed in their Sunday best, the girls in matching lavender lawn, trimmed with lace, and Philip in a light gray suit.

Sundays were almost the only time Fiona didn't wear the standard black-and-white alpaca of a maid. While her wardrobe was limited, she had good taste in clothes and today wore a dress of burgundy and white striped crepe and a small leghorn hat, trimmed with rosebuds made of burgundy sateen.

The five of them drew looks from several villagers while crossing the green by the church. Julia chose to believe it was because they were new faces, or perhaps because they looked nice, and not because people were surprised to see that they were still alive.

Saint Jude's was situated among some elms and beeches to the east of the green, which stretched out between the river and Church Street. On the medieval building's south side, a stone wall and wooden lych-gate surrounded the headstones of the churchyard. Several ancient yew trees lined the inside of the wall, conceivably planted to repel cows from wandering in from the green in earlier days. Worshipers entered the church through an arched doorway, over which the words *Watch and Pray, for Ye Know Not When the Hour Cometh* were carved into stone.

Inside, brightly colored stained-glass windows, a chancel choir, robed in white, and an organ in the gallery at the west end added to the ecclesiastical aura that so typified the Church of England. As they moved past several rows of filled bench pews in the nave, Julia was grateful to receive at least a few bashful smiles directed toward her family. Perhaps not *all* of the villagers were waiting to see if the ghost of Jake Pitt would murder them in their beds. An even greater relief came with the realization that there wasn't a servants' gallery and Fiona would be able to sit with the family.

"I see a good many children here," Julia whispered to Aleda when they had settled themselves into an empty pew near the front. The girl grimaced and shrank down farther in her seat.

"They were all staring at me when we passed. I'm sure they'll be making fun of my hair tomorrow."

"Why, they were just being friendly. And your hair is lovely."

"You have to say that because yours is the same color."

"I don't have to say anything. And let's take our minds off ourselves for a little while, shall we?" Julia admonished gently.

Vicar Wilson's sermon on the good Samaritan was delivered in a strong voice that belied the condition of his limbs, for Julia had noticed a hesitation as he mounted the step to the pulpit. She felt an immediate guilt for the two days the good reverend had helped at the *Larkspur*, even though he had taken on the lightest of duties. *He has been a true good Samaritan.*

"It actually makes Papa feel better to be moving about," Henrietta reassured Julia at the outskirts of the crowd gathered outside the church door. "His joints ache him more if he spends too much time in a chair."

Even though some villagers had been generous with nods and smiles, none ventured over to meet them save Vicar Wilson, the Worthy sisters, and Luke the gardener. "People here are a bit timid of city folk," the good vicar explained, as if worried that Julia and her family might be disappointed.

"Has the ghost anything to do with it?" Julia asked, lowering her voice.

"Well . . . perhaps a little. But we'll show them it's all in their minds, won't we?" Offering his arm, he led Julia and her group from one cluster of villagers to another and made introductions. Perhaps it was the vicar's presence that solicited a surprisingly warm welcome from the dairy farmers, shopkeepers, housewives, and factory workers they met. Their children, though, tended to hang back and give shy stares to Julia's children—who did the same themselves.

Presently Julia and her group set out for lunch at the *Bow and Fiddle*. After three days of only pastries and sandwiches, Julia decided

79

it was time for everyone to have a hot meal. She still hoped to find a cook, though, and mentally kicked herself for not making inquiries of Henrietta after church. Even after paying for groceries and a cook's wages, meals would be less expensive at home than at an inn. And she wanted to be a good steward of the money entrusted to her.

About one third of the tables at the half-timbered inn were taken when the five sat down to a lunch of the beef and dumplings that Mrs. Jewel Worthy had recommended. Mr. Pool, the owner, came over to make their acquaintance—he was a portly man wearing a fringe of gray whiskers below the jaw, extending from ear to ear. "I was worried when I heard someone was opening up th' *Larkspur* again, I don't mind telling you," he said to Julia while wiping his hands with his white apron. "There just ain't enough business for two inns in Gresham. But a lodging house . . . well, that won't affect me none at all."

"I'm sorry about the loss of coaching business," Julia told him, to which he responded with a shrug.

"I get more customers come evenings, so I can't complain. Folks still need a place to visit." He gave her a cagey grin. "And maybe your lodgers will want to supper here once in a while. I've the best cook in Gresham working in my kitchen."

Julia smiled. The meal had indeed been tasty. "The best cook?"

With a slight blush, the innkeeper confessed, "Well, second best, if you care to know th' truth. I the best won't budge from th' squire's kitchen, so there you have it."

———

That afternoon, Fiona and Mrs. Hollis devoted their cleaning efforts to the pantry. Each had bound her hair up in a scarf to keep it protected from dust and webs for the evensong church service that night. "All we need are eye patches to look like pirates," Fiona had remarked, and it was good to hear her mistress laugh.

"I would really like to hire Audrey Herrick in the kitchen," Mrs. Hollis said a little while later as she wiped down shelves with a wet dish towel. "She would be a great asset to our lodging house. But I can't offer her any wages until we've lodgers on the way, and we need a cook right now."

Fiona nodded down from the chair upon which she stood to reach cobwebs with her broom. "If only I'd learned. But an older sister took care of the cookin' at home until I was eleven, and then she left

80

to take a position at the big house."

"Eleven," her mistress breathed. "Why, that's Aleda's age. How did you bear it?"

"I had no choice but to bear it. Besides, that was the way things were. Some had it much worse, so I've no right to complain." The subject was not a comfortable one, so Fiona directed it back to the matter of the cook. "But I'd be willin' to try, until you can hire Mrs. Herrick."

Mrs. Hollis shook her head. "The guest chambers need both our attention. I've not paid much notice to what goes into shopping for food and cooking, but it seems that the whole process takes a lot of time. If I were to hire someone for the kitchen, then it wouldn't be right to dismiss her as soon as it's practical for Mrs. Herrick to come. And if I demoted someone who's had complete charge of the kitchen to a lesser position, then there would surely be some resentment."

They worked on to the sounds of broom straws swishing against walls and the squeak of a cleaning cloth against wood, until an idea presented itself to Fiona. She dropped down into the chair and smiled.

"What if you hired someone permanent to help with the cleaning now, missus? You mentioned needin' to hire other servants later. That would free me to work in the kitchen until Mrs. Herrick can come. Surely I can manage for a while."

Mrs. Hollis paused from her work to cock her head thoughtfully. "Why, of course. It's such a simple solution. But I'll help you."

That brought some doubts to Fiona's mind. Mrs. Hollis had likely never set foot in a kitchen until coming here. She didn't want to offend but couldn't help asking, "Are you sure, missus?"

"We can teach each other. And with the two of us in the kitchen, we should be back to the housework in no time."

"You shouldn't be having to do that."

Her mistress held up a hand, already beginning to redden at the knuckles. "My days of being the fine lady are over, Fiona. Besides, it could be an adventure, learning to cook. We may just surprise ourselves."

———

"This porridge seems rather thick to me," Julia said the next morning while using both hands to stir the contents of the black pot on the stove with a long metal spoon.

Fiona stopped slicing bacon at the table and walked over to take

81

a look. "How many oats did you add to the water?"

"Well, hundreds," Julia replied a bit testily, for her arms felt like lead. "I didn't know I was supposed to *count* them."

The maid took no offense but smiled. "I didn't mean individual oats, missus."

"Oh." Releasing one hand to point briefly to an empty brown bag on a cupboard shelf, she said, "I used those."

"The whole bag?"

"Wasn't I supposed to?"

Fiona looked down into the pot again. "I believe they swell as they cook. Shall I add some more water?"

"I suppose you should." Julia grimaced as she pulled the spoon through the muck. "It's like stirring glue."

Returning from the basin with a kettle of water, Fiona poured in a little at a time until Julia nodded. "Much better. But I shouldn't wonder that we'll be eating porridge for a week. Can it be warmed over?"

"I don't see why not."

"It's still sticking to the bottom of the pot. Is it supposed to do that?"

Fiona made a helpless gesture. "Could it be the fire?"

"That's it," Julia told her. With her chin she pointed to the row of knobs. "Will you turn up the one on the far right?"

"Up, missus?"

"My arms are going to fall off if it doesn't cook any faster."

"Why don't you let me stir for a while?"

"Thank you, but I'm rather determined to see this through." Julia smiled. "I never thought I would feel prideful about cooking a pot of porridge."

Fiona smiled back as she scooped several spoonfuls of lard into a pan for frying the bacon and eggs. "If only Mrs. Capshaw could see us now, missus."

————

Philip Hollis dressed quickly Monday morning, pulling on a pair of brown corded trousers and buttoning up his favorite shirt of blue muslin. He had talked his mother out of having him wear his Sunday best after hearing from Miss Wilson that most of the students were the children of dairy laborers and would be dressed in plain smocks or jerkins. He certainly couldn't fit in by parading his city upbringing.

Leaving his room at the end of the corridor, he walked down to his sisters' door and applied a rousing series of knocks. It wouldn't do to be late on their first day of school, and if he knew anything about his sisters, he knew they took much longer to dress than he did.

When no sound came, Philip knocked again. "Aleda? Grace?" he called, wondering why Mother hadn't already gotten the two up and going. *I'm sure not going to wait for them,* he thought. But then he reasoned that they'd likely had trouble sleeping after Mother had told them about the supposed ghost.

Not that *he'd* suffered any fright. Why, he could barely remember his head hitting the pillow. But Aleda and Grace, well, they couldn't help being girls. As he rapped upon the door and called out still a third time, the guilty thought hit him that he should have brought his pillow and blankets into the girls' room and made a bed upon their carpet last night. He was the man of the family now, and here he was allowing his sisters to sleep unprotected, if only from their own imaginations.

"I'm coming in!" he called before easing the door open and finding himself staring at an unoccupied bed. One corner of the coverlet touched the floor—making beds was a new experience for everyone in the house except Fiona—and it was clear to see that the girls had vacated their room some time ago.

And they didn't even care to wake me! he thought indignantly as he raced down the corridor to the dining room and almost bumped into Aleda.

"Mother just sent me to fetch you," she said, the sides of her long auburn hair drawn up into a white ribbon at the crown of her head. "We're going to take our meals in the kitchen until we have more servants."

"How long have you been awake?"

"Oh, Grace and I woke up ages ago. We wanted to give ourselves plenty of time to dress for school."

"Didn't you have trouble sleeping?"

She cocked her head at him. "Why, no. We slept like stones."

Humbled somewhat, Philip followed her into the kitchen and saw Mother at the stove, wearing a white apron over her black dress.

"Good morning, Philip," she said. Strands of red hair fell from a coil at her neck and her face was flush from the heat, but her expression was one of triumph. "I'm cooking porridge."

Fiona smiled, her appearance also slightly disheveled as she brought a platter to set on the table. "And I've fried some bacon. Eggs are still in the pan."

"Good. I'm as hungry as a bear," Philip said, giving one of Grace's brown curls a playful tug before pulling out a chair beside her.

Aleda, now seated across the table from him, was attempting to stab a strip of bacon from the platter with her fork. "It's a bit overdone," she leaned forward to whisper to Philip.

"Children, wait until we've a chance to pray," Mother warned, dishing up porridge into a bowl. A strange burnt odor wafted over from the side of the kitchen. Philip discovered its origin after Mother and Fiona sat down to join them and the prayer was said. Black specks and flakes were scattered through the porridge in his bowl, as thick as raisins in Christmas pudding.

And the eggs that Fiona had spoken of should have stayed in the pan, Philip thought, for they too were not up to Mrs. Capshaw's standards. Strings of hardened yolks had leaked into the whites, and appetite-killing grease pooled in every indentation. He raised an alarmed eyebrow to Aleda, who sent him back a helpless shrug. *You're the oldest,* her expression seemed to say. *It's up to you to say something.*

But he didn't have to, for the next sound he heard was a sniffle. He turned to his mother, seated at the head of the table on his right, just in time to see a tear roll down her cheek and drip into her porridge.

"This is inedible," she whispered.

"The eggs too," Fiona said dully from Aleda's other side. The maid's expression matched their mother's.

"Why, no it isn't." Philip took a big spoonful of his porridge, hoping God would forgive him for the lie. He gulped it down without chewing and motioned for Aleda to do likewise. She apparently wanted to spare Fiona's feelings as well, for she picked up a strip of bacon with her fingers and began to work the tip with her teeth, like an Eskimo chewing whale blubber.

Deciding to follow Philip's lead and then some, Grace spooned porridge into her mouth, gulped it down, and stretched her lips into an enraptured smile. "This porridge is heavenly, Mother!"

Philip cut his eyes to her with a warning look, but the damage was done, for another sniffle came from the head of the table. Quickly he heaped another clump of oats onto his spoon, but before he could force it up to his lips, he heard a noise that sounded suspiciously like a low chuckle. He looked at his mother—she was wiping her eyes with her napkin but smiling at the same time.

"You three are terrible actors," she said quietly.

"Why no, it's quite . . ." Philip began.

"Bless you for it, but you can stop eating now."

"Thank you, Mother!" Grace gushed, dropping her spoon into her bowl as if it had contained hemlock. Fiona put up a hand to cover a smile, and soon laughs erupted from all quarters of the table.

"All we have left from last night are some bread and cheese," Mother said presently, wiping her eyes again. "We'll have that for breakfast."

It sounded like a feast to Philip.

————

Breakfast was forgotten as the three set out for the short walk down Church Lane. The sight of windows glittering through a line of elder trees ahead and the rosy brick of the gabled school building only brought anxieties, which were heightened upon the sight of three dozen children of all ages and sizes at play in the school yard. Girls in ankle-length frocks and pinafores and colored hair ribbons joined hands for "drop the handkerchief" or scratched out play houses in the dirt; boys in corduroys or farmers' smocks played marbles or tossed a ball back and forth. Philip reckoned to himself that he'd never seen so many children together in one place. How did they all fit inside the school building?

"What if they ask about the ghost?" Grace whispered, clutching the brown paper parcel that contained her lunch—again bread and cheese—with both hands.

Aleda was quick to offer advice. "You just tell them they're ignorant rubes if they believe such nonsense."

"And I can see you're going to have lots of friends here," Philip told her.

With a toss of the head, Aleda replied, "Well, I'm sure I don't care. This is going to be such a bore."

Grace clamped a hand over her little mouth. "Mother says not to use slang."

"What slang?"

"You said 'bore.' "

"That's not slang."

"Yes it is," Philip cut in, frowning. "And try to look pleasant, will you?"

85

Aleda tightened her lips at these admonitions and turned her attention back to the activity outside the school building. The three kept to themselves on the fringe of the yard, pretending not to notice the curious stares from some of the children at play, until a pleasant-faced woman appeared in the doorway at the top of the steps and rang a handbell. There were squeals and chatter as the girls formed a line at the bottom of the steps, with the boys bringing up the rear. When the last student had been swallowed up by the building, Philip turned to his sisters and said, "We'd best be going in now."

"Now?" Grace echoed in an uncertain tone.

"It's only going to get harder the longer we wait."

The doors opened up into a good-sized schoolroom, filled with rows of desks. Queen Victoria's portrait stared regally down at them from the back wall, and a map beside it showed the large part of the world that owed allegiance to her. On the opposite wall another doorway led into a second classroom. A dozen or so of the younger children were following the schoolmistress through this doorway, and at Philip's urging, Grace solemnly walked behind them.

At the head of the main room a man rose from a desk. He had close-cropped dark hair and brass spectacles, a starched collar, and a general demeanor of authority on a medium frame as erect as a lightning rod. Captain Powell was his name, Miss Wilson had told them, adding that he'd been pensioned after losing an arm in South Africa. Philip forced himself not to stare at the pinned-up left sleeve, though it fascinated him immensely.

"You must be the Hollis children," Captain Powell said. The blue eyes that studied them were penetrating but not unkind. "Your mother has already given me your names and ages. I've prepared desks for you."

Philip and Aleda exchanged relieved glances. To have one's own desk would be like having a home away from home, an island of refuge in this sea of unfamiliarity. As he went over to the back-row desk that had been pointed out to him, Philip was grateful that the schoolmaster hadn't required the class to say "good morning" in unison, or asked him and Aleda to give short introductory speeches, or fostered any other embarrassing attention upon them.

A short stack of texts was ready upon his desk top. Reverently Philip ran a finger along the spine of the familiar *Oxford Study of Mathematics. Smith's Rules of Grammar* was there too and had never looked so good to him, mixed in with an unfamiliar-looking history text. *This isn't going to be so bad after all,* he thought. As the class rose for morning devotions, he returned the grin of the boy seated next to him, a lad wearing a brown linsey-woolsey shirt that matched the color of his hair so closely that it could have been woven from it.

"Name's Jeremiah," the boy whispered under the sound of shuffling feet.

"Philip," Philip whispered back.

"What happened to your finger?"

"Sprained it."

"Seen the ghost yet?"

"Had breakfast with him this morning."

"No!"

"Yes! Beastly table manners, but you should see him carve the bacon."

Both boys were silent for the morning prayer and joined in a chorus of voices for the Scripture recitation. Fortunately, it was the first chapter of Psalms, which Philip and Aleda had already memorized under Mr. Hunter.

"Blessed is the man that walketh not in the counsel of the ungodly, nor standeth in the way of sinners, nor sitteth in the seat of the scornful. . . ."

When the shuffling began again as students took to their seats, Jeremiah eyed Philip again. "D'you like to go fishin'?"

"Never been."

"Tomorrow?"

Philip grinned at the boy. *I may just learn to like it here.*

*T*hat same afternoon, Julia was just about to enter her bedroom to fetch a bonnet when the front bell clanged. *I wonder if that's Miss Wilson.* If so, Julia would be saved a walk to the vicarage, for she had decided to ask the vicar's daughter if she knew of anyone willing to take on a temporary position as a cook. Preparing and then cleaning up after the disastrous breakfast this morning had taken her and Fiona over two hours—they simply could not afford to take that much time away from the other desperately needed cleaning chores, even if she hired another maid.

As she hurried down the corridor toward the hall, she heard voices and realized that Fiona had answered the door. Indeed, a tall woman of about forty-five was accompanying the maid into the room and introduced herself as Mrs. Ophelia Rhodes.

Julia stepped over to extend her hand. "Julia Hollis. And this is Fiona O'Shea."

"Forgive me for not calling earlier," the woman said as she took Julia's hand. "But I just returned from Nonely last night after two days away. A cow birthed premature triplet calves and we almost lost them."

"I'm happy to make your acquaintance, Mrs. Rhodes." Julia noticed then the iron pot that Fiona was holding by the handle.

"Mrs. Rhodes brought us some mutton stew, ma'am. I'll take it to the kitchen and brew up some tea."

Julia thanked Fiona and turned to her visitor again. "How thoughtful of you. We were going to have to resort to tinned foods for supper tonight."

"Then I came just in time, didn't I?" Mrs. Rhodes said, feigning a little shudder. "Actually, Mrs. Bass, my cook, produced the stew. I can't boil an egg." She was unfashionably tanned and robust for a woman, wearing an unadorned gown of umber poplin, and her brown hair was drawn into a careless knot. The moss-colored eyes were warm, though, and Julia suspected that she'd found another friend in Gresham.

"Please make yourself comfortable," Julia said, indicating the cluster of chairs and two sofas.

Mrs. Rhodes looked around the room on her way across the floor. "Why, it looks just as it did in the old days."

"Yes?"

"Ethan Banning and my husband were good friends. Have you had many calls?"

Julia shook her head. "I suppose the ghost and all . . ."

"Oh, they'll get over that. Trust me."

"That's what Vicar Wilson says."

"There now, you see?" The two settled themselves on opposite ends of a sofa.

"Do you live on a dairy farm, Mrs. Rhodes?" Julia asked.

The woman smiled. "Hardly. I'm an amateur veterinary. When Miss Wilson told me you had been a doctor's wife, I felt compelled to meet you." Her face became sober. "I'm sorry your husband passed away. Is it terribly hard for you?"

The little ache came to Julia's chest, but this time induced by guilt. For the first time in the almost six weeks since Philip's death, she'd gone through the good part of a day without thinking about him. *He's still the father of your children,* she reminded herself.

"We're managing, thank you," Julia finally told her, and then steered the subject away from herself. "Is your husband a doctor as well?"

"He is at that. Of people, not animals."

They spent some time in small talk, with Mrs. Rhodes asking about Julia's children and her plans for the *Larkspur,* and filling in bits of information about Gresham and its townsfolk that Henrietta and Vicar Wilson had inadvertently left out. When Fiona returned with tea, Julia asked her to join them. She hoped Mrs. Rhodes wouldn't mind having a servant sit in on the conversation, but after all the recent sacrifices Fiona had made for her family, it was getting more and more difficult to think of her as anything less than a friend. And if Mrs. Rhodes *did* mind, well, she had misjudged her.

Mrs. Rhodes didn't appear to take offense at Julia's invitation, but as it turned out, it was Fiona who demurred politely, saying she had some tidying up to do elsewhere. *I'm content to stay in my place,* the eyes above the knowing smile she gave Julia seemed to say.

"How did you become a veterinary doctor?" Julia asked her visitor over their cups of tea after Fiona had excused herself and left the room.

"Amateur," Mrs. Rhodes reminded her. "And I have my husband to thank for it. It saved my life, I believe."

"How so?" Julia asked.

The corners of Mrs. Rhodes' moss-green eyes creased as she related how she'd spent twelve years grieving over the childless condition of her marriage. And then one day her husband, Isaiah Rhodes, came back from a trip to London with a stack of books on animal husbandry. "He said he was weary of being called out every time a cow suffered mastitis or a dray horse had colic. I was irritated at first. My father was a glover in Manchester. What did I know about animals?"

But she became interested in spite of herself, she said, and her informal practice grew—so much that farmers as far away as Hammerhill sometimes sent messages requiring her services or showed up at her house with a pig or favorite ailing dog in the back of a wagon. Two years ago she'd had to hire the churchwarden's nephew to assist her with calls. "I complain incessantly about how busy I am, but I wouldn't give up my little practice for anything."

"It has given you a purpose, hasn't it?" Julia said.

"As my husband so wisely assumed it would. One has to have a purpose in life." Tilting her head to study her, Mrs. Rhodes added, "And if I may say so, Mrs. Hollis, you sound as if you've learned that lesson yourself."

Julia smiled. "I'm learning it as we speak." She then told Mrs. Rhodes how making plans for the lodging house gave her new hope for the future after her husband's death. There was no need to bring up Philip's gambling—spousal betrayal wasn't a subject comfortably discussed with new acquaintances over tea.

As the three Hollis children set out for the *Larkspur* that afternoon, Philip was not surprised to learn that Aleda didn't share his opinion about school. "I think all the girls in the fourth standard are dull-witted," she sniffed. "Even if they didn't bring up that awful ghost story. And none even tried to be my friend."

Philip looked back over his left shoulder at the school building. During break he'd struck up friendships with two boys his age—Jeremiah Toft, whose father was a groomsman for the squire, and Ben Mayhew, the wheelwright's son. Some of the other boys did happen to seize upon the subject of the *Larkspur's* ghost as a method of tormenting the new fellow, but when it became obvious that their barbs couldn't penetrate Philip's armor of humor, they gave up and became sociable.

Turning back to Aleda, Philip said, "Well, of course they aren't going to be friendly if you think they're dull-witted."

"But I never said that to *them*."

"Doesn't matter," Philip told her, shifting his books from one arm to the other as they turned the corner onto Market Lane to head for the front door. "They could tell you were thinking it. And Mother says you have to *be* a friend before you can have one."

"The Good Book says that too, dearie," came a voice across the lane and off to their left as soon as an old blanket. The three turned their faces as one to where the two lace spinners sat in a patch of sunlight between a pear and a yew tree. One of the Worthy sisters— Philip couldn't tell them apart yet—nodded her head at them, while the other shook hers just as adamantly.

"It don't say that at all, Iris," the headshaker said. "What it says is that ye should show yourself friendly if ye want to have friends."

"Well, it sounds like the very same thing to me," the one who'd first spoken replied. Both sets of gnarled fingers never stopped moving even as their owners spoke. Turning back to Aleda, the woman said, "Many a smile has won many a friend, dear. Try smiling tomorrow, and things will be different."

The headshaker was now nodding agreement. "Ye can attract more flies with honey than with vinegar, dear."

Aleda, who now wore two spots of color upon her cheeks, nonetheless managed to stretch her lips into a grimacelike smile. "Thank you," she said, then indicated the two textbooks under her arm. "Well, we have homework."

Both wrinkled faces beamed. "Makes the mind grow, dear."

———

The children came through the front door from school, and after Julia introduced them to Mrs. Rhodes, Grace asked timidly if the veterinary lady could take a look at her sparrow.

"Why, I would be happy to," Mrs. Rhodes replied. Minutes later, Grace came back into the room with her bird, now housed in a roomier wire cage that Aleda had found in the gardening cottage yesterday. Mrs. Rhodes reached into the cage and scooped the sparrow into her lap. The tiny bird, which must have been all chirped out after four days in captivity, simply sat there blinking its eyes as its wing was probed.

"Hmm, this is as fine a job of splinting as I've ever seen. Is this your handiwork?"

"Jensen, our butler in London, did it," Philip told her, leaning over the back of the sofa.

Mrs. Rhodes nodded. "Well, since the bones are so light, they knit together much more quickly than other animals'. You should be able to release him in another two weeks."

"Him?" Grace asked with eyes wide.

"Why, yes. It's a male of the species." Mrs. Rhodes gave the child standing at the sofa arm an indulgent smile. "And I take it you've gone and dubbed the little fellow Florence or Helen or something in that vein?"

"Christine," Grace replied sheepishly.

"Ah, another equally feminine name. Well, I'm certain the trauma will not impede his healing in any way."

"But I should change the name, don't you think? I shouldn't like to be called by a boy's name."

"How about Bertram?" Julia asked. Back in London, Bertram was the younger brother of one of Aleda's playmates, and the girls had always seemed fond of him.

But Aleda wrinkled her nose. "Bertram always cried whenever he lost at croquet."

"I once had a parakeet named Freddie," Mrs. Rhodes offered.

Grace considered this, studying the bird, but then shook her head. "I'm sorry," she said politely. "But he doesn't *look* like a Freddie."

Fiona came into the room bearing mugs of chocolate for the children and set the tray down upon the nearest tea table. As she handed out mugs, she listened to Aleda's account of the situation. "What about Tiny Tim?" she suggested right away. "You know, from Mr. Dickens? Being crippled and all . . ."

Grace brightened, and Mrs. Rhodes clasped her hands together. "Why, it fits perfectly." To Fiona, she said, "You've obviously a gift for titles."

"Not that I'm aware of, ma'am."

"Oh, but I believe otherwise and must confess to some envy. Naming animals is a talent that has eluded me, which explains why my poor parakeet was named Freddie. And my favorite mare, Lucy, will be foaling in another month. May I send for you after it happens?"

"But I've never named a horse before," Fiona confessed.

"Well, it would do no harm for you to give it a try, would it? I can always decline if you suggest something like Nero or Jezebel, which I doubt most seriously will happen."

With that understanding Fiona agreed, saying she felt honored to be asked. Mrs. Rhodes then got to her feet and apologized for staying so long. "I hope I've not kept you from anything important," she said to Julia.

"Absolutely not," Julia said, walking her to the door. "I've enjoyed your visit tremendously." And she still had time to walk to the vicarage before supper. But it occurred to her suddenly that Mrs. Rhodes might know of a prospective cook.

"Excuse me, but perchance do you know of someone looking for a temporary position as a cook?" Julia asked.

"Why, I certainly do," the woman answered after a thoughtful silence. "Betty Moser. She's moved back to Gresham with her family, the Upjohns, just for a month or so while her husband is working as a laborer on a railroad extension in Wolverhampton. I sewed up a gash on her father's collie just last week, and Betty complained of sharing a bed with three sisters. I believe she would be most anxious to have a little peace and earn wages at the same time."

After Mrs. Rhodes was gone, Julia gathered her children around her on the sofa and listened to accounts of their day at school. Only Aleda's face crumpled with the telling. "They didn't like me."

"I'm so sorry," Julia told her. "But they don't know you, Aleda. Put forth a little more effort to be friendly tomorrow, and I know your day will be better." Thinking that a walk would cheer her up, Julia asked the girl if she would like to accompany her across the river to speak with Betty Moser, but Aleda seemed more content to stay home and mope. Grace was absorbed with her sparrow, and Philip had expressed a desire to get right to his homework, so Julia bade them all farewell and started out alone. She got no farther than the gate when she heard the front door open, and Philip caught up with her.

"I don't want you to be alone," he said protectively.

Julia was touched but resisted the urge to kiss his cheek out in the light of day—such displays of emotion seemed to embarrass this thirteen-year-old of late. "But I'll be fine. If you have studying . . ."

"I can study later."

They walked north up Market Lane, passing the Bartley Subscription Library and the smithy forge before crossing the bridge over the

93

Bryce. To their right were two red-brick barnlike buildings that housed the cheese factory, followed by three neat rows of cottages inhabited by factory workers and their families. The rest of the area was taken up by vast hedged pastures of black-and-white cows.

It was in the garden of one of the cottages that Julia found the Upjohns. Two women sat knitting on a bench, surrounded by several rowdy children of all ages, with straw-colored hair as curly as watch springs. Julia presumed the younger woman on the bench to be Betty Moser.

"Me dotter can cook just fine," Mrs. Upjohn said in answer to Julia's timidly stated question.

She had forgotten to inquire of Mrs. Rhodes if the young woman had even seen the inside of a kitchen. Mrs. Upjohn was a square-jawed woman with bad teeth and a chaotic topknot of the same straw color as the children's. She leaned forward in her chair to fix Julia with an appraising eye.

"All me gels—they can cook, clean, iron . . . even help out wi' butchering pigs come thet time o' year. Would you be needin' a chambermaid or two?"

"Not yet," Julia said, taking a backward step from the intimidating stare. When she could finally speak an uninterrupted word to Betty, she asked if the girl would care to move into the cook's chamber at the *Larkspur*. Betty's eyes widened at the suggestion.

"Thank you kindly, ma'am, but me brother can take me in every mornin' and fetch me in the cart after supper."

"Are you quite sure?" Julia asked, darting a quick look at the size of the cottage in proportion to the number of children milling about. Surely the young woman would be longing for some privacy by now.

The fair head bobbed. "Thank you kindly, ma'am," she repeated. "But I'd just as soon stay t'home."

There was nothing more to discuss, so Julia said a polite farewell and turned with her son to start back.

"Maybe if you agreed to put elder twigs in her room . . ." Philip whispered when they were almost out of hearing range.

Julia started. "Surely you don't think that's why she won't stay."

"Looks that way to me," the boy answered, then sighed. "And it's that Jake Pitt's fault. You'd think he'd have better sense than to allow himself to be carried through a door headfirst."

*B*y Good Friday, two weeks after they'd moved into the *Larkspur*, Philip had regained full use of his finger, the sparrow Tiny Tim was finally set free, and Betty Moser proved herself a fairly decent cook. And as things improved in the kitchen, they improved at school for Aleda. Once she finally faced up to the fact that longing for the past was keeping her from enjoying the present, she snapped out of her self-imposed misery and began to apply herself to making friends. She even resumed practice on the pianoforte in the hall. Upon discovering her talent for the instrument, Captain Powell had asked her to accompany the class with hymns during Monday morning chapel. Philip and Grace had acquired playmates from school as well, and it did Julia's heart good to see the children have some fun during the times that they weren't needed to help with the household chores.

And now this! Julia thought, turning the envelope over in her hand.

Fiona leaned upon her hoe. "Aren't you going to open it, missus?"

Julia had earlier declared it a perfect day to restore the front garden to a semblance of order, even though neither she nor Fiona had ever gardened. Unfortunately, they found it difficult to tell the legitimate plants from weeds and had to call upon passersby several times to seek advice.

Every villager who passed seemed to have more gardening knowledge than they did. And they all appeared willing and even flattered to share their expertise—often while sending occasional curious glances at the upper windows, perhaps in hopes of catching a glimpse of a spectral face. Mrs. Sway, the greengrocer's wife, was also kind enough to suggest that an elder tree planted on each side of the gate would be a tried-and-true repellent for ghosts.

And then Mr. Jones, the postman, had paused at the gate.

"I don't know a Mr. Norwood Kingston from Sheffield," Julia said, staring down at the return address. "This just *has* to be an inquiry about a room."

Three long weeks had passed since she'd sent off several advertisements, reading, *The Larkspur, temperance boardinghouse located in the tranquil village of Gresham, Shropshire, to let rooms . . .*

"Would you like me to open it?" Fiona asked, setting her hoe aside and wiping her hands upon her apron.

Julia gave her a nervous smile and handed it over. "If you wouldn't mind. And please read it to me."

The seconds seemed leaden as the housekeeper carefully broke the seal with a dirt-crusted fingernail. " 'Dear Mrs. Hollis,' " she finally said. " 'I read with interest your advertisement in *The Sunday Visitor. . . .*' "

The next day the postman brought two more letters of inquiry. As soon as she had the opportunity to slip away, Julia went to *Trumbles* and withdrew four pounds. She borrowed a wallpaper pattern book from Mr. Trumble and purchased three shiny lunch pails for sixpence each along with a card of fishing line Philip had requested for a half-penny. Next, she went to the butcher's and ordered a joint of lamb for Easter Sunday dinner. The rest of the money she dropped into her reticule.

She found Fiona in the hall, polishing the fireplace with leadblack. Some twelve feet away, Grace knelt upon the bench in front of the pianoforte and moved the index finger of each hand up and down upon the keys, producing inharmonious but not unpleasant sounds. Under the bench napped Buff, the yellow tabby Betty had given the girl for her sixth birthday last week. Grace was the first to notice Julia and stopped playing. "You went shopping, Mother?"

"I did indeed." Julia set her parcel down upon one of the sofas, returned Fiona's greeting, and walked over to kiss the top of Grace's head. "Did your brother and sister scatter already?"

The child turned on the bench and nodded, her bottom lip trembling just a bit. Before Julia could ask what was wrong, Fiona backed out of the fireplace and got to her feet, her chore finished. Sending a sympathetic look over to Grace, she said, "Miss Wilson asked if they would help her pick some cowslips on the Anwyl to decorate the church for Easter service. I didn't think you would mind. I'll tidy up their rooms."

Julia shook her head. "Thank you, but they'll have time to finish their chores this evening." She nudged Grace aside on the piano bench and sat down next to her. The commotion caused Buff to saunter off for more sedate surroundings. "You wanted to go with them, did you?"

Now a tear welled in the corner of one green eye. "Philip said I'm too little. He wants to look for marbles, too, and won't have time to watch me."

"Well, what if Fiona and I watched you?"

Grace's face brightened, and she held out both arms and wrapped them around Julia's neck. "Thank you, Mother!"

"You're welcome. Now, go see if you can fish your boots out of your armoire. Those slippers will never do."

"She'll need woolies too, ma'am," Fiona reminded. "The ground is still damp."

"Of course. Just look for the boots, and I'll be there in a minute."

When Grace had left the room, Julia turned back to Fiona. "You would enjoy a walk with us, wouldn't you? You've worked so hard these past two weeks."

The Irishwoman smiled but shook her head. "You go enjoy some time with your daughter. Besides, the fireplace in the dining room needs attention."

"But that's not a housekeeper's task, is it?"

"Not a housekeeper's task?" Fiona echoed.

Julia went over to the sofa, reached into her reticule, and pulled out two pound sterling notes. "Your past month's wages, Fiona," she said, crossing over to where her confused friend stood. "And well-deserved."

Fiona shook her head again. "You haven't a single lodger yet, ma'am—I can wait. And that's double what I was paid in London."

"Ah, but you weren't the *housekeeper* in London, were you?" Julia, hardly able to contain her excitement, gave Fiona a quick embrace. "And we're going to visit the dressmaker here in Gresham and see about ordering some gowns to replace those uniforms. Housekeepers should dress according to their station, don't you think?"

She stopped babbling, a little hurt that Fiona's expression did not match the joy she was feeling. "Aren't you pleased at all, Fiona?"

"Why, yes . . . of course." The maid bit her lip. "But you need lodgers. . . ."

"And as to the lodgers, well, Jensen was right. We're going to fill this house."

Fiona's violet eyes widened. "More letters?"

"Two," Julia smiled, pulling the pair of envelopes from her reticule and waving them at her. "Two beautiful, wonderful letters!"

"I wish we had better cutlery," Julia sighed as she and Fiona picked up the dishes and flatware from the oak table in the dining room. The table was inordinately long, appearing to have been crafted inside the room itself, and was flanked by ten chairs on each side, with two at each end. Out of consideration for Betty Moser, who took care of the cooking and scullery work by herself, the family still took their meals in the kitchen, but this was Easter Sunday. Vicar Wilson, Henrietta, and Dr. and Mrs. Rhodes had joined them after the morning service for a feast of lamb with mint sauce, green peas, creamed onions, potatoes, and cabbage. Now that the guests were gone, Julia and Fiona had offered to help with the cleaning up so that Betty could spend part of the day with her own family.

"At least the china's nice," Fiona consoled. "Blue goes so well with a white cloth."

"It does at that," Julia replied but frowned down at the fork in her hand. So many other pressing matters had kept her from considering the state of the cutlery, but today she'd noticed Mrs. Rhodes give her place setting an odd glance when she first sat down at the table. The carbon-and-steel cutlery discolored quickly and required routine tedious rubbings with a dry cork and scouring powder to retain a semblance of its original luster. No doubt her lodgers-to-be would have been used to dining with silver. Would they complain of being given substandard service, perhaps even demand a reduction in rent? But with having to order linens, wall coverings, and new carpets for the six guest rooms, as well as hire on more servants soon, she could not justify spending the remaining funds on new cutlery. And there were provisions to consider. The kitchen had to be well stocked before the first guest arrived.

Fiona's voice drew her out of her reverie. "Have you considered praying for some silver cutlery?"

"Praying?" Julia resumed collecting pewter into a dishpan. "I've prayed more these past two months than in all the former years of my life combined. But don't you think it would be greedy praying for silver? Sort of Judas Iscariot-like?"

Her arms laden with a tray of soiled dishes, the housekeeper tilted her chin thoughtfully. "Why, I don't know, ma'am. It doesn't seem like a greedy request to me. And Judas certainly got his silver by other means than prayin'."

"God's given me so much lately. I don't want to sound ungrateful."

"But He knows your heart. And it appears to me that you're very grateful."

Because I've so much to be grateful for, Julia thought. Never again would she take for granted that her children had food and shelter. But would it be so wrong to ask for something that would enhance the business God had provided? *And if it's something that I don't truly need, He'll know that better than I will.*

"I'll pray for the silver," she finally said. "He can always say no." And if He did, well, she had already been blessed beyond measure.

Fiona smiled, hefting the tray in her arms. "I'll do the same."

———

The weather was just perfect on May Day morning, cool enough for woolies, but with no threat of rain in the cloudless sky. Though protesting that he was too old and manly for the possession of the garland, Philip allowed Aleda and Grace to wheedle him into assembling with the other village children on the green. He was relieved to see Ben and Jeremiah there as well, sporting sheepish looks—both had also declared themselves too mature for such foolishness. Children were decked out in their Sunday finest, their hats decorated with flowers and bright ribbons. A garland of bluebells, forget-me-nots, cowslips, violets, wallflowers, and daffodils had been prepared in school the day before, and the children would take turns carrying it as they proceeded through the streets of Gresham.

A photographer from Shrewsbury was readying his tripod and camera, and Miss Hillock, Grace's schoolmistress, arranged the children in rows—smallest to tallest. Philip, Ben, and Jeremiah gladly took the back row and assumed somber expressions. It was one thing to have one's image captured in a photograph to be displayed in the schoolhouse for perpetuity, but to be pictured as actually *enjoying* the event would be humiliating beyond words.

"Let's straighten your bow, shall we?" Miss Hillock said, leaning down to aid a small girl in front. When she'd finished primping every child within reach, she stepped back and allowed the photographer to do his job. The man's head disappeared behind a black cloth. The parents who had attended the festivities admonished children to hold still, and then there was a flash, followed by a sharp sulfur odor.

"You done fine," the photographer said when his head appeared again. "Remember to tell your mothers and fathers that I'll be taking family portraits in front of the Maypole during the picnic."

The children began their procession then, with Connie Jefferies, one of Grace's little friends from the infants' school, carrying the coin box. As a matter of custom, they went first to the vicarage behind Saint Jude's, where they struck up in a timid and shrill chorus, a three-verse song beginning,

A bunch of may I have brought you
And at your door it stands
It is but a sprout, but it's well put about
By the Lord Almighty's hands.

The door was opened by Vicar Wilson himself, who slipped a penny into the money box and admired the garland, proclaiming it as being "the best ever made."

The Manor House came next, set in a framework of pine and deciduous trees, manicured lawns, shrubbery, and outbuildings. The house itself was constructed of red sandstone with a red clay tile roof, high gables, and mullioned windows. It seemed much too huge to Philip for one man. This time a servant opened the door and turned over the penny after giving a perfunctory nod at the garland. After that the chattering gaggle of children marched to cottages and farmhouses, collecting coins that would later provide a school treat on the last day before summer recess. Even the most humble of cottages managed to produce a farthing or half-penny.

Mr. Trumble, in addition to his penny, liberally handed out boiled sweets at his general shop, bank, and post. "There now, plenty for everyone," he chuckled, seeing that no child left without a bulge in his cheek. Philip found that he was enjoying himself immensely, though he would never have admitted it to his friends.

As the procession moved on, he looked back over his shoulder at Mr. Trumble, who stood on his front stoop waving farewell, and wished again that his father had been more like the shopkeeper. With so many items needed to ready the *Larkspur* for the coming lodgers, Mother had sent him to *Trumbles* often during the past week. And he was more than willing to go, not just to look at the marbles, but because the shopkeeper acted as if he enjoyed their chats—as if what Philip was saying was of the greatest importance.

Mr. Trumble treated everyone with the same courtesy and interest, young or old, but what Philip appreciated most was that the shopkeeper *listened* without seeming to be thinking about something else. How many times had he been bursting to tell Father about an exciting cricket match or something like that . . . only to have his father pat his head after a while and say, "That's fine, son. Have you seen my newspaper?"

And yet he still believed his father had loved him, which brought about immense guilt whenever he tried to understand his own sense of having been abandoned. Especially when he had no words to convey how he felt. And if he could voice them, to whom would he speak? He certainly couldn't add to his mother's grief. She'd suffered enough and was probably still suffering, even though she managed to keep a brave front.

It seemed that most villagers were beginning to lose interest in the *Larkspur*'s ghost after all. As Julia approached the green, she was stopped for pleasantries several times. *Vicar Wilson was right*, she thought. How sad she had been to learn that he would be leaving within the month for a drier climate that would be kinder to his rheumatic joints. His kind, benevolent, grandfatherly ways would be sorely missed by everyone in Gresham. Henrietta's absence would be felt as well, for she was like a doting aunt to all who knew her.

Even though she would be leaving soon, Henrietta showed no signs of slackening with her duties. She could be seen moving from table to platform to Maypole, taking care of little details that added to the success of the celebration. Julia waited until opportunity presented itself and approached the vicar's daughter.

"Everything looks so nice," Julia told her after a quick shared embrace. She could not bring herself to say good-bye just yet. "It seems the whole village is involved."

"Well, almost," Henrietta said, her hazel eyes smiling. "It's because country folk work so hard. When they have a chance to play, they take it seriously."

"What can I do to help?"

Henrietta held up a basket of violets gathered into nosegays. "Would you like to put these around the punch and cake table?"

"But of course," Julia replied.

As she pinned flowers to the edge of the tablecloth, Julia smiled at the sound of children's laughter and chatter in the distance. Earlier, she and Fiona had joined the parents following the group as it passed the *Larkspur*, but turned back to prepare food for the picnic after the children crossed over the Bryce. Betty Moser had recently rejoined her husband, and Mr. and Mrs. Herrick and the other newly hired servants weren't due until next week, but Julia was confident that she and Fiona could prepare a decent lunch of sandwiches, cheese, and fruit. As time slipped up on them and the hamper had not yet been packed, Fiona had insisted that she go on ahead to the green and not miss the return of the children.

Fiona's absence was noted, for Luke Smith, the vicar's gardener, approached Julia ostensibly to ask how she liked the fine weather and to inform her that rain had all but ruined the past two May Day celebrations. "Well, then I'm sure everyone appreciates today's beautiful weather all the more," she told him, pausing from her work to give him a smile.

"Yes . . . appreciates," came out with a faint whistle, and he shifted his feet. "Don't suppose everyone is here yet, though."

She understood then and nodded in the direction of the *Larkspur*. "Miss O'Shea will be here shortly. She's packing our lunch."

Relief washed over the man's tanned face. "Well, uh, that's good."

"Would you hand me another pin from that cushion?" Julia asked him, bending slightly to position another nosegay. He obliged right away. She had assumed she'd found herself an assistant, but when she asked for another pin, there was no answer. "Mr. Smith?" she said, turning, only to come face-to-face with Mrs. Rhodes.

"Lovely table, Mrs. Hollis. Could you use some help?"

"Why, thank you."

They formed an efficient team, with Julia positioning nosegays and Mrs. Rhodes pinning. Ten minutes later, the last violets were set in place. Julia and the veterinary doctor took a step back to admire their work.

"Would you like to share our picnic?" Julia asked her, assuming Dr. Rhodes was out making a call.

Mrs. Rhodes flashed her a grateful smile but shook her head. "I just nipped over to see the decorations. Lucy's going to foal any day now, and I want to stay close to home. But do stop by later today, if you have the time. I've something that may interest you."

*N*ow then, stay put," Fiona muttered to the hamper lid as she trimmed the ends of the twine she'd used to make repairs. Philip had found the dusty old hamper last week while foraging about in the empty groomsman's apartment over the stables. Now that Fiona had it cleaned, it looked practically new, but she hadn't realized until this morning that the catch was broken. *At least it holds enough food*, she thought, lifting the hamper an inch from the table to test the patch job. It was quite heavy, causing her to smile at her mistress's earlier worries that they would all starve. *It's cutting back we'll be needing to do soon, or we'll lose our figures for sure.*

She was untying the apron from around the waist of her saffron-and-white checked gown when the bell tinkled at the courtyard door. Patting her straw hat down upon her crown, Fiona walked across the corridor to open it. Luke Smith stood there with an anxious smile across his clean-shaven face. He wore a black Sunday suit instead of his usual work clothes and had slicked back his hair with oil.

"Why, good day, Mr. Smith," Fiona said.

He seemed to take encouragement from her greeting, relaxing his smile a little. Nonetheless, his hands seemed to want for something to do; they alternated between dangling at his sides and hiding in his pockets. "Thought you might be wantin' some help toting your hamper."

"Why, that's very kind of you," Fiona had no choice but to declare. The hope in his expression saddened her—Luke was a decent person and she had no wish to hurt him. She was aware that allowing him to carry the hamper was only encouraging him, yet he would have felt humiliated had she turned him down.

He followed her into the kitchen and went over to the hamper on the table. "Had to fix it, did you?" he asked, surveying the twine.

"At the last minute, I'm afraid."

"A basket weaver lives down Worton Lane, past the old mill. Keegan's his name."

Fiona raised an eyebrow. "Irish?" She'd thought herself the only Irish person in Gresham.

"He could fix it up right fine for you." Luke's face brightened. "Why, I'll be happy to bring it over to him after the picnic."

"Oh no . . . thank you. I believe I would like to meet him anyway."

Panic flickered across Luke's expression, and perhaps a fair amount of jealousy. "He's got a wife and family too, he has."

"All the better," Fiona said. "I don't often have the opportunity to visit with other Irish folk."

He was obviously relieved to hear her intentions stated in the matter. Lifting the basket, he walked ahead of her to hold open the courtyard door, then accompanied her down the carriage drive. It was too late when Fiona saw the Worthy sisters in their usual places in the sun. Had she known they weren't going to join the festivities, she would have taken Luke out the front door. She sent a reluctant wave at the sisters and steeled herself, knowing what was coming.

"Why, don't you two look smart!" Iris beamed.

"Thank you," Fiona returned in a flat voice.

Jewel nodded, her smile just as enraptured as her sister's. "Just like a prince and princess, don't they, Iris?"

"They do indeed! A prince and princess!"

Thanking them again, Fiona waited until they were out of earshot to turn to Luke. The compliments had obviously embarrassed him as well, for his clean-shaven cheeks flamed red.

"I'm sorry about that. They do mean well."

He ducked his head and laughed. "Well, they was half right."

"I beg your pardon?"

Now the look he gave her was plainly adoring. "You do look like a princess, Miss O'Shea."

Fiona's heart sank, and she thought, *You can't keep giving him hope.* Her steps halted. "Mr. Smith."

"Huh?" He had taken another step but turned back to look at her. "Miss O'Shea?"

Fiona glanced up at the sky, powder blue and almost cloudless. Birds trilled choruses in branches overhead, and a timid breeze fraught with green and growing things bathed her face. *Why does it have to be such a perfect day?* She drew in a fortifying breath. "I think you're a good and decent person, Mr. Smith."

"Yes?" he said, raising his eyebrows anxiously.

"But we can never be anything but friends."

Luke's face fell. "We can't?"

"I'm so sorry."

He shifted the hamper to his other arm. "You don't care for me?"

"I care for you very much. You've been very kind to us."

"Maybe if I came to call more often? We could go for rides, even—the vicar would lend me the—"

Putting a hand on his arm to stop him, Fiona said, "I'm sorry, but that wouldn't be a good idea. Visiting and taking rides would only lead to courting. And there's no use in courting when I can never marry."

"You can't ever. . . ?" He could not go on, but opened and closed his mouth several times like a fish on land. Finally, she finished for him.

"I can't marry, Luke. You or anybody."

The children returned slightly bedraggled from their long trek, but most with glowing faces. They scattered to their parents and helped roll out quilts for the picnic. Fiona appeared with the hamper just as the small brass band hired from nearby Ellesmere began to perform on the steps of the town hall.

"Are you all right?" Julia asked, eyeing her drawn expression.

The housekeeper glanced at the children nearby and answered, "Fine, missus. Just a bit tired."

"I should have stayed and helped you. I didn't realize the basket would be so heavy."

"Not at all, missus. I'll be fine, truly."

"Well, you just sit there," Julia ordered. "I'll serve the sandwiches." She was surprised that Luke Smith did not join them. And even more surprised when he passed close by the quilt some quarter of an hour later, holding hands with one of the greengrocer's daughters. Julia looked over at Fiona to see if she'd seen, and Fiona gave her a strange half smile and shook her head slightly, as if to say, "It doesn't matter."

When the festivities were over, the children continued to play upon the green, squeezing the last remaining drops of sunlight from

the day. Boys fielded cricket balls, girls constructed jewelry from clover flowers, and small children, under the watchful eyes of parents or
older siblings, caught minnows with jars at the river's edge. Grace was
the first to feel the strain from all the day's activities and came back
over to the quilt.

"When are we going home?"

"I'll walk her home if you'd like to stay," Fiona told Julia. "I'm
a bit worn out myself."

Julia thanked her, but remembering Mrs. Rhodes' invitation, she
accompanied the two as far as the *Larkspur*. She sent a wave to the
Worthy sisters, then walked on alone up Walnut Tree Lane. The cottage that housed Dr. Rhodes and his wife was a quaint mixture of
stone and cob, the whole snugly thatched.

"Come inside, dear," Mrs. Rhodes said, answering her own door.
"The servants are still at the picnic—I told them to stay as long as
they wished."

"Are you sure you can take time away from Lucy now?"

"Dr. Rhodes is taking a turn with her. Please, come on in." She
led Julia into a parlor filled with a comfortable but chaotic mixture of
old furniture and scattered medical books for ailments of both man
and beast.

"How is Lucy bearing up?" Julia asked as she sank into the cushions of a rust-colored horsehair divan.

"Like a soldier, thank you." Mrs. Rhodes then excused herself,
promising to be back in a minute. She returned with a flat wooden
box in her arms and a enigmatic smile on her face and sat down next
to Julia. Opening the lid, she said, "This was passed down to my husband from his grandmother. She loved to entertain, so there is service
for sixteen here. It would give me great pleasure if you would use it
at the *Larkspur*."

Julia's breath caught in her throat at the tarnished but beautiful
cutlery that lay cushioned in scarlet velvet in the box. "I can't possibly
borrow something so valuable, Mrs. Rhodes."

"Oh, but you must. This set has been in a drawer for twelve years
now. It's a shame to keep something so lovely under a stack of table
linens, when it could be put to good use. I don't want to be like that
fellow in Scripture who buried his talent."

"But why aren't you using it?" Julia picked up a dessert spoon
and studied the intricate rosebud pattern. It would indeed look lovely
after an application of silver polish. A chill caught her shoulders.

Could this possibly be a coincidence, Mrs. Rhodes offering silver cutlery just two weeks after she and Fiona agreed to pray for it? *This is no coincidence,* she admonished herself right away. *You didn't expect spoons and forks to drop from the sky, did you?*

"We have the set my husband's mother passed down to him," Mrs. Rhodes went on, her eyes crinkling at the corners. "His family had some wealth, you see. Mine had only tin cutlery and crockery dishes, but when there was food to be had, we cared little about the plain trappings."

"I would be anxious about losing a piece," Julia told her.

"I surely wouldn't grieve over a missing spoon or two. But if it would make you feel better, Royal Sterling is still conducting business in Sheffield. Just order replacements if that happens."

An overwhelming sense of calm enveloped Julia, accompanied with the knowledge that this was indeed the way God chose to answer her prayer. The spoon in her hand, cool and smooth, was a tangible reminder of His benevolence. "I would be honored to use this silver," she said, reaching with both arms to embrace the woman beside her. "And your thoughtfulness means more to me than I can say."

She left then, so that her hostess could see about Lucy. "Please remind Fiona to come around in a day or two so we can name the colt," Mrs. Rhodes called to her from the door as she unlatched the front gate.

"I will," Julia called back. All the way down Walnut Tree Lane she hugged the box to her chest, barely noticing if her feet touched the ground. She thought about how God had used people, like Fiona and Mrs. Rhodes and Jensen, to answer some of her most urgent prayers. What if one or another had declined to follow His prompting? Mankind had been allowed free will ever since Adam in the garden. Would God have found another aqueduct for His blessings, or would that particular prayer have gone unanswered?

While her mind mulled over the subject, she tried to think of a time when God had used *her* to answer the prayer of another person. She was disheartened to find herself unable to recall even one instance, but then she remembered the day Fiona was hired. Surely it had been no coincidence that she'd been in the kitchen garden that day. What if rain had prevented her from leaving the house?

And my life was changed for the better that day as well, she thought. Just like the widow who fed Elijah and found herself with perpetual food during a famine, she had been blessed while allowing God to use her to bless another.

Oh, Father, thank you that Mrs. Rhodes and others were submissive to your will, she prayed, hugging the box more tightly. *And please help me to keep my heart open to know whenever you wish to use me in other people's lives.*

"What have you there, dearie?" Jewel Worthy called out when Julia came in sight.

"Why, it's an answer to prayer."

"Do tell?" Iris smiled, her deft fingers never slowing at their delicate spinning. "May we see it?"

"Of course." Julia paused so that the two could admire the silver, then bade them good-day and started for the carriage drive.

But the sisters were reluctant to let go of an opportunity to chat. "Miss O'Shea and Luke Smith looked so nice together, didn't they?" Jewel called from behind.

Julia turned. "I beg your pardon?"

"Just as if they'd stepped out of a picture," Iris gushed. "He was carrying the hamper for her."

Jewel nodded. "Just like a proper gentleman."

———

Fiona was just easing shut the door to the girls' bedroom when Julia walked into the family corridor. "I just looked in on her, missus. She's fast asleep."

"Thank you, Fiona." Julia held out the wooden box. "Would you like to guess what's in here?"

A hand went up to Fiona's chest. "Why, that's a cutlery box!"

"Indeed it is. Mrs. Rhodes says we may use it for as long as we like. Let's find a place to sit and I'll show it to you."

They decided on the tiny parlor in the housekeeper's quarters. It was simply but comfortably furnished with a small stove, two overstuffed chairs that took up most of the floor space, and a tea table. Julia set the box upon the table and opened the lid for Fiona's inspection.

"God is so good," Fiona breathed, picking up one piece and then another.

"So good," Julia echoed. But then she noticed a tightness about Fiona's lips, as if she were struggling to keep her composure.

"Fiona? Is something wrong?"

Fiona avoided Julia's eyes as she set a butter knife back in the box. "I suppose the sisters told you about Luke."

"They did." Julia bit her lip. "I should never have told him you were back here packing the hamper."

Fiona looked up at her. A little smile had replaced the tightness in her lips, but it was not a happy one. "It's not your fault, missus. But there is something I should tell you."

"There is? Fiona, if Luke said anything to hurt you . . ."

"It was I who hurt him," Fiona said, shaking her head bitterly. "I told him we can never be more than friends. I know it hurt him badly, especially when I wouldn't give him a good reason. But I didn't want to tell anyone else something that I've kept from you for years and should have told you a long time ago."

It pained Julia to hear the sorrow in her voice. "You don't have to tell me anything, Fiona. Not if it makes you sad."

"Actually, ma'am, it'll be a relief to come out and say it. Secrets are a weighty burden to carry around for so long."

"Yes?"

Fiona took a deep breath, then said, "I'm married, Mrs. Hollis."

"You are?" Julia gasped, unable to keep the shock from showing. "I am."

"But how can you be married? And to whom?"

"I'll tell you, ma'am." Resting her head against the back of the chair, Fiona allowed several seconds of silence to pass, then said in a voice dead of emotion, "When I was fourteen years old, my da married me off to a much older man from the neighboring town of Callan. John Dougal is his name. He was wealthy, compared to most families, and my father got a mule and wagon out of the bargain."

"Fiona . . ." Julia breathed, her hand up to her heart.

"It happens, ma'am. More than you think." Now that the story had begun, she seemed anxious to have it over and done with and went on with scant pause. "I soon became in a family way and scarcely knew what was happening. But weeks before the child was to be born, I woke one mornin' in severe pain. There was a doctor in Thomastown, but my husband didn't want to spend the money, so he put the cook to tending to me. When she saw I was in trouble, she finally convinced my husband to fetch the doctor."

"And the baby?" Julia asked, holding her breath, though she already knew what the answer would be.

"Born dead, finally. A girl, ma'am. And I hovered between life and death for days. The doctor said I would bear no more children. Young and afraid as I was back then, I was glad to hear it. Truth is, I wanted to die myself. I thought God had deserted me, and I could see no reason to keep on living.

"My husband had five grown children already," Fiona went on, "and didn't mind about the baby. You see, a mule and wagon are a cheap price to pay for a maid who'll work without wages for the rest of her life. And without having to give attention to a brood at the same time."

Her voice broke. "I was already used to the hard work, ma'am. It was the other things I couldn't bear."

Julia pressed her hands together, stung by her own selfishness. Here she had been crying on Fiona's shoulder since Philip's death, accepting her comfort, and all along unaware that Fiona could have used some comforting herself. "He mistreated you?" she whispered.

"Aye, he did. When I was eighteen, I could bear it no longer, but my da warned I couldn't humiliate him by comin' back home. So I stole some money from my husband, just enough to get myself to England."

She wiped a wet cheek with the back of her hand and looked across at Julia. "There was much more money, missus. But I didn't take it. I thought it would be easy to find a position in London . . . having worked all my life."

"Fiona, you're not a thief. You earned that money."

"No, ma'am. I stole it. But I sent it back piecemeal over the years. Didn't dare to write a return address on the envelope, for fear he would come and find me. Only Breanna knows where I am, and she won't tell."

"And so you finally came to my house."

Wiping the other cheek, Fiona said, "I was just about to give up, when someone said those fancy houses on Park Lane might be hiring. But after knocking on some back doors, I found out those houses only hired through agencies. Something told me to keep on knocking, though."

"God told you, didn't He?" said Julia and felt goose prickles down her arm.

"I'm convinced of that." Finally, something resembling a smile crept into Fiona's expression. "When you spoke so kindly to me in the garden that day, I found out that He hadn't given up on me after all."

Julia got up from her chair, walked over to the housekeeper, and leaned down to embrace her. "You poor dear. You must have suffered terribly going through all of that."

"It's all right, ma'am," came a muffled cry against her shoulder.

Straightening, again, Julia said, "You sit right there, Fiona. I'm going to see about Grace and then brew us some tea."

Fiona started to rise from her chair. "No, ma'am, I can't allow—"

"Stay there, Fiona."

When Julia returned, the two sipped quietly for a while, then Julia asked Fiona if it grieved her that she wasn't free to marry again.

Fiona, clear-eyed now, took no offense at the question. "Perhaps it would grieve me if I allowed myself to dwell upon it. But even if I were free, that doesn't change the fact that I can't bear children."

"But a happy marriage is possible without them. Look at Dr. and Mrs. Rhodes."

"Perhaps," the maid said with no conviction in her voice.

"You said your husband was much older. Perhaps he'll die soon." Julia knew she would have to repent for that later, but for the moment she hated Fiona's husband with a passion for the abuse he'd inflicted upon her.

Fiona stared across at her with a stunned expression. "Mrs. Hollis . . . don't say such a thing."

"I'm sorry," Julia told her. *But only for saying it. Not for meaning it.*

*O*n Saturday the fifteenth of May, Julia woke up well before the sun and found herself too excited to go back to sleep. *Our first lodger!* She hummed all the way to the kitchen, carrying a candle before her, and thought about the cup of tea that would soon be warming her insides.

Any sleep-robbing doubts about opening a lodging house had been quieted weeks ago as more than a dozen letters of inquiry occupied the top drawer of her writing table. Obviously, more people than she had imagined were interested in trading the noise and hurry of the cities for the sedate setting of a small dairy village.

And the *Larkspur Inn* was now ready to accommodate them, refurbished, stocked, and sparkling clean. Some less-than-urgent improvements still needed to be made in the gardens and stables, but now that the inside was finished, Karl Herrick would finally have the time to devote to those chores.

Other servants recently hired, aside from the Herricks, were Mildred and Gertie in the kitchen, Ruth and Willa, first cousins who served as upstairs chambermaids, and Georgette and Sarah, parlor-maids.

Fiona had expressed some misgivings about her ability to take charge of a houseful of servants, but it came as no surprise to Julia when her Irish friend proved herself most competent. Without doubt it was because she had worked for so long on the bottom end of the hierarchy and understood a servant's longing to be treated as a person and not some domestic contrivance. She calmed their initial fears concerning Jake Pitt, saw to it that they received adequate rest, and praised them for jobs done well. And she was wise enough to allow Audrey Herrick complete control over the kitchen.

Later that morning, after the older children had set out to play with friends and Grace was occupied with "helping" Mrs. Herrick and Mildred roll out pear tarts, Julia picked some blue forget-me-nots she and Fiona had managed to coax out of the soil in front. She was just putting the finishing touches to an arrangement in the first bedroom past the landing when Fiona appeared in the doorway. "Mrs. Kingston is downstairs, missus."

"Already? I didn't even hear a coach." Julia smiled. She still wasn't quite used to seeing Fiona perform her duties in regular dress instead of uniform, with only an apron to signify that she was a servant. Today she wore a becoming plum-colored calico. Julia suffered a twinge of envy. She was so weary of dressing like a chimney sweep. She then had to remind herself that there were people with worse problems than being obligated to wear black for twelve months.

It was not so much that she cared about looking attractive—in fact, that was the least of her concerns at present. But every morning for over three months she had clothed herself with a garment of mourning, a reminder that her husband was dead. And remembering that he was dead only caused her to remember how he had failed them. She wanted to forget. For the sake of the children and propriety, however, she knew she would continue to wear the banner of widowhood until the year had passed.

She stepped back from the bedside table and gave the room a quick going-over with her eyes. Surely even the fussiest potential lodger would approve of such a cheerful room, with its warm oak furniture, William Morris wall covering, and colorful Brussels carpet. Turning to Fiona again, she pressed her hands together and asked, "What is she like?"

"The new lodger?" There was a slight hesitation. "To be truthful, a bit on the imperious side."

"*Imperious?*" In spite of her anxiety about the visitor downstairs, Julia had to smile. "And what novel have you gotten yourself absorbed in now?"

"I'm muddlin' my way through *The Arabian Nights*," Fiona answered, covering a yawn.

Since moving into the *Larkspur*, it was not unusual for her to lose track of time and stay up half the night lost in the pages of a novel. It seemed she was determined to make up for the time when books were a rarity to her. Her household responsibilities did not suffer, and Julia was happy to see Fiona get some enjoyment out of life. She felt even closer to the housekeeper since hearing about her wretched past.

"Well, putting her *imperiousness* aside," Julia persisted, "do you think Mrs. Kingston will be impressed with the room?"

Fiona's eyes moved from the freshly arranged flowers to the fireplace, where a wood fire spread its warmth over the morning chill of an open window. Through the opening in the dimity curtains, the dignified Anwyl could be seen, crisscrossed with footpaths and bridleways and frosted by blue, pink, and white milkwort. " 'Tis a fine room. Most anyone would be impressed with it."

Catching the slight evasive tone of Fiona's voice, Julia folded her arms and leveled a stare at her. "I know you, Fiona. What's wrong?"

"Well . . ."

"You don't think *she's* going to like it, do you."

"I hope I'm mistaken, but she just seems a mite hard to please."

"Oh dear. Perhaps she's weary from the trip from Shrewsbury?"

Another slight pause, then, "That could be it."

"Then I shouldn't keep her waiting." Julia took a quick peek in the wall mirror to tuck some stray strands back into her chignon. "Would you ask Mrs. Herrick to send a tray?"

"I've already done so, missus."

In spite of Fiona's misgivings, Julia's steps on the staircase were as light as her spirit had been lately. How could Mrs. Kingston, or anyone else for that matter, be anything but smitten with the *Larkspur Inn?*

It's likely she'll want to move in right away, Julia thought, hurrying down the staircase to the hall. And Mrs. Kingston was only the tip of the iceberg. Five other potential lodgers would be arriving within the next four weeks.

Not wishing to startle her visitor by barging into the room, she paused in the doorway leading into the hall. She had surmised by Norwood Kingston's letter that his mother was on in years, so Julia expected to find the woman settled in a sofa or in one of the chairs. Julia was surprised to find a woman dressed entirely in black standing at the fireplace with her back to the stairs. Julia blinked as a flash of white handkerchief swept across the chimneypiece. *Why, she's checking for dust!*

"Well, at least this room is clean," the woman muttered to herself. "But I intend to inspect the mattress for bugs at first opportunity."

Julia stepped inside the room. "Mrs. Kingston?"

The woman turned around with no trace of chagrin upon her face.

She was, as Julia had suspected, elderly, with steel-gray hair peeking from her bonnet. Her shoulders were surprisingly broad, her tall figure as erect as that of a much younger person. Commanding blue eyes, the sort that must have reduced many a parlormaid to tears, peered down a hawkish nose. "You are Mrs. Hollis, I trust?"

"I am," Julia answered, assuming her most welcoming smile as she motioned toward the chairs. "Tea will be here shortly. Would you care to—?"

"I wish to inspect the room first."

Julia's smile did not waver at this interruption. "Of course. I'll show you the way."

They walked to the staircase together, with Julia stepping back to offer the woman the lead. "I had pictured a more modern facility," Mrs. Kingston muttered after one look at the worn oak of the banister railing. Karl Herrick had varnished it to a high sheen, but there was no hiding the nicks that gave away its antiquity.

"You'll find that the *Larkspur* is as well built as any modern home," Julia replied. "All the conveniences are here as well. Each floor has a water closet and lavatory with running water."

Just then, the step under Mrs. Kingston's foot let out a squeak. The woman froze, shifted her weight to produce another squeak, then turned to raise an eyebrow at Julia. "Well built, you say?"

Again Julia smiled, though her lips were beginning to feel some wear at the corners. "The wood was recently replaced on that step, but unfortunately, it didn't stop the squeak." A sudden memory took the effort from her smile.

"The house I lived in when I was a child," Julia told her, "had a stair that squeaked too. My father would tell me that a mouse napped underneath it and was startled awake at the sound of footsteps on 'his' step. So it was the mouse that squeaked, you see? I always made it a point to skip over that particular step, out of courtesy to the little creature. Why, even now in this house, I sometimes find myself automatically doing the same thing."

The effect this recollection had upon Mrs. Kingston was hard to tell, for the elderly woman simply leveled a bemused stare at her before continuing up the staircase. Giving a quiet sigh, Julia followed. She ran her hand lightly upon the banister that her visitor had looked upon with obvious scorn, appreciating the richness of the wood beneath her fingers. How many thousands of hands had run along that same banister?

Though Jensen's loan had been enough to make any structural improvements that the house warranted, Julia had asked Karl to only take care of the repairs necessary for convenience and safety. The banister had just needed a sturdying nail or two and a fresh coat of varnish. In Julia's opinion, the signs of the house's two centuries of existence added character and were to be respected, like the wrinkles on an aged person's brow. Take away the nicks and flaws, and the atmosphere would be as sterile as any modern hotel.

Having reached the landing, Mrs. Kingston paused to catch her breath. Julia waited at her side.

"How long have you been a widow?" the woman asked suddenly, eyeing Julia's black cashmere gown.

"Three months, Mrs. Kingston."

"Does that mean you oversee the operation of this establishment alone?"

"This is my home as well as a business establishment," Julia answered, forcing her carriage up into a more confident posture. "And we've an extremely competent housekeeper."

"And what about a gardener? I must say that I was not in the least impressed with that flower garden in front."

"I apologize for that. Our caretaker, Karl Herrick, has had to spend most of his time on repairs and refurbishing. When we've established a routine, I'm certain he'll have time to devote to gardening." She then changed the subject. "Would you care to see the room now?"

"Very well."

As they advanced upon the first chamber to their left, Julia could already feel the fresh breath of spring wafting through the open doorway. "We opened a window this morning to—"

"And why was it necessary to air the room out?" Mrs. Kingston interrupted. "I will not stay in a place that reeks of pipe tobacco."

"Not at all, Mrs. Kingston." Julia walked in behind her and pointed to the wall on her right, papered in shades of rose, hunter green, and gold. "This morning I detected the faint odor of paste in the air. You see, the wallpaper was hung just last week."

The woman stepped over to the wall and squinted her eyes at the floral design. "William Morris?"

"It is." The approval in her eyes made Julia feel less uneasy about the squeak on the staircase. William Morris was the most revered designer of tapestries and wall coverings in Great Britain. Deciding it was now time to settle the bedbug question, she walked over to the foot of the bed and pulled back the covers. "As you can see, the mattress is new as well. And we change linens every Monday."

Mrs. Kingston came over to give the mattress the same scrutiny that she had given the wallpaper. She then seated herself on the side of the bed and gave a little bounce. "Bedsprings, Mrs. Hollis?"

"Of course," Julia answered as she tugged the covers at the corner back in place. "Would you care to lie down and see how comfortable it is?"

"I would indeed." Still clutching her reticule in both hands, Mrs. Kingston eased her full height upon the bed, straightening out the folds of her black skirt. After a moment, something resembling satisfaction spread across her sharp features. "All right," she said, hoisting her feet back to the floor. "I shall give this establishment a try."

Julia swallowed, amazed that at the age of thirty-one she could still find herself so intimidated. "Of course we will need to discuss the policy of the house first."

"Policy?"

"As I mentioned in my letter, I have three children, and—"

"Just keep them quiet and out of my way and we'll have no problem." Mrs. Kingston pulled a note from the bag in her lap and held it out to Julia. "Give this to the coachman and have him deliver my trunk up here right away. I wish to change from these traveling clothes."

Julia took the half-sovereign from the woman's hand and stared blankly down at it. For the fraction of a second the face upon the note, King Charles I, changed shape and blurred into Mrs. Kingston, peering at something ahead with a disdainful expression. Giving a quiet sigh, Julia wondered again if turning the *Larkspur* into a lodging house had been the actions of a sane woman. How could she bear it if the other lodgers turned out to be as overbearing as Mrs. Kingston? *How can I live with even one like this? Why, it would be like living at the London house again.* The vision she'd had, however naively, of a happy extended family under one roof faded like breath upon a mirror.

"Mrs. Hollis?"

The voice interrupted her thoughts. Again Julia blinked. "Yes?"

Mrs. Kingston still sat there, blue eyes regarding her. A hand raised in a gesture of dismissal. "The coachman? He'll likely charge double if he's kept waiting too long."

"I'm sorry, I . . ." Midway through her apology, Julia clamped her mouth shut. She handed the money back to the woman and shook her head. "It's imperative that we first discuss policy, Mrs. Kingston."

"Oh, very well," Mrs. Kingston said, expelling a martyred sigh. "What is it you wish to say, Mrs. Hollis?"

"Regarding my children . . . they're well behaved and courteous and will certainly not be allowed to intrude upon the guests' lives. But this is their *home*. I will never demand that they stay out of sight and stop being children."

"And what about my privacy?"

"Your chamber will, of course, be off-limits to them, as well as the sitting room on this floor. They will join us for meals, but since I believe children should be silent at the table unless spoken to, you'll have no cause to resent their presence."

The woman waved a hand again. "I suppose I can live with that." She got to her feet and pressed the half-sovereign back into Julia's hand. "Now, my driver, Mrs. Hollis. . . ?"

Fiona appeared herself with a tray. Julia wondered if the housekeeper were attempting to shield the maids in her charge from this fractious woman.

"I'm sorry this took so long. I upset the creamer on my first trip up the stairs."

Before Julia could speak, Mrs. Kingston turned to Fiona and motioned toward the writing table against the wall. "You may set it there and pour. And I will require your help with unpacking when my trunk arrives."

Julia could stand it no longer. *I still have those dozen letters*, she reminded herself. *Even if I didn't, it would be better to take in washing than to allow someone like this to rule over the household*. Again she gathered up her nerve and handed the money back to the woman. "I'll pay your driver myself, Mrs. Kingston."

"Why, there is no need to do that." Mrs. Kingston said, and for the fraction of a second her features actually seemed to soften.

Steeling herself, Julia continued in a polite but decisive tone. "I will reimburse you for your railway ticket as well, because your trip out here has been in vain. I cannot accept you as a lodger." She could hear Fiona give a short gasp behind her, and some color sprang into Mrs. Kingston's cheeks.

"Accept *me?*" the woman sputtered. "Why, I never—"

"You would be happier somewhere else," Julia said, although she

119

couldn't imagine where that place might be. *The Taj Mahal?*

"Indeed I would!" Raising her chin, Mrs. Kingston gathered the shawl tight around her stout shoulders. "Keep your money—for now. I've a good mind to take you to court for false advertising!"

"Do whatever suits you, Mrs. Kingston."

"Oh, you haven't heard the last of me!" the woman huffed on her way across the room. She paused at the door long enough to give the walls a contentious scowl. "I'll wager that wallpaper isn't William Morris' at all. And it's just a matter of time before someone falls through that rotten staircase!"

"Then, I would advise you to tread lightly on your way down." As soon as the words left Julia's mouth, she felt ashamed for their sharpness . . . and for the brief feeling of satisfaction they'd given her.

When Mrs. Kingston's formidable figure had disappeared through the doorway, Fiona recovered enough to set the tray down on the writing table. "Are you all right, missus?"

"I'm not quite sure." Julia held up a hand and stared curiously at it. "Why, my hands are shaking. That was quite a scene."

"Perhaps I should see her out."

Julia nodded and sank into a chair. "Thank you."

Two hours later she sat in her favorite overstuffed chair in the library reading *The Dwellers of Clover's Forest* to Grace, who sat in her lap.

> *. . . and Mister Hare, jumping high*
> *will lead us to his warren nigh . . .*

"Mrs. Hollis?"

Julia looked up from the book. This time it was Georgette, one of the two parlormaids, who stood in the doorway peering owlishly through thick spectacles. She was Mildred the kitchen maid's second cousin, a girl of about nineteen who had a practice of slipping her spectacles into an apron pocket whenever an eligible male was about. Those times had been few and far between so far, limited to the Duncan brothers who had come up from Shrewsbury to deliver and hang the wallpaper.

"Yes, Georgette?"

"You've got a visitor in th' hall," the girl announced. "It's that Mrs. Kingston again."

Julia gave a deep sigh. "Did she happen to say why she's come again?"

"No, ma'am. Do you want me to ask her?"

It was tempting, but Julia shook her head. "Tell her I'll be there shortly." When the maid was gone, Julia closed the book and pulled Grace closer. "Why don't you play with your dolls for a little while? If I'm not back soon, we'll finish the book at bedtime."

"But we're only supposed to read the *fairy tale* book at bedtime."

Julia turned the girl around to face her and smiled. For a happy child who was loved by family and servants alike, Grace could wear the most serious expressions. Julia knew that the thoughtful look on her face now was because the normal bedtime routine would be altered. Grace was the only one of her children who had inherited Philip's love of order. Even her dolls had to be arranged a certain way in their crib before she would close her eyes to sleep.

"Then why don't you find Fiona and ask her to finish reading this to you?" Julia suggested.

The green eyes brightened. "May I?"

"Of course you may," Julia answered, giving her another squeeze. "Just don't ask her to read the fairy tales."

Finally a smile turned the corners of Grace's mouth upward, though her eyes were serious again. Pressing small hands upon Julia's cheeks, the child brought her face closer and said, "Only *you* are supposed to read fairy tales."

———

This time Mrs. Kingston was seated on a sofa when Julia walked into the hall, her bonnet slightly askew and her face haggard. Julia noticed that her eyes looked an even sharper blue and realized it was because they were rimmed with red. *Has she been crying?*

Lowering herself into the facing sofa, Julia said as cordially as possible, "I didn't expect to see you again."

"Yes," Mrs. Kingston said, dabbing at her eyes with her handkerchief.

For a brief, cynical second, Julia thought that it was a good thing that the chimneypiece hadn't been dusty earlier. Again feeling ashamed for her hardened attitude, she waited for the woman to continue.

"I wish to apologize for the way I conducted myself earlier."

"I beg your pardon?" Julia couldn't imagine those words coming from the woman in front of her, who only hours earlier had been so pompous and demanding.

"My behavior was inexcusable." Mrs. Kingston dabbed at her eyes again. "And I don't blame you one whit for feeling anger toward me."

Feeling a sudden unexpected surge of pity, Julia replied, "As I recall, I was a bit sharp myself."

"You had every right to be," the older woman sniffed. She looked away for a minute, then went on. "When I left here, I had the coachman take me to the other inn in town for tea. You know, the . . ."

"The *Bow and Fiddle*," Julia offered, and Mrs. Kingston nodded.

"After I had my tea, I asked to see a room. The proprietor's wife led me down an empty corridor to a room that wasn't nearly as nice as the one you showed me upstairs and told me I would be the only guest so far today."

"That's typical," Julia said. She opened her mouth to explain what the railways had done to the coaching inn business but then decided that the "why" really didn't matter to Mrs. Kingston at the moment.

"Anyway, I immediately told her that I'd changed my mind about the room," Mrs. Kingston went on. "It was quite unsettling, the thought of myself being the only person on the whole chamber floor, and for no telling how long."

"Then why didn't you go back to Shrewsbury, if I may ask?"

"Because I would have to find a place to stay there as well. I have lived in the country all of my life, Mrs. Hollis, and the cities frighten an old woman alone like me." She looked down at the gloved hands folded in her lap.

"Alone?" Julia recalled the correspondence she'd had with Mr. Kingston concerning arrangements for his mother. "But you were living with—"

"My son, Norwood, and his family," the woman nodded, the splotches on her cheeks deepening. "But I was asked to leave once Norwood received your response to his query. Ordered to leave, actually."

"*Ordered?* By your son?"

Mrs. Kingston raised her chin and pressed her lips together. "He offered to escort me, but I told him to stay with his precious Lucille. It's her fault, you see. My daughter-in-law doesn't even try to get along with me. She says I'm critical and interfering and . . ."

The words were left hanging in the air as she paused to draw in a shuddering breath. For several long seconds the woman's face assumed a look of painful introspection, and when she finally spoke again, her voice came out barely above a whisper. "And I'm afraid she is correct."

Compassion moved Julia across to the other sofa. She sat down beside the woman and put a hand on her shoulder. "There, there now. Surely it's not too late to apologize."

Mrs. Kingston mopped her whole face with the handkerchief this time. "It is to my son's family. I would have destroyed his marriage had he not finally gathered the courage to order me to leave."

Gently, Julia asked, "Have you no other children?"

Again she shook her head. "None that lived past the age of three."

No wonder she's so bitter, Julia thought. "I'm so sorry."

"When Norwood . . ." She looked at Julia again. "My husband, Norwood. My son was named after him. When my husband died, my son asked me to live with him." A ghost of a smile touched Mrs. Kingston's lips, but then it faded as the sadness in her eyes deepened. "Norwood has three precious young children. My grandchildren."

It was the way Mrs. Kingston's voice caressed the words *my grandchildren* that brought a lump to Julia's throat. She was groping for some words of comfort when Mrs. Kingston spoke again.

"I dare not ask them to take me back, Mrs. Hollis, at least not now. My son's marriage must have time to heal."

Julia had never met the son and daughter-in-law involved, of course, but she had the fresh memory of the way Mrs. Kingston had acted upstairs. Very likely they'd had no other choice. It was so tempting to offer the room again, but she had to consider her own children, her servants, and the other lodgers that would be forced to keep company with her. "I don't quite know what to say," she told the woman frankly.

Mrs. Kingston's bottom lip trembled again. "I can't fault you for that, Mrs. Hollis. But if I keep myself out of everyone's sight, will you allow me to stay until I find another place? I'll pay double."

"The board I advertised is satisfactory, Mrs. Kingston, and I don't wish for anyone here to have to 'keep out of everyone's sight.' As I said earlier, this is a home, not just a place of business. But if you were to stay here, how would you find another place to live?"

"There were other advertisements in *The Illustrated Times*, along with yours. I can have some letters of inquiry posted by morning."

Julia considered this, and then felt compelled to ask, "And what will happen when you visit these other lodging houses?"

"You mean, will I behave the way I did here?"

"Well. . . ?"

Giving a somber nod, Mrs. Kingston replied, "I would surely hope not, Mrs. Hollis. Just a short while ago, when I was having tea at . . ."

"The *Bow and Fiddle?*"

"Yes, that place." Mrs. Kingston's face clouded up again. "I've never felt so alone in all my life. And now I realize that *I'm* the cause of it." She blew her hawkish nose into her handkerchief. "Even when Norwood—my husband, that is—was alive, he spent most of his time in his study, or out with his horses. Why didn't I realize what a shrew I was?"

Just a couple hours ago, Julia would have thought it impossible to feel pity for the woman who had been so obnoxious upstairs. *Everyone should be given the opportunity to change,* she told herself now. And hadn't she prayed just days ago for God to use her to bless others' lives?

"Mrs. Kingston . . ." she began tentatively.

A faint glimmer of hope appeared in the woman's eyes. "Yes?"

"Why don't we go over policy again?"

The hopeful expression turned incredulous, and then Mrs. Kingston seized Julia's hand and held it against her wrinkled cheek. "Bless you, dear! You'll not be sorry."

Julia wasn't quite sure about that, but then, faith would not be necessary if one could be sure about everything.

*N*ow go fetch me a nice fat one," Philip commanded the grub he'd just impaled upon his fishing hook. Philip, Jeremiah, and Ben had gotten up early to dash through their chores and take advantage of every minute of daylight they could wring out of a May Saturday. Fishing from the stone bridge over the River Bryce in the late morning and an afternoon cricket match on the green were the main events on their itinerary, with a hurried lunch wedged in between.

The Bryce stretched out before them like a blue ribbon. Waterbugs darted through overhanging willow branches stirring lazily with the current. In the shallow waters off the north bank, the familiar lilting cadence of Irish voices floated to Philip's ears as a half-dozen young children pulled osier reeds from willows for their father, Alan Keegan, to weave into baskets. Philip took a deep breath of the fresh morning air and wondered how he'd ever been content living in the city.

"Hey, Philip, if my mother or papa comes by this way, don't look like you're enjoyin' it so much," Ben warned good-naturedly from his right while threading his line through the end of a hook. "I've got them believing that fishing is just like my other chores." His red curls made Philip's auburn and copper mixture look almost muted, and his face wore ten freckles for every one of Aleda's.

Philip shook his head. "I believe the way you flew out of the house with your pole gave you away, Ben. I'll wager you don't run to your other chores like that."

"Well, it puts food on the platter, doesn't it? It's not our fault if it's fun."

"Great fun," Jeremiah agreed. "In fact, I think the catching is more fun than the eating."

Philip agreed. But then he thought of the way Mrs. Herrick prepared river trout—seasoned with pepper and Worcestershire sauce and baked with slices of lemon and onion—and almost changed his mind. *Almost*, for the activity gave him a sense of satisfaction that went beyond merely having a good time.

He would always savor the memory of the first time he carried home a string of bream. Even though Betty Moser had fried them for so long that the meat was dry, Philip had thought it the most delicious meal he'd ever tasted. As the man of the house, he had provided food for the table—had fed his family with the fruits of his own labor. And even now, with more lodgers on their way and money not so dreadfully tight, he still experienced a sense of well-being when his fishing was successful.

"Hey, Jeremiah." Ben's voice cut through his thoughts. "How did you get away from your brothers this time?"

Jeremiah rolled his eyes. "Same way." To go fishing or do anything fun, Jeremiah had to slip away when David and Seth, ages seven and nine, were occupied with other activities. His usual exit was through an upstairs window and down a beech tree with branches sturdy enough to accommodate him.

A rumble of wheels and a ring of hoofbeats against the cobblestones grew louder and louder from the south. The bridge was wide enough for both the boys and the red-and-white carrier wagons that traveled incessantly back and forth from the cheese factory to Shrewsbury, so Philip took little notice of the sound. It was only when Jeremiah snatched off his cap and said, "The squire!" that Philip looked up over his shoulder.

He was met with a pair of eyes glaring so viciously that it gave him a start.

Of course he recognized Squire Bartley's barouche and driver and footman in full livery. But he had never seen the squire up close before and surely couldn't understand the anger in his gaze. The man hadn't even given the other boys a glance as the carriage passed behind them.

"Whatever did you do to him?" Ben asked, his cap in hand as well.

"Don't know," Philip answered. He leaned back to get a clear view of the carriage moving on toward the cheese factory. "I've never even met him."

"It's because yer mum stole his cook and gardener," said Jeremiah.

Philip turned to Jeremiah and defended his mother. "The Herricks gave him fair notice. Besides, they worked at the *Larkspur* before they worked for him."

His cork bobbed below the surface of the water, and he gave the line a quick jerk, then frowned at the sight of his bare hook glistening in the sunlight. While his attention was diverted by Squire Bartley, some plump trout had nibbled away his bait. *At least we're not beholden to the old grouch.*

Which made his family a decided minority in Gresham. From the factory workers to the dairy farmers to the smithy, joiner, carrier and wheelwright, to even the greengrocer and baker, most livelihoods were linked either directly or indirectly to *Anwyl Mountain Savory Cheeses.*

"Hey! Lookit the Micks playin' in the mud!"

Philip looked to his left, from where the sound had come, and saw two Irish children standing frozen like statues. On the bank stood Oram and Fernie Sanders, boys of about thirteen and fourteen years old. They had tanned, smug faces and strapping physiques, and Philip had learned his first week in Gresham that most village boys gave the Sanders brothers wide berth. Fortunately, their father, Willet Sanders, considered it foolish to send his daughter and six sons to school when they could be put to work on his dairy farm, so the boys had little free time to devote to bullying.

"Why are they always so disagreeable?" Philip asked Ben.

"Something to do, I reckon," Ben muttered, shaking his head with disgust.

"Hey, Micks! You too good to go to church with everyone else?"

"They're papists, the Keegans are," Jeremiah whispered. "They go off to Shrewsbury for church most weekends."

"Well, where do the Sanders go?" Philip had never seen them at Saint Jude's, but there was a Baptist chapel on Short Lane that the Herricks attended. He didn't know much about Baptist theology but didn't think they were the Sanders' type. In fact, he doubted that any denomination would suit the Sanders. *Chapel of the Philistines, perhaps?*

"Sanders? Church?" Jeremiah snorted. "They don't go nowhere, the lot of them, except for their sister Mercy. She's Wesleyan."

"Then why does it matter to them?"

"It doesn't," said Ben. "If it weren't that, they'd find another reason."

On the bank, Philip watched the Sanders brothers hoot away, slapping each other on the back in congratulations for particularly barbing insults. His eyes moved to the children. Four were back at work again, obviously trying to ignore the barbarians. But the youngest, a boy about Grace's age, had broken into tears and was being comforted by an older sister. Pulse racing and cheeks burning fire, he opened his mouth to challenge the two bullies, but Ben beat him to the draw and shouted, "Hey! Why don't you two push off!"

The effect upon Oram and Fernie was immediate, for the two stopped hooting and glared in their direction.

"Get ready, gents, I believe we're about to die," Ben whispered.

Philip nodded, watching the two advance down the bank. "It appears so."

"Think we should run?" asked Jeremiah.

"Not on your nelly. We'd have to leave our poles and tackle. And you know what they'd do to them."

"Just ignore them and maybe they'll go away," Ben advised.

The brothers did not go away but fortunately stopped where the bridge met the bank, and Philip wondered if it was because the bridge was in plain sight of the cottages lining the west end of the village green—particularly Constable Reed's. From what he had gathered about the behavior of bullies, they preferred practicing their craft with few witnesses about.

But they certainly didn't mind verbal sparring. "Well, well!" Oram called out. "Lookit 'em tryin' to catch minnows wi' poles!"

A loud *pul-ump* accompanied his taunt, followed by a spray of water that reached as high as Philip's chin. He glared over at the two and saw that they were holding rocks as big as croquet balls.

"Whatsa matter? Fish got away?" Fernie aimed and fired his weapon. The rock fell short by a good five feet, but the boy strutted about as if he'd scored a bull's-eye.

"Why don't you go bother somebody else!" Ben shouted. "Like Constable Reed!"

"Oo-eee! The constable! Maybe *you* oughter go tell 'em that some bad old boys is throwin' rocks in the river and got a little water on your aprons!"

This came from Fernie, obviously the more eloquent of the two. "Hey, Mr. Hollis, sir!" came another jeering cry. "Do you sleep with a blanket over yer head so's you won't be scared of old Jake?"

Philip was just opening his mouth to send back the suggestion that the Sanders brothers should wear blankets over their heads during the day so that *other* people wouldn't be frightened, when Jeremiah cautioned, "Don't say anything. They're hoping one of us'll set out after them."

Another *pul-ump!* showered the three with water, causing Philip to pull in his line. "Guess fishing's over for the day."

"Guess so," Ben said, but then did a curious thing. Ignoring the third *pul-ump!* he turned and sent a quick furtive motion toward the Anwyl.

"Look over at the hill for a second," he whispered through his teeth. "Not too long, Jeremiah!"

"What was that abou—" Philip started but was silenced by a warning look.

"Now let's go." Ben stood and then said in a loud, but not *too* loud, voice, "Well, I've *chores* to finish anyway."

Jeremiah's mouth opened. "But you already did—" He stopped himself short, knowledge dawning in his eyes. "Me too. Guess I'll be workin' at *home* the rest of the day."

Now Philip understood the plan. "Gipsy Woods?" he whispered to Ben as he packed up his fishing equipment.

"Half an hour."

Philip stole a glance at the Sanders brothers. Their heads were together as if puzzling over something, but he noticed that Fernie sent a quick nod in the direction of the Anwyl. Then, in what was supposedly some brilliant tactical maneuver, Oram slammed his rock to the ground. "Aw, there's more to do at home," he said in a voice so loud that the Worthy sisters were likely nodding agreement as they spinned their lace.

"Boring is what this is, watchin' these girls try to catch a fish." The Sanders boys turned and shuffled off north in the direction of their farm, while Philip and his friends separated and walked on to their homes.

Forty-five minutes later, the three sat on a bank in the south bend of the River Bryce. The northern edge of Gipsy Woods shielded them from sight of the Anwyl—which was likely being explored that very moment by the Sanders boys. It was a fine picture, Philip thought, to imagine blond heads peering behind shrubbery and between rocks. And pulling off a successful subterfuge made the fishing even more fun.

Ben and Jeremiah had already pulled in a trout apiece, between bites of the ham sandwiches that Mrs. Herrick had packed up for the three to share. Philip, however, waited to finish his sandwich before tending to his line. While he had no qualms about baiting a hook with some wriggling slug or cricket, it was not the most appetite-inducing sight.

"Have they always been like that?" he asked presently, wiping his hands upon his trousers and picking up his line. He did not have to say to whom he was referring, for straightway Jeremiah gave a nod.

"Even the two oldest, Harold and Dale, were bullies in their day, accordin' to Thomas." Thomas was Jeremiah's older brother, who also worked in the squire's stables alongside his father. "And they still pick fights at the *Bow and Fiddle* when they're in their cups."

"And their papa as well," said Ben. He was reflectively quiet for a 'minute, then tapped his forehead. "*Now* I know what that saying means."

Philip blinked. "Beg pardon?"

"You know—my grandmother says it all the time. 'The fruit doesn't fall far from the tree'. I always wondered why she would say that, and always after discussing with my mother something awful that somebody did. She'd have that 'look' about her too, and I had a feeling she wasn't just talking about apples or pears. But when I'd ask, she or mother would send me off to play."

"*What* look?" Jeremiah asked, clearly puzzled.

"I'll show you," Ben replied. First, he pursed up his lips primly, then arched an eyebrow while giving a slow nod. Philip burst out laughing.

"You've got it, all right. You'll make a fine grandmother, Ben."

"*Grandmother!*"

They traded cuffs for a minute, and then Philip patiently explained the old adage about the fruit and tree to Jeremiah. As the early afternoon approached and the fish seemed to be less inclined to bite, the boys packed up to go. Their patience had been rewarded and all three of their tables would boast fish tonight. Philip had the least to show for his efforts, but the three decent-size bream and large trout would be ample supply for one of Mrs. Herrick's savory chowders.

On his way around back to the gardening cottage to put away his pole and tackle, he automatically lifted a hand to wave to the Worthy sisters off to his left. He did not even have to wonder if they'd seen him. Their keen eyes never missed any movement within seeing distance. How they managed to spin lace at the same time was still a mystery to him. As usual, the two elderly women weren't about to allow him to enter their range of sight without comment.

"Ye've a guest inside, Philip," Jewel called out in her raspy voice.

Philip paused and nodded. "Mrs. Kingston. She's boarding with us now."

"Not Mrs. Kingston." Iris shook her head. "She came last Saturday. Ye've another guest today."

"A gentleman," Jewel said. "And he sent his coach away, so he's likely planning to stay. Had two trunks ye could ha' buried horses in."

"Now, why would a gentleman need two trunks of that size?" asked Iris.

With a fair touch of resentment in her voice, Jewel said, "He ain't the friendly sort, if ye ask me. I asked him his name, and he wouldn't even look my way."

"And your mother and sisters aren't home," Iris said. "They left for a walk about an hour ago with your housekeeper and that Mrs. Kingston."

Jewel nodded, her fingers still moving with their usual swiftness. "And your sister, Aleda, left earlier. Said she were going to play at a friend's house. We've decided it must be Josiah Johnson's girl, Helen, over at the bakery. They spend a lot o' time together. Sweet child, that Helen."

After all of this information had been reported, the sisters silenced themselves and watched Philip expectantly. All he knew to do was to hold up the string of fish in his hand. "Well, I should put away my things now. Have a pleasant afternoon."

They bade him the same, and he could feel both sets of eyes upon him as he neared the gardening cottage. Inside, Karl Herrick's quick brown eyes looked up from the shovel he was sharpening with a file. He was short like Mrs. Herrick, but with a long torso and powerful-looking arms. "You haff caught some fish, *ja*?"

"Four." Philip held them out for him to admire.

"You're a fine lad, Master Philip." He nodded toward the direction of the Worthy sisters' cottage. "They tell you all about the visitor?"

"More than I wanted to know," Philip answered. "But I didn't think any more lodgers were expected until next week. Who is he?"

"My Audrey says he is not one for speaking. She and the others are in . . . how you say? A *tumult* . . . wondering what to do with him."

"Is that why you're hiding out here?"

131

"Hiding?" The brown eyes blinked over a spreading grin. "Why, Mrs. Hollis has asked me to plant a vegetable garden. My first duty is to my employer, *verstehen?*"

"I understand," Philip smiled back.

Mrs. Herrick was standing on her stool at the worktable preparing a tray when he walked into the kitchen. "Oh, I was hoping you was your mother!" the cook blurted out.

Philip opened his mouth to give a joking reply but stifled it upon noticing the worry in her expression. "Shall I go look for her?"

"Don't know how long that would take. You'd do better to entertain Mr. Clay in the hall. He's been waitin' in there by himself for a good quarter of an hour now."

"Wouldn't you like me to clean the fish?" He held up the string, his pride a little injured that she hadn't noticed.

"I'll ask Karl to do that in a bit." A twinkle finally lit the hazel eyes. "I suppose you'll be wantin' chowder for supper?"

"I can already taste it." Looking down at his soiled blue muslin shirt, Philip asked if he should first change.

"No time for that, Master Philip," Mrs. Herrick answered but clucked her tongue at the state of his clothes. "But here . . . pop into the scullery and let Gertie help you wash those hands. You've mud on your chin as well. Now remember, his name is Mr. Clay."

Philip did as instructed, then, leaving the fish in the basin, he walked down the corridor to the hall. At first he thought that Mrs. Herrick was mistaken, that the gentleman had left for some other part of the house. A second later his eyes found the visitor on the sofa closest to the empty fireplace and farthest away from any lamp. Philip's heart skipped a beat at the sight of the thick, dark brown hair, but then the man turned his face toward him and all resemblance to his father vanished.

"Mr. Clay?" Philip asked. He could not recall ever being called upon to entertain an adult visitor alone and wondered what he could possibly say that would be of any interest to him.

"Yes?" Mr. Clay had a handsome face with well-defined, aristocratic features, but his posture seemed that of a person who had been wrung out by life. His shoulders, neither broad nor slim, sagged slightly, and both hands rested motionless on the cushions at each side.

Philip advanced reluctantly, wishing he'd paid closer attention back when Mr. Hunter read a daily page from *Etiquette for Good Boys and Girls.* Was the younger supposed to offer a hand, or wait until his elder did so? He decided upon a quick bow and said, "I'm Philip Hollis. My mother owns the *Larkspur.*"

Mr. Clay solved his dilemma by stretching out his right hand. A cultured voice said, "Ambrose Clay."

They shook hands, and Philip recalled some bits of information Mother had given about the query letters she'd received. "You're an actor, aren't you?"

"Yes."

Philip shifted his feet and looked about the great room, wishing that by doing so he could cause his mother to materialize in some corner. "Well, I suppose you've been told my mother isn't here now. She wouldn't have left had she known you were to arrive today."

That sounded like an accusation, he realized with horror after the words left his mouth, and he tried to correct himself. "I meant to say . . . Mother will be happy to find you here, just surprised." He cleared his throat. "Pleasantly so, of course."

"Thank you."

Should I offer to show him his room? Philip wondered, for surely the two trunks had already been delivered upstairs by the coachman. A footstep sounded from behind him and Philip turned, awash with relief. But instead of Mother, it was Georgette who stood in the doorway with a tray, and he could now understand the disappointment Mrs. Herrick had felt when he'd walked into the kitchen earlier. The maid searched the long room from side to side with her short-sighted eyes squinted.

"Over here," Philip told her.

She advanced with a wide smile but stopped halfway across the room and seemed confused. Two blinks later, the short-sighted eyes seemed to focus upon the figure seated upon the sofa. "We've all kinds of little cakes and sandwiches," she said cheerily as Philip pushed forward one of the tea tables.

"Just tea, please," Mr. Clay told her, as if the effort of speaking were almost too much for him.

"Milk or lemon?"

"Plain. But do thank your cook for the tray."

When she was gone, Mr. Clay looked up at Philip as if noticing him for the first time. "You don't have to wait here with me."

"Oh, I don't mind," Philip said, wincing inside at the lie. Vicar Wilson's sermon last Sunday evening had been about how a person's yea should mean yea, and his nay mean nay. A poor man who possessed integrity of speech, the vicar had said, had something that all the gold in the world couldn't purchase. Inspired by those lofty words, Philip had determined he would never again allow a falsehood to pass his lips. He was glad the vicar couldn't hear him right now, but the unsettling thought crossed his mind that God could.

"Aren't you having anything?" the man asked with a nod toward the tray.

"No, thank you." Actually, Philip thought a couple of seed cakes would be a fine finish to his early lunch of ham sandwiches, but he was too nervous to gobble them down in front of this visitor.

"Why don't you sit down?" Mr. Clay said presently.

"Yes, thank you." Philip backed into a chair. He watched Mr. Clay finish his tea and then felt compelled to break the silence again.

"Do you enjoy acting?"

Mr. Clay looked at him again. "Acting? Why, yes."

"Where have you performed?"

"Oh, Oxford when I was a student. London, for the past fifteen years, with a tour of the States before the war."

Then why are you here? Philip thought, but said instead, "Have you performed any Shakespeare?"

"Quite a lot, actually."

While it seemed that Mr. Clay didn't resent being questioned in such a manner, it became obvious to Philip that he was too weary to volunteer any information. In spite of the refreshment he'd just taken, the man looked as if he'd *walked* from Shrewsbury, trunks and all. Philip decided that, as the man of the house, he was just going to have to plan a course of action in the absence of his mother.

"Mr. Clay?" He cleared his throat again. "Would you like to go upstairs and rest?"

"Do you think that would be all right?"

"Yes, sir."

Relief washed across the man's face. "I would like that very much, thank you."

I would like to purchase a carriage and team before winter," Julia said apologetically to Mrs. Kingston as the party of four made their way down Walnut Tree Lane, the farthest north-south road to the west of Gresham. Mrs. Kingston had expressed a desire to see the village that would be her new home and said she didn't mind if Julia asked Grace and Fiona along. A May breeze eddied about them, full of promise and sweet scents from the cottage gardens that they passed.

"Humph!" Mrs. Kingston snorted while keeping the lead she'd enjoyed for the past half hour. "God gave us legs for a purpose. Horses and carriages are going to be the ruin of England. And the trains as well."

Julia sent a wave to Dr. Rhodes' gardener, who was weeding a patch of hollyhock. She wondered if Mrs. Rhodes were out on a call or in the stable tending the colt, Gabriel, recently named by Fiona because of the white circle adorning his forehead. "Surely you'll agree that they make life a lot more convenient," she reasoned to the back of Mrs. Kingston's black bonnet.

"Sometimes, but everyone has gone soft because of it. I've walked three miles daily for the past twenty years . . . weather permitting. Haven't had an aching joint or even the sniffles since I don't remember when. Convenient indeed!"

Grace apparently mistook the gruffness in the new lodger's tone as anger, for the tender-hearted girl took a couple of quick steps to catch up and slipped a hand in Mrs. Kingston's. "Do you like hills? I'll ask Philip to show you the best paths to take up the Anwyl if you'd like."

Taken off guard, the elderly woman peered down at her and softened her tone. "Why, that's very kind of you."

"Blessed are the peacemakers," Fiona murmured from Julia's side.

As they turned left on Church Lane and headed back toward the *Larkspur*, Julia could see Karl Herrick clearing away shrubbery from the patch of ground behind the courtyard which was to become the kitchen garden.

Mrs. Kingston had obviously seen him, too, for she suddenly released Grace's hand, quickened her steps, and advanced toward him, returning the Worthy sisters' greetings with a cursory nod. The two managed to wave Julia to a halt, though.

"You've a visitor, Mrs. Hollis," Iris said. "A gentleman."

"Not a friendly sort, if ye ask me," Jewel added, nodding in the direction of the kitchen garden. She peered up at Julia with a critical eye. "Just like yer Mrs. Kingston there. Do ye intend to fill the *Larkspur* up with unsociable people, Mrs. Hollis?"

"Of course not," Julia told them, avoiding glancing over at Fiona, lest she give way to the smile she was struggling to keep inside. "And once Mrs. Kingston becomes better acquainted with you, I'm sure you'll get along famously."

"I don't know about that, dear," Iris sighed. "We had a chat with her yesterday, and she mentioned that we ought to mind our own business."

Jewel drew her lips together. "All we did was ask her why she moved to Gresham. Never once did we say she wasn't *welcome* here!"

This time Julia sent a pleading look to Fiona, who took a step closer and came to the rescue. In her most soothing brogue, she said, "We all have days when we feel out of sorts. And some people are more sensitive to questions than others." She nodded down at the strips of lace upon the women's cushions. "My, my! Isn't it amazing that something so lovely can come from simple threads."

As the Worthy sisters brightened and pointed out the intricacies of their patterns, Julia suddenly recalled that they had mentioned a visitor. She wasn't expecting her second lodger, a Mr. Clay, until three days from now but wondered if he'd come early. She didn't want to ask the Worthy sisters for details, or she would be delayed for another ten minutes.

"Have a pleasant afternoon," she told them, even though they were too busy discussing their lace with Fiona to notice. Taking Grace's hand, she hurried up the carriage drive. She felt guilty for leaving Fiona at their mercy but knew the housekeeper would be able

136

to extricate herself tactfully after another minute or so.

Oh dear! Is she giving orders to the servants again? Julia wondered, approaching Karl and Mrs. Kingston at the garden site. But when both heads turned to her, their expressions seemed pleasant enough.

"So you've gotten yourself away from them," Mrs. Kingston said. "I hope you don't mind my asking Mr. Herrick here to move this rose bush."

"Rose bush?" Julia stepped forward to peer down at the straggled bit of thorns and reluctant buds growing near the stones of the gardening cottage. "Why, I've never even noticed it."

"You don't happen to know which variety of rose it is, do you?"

"I'm afraid I don't. My gardening skills are lacking, as you've already noticed."

Mrs. Kingston nodded agreement to that point. "Well, it's not the proper time to transplant anything green. But the poor plant needs the morning sun most desperately, so Mr. Herrick is kindly moving it to the front. I shall just have to nurse it along and try to keep it alive."

To Karl, she said, "Careful now—a good wide circle. You don't want to shock the roots." Mrs. Kingston looked at Julia again and nodded toward the Alcorn's cottage, next door to the Worthy sisters.

"I wonder if that family would let me have some rabbit droppings to use as fertilizer?"

"I'm sure they would. But how did you know. . . ?"

"That they raise rabbits? Why, those two lace spinners told me just yesterday. Excellent work they do, by the way. I plan to purchase some lace to send to my grandchildren come Christmas."

Julia thought about the ghost story and wondered if rabbits were all that had been discussed. "So, you had a chat with them?"

"A good long one." Mrs. Kingston's blue eyes shone with just a bit of mischief. "And I can assure you of this, Mrs. Hollis. If I come across Jake Pitt in some dark corridor, I shall give him what-for."

And I'll cheer you on, Julia thought. When she finally hurried through the kitchen doorway, Mrs. Herrick sent a mild reproachful look from atop her stool. "So you've finally decided to come home."

"Is it Mr. Clay who's here?"

"Aye. And he's been waitin' for an hour now."

"He's the actor," Mildred volunteered as she paused from chopping up turnips. She was a tall and broad woman with a warm nature that belied her perpetually anxious expression. Her hair was covered with a frilled cap, except for two reddish-brown curls that bobbed over each ear. "A most handsome fellow too. Georgette is black and blue from runnin' into tables and doors."

"But he wasn't due until Tuesday. Where is he now? In the hall?"

"Up in his room," the cook answered. "Master Philip said the man looked like he needed to rest. He sure didn't touch a thing on my tray."

Julia found Philip pacing the hall with his hands gathered behind his back. He looked greatly relieved at her presence, and after repeating what Mrs. Herrick had already told her, he asked if he could leave to play cricket with his friends. She thanked the boy for taking care of matters and allowed him to go. "Just be back by suppertime."

Philip did indeed return as ordered, but as the evening wore on, Mr. Clay had yet to put in an appearance. After contemplating the matter, Julia finally went upstairs and knocked softly upon his door. Normally she would not have dreamed of visiting a gentleman's room, but she reminded herself that she was the landlady of this establishment and had a duty to know what was going on.

Besides, Mr. Clay's actions, as described by Philip, were not those of a well man. If he were carrying some sort of contagious disease, she had to think of the welfare of her children, the servants, and Mrs. Kingston. Perhaps a coach would even have to be hired to take him to the hospital in Shrewsbury.

She sent up a quick prayer. *Please show me how to deal with this, Lord.*

"Come in," said a voice from the other side.

Judging by the dimness of the room as she pushed open the door, Julia expected to find Mr. Clay still abed. But a face turned to her from one of the two wing chairs by the window. She could tell little about the man while standing in the light of the hallway, but the voice had been of someone perhaps a little older than herself.

"I'm Julia Hollis," she said, taking a step into the room. "We corresponded about your taking a room here."

"Yes, of course."

She cleared her throat. "I've come to inform you that supper will be served at seven. And to discuss certain things with you, if I may."

"Please, do come in," he repeated, getting to his feet. Julia crossed the carpet to offer her hand. The man was clad in a plain white shirt and dark trousers, with a scarf tied loosely at his neck. A frock

138

coat hung upon the back of the chair in which he'd been seated. The hand that he offered didn't feel overly warm or clammy, and though his face appeared drawn, there seemed to be no flush of fever. Julia sat down in the chair adjacent to Mr. Clay's, and he took his seat again.

"I apologize for not being here when you arrived, Mr. Clay," Julia told him. "But I wasn't expecting you until Tuesday."

"The fault is mine, I assure you," he said in a refined voice colored with a trace of Cornish accent. "I simply felt compelled to get out of London. If you'd prefer, I can go somewhere else until then."

Julia shook her head. "Of course not." *You have to ask him now,* she ordered herself. "But I must confess some concern about the state of your health. Why are you sitting here in the dark?"

He gave a long sigh. "I suppose you wonder if I'm ill. Not with anything that should alarm you."

"Then you *are* ill."

After a hesitation, he replied, "I suffer from periods of overwhelming despondency, Mrs. Hollis. It has so affected my career that I've found it necessary to get away to a place where I can rest. When I came across your advertisement in *The London Times,* it seemed to be the answer."

His expression was so bleak, his tone so hopeless, that Julia's heart went out to him. "Have you considered . . ."

"A sanitarium?" A corner of Mr. Clay's mouth quirked. "I spent several months in one some years ago in Bath. But I left there in far worse condition than when I was admitted. I do not wish to be in the company of other people who share the same affliction."

His eyes appeared to be slate gray in the fading daylight, heavily fringed with dark lashes that a maiden would have given her last hair ribbon for. Right now, though, they appeared as opaque as marbles, as if shielding a hurting soul inside.

"I assure you I'll not cause any trouble, or ask for any special privileges," he went on, directing an entreating look at her. "I just need a place of respite where no decisions are required of me, and where I can be alone whenever I wish."

Julia's eyes swept around the dim room. While the bed had obviously been slept in, Mr. Clay had made a clumsy but thoughtful attempt to straighten the coverlet afterward. But was a dark room the atmosphere that someone like Mr. Clay needed? Was he to become a hermit in her home? What if he became suicidal?

Be honest with him, Julia told herself. *If he moves in here, it's going to be much harder to ask him to leave.* She sighed. "I confess that I don't know what to make of this, Mr. Clay. A despondency of this magnitude—"

"It lightens dramatically at times, I assure you."

That struck a suspicious cord with her. "You're aware that this is a temperance establishment, aren't you?"

"Yes," he nodded. "That's another reason I responded to your advertisement. I discovered years ago after almost wrecking my career that strong drink only made my condition worse. I would rather not have the temptation about."

When Julia did not answer right away, he leaned forward slightly and said, "Won't you allow me to stay, Mrs. Hollis? You can send me packing if you find my presence too disagreeable."

The longing in his voice stirred compassion in Julia's heart, and she thought again of the people who had allowed themselves to be used of God to bless her life. Was He now impressing upon her to help Mr. Clay? Surely it had been no accident that a well-traveled actor chose her unassuming establishment. If she only had a little more time to be sure before making a decision that would affect the whole household. *Perhaps we aren't always allowed to be sure,* she thought. Again, wasn't that where faith came in?

"Yes, you may stay here," she finally answered, then gathered up the courage to add, "But under certain conditions, Mr. Clay."

"Yes?"

She had already covered the matter of the children in their correspondence, so she had only to add to that. "I ask that you take meals downstairs with us. My servants have enough responsibilities without delivering trays to someone capable of walking down to the dining room."

After just a brief hesitation, he said, "Reasonable enough, Mrs. Hollis."

"*And,*" she continued in a firm but gentle voice, "that you vacate your room for half an hour every morning so that it can be cleaned. We've a comfortable sitting room on this floor, as well as a library downstairs where you can go for some solitude during that time."

Mr. Clay nodded with apparent relief that her requests had been simple ones and turned to take something from the pocket of the frock coat hanging behind him. "My cheque," he said, handing it over to her.

"But this is too much, Mr. Clay."

"I find it rather overwhelming to keep up with accounts and the like, so I made it out for three months. Please remind me when that period is over, and I will draft you another."

There seemed nothing more to discuss, so Julia thanked him and got to her feet. Mr. Clay rose as well, saying that he should freshen up for supper. Before Julia reached the door, however, he spoke to her again.

"Mrs. Hollis?"

She turned back to face him. "Yes, Mr. Clay?" His expression, from what she could tell at that distance, was apologetic.

"I am inclined toward self-obsession during times of despondency. But it has just come to my attention that you are in widow's dress. I feel rather embarrassed. No doubt life is difficult for you at times as well."

It touched Julia that he would consider her feelings when he seemed so defeated by his own dark emotions. She smiled consolingly at him. "I still have my children, Mr. Clay. And God has shown himself to be the most tender of companions."

A slight nod was his only reply, so she turned and left him. When Mr. Clay came downstairs for supper he was quiet, but not unpleasantly so. He even lingered after the meal long enough to answer Aleda's and Philip's questions about the London stage before excusing himself and returning to his room.

"What is wrong with the poor boy?" Mrs. Kingston asked Julia later as they sat over needlework in the library while the children were occupied with other things.

Julia cocked her head at her. "Philip?"

"No, not Philip. That Mr. Clay upstairs."

She had to smile. "He's well into his thirties, Mrs. Kingston."

With a shrug the older woman said, "Well, to a woman well into her sixties, Mrs. Hollis, people of that age seem as children."

"He suffers from despondency," Julia said after a moment's thought. She certainly couldn't keep Mr. Clay's condition from the rest of the household.

"How sad."

This utterance of sympathy surprised Julia, who halfway expected Mrs. Kingston to mutter something like Mr. Scrooge's "humbug!"

Later, after she had prayed with her children, Julia found that her own private prayers were becoming longer. In a little over a week she'd added requests that Mrs. Kingston's son and daughter-in-law forgive her, and now, that the quiet man in the room upstairs would find peace of mind.

Vicar Wilson's last official duty in Gresham would be to give a short devotion at the school awards ceremony in the town hall on the evening of June first, a Tuesday. The children spent the last day of school helping to tidy the classrooms before the summer months. They were allowed a longer break in the school yard and found punch and biscuits waiting for them upon their return.

None of the boys dared assemble for cricket, nor did the girls for "drop the handkerchief" after the dismissal bell, for mothers had warned that they were to stay clean for the assemblage tonight. After bidding his friends good-bye, Philip went straight to *Trumbles*.

"And what might I do for you today, Mr. Hollis?" the ever affable shopkeeper asked, hooking his thumbs under his suspenders.

From his trousers' pocket Philip took the two shillings that Mother had given him this morning. "I'd like to buy some hair pomade."

"Ah. Running errands for that new lodger, are you?"

He almost nodded, for even though the pomade had been his idea, he now felt a little embarrassed about it. *But you live in a lodging house . . . so you're a lodger in a way,* said some less-than-honest voice in his mind. But he just couldn't make himself act out the lie. Trying to assume as manly an expression as possible, he deepened his voice just a bit and said, "It's for me, Mr. Trumble."

Thankfully, Mr. Trumble did not appear to find this amusing. "Ah, awards ceremony tonight, isn't it? You must be expecting to be called up, a bright fellow like you."

Philip hung his head. "Thank you, sir. That would be nice, all right."

"Well, I've just the thing for you, young Mr. Hollis." The shopkeeper brought out a blue glass bottle from behind the counter. "*Pearce Brothers' Fine Oil,*" he said.

"Is it any good?"

"Is it any good?" Mr. Trumble echoed incredulously. "Why, it's the brand used by the most extinguished gentlemen in England."

142

After dressing in his Sunday best and spending a good ten minutes combing a dab of pomade through his auburn hair, Philip practiced making expressions of surprise in the mirror above his chest of drawers. *Don't overdo it,* he told himself. In a way, he wished Captain Powell didn't have the habit of announcing the results of examinations and compositions in class, for no student at Gresham school, save possibly the infants in Miss Hillock's class, would be fooled by any surprise he feigned. Yet if he appeared to be actually expecting one of the medals awarded to the students in the fifth standard, people would think him conceited.

He settled for a pleased-but-humble-looking smile and left his room to find his mother. She was in the hall, chatting with Mrs. Kingston—the two women looked like a pair of rooks in their black gowns, gloves, and bonnets, and Philip had the disloyal thought that he would be glad when Mother didn't have to wear black anymore.

"Don't you think it's time we were leaving?" Philip asked his mother when a break occurred in Mrs. Kingston's flow of words. Both women turned to look at him.

"It's a bit early," Mother replied.

"But we'll want to sit up front, won't we?"

"It's always nicer when you can see what's going on," Mrs. Kingston remarked, and Philip gave her an appreciative smile.

After two weeks now, he was still not quite at ease in the elderly woman's presence. Even though she had never been unkind, her tone of voice could still be sharp at times. It had surprised him greatly to learn that she was eager to attend the awards ceremony.

"All right, then," Mother said to him. "Step into the kitchen and tell Miss O'Shea we're ready, then you can fetch the girls." So that Fiona would be respected as the housekeeper, his mother referred to her as "Miss O'Shea" whenever lodgers or other servants were present and had instructed Philip and his sisters to do the same.

"Thank you!" Philip threw over his shoulder on his way up the corridor. He delivered the message to Fiona in the kitchen and hurried back down to the family corridor. He was just about to knock on his sisters' door when a strange sound met his ears. He thought it was Buff the cat at first, but then his heart jolted in his chest. *Grace?*

Her sobs grew louder as he threw the door open. She was standing in front of the dressing table and mirror, her hands covering her face while Aleda looked on with a frown.

"What happened?" Philip asked Aleda.

"Just look at her hair," she replied in a disgusted tone.

Philip heard panicked voices behind him and moved aside to allow Mother and Mrs. Kingston in the room. Then he studied the object of Aleda's scorn more closely. Grace's brown curls lay plastered against her scalp in an oily sheen, while the odor of pomade, *his* pomade, hung heavy about her.

"Grace?" Mother said, stepping over to her. "Whatever did you do?"

"She said she wanted to look nice for the ceremony," Aleda replied, arms akimbo. "She went into Philip's room just a minute ago and got into that bottle of oil he bought. She's supposed to win the 'Good Citizen' award, but I don't think Miss Hillock would give it to her if she could see how sneaky she's been."

"That's enough, Aleda." While Mother attempted to soothe Grace, Mrs. Kingston, who appeared to be oddly struggling with the corners of her mouth, said that she would get a towel from the water closet. Philip didn't know quite where he fit into the picture. On any other day he would have been angry at Grace for wasting something that belonged to him—but this evening he just wanted to get to the town hall. Even if she'd shaved her head, he would probably just ask Mother to cover it with a bonnet and get everyone going.

And as it turned out, that was all she could do, for it would have taken hours to wash the oil out of Grace's hair. When Mrs. Kingston returned with the towel and Fiona in her wake, Mother blotted as much of the pomade as possible from Grace's hair and tied a bonnet under her chin.

"I'm sorry, Philip," Grace whispered as the group left the *Larkspur*'s front door. She had stopped crying, but her expression was one of misery.

"You could have asked, you know," he felt compelled to lecture.

The corners of her mouth drooped even more so. "But you weren't in your room. And I didn't mean to pour out so much. It came out so fast."

It was impossible to hold any grudge against her.

"That's all right, Grace," Philip told her. He thought about Mr. Trumble's recommendation of the product and added, "It did make you look rather extinguished."

"What?"

He patted her shoulder. "Never mind."

Even though they arrived early, the benches in the town hall, a red-brick building with a weathervane of a horse above its steep roof, were three-quarters filled. Miss Hillock's students were first to receive their awards when the ceremony began. As it turned out, small bronze "Good Citizen" medals were given to every one of the younger students, who each beamed with pleasure upon receiving it. No one seemed to notice anything amiss about Grace's appearance when she walked up to the platform to join her classmates, and she smiled just as broadly as the others during the applause.

When it came time for the older students, Aleda was awarded a medal for spelling in the fourth standard, as well as a special certificate of recognition for playing the piano during chapels.

Philip was indeed called up on the platform by Captain Powell to receive both the arithmetic and science medals for the fifth standard. He found that making the correct facial expression was not a problem after all. Even though he was expecting some honor, he could not stop smiling his sincere pleasure as the medals were pinned to his coat. Having spent the bulk of his schooling years under the direction of a tutor, he'd never had the opportunity to compete with children his own age and found that he liked it very much.

Penelope Worthy, a factory worker's daughter and distant relative of the Worthy sisters, was announced the winner of the coveted "Top Student in the Sixth Standard award." It was the highest honor at Gresham School, for which only students in the final standard were eligible. Any students who had the means and desire to continue their education after that were sent away to preparatory schools.

Philip watched with awe as Captain Powell presented the trophy. It was a silver two-handled cup atop a polished wooden base. On the front of the base was attached a silver plate, upon which were engraved three lines:

Penelope Worthy,
Top Student, Gresham School,
June 1, 1869.

Though proud of his medals, Philip could hardly stop looking over at the trophy that the radiant-faced girl held up for all to admire. His eyes caressed the gleaming metal, and he formed a mental picture of himself cradling it in his arms to the applause of everyone present. *I'm going to win that next year,* he determined. Even if he had to study every minute of his free time, those few minutes of triumph on the platform would be worth it.

Cambridge
June 2, 1869

Andrew Phelps, rector of Saint Benett's, sat back in his favorite wing chair and listened to the banter of the two young people seated at the other end of the drawing room.

"You can't expect me to believe that your uncle brought an elephant all the way to Kensington!" his eighteen-year-old daughter Elizabeth was saying to the well-dressed young man. Her cheeks were flush, her brown eyes alive with life, and Andrew felt a pang at her happiness. It was only a matter of time before Jonathan Raleigh proposed. How did other parents adjust to losing their children?

"Even after you've seen proof with your own eyes?" Jonathan argued back.

"That photograph could have been taken in India."

"You say? And how would you account for the spruce trees in the background?"

Elizabeth's eyes widened. "You're serious, aren't you?"

"Serious as taxes." The young man chuckled. "I'll spare you the details of the poor beast's journey across the channel, however. Suffice to say, his equilibrium did not cope well, especially when a storm whipped the water to new heights."

"You can't mean . . ."

"Well, we have to take my uncle's word about that. He mercifully took no photograph of the event."

Andrew frowned at the letter in his hands. It had arrived by post today, bearing no return address. *Someone jealous of Mr. Raleigh,* he told himself again, for Jonathan Raleigh was the type who inspired envy. The nephew of a duke, third cousin to the Lord Chancellor, he

147

was one of those golden students who excelled at his studies and was even captain of the archery team. The upperclassman had met Elizabeth at a church fete and swept the girl off her feet. Even Andrew had been impressed. Mr. Raleigh's manners were as impeccable as his family credentials, and so he allowed the young man to call upon his daughter.

I'll throw it in the fire, Andrew thought. Anyone spineless enough to send an anonymous message such as this was surely no one who could be trusted. Instead, he folded the page and held it. The five lines had contained only an address on Locke Street in the seedier part of Cambridge and a warning that Jonathan Raleigh was seeing the wife of an army sergeant there.

Thirteen-year-old Laurel came from upstairs and perched herself on the arm of Andrew's chair. "Have you been missing anything lately, Papa?" she asked.

He had to think about that one, for he had a tendency to misplace things. "Why, not that I can recall."

She grinned and drew his favorite pen from behind her back, the one he had long given up hope of recovering.

"Where did you find it?" he asked as she handed it to him.

"In the dirt under the garden swing. Along with two shillings. May I keep them, Papa?"

"Well, I suppose a reward *is* in order."

"Thank you!" she said, giving him a quick embrace. Like Elizabeth, Laurel had her mother's dark brown eyes and delicately carved oval face. Andrew felt grateful, for his daughters' sakes, that both had inherited most of their looks from Kathleen. In fact, his only contributions toward their appearances were the dimples in their cheeks and the straight, wheat-colored hair. Most people were unaware of his own set of dimples, however, for he'd worn a beard ever since he was a young curate.

He was fully aware that he could never be regarded as a handsome man in the classical sense. For one thing, his height was too nondescript at five feet eight, and his body, though solid, was thick almost to the point of stockiness. His nose, once broken by an errant paddle during his university days on the rowing team, would appear more natural on the face of a prizefighter than of a man of the cloth. But since he seldom looked in a mirror except to make sure that he'd parted his hair correctly, it didn't matter.

"What have you there, Papa?" Laurel asked, reaching out to scratch his bearded chin.

Andrew slipped the folded page in his waistcoat pocket. "Nothing that would interest you, Pet. I thought we were going to have to send someone up for you. Dinner is almost ready, Mrs. Orson says."

"I was studying and lost track of time. Where is Grandmother?"

"She's at one of those ladies' meetings—'The Society to Promote Hummingbird Table Etiquette' or something of that sort."

Laurel giggled. "I'll tell her you said that."

"To your peril, if you do," Andrew said, feigning severity. He could tell that she wasn't the least bit alarmed and wondered for the hundredth time since Kathleen's death if he were doing his girls a disservice by not being a sterner parent. His own father had been eager to point out the character flaws of his six sons. Too eager, Andrew had thought while growing up, but he could see now that the criticism had made him strive to become a better man, if only to prove his father wrong.

But the feminine mind was still such an enigma to Andrew. He wasn't certain if his daughters' delicate egos could take the severe regimen by which he had been raised. Blessedly, Elizabeth and Laurel were tender-hearted children, eager to please, and had never tried to take advantage of his mild discipline. He had visited households, in the course of his duties, where children had been permitted to become little tartars, ruling parents and servants with self-important contempt. One could only imagine what sort of disagreeable adults those children would become, and chiefly because the parents failed to exercise a restraining hand.

The only times Andrew could remember being in the company of his own parents were when the boys were brought down to the drawing room for brief evening visits before bedtime, or to recite for guests. Andrew did not consider himself deprived during those early years in Gloucester. His nanny was kind and attentive, and besides, it was the same way with most families of the upper classes. At the age of eight he was sent to join his older brothers at a boarding school in Huntingdon. That was when a longing for the attentions of a loving mother and father took root in his heart and began to grow.

And that was the other reason Andrew could not bring himself to be as stern as he knew he should be. Perhaps the primary reason. A sudden attack of apoplexy had taken his beloved Kathleen from them six years ago. He felt great empathy for his daughters, growing up without the tender ministrations of a mother. Even his widowed mother, who had agreed to come to live with them in Cambridge, could not fill the void that Kathleen had left. *But God hasn't sent anyone into my life to take her place.*

"Father?"

Realizing he'd drifted off into one of his "hazes," as Elizabeth called them, he looked at Laurel again. "Yes?"

The girl motioned toward Elizabeth and her beau, both heads bent over a globe. "They don't even realize I've walked into the room, do they?"

" . . . of the elephant's journey was by rail," Jonathan Raleigh was explaining to Elizabeth. "My uncle hired a whole steerage car."

"I'm afraid they don't, Pet." Andrew agreed. He cleared his throat, and the two heads turned in their direction.

"Will you stay for dinner, Mr. Raleigh?"

The young man gave a reluctant shake of his dark head. "Thank you, sir, but I'm afraid I've already been invited to dinner. One of those stuffy faculty-student affairs. In fact, I should be leaving now."

When Mr. Raleigh was gone, Andrew sat to dinner with his daughters, himself at the head of the table, Elizabeth on his right and Laurel his left. The pocketed letter was a hot brand on his chest, and he wondered again why he was unable to dismiss it as petty jealousy. Perhaps it was because Elizabeth seemed to be so completely in love.

"You know," he began awkwardly after carving the roast duck, "we should invite other gentlemen to dinner sometime. Take Mr. McCready's son, Bruce, for example. I find his knowledge of the Scriptures most impressive. He'll make a fine minister one day."

"Yes, he seems to be very pleasant," Elizabeth replied, toying with her food, as was her habit of late. But then she looked up at Andrew and smiled. "Did you know that Jonathan's uncle keeps an elephant on his estate in Kensington?"

"What does he feed it?" Laurel asked with wide eyes.

"Why, I'm not sure. I'll have to ask Jonathan."

Andrew dabbed his mouth with his napkin and went cautiously ahead. "It would be good for you, making the acquaintance of other young gentlemen. You'll have less time for such things when you start at Eton this fall."

Elizabeth lowered her eyes to study the place setting in front of

150

her for several seconds, prompting Andrew to ask her if anything was the matter.

"I don't want to go to college," she whispered after some hesitation.

"Don't want to go to college?" Andrew echoed, uncomprehending. "But you're doing so well at Brunswick." Brunswick was the preparatory school for girls on Newmarket Road operated by the Sisters of Saint Anne, whose creed was that idle minds were the devil's playground.

Finally raising her chin, she met his gaze. He could see the tears shining in her brown eyes. *That's not fair!* Andrew thought, even as his heart began to melt. He set down his fork. "Elizabeth, what is wrong?"

"Nothing," she whimpered while dabbing her eyes with her napkin.

"Nothing?" He tried coaxing a smile from her. "Come on now. You've spent too much time studying for exams lately. Why don't you take a day or two and rest?"

"I want to take a year away from studying, Papa. Perhaps longer. Perhaps forever."

"But college . . ." Andrew could only mumble stupidly, glancing at Laurel for help.

His younger daughter gave him a somber nod and turned her face back to Elizabeth. "Is it because of Jonathan?"

Elizabeth blew her nose. "N-No."

"Then, why?" Andrew asked, not quite believing her half-hearted denial.

"I just don't want to go," she said, then gave a sigh that belied her tender years. "I'm so weary of Latin and mathematics and French—all of it."

"But you may not feel that way in another month or so." Which was very likely, Andrew thought, for Elizabeth had a history of taking up projects and abandoning them later, such as the flute and riding lessons. He certainly couldn't allow her to abandon her education on a whim.

The light in her brown eyes seemed to dull in front of him, and she stretched out her hand upon the tablecloth to touch his. "I want you to be proud of me, Papa. That's why I've studied so hard all these years. But I feel like I've become a shell, full of facts and figures. There has to be more to life."

She looked so much like her mother, staring at him with tears still hanging to her lashes, that a painful lump swelled within Andrew's chest. "I have always been proud of you, Elizabeth," he said gently. "You never had to earn that."

She heaved another deep sigh. "I know."

"What is it, then?"

Fixing her eyes again upon the filled plate still in front of her, Elizabeth answered in a small voice, "I want to be like Mother was. I want to marry . . . and have children."

Jonathan Raleigh, Andrew thought. *I knew it.* Now it was he who sighed. "You're that much in love with him?"

"Yes," she whispered.

Andrew glanced again at Laurel, who returned a helpless shrug of her shoulders. He turned back to his elder daughter. "Has he asked you, Elizabeth?"

She shook her head. "But I know he will. He's hinted as much. And he's asked us all to come to Kensington this summer to meet his family."

"We could see the elephant?" Laurel perked up, then grimaced at Andrew's warning look.

"There is a gazebo on the grounds," Elizabeth went on. "It was there that Jonathan's father proposed to his mother. Jonathan says he wants to show it to me."

"Oh." Andrew rubbed his forehead absently. "And if . . . if he proposes?"

The blush across her cheeks gave her answer, even before her lips responded, "I would accept. I do love him, Papa."

———

He spent the next hour in his library chair, staring unseeingly at the same page of *The Cambridge Chronicle.* Yes, he'd expected that Mr. Raleigh would eventually propose. But now that the day seemed to be rushing toward him, he wished with all his heart that he could turn the clock back to the time when his girls did not have thoughts of leaving home. *This summer? I didn't know it would be so soon.*

"Andrew, dear?" Lydia Phelps, his mother, came into the room with a rustle of silk. "Where are the girls?"

"They're upstairs."

She came closer, her eyes narrowing suspiciously. "And when did you become interested in the fashion page?"

"Huh?" Andrew looked down at the newspaper in his hand, then set it aside. "Did you enjoy your meeting?"

"Marvelous," she replied, ostrich feathers quivering from her hat as she spoke. She settled into a chair. "I find society at Cambridge far more stimulating than back at Gloucester. Vastly more cerebral."

"Yes?" He hoped she would not launch into a description of the evening's events, for he found her social acquaintances rather pompous and self-absorbed.

His mother fixed him with a mildly calculating look. "You know, Mrs. Keswick was there. She's having a dinner party next month and will be sending you an invitation to act as my escort."

"Mrs. Keswick?"

"Oh, don't look at me with that blank expression. You met her at my little luncheon last month. She's a widow, you know, and well situated."

Andrew vaguely recalled a set of predatory eyes beneath the brim of a hat *à la Reine* and felt a little shudder.

"She found you quite interesting," his mother went on. "With just a little encouragement from you, you could have those girls a mother."

And wishing Mrs. Keswick good day would likely be encouragement enough, Andrew thought. He always found himself puzzled whenever a woman expressed interest in him. He was certainly no Adonis and did not have the polish and charm necessary to woo them. It was still a wonder to Andrew that Kathleen had loved him so completely.

And that was the reason for his hesitancy in responding to the occasional flirtations that were directed his way. Not only had Kathleen been his helpmate and the mother of his children, but she was also his friend . . . his best friend. Which made the marriage all the sweeter. While he could appreciate a woman's attractiveness and femininity and would like to have a wife again, he had yet to feel anything close to the bond of friendship he had enjoyed with Kathleen. And certainly not with those women who so arduously cultivated his courtship, for it seemed that they had neither the time nor the patience to develop a friendship.

"*Andrew?*"

Realizing he'd drifted again, Andrew looked at his mother. "I beg your pardon, Mother?"

She gave an impatient sigh. "Don't you *want* to marry again one day?"

"Of course," he told her gently. He could not fault her for trying to better his life. "But not just for the sake of marrying. I've witnessed too many disasters that have resulted from haste."

His words brought Elizabeth and Mr. Raleigh back to his mind, and he suddenly got to his feet. "Would you mind hearing the girls' prayers?"

"Why, where are you going?"

Andrew touched his waistcoat pocket. "I've an errand. Please don't wait up."

Fourteen Locke Street turned out to be an old building carved into flats, dark except for lights shining from three windows and the glow of a streetlamp near the stoop. Across the street lay a wedge of ground that could loosely be described as a park. Andrew sat down upon the lone bench there and waited, elbows propped upon knees, not even sure what he wanted to happen. If it turned out that the anonymous note was true, then Elizabeth would be devastated. And if he found no evidence to support the accusation, did that mean Jonathan Raleigh was innocent? Or that he'd managed not to get caught this time?

"Am I being foolish, Kathleen?" Andrew mumbled. He could clearly imagine her watching from heaven with that indulgent smile she used whenever he worried about anything. *If only you were here to help me keep my thoughts straight.*

A cough broke through his reflections, and he looked up at the figure standing at his left. She wore a gown of garish purple and a hardened expression, making her look anywhere from twenty to forty years old. He could tell even in the semidarkness that the smile she was giving him did not travel up to her world-weary eyes.

"You look lonely, mister," she said, taking a step closer to his bench.

Annoyed, he opened his mouth to snap at her. Even in such a cerebral city as Cambridge, there were certain sections where a gentleman simply could not walk without being accosted by such as the woman before him. Then the thought crossed his mind, *She's someone's daughter.*

"What's a handsome fellow like you doin' all alone?"

Andrew couldn't help but chuckle at the absurdity of this flattery. That seemed to encourage her, for she took a step even closer and said, "There's a pub over the road a bit. How'd you like to buy me a drink?"

"What is your name?"

"Annabel," she shrugged, as if to say, *what does it matter?*

"Annabel," Andrew echoed. "A lovely name."

"Well, I can show you a lovely time too."

He shook his head. "Ah, but it wouldn't be so lovely for you, would it?"

Frowning, she said, "What are you talking about, mister?"

"How many men have given you anything back for all they've taken from you?"

"I get paid." After her eyes scanned the vacant street in vain for a more likely prospect, she turned back to Andrew and feigned another smile. "Hey, are you going to buy me that drink or not?"

"Why don't you let me tell you about some living water instead?"

The woman went as rigid as a statue. "You're a preacher, ain't you?"

"I am."

"Why didn't you tell me straight off?" She spat on the ground near his feet. "I wouldn't have wasted my time."

With that, she turned and was swallowed up by the night again. *God, lead her to you somehow,* Andrew prayed silently, his already troubled heart now heavier with his failure to reach the woman.

Another two hours went by, with Andrew studying every face that passed, straining his ears at every voice. It was a familiar masculine laugh that finally caused his pulse to quicken. He got to his feet and watched a couple enter the amber glow of the lamp in front of number fourteen. Their arms were linked, and their attention was absorbed with some mutual joke. The woman—obviously much older than the young man—giggled to match his laugh.

His fists balling at his sides, Andrew stepped out into the street. "Mr. Raleigh?" he called out, still hoping his sight and hearing were mistaken.

The laugh stopped abruptly, and the giggle trailed to a halt. "Who's there?" the young man replied in a slurred voice, squinting in Andrew's direction.

"Andrew Phelps, Mr. Raleigh!"

"Reverend Phelps?" It appeared as if Jonathan was trying to detach himself from the woman, but she clung to him and they both stumbled. When the young man found his feet again, the shock seemed to have sobered him a little. "I can explain, sir," came out in a slightly more stable voice.

"And I'm listening, Mr. Raleigh."

"Tell him I'm yer sister," the woman whispered loudly, then burst into another spate of giggles.

Jonathan gave her a murderous look. "Shut up!"

Having seen all that was necessary, Andrew had no desire to witness any more of this spectacle. "Stay away from my daughter, Mr. Raleigh!"

The young man's jaw fell, and for a second it looked as if he would step toward him. But then resignation seemed to set in. Jonathan Raleigh touched the brim of his bowler hat in a mock salute. "And good evening to you, Reverend Phelps! I'll not darken your door again."

———

Two weeks later, the young man once again proved himself to be lacking in integrity, for he did not keep the vow he'd made on that dark street. Claire, the parlormaid in the vicarage, knocked on the door to Andrew's study as he was preparing to pay calls to the sick of the parish. "That Mr. Raleigh asks to see you, sir."

The name issued from her lips as if she'd said, "Napoleon," or "Mary, Queen of Scots," and Andrew could see the scorn in her eyes. There was no keeping secrets from the servants, especially with Elizabeth moving aimlessly about the house as if someone dear to her had died. *You had no other choice,* Andrew reminded himself, but the memory of how her face had crumpled when he gave her the news would haunt him forever.

"Please tell Mr. Raleigh I am unavailable," Andrew said to the maid, but then shook his head. "Never mind. I have a feeling he'll only come back if I don't see him."

"Oh, I wouldn't say that, sir," Claire said, her lips forming a tight line. "If you'll allow me to give him a piece of my mind, he'll make tracks. Or Mrs. Orson would be happy to take her rolling pin to him!"

"Indeed?" Andrew had to smile. "If I need reinforcements, I'll be sure to call the both of you."

"Well, he's out there on the portico, then. I wasn't about to ask him in."

Jonathan Raleigh was indeed waiting out front, hat in hand, and looked up when the door was opened. Unmoved by the misery across the young face, Andrew fought the urge to reach out and grab him by the throat. "What do you want, Mr. Raleigh?"

The chin quivered. "I came to apologize, sir."

"Elizabeth is at school. And I wouldn't allow you to speak with her anyway."

"I know that. That's why I'm here now."

Andrew raised an eyebrow. "So . . . you've added truancy to your list of vices?"

"Don't say that, sir!" Jonathan winced painfully. "I wanted you to know that I haven't seen . . . haven't been to Locke Street since that night."

"That is good to know, for your sake. But again, you may not see my daughter."

Fretfully the young man wrung the brim of his hat with both hands. "I've wronged her. I should be allowed to beg her forgiveness."

"No, you should not," Andrew replied. "And the best thing you can do for yourself is to forget about Elizabeth."

"Don't you think I've tried!" Jonathan's dark eyes brimmed with tears. "You preach about forgiveness, don't you? Well, why won't you—"

"There is a difference between forgiveness and foolishness, young man. I bear you no ill will and pray your waywardness has taught you to stay upon the straight and narrow. But my sainted wife didn't suffer through the valley of the shadow to bear this child just to have her ruined by the likes of you. Good day, Mr. Raleigh."

Ignoring the sob that tore from the young throat, Andrew stepped back and closed the door with a final click.

Five minutes later, the parlormaid's voice broke into his thoughts. "Reverend?"

"What?" Andrew blinked, surprised to find himself still standing in the foyer by the hall tree. He straightened and asked, "What is it, Claire?"

The maid eyed him with a worried frown. "May I fetch you a cup of tea?"

"Tea would be nice," he answered but then shook his head and reached up for his hat. "Wait . . . no, thank you. I'll be back by supper."

"Going to make your calls now, sir?"

"Yes." Andrew opened the door again. Making his way up King's Parade, he eyed the under- and upperclassmen scurrying across the

157

grounds of Trinity College with books under their arms and wind in their Norfolk jackets. It was a classic picture of academia; students absorbed with the quest for knowledge. Yet he knew that for every young man who had come to the university seeking to be educated, there were three of Jonathan Raleigh's ilk—sons of wealthy peers and businessmen, enjoying more unsupervised freedom than ever before in their lives. Their numbers filled the pubs and gin palaces most evenings. *Why did I ever think Cambridge would be a good place to raise daughters?*

His steps slowed until he came to a complete halt on the walkway in front of *Bromley's Baked Goods.* Ignoring the passersby on both sides and the street sweeper's curious looks, Andrew rubbed his beard absently while mulling over his family's situation. He moved on after several seconds, but instead of proceeding as before, he made an abrupt turn in the opposite direction and headed toward Saint Mary Street. He would indeed make his calls to the sick, as was his duty. But his very first call would be to Bishop Myers. He needed some advice about the future.

*I*t seemed that all of Gresham had turned out in front of the vicarage to bid farewell to Vicar Wilson and Henrietta on the morning of June fourth. Even Squire Bartley, whom Julia had still not met personally—and was in no hurry to do so—was there, keeping himself at a distance from the assemblage. He was a tall man for his elderly years, bald as a Druid with thick white eyebrows that seemed to be formed into a perpetual scowl. Why someone with his disposition even attended church was a mystery to Julia. He seemed to get no pleasure from it as he sat alone in his pew, one row ahead of his servants.

There were more than a few teary eyes present as the good reverend and his daughter exchanged embraces with the well-wishers. Luke, who was to drive them to the railway station in Shrewsbury, sat somber-faced at the reins of a borrowed landau, while housemaid Dora and the cook, Mrs. Paget, sobbed openly. Finally the landau moved away, with several boys chasing it down the vicarage lane. Behind, people called out final farewells, raising handkerchiefs. And then the sound of carriage wheels and horses' hooves faded away, and people turned back toward their houses to tend to the duties of the day.

"I'm going to miss them so much," Fiona said as she and Julia walked back home, accompanied by Aleda, Grace, Mildred, and Mrs. Herrick. A gentle breeze, fragrant with the scent of hay drying in the fields, blew around them.

"They'll be missed by us all," Audrey Herrick agreed. Though the Herricks were members of the Baptist chapel on Short Lane, the cook had become closely acquainted with the vicar during his visits with Ethan Banning over the years.

"When's the curate coming?" Mildred asked.

"I believe Luke is to bring him back here this evening," Julia replied. The congregation had been told last Sunday that a curate from Saint Margaret's in Shrewsbury would handle church duties until a new vicar could be assigned.

The kitchen maid's lips drew together bitterly. "Well, won't either of 'em—the curate or the new vicar—be able to hold a candle to Vicar Wilson."

There were general murmurs of agreement. Julia made one herself, even though she was aware that she wasn't being quite fair. It wasn't either minister's fault that their beloved Vicar Wilson could no longer cope with the weather here. But she was afraid there would be some resentment toward the two, particularly the new vicar.

Fiona was obviously of the same mind, for as they ambled pass the empty schoolhouse, she commented, "Perhaps it's for the best, sending a curate first. Then it won't seem so much that the new vicar is taking Vicar Wilson's place."

That sounded reasonable to Julia, and she said so. She then caught sight of Ophelia Rhodes walking up ahead of them. Mrs. Rhodes was kept so busy with her veterinary duties that Julia hadn't had opportunity to tell her how much they were enjoying the use of the silver cutlery. "I'll see you at home later," she told the group and walked quickly to catch up with her friend.

The walk home together turned into coffee and biscuits at the Rhodes' cottage. When Julia finally stepped back through the *Larkspur*'s courtyard door, she was met by the strains of a piano and a male baritone voice with perfect pitch.

"It's that Mr. Clay and Miss Aleda," Mrs. Herrick said from the kitchen doorway, her face beaming.

Mildred and Gertie nodded from behind each shoulder, their faces likewise enraptured. "Who would ha' thought it?" said Mildred.

Who indeed? thought Julia. "Well, shall we go see?"

She hurried down the corridor, with the three servants following close behind. Julia stopped just inside the hall and blinked at the scene before her eyes. Aleda sat at the pianoforte, her slender fingers prancing over the keys like circus ponies, while Mr. Clay stood at the piano's side. Their audience consisted of Mrs. Kingston, who smiled over her needlework, one foot actually tapping, and Grace, next to her on the sofa with Buff curled up in her lap. Across the room, Fiona stood at the empty fireplace and watched with a bemused expression.

Upon seeing that his audience had more than doubled, Mr. Clay did not appear abashed but winked at the four newcomers and continued to sing:

A good sword and a trusty hand!
A merry heart and true!
King James' men shall understand
What Cornish lads can do.
Out spoke their captain brave and bold,
A merry sight was he
If London Tower were Michael's hold,
We'll set Trelawny free!

When the song was finished, he accepted the applause with grace but politely turned down requests for more songs. "And I must compliment young Miss Hollis here for her most excellent accompaniment."

The kitchen servants returned to their duties, still smiling, and Julia approached the piano with wonder. "Where did you get the music for that song?" she asked her daughter. "Do you sing it at school?"

Her face flushed with pleasure, Aleda looked up at the actor. "It's Mr. Clay's."

"A souvenir from *Trelawny*, a little comedy that ran a year or two in the Strand Theatre." Mr. Clay picked up the score from the pianoforte. "I'm afraid I'm a bit of a pack rat concerning mementos from the stage."

"Quite wonderful, if you ask me," came Mrs. Kingston's voice from behind.

"You were both wonderful," Julia agreed. To Mr. Clay, she added, "And I must say I'm delighted to see you're feeling better."

"Thank you." His smile did not waver, but a touch of sadness came into his slate gray eyes. "If only I knew how to hold on to it somehow, Mrs. Hollis."

Mrs. Kingston drew Julia aside in the library after supper, a strange glow to her face. "Mrs. Hollis, are you aware that there is to be a flower show on the green this coming Saturday?"

"Why, I believe it's posted in the vestibule at church," Julia replied. With so many duties to attend to lately, she had given the notice little more than a cursory glance but happened to recall that some members of the Shrewsbury Floral Society would be in attendance as

161

judges. "But I must confess I paid it little mind. Are you interested in attending?"

"Oh, Mrs. Hollis!" Mrs. Kingston clasped both hands together over her heart. "We had them annually in Sheffield, but I was afraid a village this size would not. I won the 'geranium' ribbon three years running."

She seized Julia's arm, her blue eyes intense. "Mrs. Hollis, Karl Herrick is a most capable man, but it's obvious that he has overwhelming responsibilities. Why don't you allow me to assume the cultivation of the flower garden? It would make me very happy."

"But, Mrs. Kingston, you pay for your lodgings here. You shouldn't feel obligated to—"

"How can one feel obligated to do something one enjoys? Please, Mrs. Hollis. Why, it would free Mr. Herrick to tend the vegetable garden and his other duties. And didn't you say yourself that you plan to buy a carriage and horses? Unless you plan to hire a groomsman, he'll have that to do as well."

In the face of such determination, Julia could do nothing but acquiesce, adding, "But I'm sorry you'll have nothing to show at the competition this year."

Mrs. Kingston didn't appear sorry at all. In fact, a content smile appeared on her face. "Ah, but there is always next year now, isn't there?"

———

Three nights later, Ambrose Clay lay on his side and drew his knees up to his chest, more wide-awake than when he had climbed into his bed two hours ago. That was the most perplexing and discouraging thing about the condition that had all but ruined his career. When despondency had him in its grip, he felt so weary that he would gladly stay in bed for days at a time. If he could *sleep*, that is, for insomnia went hand-in-hand with the fatigue to form an incongruous partnership.

He often wondered why it had been his lot in life to suffer such madness. He had no doubt that he was as mad as a dervish. How else could he explain the extremes in his moods? There were days at a time when he felt he could conquer the world, when energy suffused his limbs and creativity his mind. If only he could cling to those glorious days, as a child clings to his mother, refusing to allow them to slip away! But no effort of his will could keep the despondency from returning—he knew, for he had tried many times.

Sometimes the temptation was strong to put an end to the suffering once and for all, as his father had done, yet he could not bring himself to take that drastic step. What if he succeeded in only injuring himself, to the point where he became like one of those poor wretches who hover in doorways, begging alms of passersby?

And so he looked upon the remainder of his days as a cruel life sentence to endure. He could not go back and undo the event of his birth. Were such a thing possible, yes, but it served no good to dwell upon fantasies. With a sigh, he threw aside the bedclothes and got to his feet. Reading late at night often distracted his mind enough to allow a natural sleepiness to come over him. He slipped a flannel dressing gown over his pajamas, pushed his feet into corduroy slippers, and picked up the copy of Trollope's *Barchester Towers* from his night table. He'd finished it late last night during another bout with insomnia and would save the chambermaid the trouble of returning it to the library.

As he held a candle in front of him on his way down the dark staircase, the stillness of the house only served to increase his melancholia. With envy he could imagine the others upon their pillows, caught up in the slumber that so eluded him. That was another paradox of his condition. While the despondency caused him to closet himself away from the company of other people, he felt at the same time overwhelmed by loneliness. *I'd welcome even Jake Pitt's company right now,* he thought, a bitter smile twisting one corner of his mouth.

The library door was closed, as usual, but with a thread of light visible underneath. *Surely someone hasn't left the lamp burning.* A room filled with books, some of them quite old, would be a certain fire hazard. He turned the knob to open the door and saw the startled face of Miss O'Shea.

"I'm sorry, sir," the housekeeper said, averting her eyes as she rose from her chair.

Her apology annoyed him a little, and her aversion to look at him much more. "Sorry for what?"

"For disturbing you," she answered in a soft Irish brogue. "I'll leave now."

He shook his head, still annoyed. "But how could you have disturbed me, when you were here first?"

"I just—"

"And please—I'm as fully clothed as you."

"Yes, of course you are," she nodded and turned her eyes to him.

He realized then that she was waiting for him to move from the doorway so she could quit the room. As annoyed as she had made him, she was the only other conscious person in the whole house, and he suddenly felt loathe to let her go.

"Would you mind keeping me company for just a little while?" he asked in a more gentle tone.

She hesitated but then lowered herself back into her chair. Ambrose took a chair about five feet away—a safe distance, so she would see that conversation was his only motive. He had never really noticed her as a *person* before, he realized, ashamed of his own elitism. Like the other servants, she had only been someone in the background— a calm little apron-clad figure who moved unobtrusively in and out of rooms to oversee the functions of the house.

Now she wore a simple housedress of a light rose color, and raven-colored hair fell about her shoulders with a healthy shine. The eyes, as purple as orchids, showed a keen intelligence that he admired in a woman and a modesty that he found charming. *She could be beautiful,* he thought. *If only someone would tell her so.*

"What were you reading?" he finally asked her.

She glanced down at the book in her hands. "*The Newcomes.* Have you read it?"

"Ah, Thackeray. Yes, I have." Actually, he'd acted the role of Clive Newcome in a student production at Oxford and could still quote entire paragraphs. "Are you enjoying it?"

"Quite so, sir." She appeared ready to add something to that, but then her expression veiled and she lowered her eyes to the book again.

"What were you going to say?" he felt compelled to ask.

"Just that I enjoyed *Henry Esmond* more."

"And what is wrong with saying that?"

A corner of her mouth flicked in an awkward manner. "I am not an educated person, Mr. Clay. It is not my place to critique novels."

"And yet you read Thackeray. Not all knowledge is hoarded by the universities, you know." He started to explain further but could see in her expression that she understood his meaning. "Is it very difficult for you?" he found himself asking instead.

"Difficult, sir?"

"Being in service." Quickly, he added, "I hope that question doesn't offend you."

"It does not offend me," she replied with soft frankness. "And

164

while being in service can be difficult in some households, I've been blessed in my station. Mrs. Hollis treats me very well."

"Then you are happy with your life just as it is?" Ambrose was aware that his questions were too personal, but he could not stop himself from voicing them. With happiness so elusive during his dark moods, he had to figure out how others managed to achieve it. The secret was out there, barely out of his grasp, and he just had to keep reaching for it.

After fixing her magnificent eyes upon something past his shoulder for several seconds, Miss O'Shea answered, "There are circumstances I would change if I could, sir, but I'm content."

There was a finality in her answer that did not invite questions, and he nodded understanding. A lengthier silence stretched between them until she turned her face in his direction again.

"You were having trouble sleeping, Mr. Clay?"

He shrugged and replied self-consciously, for his condition shamed him greatly, "It seems the only time I can sleep is when I'm supposed to be awake."

"Perhaps some hot chocolate?"

Ambrose was about to thank her anyway but then realized that if he turned down her offer, he would have to allow her to leave presently. He could not bear the thought of being alone again and so, while chiding himself for his selfishness—for she was likely growing sleepy—he replied that perhaps that would help.

She got to her feet and asked to borrow his candle. "I'll bring it to you here," she said, but Ambrose got to his feet as well.

"I may as well go with you."

From the kitchen worktable in the amber light of a single lamp, Ambrose watched the housekeeper carry a small copper pot of milk to the stove. "Have you worked as a cook before?"

"I have, sir." She sent him a brief smile while opening a tin of *Cadbury's Cocoa Essence*. "But for only a day."

It was the first time he could recall noticing her smile, and he found himself smiling back. "Why only one day?"

"I had no talent for it."

"Then, how do you propose to manage hot chocolate?"

"I've watched Mrs. Herrick a number of times. But I cannot guarantee that it will be as palatable as hers."

"Aye, that's a fact," came a voice from Ambrose's left. The cook's flannel-swathed little figure stood framed by the doorway, Buff the house cat staring at them from her arms.

"Oh, Mrs. Herrick," the housekeeper said, turning in her direction. "Did we wake you?"

"It's my fault," Ambrose said gallantly. "I couldn't sleep, so—"

"Just leave the kitchen as you found it. Tha's all I ask." The cat stretched up to lick her cheek, and Mrs. Herrick grinned. "She knows who butters her bread, don't she?"

The cook was gone, and they traded smiles again. Ambrose said in a lower voice, "I'll help you tidy up afterward, Miss O'Shea."

"Thank you, but it'll take me only a minute." She brought a steaming crockery mug to the table. "The mug's not fancy, but it holds more than the china cups."

"Aren't you having any?" He saw the hesitation in her face and wondered if it was because servants and non-servants generally did not share tables. "Please, don't make me drink alone." When she had seated herself across from him with a mug of her own, he took a sip.

"Just the way I like it. Not tongue-scalding hot." He chose to ignore the fact that it was rather heavy on the sugar and could use a pinch of salt.

"Thank you, sir."

Miss O'Shea asked him how he chose the stage for a career, and Ambrose found himself telling her all about his earlier years. "I was determined not to be an actor. I saw what the instability of a touring life did to my family. Most of the time we children were sent to my mother's parents in Cornwall. Father couldn't manage without my mother, you see."

"Your father was an actor?"

"A quite successful one, actually."

First taking a sip of her chocolate, she said, "Then what were you intending to be?"

"An engineer," he answered with a little laugh. "One term of heavy mathematics at Oxford killed that notion."

"But don't you enjoy acting?"

He wrapped both hands around his mug, absorbing the warmth it produced. "Actually, I love it. I suppose it's in my blood."

Her eyes became grave. "If I may ask you, sir . . ."

"Why am I not acting?"

"Yes."

Raising an eyebrow, he said, "Don't you know? I assumed my . . . affliction was common knowledge in the house."

166

"But you're still capable of walking about, and you can still speak . . ."

"Ah," he said, nodding. "So why can't I do those same things on the stage?"

No doubt she mistook the irony in his voice for mockery, for she lowered her eyes and said, "I must ask you to forgive my naiveté, sir. I've never been to the theatre."

"No, that's quite all right," he hastened to assure her. "That was a very sensible question. But you see, acting requires more than the ability to memorize lines and deliver them. One must put one's whole identity into a role if it is to be portrayed with any credibility. That requires a tremendous amount of energy and emotion."

He shrugged then, absently tracing the handle of his mug with a forefinger. "And that's the trouble, Miss O'Shea. I spend half my life with barely enough energy to groom myself. And as far as emotion goes, well . . ."

"I'm so sorry, sir," she said after a lengthy silence. "I wish I knew what to say."

"Just keeping me company now is more help than you can know," he said with a grateful little smile. "But you should go on and get some rest."

"I'm fine, Mr. Clay. Please tell me more."

"Are you sure you want to hear it?"

She nodded, and it was obvious from the compassion in her eyes that she was not just humoring him. "How long have you suffered with this?"

"Since I was a young man, barely twenty. You know, I was determined not to end up with the emotional sickness my father suffered, but determination is sometimes not enough. Not only has this affected my career, but I can never think about having a family for fear of passing down my father's fragile nature to my children."

"But you can't be sure of that happening."

"But I can't be sure of it *not* happening either. Besides, no child deserves to have a father who can barely function on some days." Giving a shrug, he said, "I've accepted that as a necessary fact of life, Miss O'Shea. And I have imposed upon your kindness long enough. Thank you for sitting up with me."

"I didn't mind, sir." She started to push out her chair but grimaced and stopped when the legs scraped loudly against the flagstone floor. Both sets of eyes darted immediately toward the doorway.

167

"I'd hate to be put to work in the scullery tomorrow for waking her a second time," Ambrose whispered after several seconds when the cook had not appeared.

Miss O'Shea smiled. "I don't think she would do that."

"Well, I'd like to stay on her good side, just the same. I know who butters my bread as well." When both chairs were pushed out as silently as possible, he said, "Won't you allow me to help you tidy up?"

"No, thank you. And please . . . take your candle. There are more in the cupboard."

"Thank you." He shifted his weight on his feet, wishing for an excuse to stay longer. "Well, good night, Miss O'Shea. Again, thank you for sitting up with me."

"May you have pleasant dreams, sir," she replied.

The compassion in her voice accompanied him all the way back along the corridor. Ambrose had no respect for people who broadcasted their troubles in the hopes of receiving pity—which was why he rarely spoke of his condition. But just for an hour or so, someone else had shared his burden. While sympathy could not alter the facts, it did make them more bearable.

*J*ulia wrote one month later in early July:

Dear Mr. Jensen,

Enclosed you will find a cheque in the amount of twenty-five pounds, the first payment for the loan you so graciously extended to me. I shudder to think how my family would be faring now, were it not for your generosity, and I want you to know that you are in my prayers daily.

I must confess that the first sight of the Larkspur caused me to doubt the feasibility of a boardinghouse, but I wish you could see it now! By the way, we have turned a linen room on the north side into a bedchamber, in the eventuality that you would ever wish to holiday or even take up permanent residence with us. The room is small but comfortably furnished, and from the window you can see dozens of quaint stone cottages and the lovely River Bryce in the background. You will find the rent extremely reasonable, for I would not dream of charging our dear benefactor one farthing.

She wrote on to inquire about his health, told him more about some of the improvements that had been made in the inn, how the children and Fiona were faring, and the names and positions of the new servants. Next came a brief description of each new lodger.

Mrs. Kingston, a widow, was our first. She can be too frank at times but has a tender heart, and I have come to enjoy her company. Our flower garden has benefitted from her residence here. She cannot bear to be idle and has a knack for coaxing blooms from the most hopeless looking of plants.

Perhaps you have heard of the actor Mr. Ambrose Clay. He has temporarily absented himself from the stresses of the stage, but when his constitution permits, he can be persuaded to deliver a soliloquy from Macbeth or a modern ballad at the piano. The children adore him, and Mrs. Kingston treats him as a son.

Miss Rawlins from Staffordshire was the next to arrive. She and Mr. Clay are the only lodgers who are not elderly. A former schoolmistress, Miss Rawlins now composes penny novelettes under the name of Robert St. Claire and so must sequester herself away when inspiration strikes, only coming downstairs for meals. Aleda has become her greatest admirer, even though she is not allowed to read Miss Rawlins' works. Please do not misunderstand—the books are not indecent, but I do believe eleven years old is too tender an age for romance stories.

Mrs. Dearing is also a widow. She has led a most interesting life, having accompanied her husband to the gold fields of California twenty years ago. They discovered very little gold but ended up founding a restaurant in Sacramento that became a profitable business. When her husband passed away two years ago, Mrs. Dearing decided to return to England. Her appearance is most interesting, by the way. Her white hair falls down her back in a long braid, Indian-style, and she has a beautiful collection of turquoise beads and bracelets.

Julia stopped writing to re-ink her pen, then scanned the two pages already written. How odd that for the years she'd had daily contact with Jensen, they might as well have been strangers. Now here she was pouring her heart out to him, as if he were a benevolent old uncle. And she knew instinctively that the butler would read every word and be happy to hear from her. She felt a pang for the wasted years they could have been friends but reminded herself that at least she'd not left London without seeing the softer side of the man.

Mr. Durwin's name may be familiar to you. He is the founder of Durwin Stoves, which he recently passed down to his sons. A widower, he appears far younger than his seventy years and credits herbal teas and a semi-vegetarian diet for his longevity. On most fair weather mornings he takes a basket up the Anwyl to search for herbs among the Roman ruins, and indeed, recently cured our cook's fever with some white mustard tea. Mrs. Herrick was very grateful.

Mrs. Hyatt, another widow, was the last lodger to arrive.

She is quiet and unobtrusive but bold enough to give an encouraging word to everyone she meets. Her late husband was in the shipping business in Liverpool, and after his death, Mrs. Hyatt could no longer bear to live by the sea. She and Mrs. Dearing are quite talented with needlepoint. They recently started a joint project that they alternate turns constructing—an ambitious three-foot-squared wall tapestry of Noah's ark!

And so you see, my friend, that we are thriving here in Gresham. And if you will forgive my redundancy, we owe it all to your kind benevolence and God's tender provision. May His mercy and grace accompany you all the days of your life.

With highest esteem,
Julia Hollis

————————

The hall, with its centrality to the rest of the house, was the usual gathering place for Julia's lodgers whenever they weren't occupied with other activities such as writing, in Miss Rawlins' case, and collecting herbs, as in Mr. Durwin's. And the after-supper hours seemed to be when everyone felt most sociable.

Julia was on her way down the family corridor one night in mid-July, after tucking in her children, when she caught the sound of Mr. Clay's animated voice. She always felt relieved, for his sake, whenever the actor's despondency loosened its grip.

If only he could know you, Jesus, she prayed silently. She was not so naive as to think that every problem troubling Mr. Clay would vanish the instant he became a believer. Surely miraculous things like that did happen. But as she'd grown closer and closer to God these past few months, she'd come to believe that most conversions resulted in a taking on of heavenly grace to help cope with life's burdens, not a complete erasure of them. Even so, the promise of a brighter eternity would surely be a comfort to someone whose present seemed so dark.

But the time she'd broached the subject, he'd cut her off politely. "I'm grateful for your concern, Mrs. Hollis," he'd said with a little smile, "but dear Mrs. Kingston has already presented me with a Bible in an attempt to save my soul. I would appreciate the courtesy of being left alone as far as my spiritual life is concerned."

She was compelled to respect Mr. Clay's request. He lived under her roof, true, but as long as he paid his rent, the man was due the privacy he'd come here seeking. Yet he could not stop her from praying that someone would reach him with the Gospel.

"Mrs. Hollis." Miss Rawlins beamed when Julia walked into the hall. With little time or concern for primping, the thirty-three-year-old writer wore her coffee-brown hair unstylishly trimmed just above the collar. The face behind her round spectacles was too angular to be called pretty, but nonetheless Aleda thought her quite exotic looking. "You're just in time to hear my idea."

Julia smiled and sat in one of the empty chairs. She glanced around the room, appreciating the homey scene. Georgette or Sarah had been in earlier to pass out mugs of hot chocolate, and every boarder save Mr. Durwin sipped from one. He and Mr. Clay were now positioned at opposite ends of the draughts table; Miss Rawlins lounged at the end of a sofa with her feet tucked up under her gown; Mrs. Dearing and Mrs. Hyatt sat on the facing sofa, with an oval needlework hoop across Mrs. Hyatt's lap. And in an overstuffed wing chair, Mrs. Kingston was reading from one of the gardening books she'd ordered from London.

"You've thought up another plot?" Julia asked the writer.

"Miss Rawlins is constantly spinning plots," said Mrs. Dearing. "I'm trying to persuade her to write a story about the gold rush in California. She would have scant research to do, what with my having been there."

"You can't do better than firsthand experience," Mrs. Kingston advised, not looking up from her gardening text.

"I know," Miss Rawlins sighed. "But I just don't find that a romantic setting. *Castles* are what young women want to read about, and mysterious old houses on the moors."

"Romance can be anywhere you look for it," Mr. Durwin said from the draughts table. He was a tall man with a full head of white hair and carried himself with a sureness that belied his seventy years. "I met Mrs. Durwin at Billingsgate when I was only sixteen, and it was love at first sight. Yet who would imagine a fish market to be a romantic place?"

Mr. Clay tilted his head thoughtfully. "There you have it, Miss Rawlins! Your next novel could be titled *Salmon d'Amour* or *The Codfish Brought Them Together*."

"Mock if you will, young man," Mr. Durwin snorted. "But since you haven't forty years of wedded bliss behind you, it would serve you well to learn from your elders' experiences."

"And I believe you're right," Mr. Clay offered in an humbler tone.

Deciding this would be a good place to change the subject, Julia turned to Miss Rawlins again. "And what is your idea, Miss Rawlins?"

The writer smiled. "Well, I'm intrigued with the story of that poor knife sharpener who died here, Jack Pitt."

"I believe it's Jake, dear," Mrs. Hyatt corrected gently, pulling a length of cobalt thread through the canvas. "Isn't it, Mrs. Hollis?"

Julia smiled through clenched teeth. "Yes."

"Thank you." Miss Rawlins nodded to the older woman, then stared into space with a dreamy expression. "Just suppose an eccentric old duke leaves his estate—let's see, the Vale of York would set an ethereal tone—to a penniless but proud niece, on the condition that she occupy the place herself for a year. And if she doesn't, the estate goes to his next heir, a ne'er-do-well distant cousin."

"Penelope St. John would be a good name for the niece," Mrs. Kingston suggested. "And you could name the cousin something ominous, like Angus Saxon. I wouldn't trust anyone named Angus."

"Let me guess," Mrs. Dearing said. "The ne'er-do-well cousin decides to frighten Penelope into leaving before the year is up. So he secretly moves into the house before she does."

"But what would that have to do with a real ghost?" asked Mrs. Kingston.

Miss Rawlins absently twisted a short strand of her hair around a finger. "Well, let's just assume there *is* a real ghost in the house. He could have even been a knife sharpener in his former life. And after he toys with the evil cousin for several chapters, the ghost murders him with an ax."

"You could have Angus cut eye holes in a portrait on the staircase so that he can stare at Penelope as she passes by," the unassuming Mrs. Hyatt offered in a hushed voice. "Only, have the ghost later pull the same stunt on Angus."

From the draughts match, Mr. Durwin asked, "But surely the young woman would be in danger as well. If he's the killing sort, why would the ghost spare her?"

"Because the ghost knows that she's good," Mrs. Hyatt suggested, then darted an anxious glance over to Miss Rawlins to see if she approved. Her face relaxed into a smile when the writer nodded.

"But where is the romance in that story?" asked Mr. Clay. "Surely you can't have a ghost fall in love with a flesh-and-blood woman."

The twisting of the lock of Miss Rawlins' hair intensified. "Well, suppose the evil cousin's twin brother comes searching for him? Before his brother—Angus—left, he made him promise not to tell anyone his plans, but now the twin's conscience won't allow him to sleep."

"John is a good Christian name for a hero," Mrs. Kingston advised. "Or Richard."

"Wait a minute!" Mr. Durwin said in an annoyed tone. "If this John or Richard is Angus' twin brother, how come *he* wasn't also left a share of the estate, providing the girl leaves before the year is up?"

"He . . . Angus, I mean, could have discredited his brother years ago," Miss Rawlins replied. "That would be the genius in having them twins, you see? Angus could have done something terribly wicked or illegal in the past and blamed it on John."

"You should make them identical twins, in that case, dear," Mrs. Hyatt suggested. "I'm sure you're aware that not all twins look alike."

Mrs. Kingston, not to be outdone, said, "It would add a nice touch to your story to give Penelope a beautiful singing voice. That is how the good twin discovers he loves her, you see? He could be a pharmacist—you know, someone who is devoted to music."

"I believe you mean a *philharmonic*," Mr. Clay corrected tactfully. "A pharmacist is someone who dispenses medicines. Of course I'm not implying that a pharmacist cannot also be devoted to music."

"Well, what are you going to do with the ghost?" asked Mrs. Dearing.

"The ghost," Miss Rawlins sighed. "I would need to resolve that part of the plot somehow, wouldn't I?"

A contemplative silence settled about everyone, until Mr. Clay snapped a finger. "Have an attractive, eligible *female* ghost move into the house—" He stopped himself when Mrs. Kingston turned to him and frowned.

"Would you please be *serious*, Mr. Clay?"

"My apologies," he said, but Julia noticed the amused look that he and Mr. Durwin exchanged.

"What do you think, Mrs. Hollis?" Miss Rawlins asked. "We haven't heard your opinion."

It was so tempting to answer with an evasive and appeasing, "I wouldn't know how to begin to plot a novel." After all, the people assembled in this room provided her livelihood, and they were all obviously caught up in this story. But she had a definite thought on the matter, so why shouldn't she tactfully express it? If she began stifling her opinion when it was *asked* for, she was in danger of turning into one of those landladies who hover about with perpetual ingratiating smiles. There was a difference between being tactful and sniveling, and surely her lodgers would prefer the former. And she could not live with herself as the latter.

"Having the evil cousin attempt to frighten away the niece is quite suspenseful," Julia answered in all honesty. "But I must confess that I'm not fond of ghost stories."

"But why?" asked Miss Rawlins. "Didn't you love a good scare when you were a young woman? Don't tell me you haven't read Poe."

Julia smiled. Of course she'd read Poe. Every English female who went to finishing school had participated in at least one clandestine post-bedtime reading of the American writer's short stories. One of the girls who shared her room had become so discomposed while listening to *The Cask of Amontillado* that she'd cried out, upset the candle, and burned a hole in the bed curtains.

"It just can't be healthy to be obsessed with the macabre," she finally replied.

"Would a certain Jake Pitt have anything to do with that?" Mr. Clay asked.

"He would," Julia admitted. "I've grown weary of hearing about the man, to be truthful. I'll be happy when the villagers forget all about him." She got to her feet then and smiled again at the faces turned in her direction. "And if you'll excuse me, I'm rather tired, so I must bid you all good night."

They all protested, offering to change to a different subject, but she thanked them anyway and took up a candle from the chimney-piece. The lodgers took daily naps and could bear sitting up until eleven or so, but she found herself stifling yawns by nine every evening. Nonetheless, for a couple of weeks after they'd all arrived, she'd made herself sit up with them, for what kind of hostess went to bed when her guests were still awake?

Fiona had finally taken her aside and suggested with her typical gentle frankness that if she truly wanted the lodgers to feel that the *Larkspur* was their home, she should stop hovering over them. It was such a relief to hear those words. That very night Julia forced herself to go to her room at ten. When no one reproached her about it the next day or even mentioned that she'd gone to bed early, she had walked to *Trumbles* and ordered Fiona a new hat. And turned in by nine o'clock that night.

Come, let us join our cheerful songs
With angels round the throne,

Fiona sang, the rug beater in her hand, as she swatted the Brussells carpet in time with the lively rhyme of the hymn. The large carpet overlapped a frame Mr. Herrick had erected between the stable and gardening shed.

Ten thousand are their tongues,
But all their joys are one!

She took a deep breath and was just about to plunge into the second stanza when a male voice said from behind her, "That was a fine song. Will you sing it again?"

Swallowing the breath she'd just inhaled, Fiona spun on her heel and gaped at a smiling Mr. Clay. "Mr. Clay! How long—"

"Only for a second or two. I give you my word. Why, I had no idea you could sing so well, Miss O'Shea."

Fiona had to smile, even though embarrassed at being caught. "Thank you, sir. It's the Irish in me."

"Are you saying that all Irishmen can carry a tune?"

"If one can't, he doesn't admit to it."

The actor chuckled, hooking both hands under his arms. "Then that means you'll be happy to deliver an encore?"

"I'm afraid it doesn't mean that, sir."

"Oh well, I'll just have to sneak up on you again the next time you're beating a rug," he drawled. "The maids must love you, Miss O'Shea. I didn't think that was a housekeeper's chore."

She pulled the cotton scarf she was wearing to keep dust out of her hair down a little lower on her forehead—it tended to slip as she worked. "Sometimes I get caught up on my duties and help them with theirs. And it's not as hard as it looks."

"Truly? It looks terribly difficult to me."

Fiona's lips tightened at what seemed to be mild condescension in his voice. While she was aware that being in service was not one of the more scholarly occupations, it did not deserve scorn from those in the more genteel classes. Quietly, she said, "Now you're making fun of me, sir."

Mr. Clay's face fell, a hand going up to his chest. "I do apologize, Miss O'Shea. My word, do I sound *that* condescending?"

Now Fiona felt embarrassed at overreacting, when Mr. Clay had been nothing but kind to her. "No, sir. I'm sure you meant no harm."

"I meant exactly what I said, Miss O'Shea. Being brought up on the stage, I've never done manual labor of any kind. I came out here and saw the size of this carpet versus the size of that instrument in your hand, and my first thought was that it looked difficult."

"I must beg your forgiveness, Mr. Clay," Fiona told him, her cheeks warm.

"No, it is I who must beg forgiveness for coming out here and talking like an idiot. And I'm ready to pay my penance."

"Sir?"

He stepped over to take the carpet beater from her hand. "I'm going to beat every speak of dust out of this carpet, Miss O'Shea."

"Mr. Clay, that's not—"

"Oh, but it is. And what else have I to do?" His gray eyes narrowed. "But I draw the line at wearing that scarf, because frankly, Miss O'Shea, it even looks a little silly on you. And now, will you please stand back?"

She could do nothing but obey, grateful that the stables blocked the two of them from the Worthy sisters' line of vision. The actor tackled the carpet with a relish, facing her and grinning like a butcher's dog while pounding it with backhand strokes that produced loud *whomps*.

Presently he began to sing, with no self-consciousness to his manner:

In coming down to Manchester, to gain my liberty . . .
I saw one of the prettiest girls that ever my eyes did see;
I saw one of the prettiest girls that ever my eyes did see,
At the Angel Inn in Manchester there lives the girl for me!

When one side finally ceased to produce clouds of dust, he went to the other side and continued. Sweat beaded on his forehead, but he continued to work until Fiona insisted that the chore was finished.

"Did I do a good job?" He looked so much like an anxious little boy that she had to smile again.

"An excellent job."

"May I help you carry it inside?"

"No, thank you. Mr. Herrick will do it when Sarah's finished polishing the dining room floor."

"Polishing the floor? Seems like a waste if you're just going to cover most of it with a carpet, doesn't it?"

"Clean has to go all the way through, Mr. Clay."

"I see," he said, handing the beater over. "Well, I shouldn't take any more of your time."

"Thank you again, sir." Impulsively she added, "It's good to see that you're having a good day."

Her comment seemed to startle him, for he cocked an eyebrow at her. "A good day? Actually, it has been a wretched one. I only came outside so my room could be cleaned and heard you here at work. I guess for a little while I seemed to forget it was a bad day. Thank you for that, Miss O'Shea."

"Why . . . you're welcome, sir."

Giving her another smile, he turned and ambled back across the courtyard with hands pocketed. After a few steps he began whistling the tune of the hymn she'd been singing.

Fiona realized she was staring when the actor turned to wink at her before disappearing through the courtyard door. She found herself thinking that for all Mr. Clay's dark moods, he surely had a knack for producing smiles from others.

You shouldn't enjoy his company so much, an inner voice warned.

178

*T*he willow peeling season ran from the end of April to June, but the riverbank chores of the Irish children continued on through July, for now the rushes were ready to be harvested. Philip twisted around to watch the Bryce behind him. A hundred feet west of where he sat on the bridge, Tom and Jack Keegan waded barefoot through the shallow water with short, curved sickles. Each boy gathered together with one arm as many long green blades as possible, then after a low, swinging motion of the sickle, tossed the bunch to a younger sibling on the bank. They chatted, bantered, and sometimes even sang as they worked.

When his neck began to ache, Philip lowered his legs back over the side of the bridge and turned his attention to his fishing cork. "They don't seem to mind working so hard, do they," he said to Ben, who lived up Worton Lane from the Keegan family.

"I expect they're glad to get out of their cottage. They help their mother and papa weave baskets when there's nothing to harvest."

"I wouldn't mind weavin' baskets if I could stay home from school all the time," Jeremiah muttered from Philip's other side. Jeremiah often let it be known that the pursuit of education was low on his list of priorities.

"It's a shame the boys never join our cricket matches." Philip raised his stringer to make sure the trout and two pike were still attached. "Those oldest two look hardy. Maybe we should ask them."

Ben shrugged his shoulders, the sunlight tinting his hair the color of fire. "You can ask if you like, but it won't do you any good. They don't seem to want to call attention to themselves—they know folks aren't quite used to them yet."

"You mean because they're Irish or Catholic?"

"Both. But one or the other would be enough to most folks."

"How long have they lived here?"

Chewing on his lower lip for a second, Ben finally answered, "About four years."

"And people aren't used to them yet?" Philip snapped his line out of the water and frowned at the undersized grayling flipping about on the other end. "How long is it going to take?"

"It takes a long time, I expect. Look at your German gardener. My father said there were years when no one would speak to him."

"Well, people speak to Fiona, and she's Irish."

"That's different—she's not a whole group." A wistful smile crossed Ben's face, for he was overcome with a schoolboy's infatuation for the housekeeper. "And she's a mite prettier than Mr. Herrick."

Philip tossed the freed grayling back into the water. "They must be terribly lonesome."

"With a family that big?" Jeremiah shrugged. "It's likely they wish they could be lonesome once in a while. I'd gladly send over my little brothers."

Philip caught Ben's eye and smiled. A squeal sounded, and all three heads jerked around at once. From the distance, it appeared that someone had startled a grass snake, for one of the younger Keegan boys held up something green and writhing for the others to inspect.

"I don't think they're lonesome at all," Ben said after the three returned to their fishing. "At least they get to do some traveling. I've never been out of Gresham."

"Where do they go?"

"Whenever weather allows it," Ben answered, "the family hitches up their wagon on Saturday mornings and goes to Shrewsbury to peddle their baskets. They stay overnight with kin, then all go to church together the next morning."

"How do you know all this?"

"I chat with them sometimes," Ben replied with another shrug. "Even been inside their cottage once. My mother had me bring a chair over there to get the seat rewoven."

An hour later, when the fish appeared to be occupied with things other than baited hooks, the boys pulled in their lines. While each had been successful, none had enough to feed a whole household. When this happened, usually the three took turns hauling the catch home, but Philip glanced back over his shoulder at the Irish children and came up with another idea.

"Why don't we give them our catch," Philip suggested after they'd washed the grit from their hands in the shallow water by the riverbank.

"But why?" asked Jeremiah, holding his string of fish a little closer. "They practically live on the river. They can catch their own."

"Just to be friendly."

"We say hello every time we see them up here. Ain't that friendly enough?"

"But we can always catch more tomorrow," Philip persisted. With a look at his friends' doubtful faces, he said, "I just remember how frightened we were to move here from London and how good it felt when people made us feel welcome. I feel sorry for them."

"Well, you know, people don't exactly throw rocks at them," Ben said, "except perhaps the Sanders, sometime. They aren't *that* abused."

Philip searched his mind for a rebuttal and finally came up with, "Not abusing isn't the same as accepting."

Ben looked ready to argue again but then glanced down at his string of fish and blew out his cheeks. "Oh, well, why not? Guess there's plenty more where these came from."

They both looked at Jeremiah, who screwed up his face into a frown. "We get to keep any fish we catch tomorrow, right?"

"Right!" Philip agreed.

He gave a reluctant nod, and with each holding his own string of fish, basket, and pole, the three crossed the bridge and turned right on Worton Lane. They heard the grind of a handsaw as they passed Ben's father's wheelwright's workshop attached to their house. Farther on near the end of the lane they heard a man's lofty tenor voice singing a melancholy ballad.

Oh, Paddy dear! and did ye hear the news that's goin' round?
The shamrock is forbid by law to grow on Irish ground!
No more St. Patrick's day we'll keep; his color can't be seen,
For there's a cruel law ag'in' the Wearin' o' the Green!

They stopped at a stone cottage with a thatched roof, where Mr. Keegan, flaxen-headed and as wiry as the reed in his hand, sat on a rough bench under a birch tree weaving a bushel basket. Close by was a wide wooden trough for soaking reeds, and on the ground a barefoot tot squatted next to a little handmade cart.

I met with Napper Tandy, and he took me by the hand,

181

*And he said, "How's poor ould Ireland, and how does she
stand?"*
*"She's the most distressful country that ever yet was seen,
For they're hanging men and women for the Wearin' o'
the . . ."*

The Irishman stopped singing and raised his head curiously as they
approached.

"How are you, Mr. Keegan?" Ben greeted the Irishman.

A smile split the man's face. "On top o' the mornin', Mr. Mayhew.
And yer folks?"

"They're well, thank you. We—" He paused to motion on either
side of him, "These are my friends, Jeremiah and Philip. We thought
you might like some fish."

Mr. Keegan glanced down at the strings of fish. "Well how much
would ye be askin' fer them?"

Jeremiah, who'd been the most reluctant to turn over his catch,
now held out his string in a grand gesture. "They don't cost nothin'."

"Nothing?" asked the man, cocking his head.

"They're a gift."

"Are you sure, lads?"

"Yes, sir."

A smile widened the Irishman's face again. "Why, thank ye kindly!
And may the good Lord bless ye!" Turning his head to the cottage's
open door, he called out, "Leila darlin'! Come and see!"

A fair-haired woman appeared in the doorway to the cottage, wiping her hands upon her apron. Giving the boys a timid smile, she answered, "Yes?"

"Would ye bring out a pail, darlin'? These kind lads are offerin'
us some fish!"

She disappeared from the doorway and returned seconds later
with an empty tin pail. "Thank you kindly, sirs," she said, giving a
little nod while her husband collected some water from the soaking
tub. As the fish were dropped into the pail, she clasped both hands
together. "Why, they'll make a fine supper!"

"Aye, they will indeed," agreed Mr. Keegan. He brushed the grass
from his brown corded trousers and motioned for the boys to follow.
Not knowing what to expect, Philip and his friends followed past a
stable that housed the Keegans' wagon and a pair of mules to a shed
of about sixteen square feet. It was apparently a more recent addition
to the property, for it was the only building not constructed of stone.

The Irishman pulled open the door and took a step inside. When he backed out again, he held three small oval baskets with lids.

"You don't have to give us anything," Ben protested.

"Aye, but it would give me great pleasure to do so." His smile was coaxing, and reluctantly Philip took the basket that was pressed upon him. It was intricately woven of fine reeds and narrow pink ribbon. The lid was hinged and had a small reed latch, like a hamper.

"This is very nice," Jeremiah told him, opening and closing the lid.

"Ye can give it to yer mothers for to keep pretties in," Mr. Keegan explained.

At that, Philip brightened. "It's Fiona's birthday next Wednesday. I'm sure she would like it." It wasn't that he cared less for his own mother, but the need to find something for the housekeeper's birthday had occupied the back of his mind for a couple of days now.

"Yer speakin' of Miss O'Shea from Kilkenny, are ye? She comes by occasionally for a cup o' tea with my Leila. Fine lady, she is." He stepped back into the shed and brought out another basket. "Ye give this one to Miss O'Shea, and that one to yer mother."

After exchanging another round of thanks with both Mr. and Mrs. Keegan, the three boys carried their tackle hampers, poles, and new baskets back up Worton Lane. They walked silently, because to speak would break the spell that the couple's humble gratitude had cast. Ben waved farewell as he dropped out at his house, and Jeremiah did the same at Church Lane. By the time Philip reached the *Larkspur*, he was feeling so at peace with the world that he tarried to chat with the Worthy sisters instead of returning their greetings in his usual perfunctory manner.

But when Jewel launched into a description of the chilblains on an unfortunate cousin's feet, so thick they had to be shaved with a razor, he suddenly remembered an errand he had to attend. There was only so much goodwill that a boy had available to spread around, after all.

"Are you busy, Mother?"

Julia smiled from her writing table at the boy standing in her doorway. "Not anymore." Actually, she had just started drafting cheques to clear the *Larkspur*'s July accounts. "Come in, dear."

She caught the odor of fish as he walked in, and she didn't mind that. But there seemed to be an aloofness to Philip lately that she didn't understand and it hurt her. He did not seek out her company nearly as much as he did when they first moved to Gresham. And when he did, it was usually because he needed something.

Oh, she was happy that he'd embraced country life so completely, and that he had so many new friends. But did a boy ever outgrow his need for a mother? Sometimes she wondered.

"You *are* busy, aren't you?"

"No, not at all," she replied, aware of an eagerness in her voice that was almost pathetic. She got up from the desk and put a hand on his shoulder, half expecting him to stiffen with distaste, although Philip had never done such a thing before. "Why don't you sit for a while so we can visit?"

"Oh . . . may we do that later?" Philip lifted a hand to show her what he was holding—a charming little basket with a lid. "I want to see if Mr. Trumble has some ribbons to put in here for Fiona's birthday. She'd like ribbons, wouldn't she?"

Though flattered that he still respected her opinion, Julia couldn't help feeling a little disappointed again—he had sought her out again only because he wanted something. *But you're being foolish,* she had to tell herself. *Can't children have moods too?*

"Why, it's lovely," she said, taking it from his hand. "Where did you buy it?"

"I didn't." With a pleased smile he told her about bringing fish to the basket weaver's family on Worton Lane. Though Julia had never met them herself, Fiona had told her weeks ago that she'd commissioned Mr. Keegan to make floor mats for the larder and scullery. "He gave me two baskets so I could give one to Fiona."

She felt a pang but really didn't know why. "Fiona will like it very much. And she'll be even more pleased that you thought of her."

"But what about the ribbons?"

"Well, I'm afraid she doesn't wear them. But she likes combs."

"Are they expensive? I only have twelvepence."

"Not very expensive. And you can buy a nice one for about the same as three or four ribbons."

He looked relieved at this. "Well, I should go do that now while I'm thinking about it. Thank you, Mother."

"You're welcome." Before the boy reached the door, Julia remembered the basket in her hand. "Philip?"

He turned again. "Yes, Mother?"

"You're forgetting this."

"Oh, that one's yours."

"For me?"

"Mr. Keegan gave me two, remember?"

Her eyes began to smart. "Why, thank you."

"You're welcome." He seemed ready to leave again but then narrowed his eyes to study her. "Are you all right, Mother?"

"I'm fine, dear." Julia smiled. "Give my regards to Mr. Trumble."

When he was gone, she sat back in her chair. *You're a silly woman,* she thought, tracing the ribbon woven through the lid with a finger. *He's your son and he'll always love you.*

But she still could not let go of the feeling that something was wrong. If only he had a father in which to confide! Even Philip, as preoccupied as he had been with his own career and amusements, would have at least been able to understand the emotions of a thirteen-year-old boy.

And then the thought struck her that perhaps that was the very thing troubling the boy. Because the children had no idea their father had gambled away their livelihoods, Julia had assumed that their mourning was a simple sorrow over the loss of a loved one. It was not mixed with misgivings and even downright bitterness, as was hers.

Or so she had assumed. She stared across at the closed door and after a while prayed, *Father, please help him to understand that we aren't meant to carry burdens alone—just as you taught me.*

ℱour days later, Fiona sat at the dining room table and held up a polished soup spoon for a final inspection. *I'm rich,* she thought. Perhaps not in material things, but how many housekeepers were made to feel so beloved by the families they tended? Last night's cake, her first birthday cake ever, had been painstakingly trimmed with dozens of iced violets. And yesterday morning Mrs. Hollis insisted that she take the day off and had presented her with a ready-made dress of cornflower-blue silk. Even the children had given her gifts; Philip, a lovely basket and comb, Aleda, an alphabet sampler she'd stitched under Mrs. Hyatt's tutelage, and little Grace, some sachets tied with lace. The female lodgers and servants had surprised her with little tokens as well. Fiona had wondered if Queen Victoria herself had ever felt so honored.

How could she have guessed, ten years ago, that life would be so peaceful and the people in her life so kind? There was a lesson to be learned from that. *Valleys don't last forever.* Neither did the mountaintops of life, but if a person just had faith and held on, each valley would eventually end. "You're rich indeed, Fiona O'Shea," she murmured.

She held up another spoon and was startled as a strangely distorted reflection of a person appeared on the back of the bowl. Mr. Clay's voice came from the doorway just as Fiona was turning in her chair.

"Miss O'Shea?"

"Mr. Clay." Embarrassed this time at being discovered talking to herself, she asked, "How long have you been standing there?"

"I just now walked up," he said, holding up the palm of his hand in a pacifying manner. "Please forgive me for startling you."

It was impossible to do otherwise, and Fiona's face relaxed into a smile. "Of course, sir," she said while pushing out her chair.

"Please don't get up, Miss O'Shea. May I join you for a little while?"

"Join me?"

He walked over to the side of the table, and she could see now that he held a hand behind his back. "I wasn't aware of your birthday until the cake was served last night. I felt badly that I had nothing to give you."

"But, Mr. Clay, you know I can't accept any gift from you."

"Just wait until you see it." He put a hand on the back of the chair he was standing behind. "May I sit?"

"Of course." She waited until he had done so to protest again. "Mr. Clay, it was kind of you to think of me, but—"

"And yet you accepted gifts from the women lodgers."

"Begging your pardon, sir, but you know there's a difference. You can't be buying gifts for me."

"But I didn't *buy* anything, Miss O'Shea. And are all Irish as stubborn as you?"

"I believe so, sir. Now please . . . don't offer me anything."

He rolled his eyes and was silent for several minutes while she continued to polish the silver. Then he picked up the tin of hartshorn powder and sniffed. He wrinkled his nose at the sharp odor. "Ammonia?"

"Alcohol too." Fiona showed him the fork she'd just finished. "You get used to the smell. And it does the job."

"So it does." Now a corner of his mouth quirked. "Aren't you even curious, Miss O'Shea?"

"About the gift?"

"You could have just turned down a diamond tiara, you know."

She couldn't help but return his smile. "If I admit to some curiosity about what's behind your back, Mr. Clay, will you give me your word not to offer it again?"

"Oh, if you insist," he grumbled. "But I certainly wouldn't begrudge you the pleasure of giving *me* a birthday gift." From behind his back he brought a leather-bound book and held it up to show her. "*Our Mutual Friend*," he said, "signed by Charles Dickens himself."

Fiona put down her cloth and reached out to touch the fine tooled leather. "You've met Mr. Dickens?"

"I have indeed. It's quite an interesting story. Have you read it?"

"No, sir, I haven't."

A mischievous light came into his gray eyes. "Care to change your mind, Miss O'Shea?"

"I can't, Mr. Clay." Again she smiled at him. "But it's beautiful. And so kind of you to offer it."

"Then I suppose I should get out of your way."

Fiona wondered if she were imagining things. There seemed to be a question in that statement, a hope that she would contradict him and insist that he wasn't in her way at all.

But she could only thank him again and pick up another fork. As his footsteps faded behind her, she discovered that the contentment she had experienced just minutes ago had vanished. In its place was the old familiar longing for something as unattainable to her as the moon.

————

"I do believe I have you again, Mr. Clay," Mrs. Dearing said one afternoon in late July, snatching another of Ambrose's red wooden pieces from the draughts board. She spoke a little louder than usual, for a heavy rainstorm lashed against the windows of the *Larkspur*, and claps of thunder rattled the glass. "Your other two are cornered. Will you concede defeat?"

"Have I any choice?" Ambrose asked but smiled at the elderly woman. His mood had lightened enough this afternoon to allow him to spend some time in the hall in the company of the other lodgers. "You're rather merciless, aren't you?"

"Quite so," she smiled. "Which is why Mr. Durwin refuses to play against me anymore." She nodded toward the gentleman, who was at that moment seated next to Mrs. Hyatt on one of the sofas, allowing her to wrap knitting yarn around his upheld hands. "Isn't that right, Mr. Durwin?"

Mr. Durwin's reply was delayed by a rumble of thunder. When it had passed, he said, "What Mrs. Dearing isn't telling you, Mr. Clay, is that she and the late Mr. Dearing were professional draught players in California."

"Is that so?" Ambrose asked the woman across from him, who wore not a trace of guile in her matronly face.

"Not quite, dear." She expertly snapped the black and red draughts into their squares as she spoke. "But the winters in Coloma could be harsh. When the weather prevented panning for gold, prospectors would spend hours around the fire at our place of business.

There wasn't much else to do, and so to give them something to help keep boredom at bay, we organized draughts tournaments. By the way, it's called checkers over there."

"Well, in that case, I believe you should allow Mr. Clay some advantage," said Mrs. Kingston from her chair near the pianoforte. She had been reading so intently from the gardening book she'd gotten from the subscription library that it was a wonder she had heard the conversation around her. "It isn't quite fair, do you think?"

Ambrose turned to nod at her. "I wholeheartedly agree, Mrs. Kingston. What do you think—shall we blindfold Mrs. Dearing?" There were smiles at this, even an indulgent one from Mrs. Kingston.

"That sounds reasonable to me," Mrs. Dearing said after a thoughtful second or two. "I would rather play with a handicap than frighten off all contenders. Shall I remove two pieces?"

All eyes swiveled to Mrs. Kingston, who waited for another clap of thunder to subside before answering with a simple word. "Three."

Miss Rawlins walked into the room from the corridor as Ambrose and Mrs. Dearing were beginning their game. "I can't possibly work with all of that noise," she sighed, dropping into a chair.

"Poor dear," Mrs. Hyatt said sympathetically.

"Oh, well. Suffering sharpens creativity, or so I'm told." The writer looked over at Mrs. Kingston. "Who was that young man with you in the garden, Mrs. Kingston?"

"I beg your pardon?" was the elderly woman's reply, her eyelids blinking as if she hadn't understood the question.

"You know, this morning, before the rain. I saw you both from my window. He didn't look like anyone I've seen around Gresham."

"Oh, *that* young man."

Ambrose caught the evasive tone of her voice and noticed that the others had as well, for all activity had ceased in anticipation of a forthcoming answer. *If she'd have just acted normal, we wouldn't have paid the subject any mind,* he thought, then reminded himself that she'd not had the benefit of almost twenty years on the stage. Deciding to come to Mrs. Kingston's rescue, as she had come to his only minutes ago, he said lightly, "I'll wager it was some learned botanist who heard about Mrs. Kingston's gardening skills and came to learn at her feet."

But the rescue was ironically ineffective. She made a startled blink of the eyes and then paled a little when Mr. Durwin said, "Actually, there is a young man staying at the *Bow and Fiddle* for a week or so—

189

a Scotsman. He's studying the flora and fauna of Shropshire, according to Mr. Pool, but I daresay he's not out gathering in this deluge. Was he your visitor, Mrs. Kingston?"

"Yes," she answered a little *too* casually for Mr. Clay's ears, but it seemed that no one else had noticed. "When I learned about the young man's residence among us, I simply asked him to lend me some of his expertise regarding the spots on the begonia leaves. If one cannot trust a botanist for gardening advice, then what is this world coming to?"

No one seemed to care to rebut that, and the lodgers resumed their draughts game and yarn winding. Miss O'Shea came into the hall bearing two periodicals the post had delivered earlier, *The New Monthly Magazine* and *Bentley's Miscellany*. She returned Ambrose's smile in a polite if not somewhat distant manner, as if she had never made him hot chocolate at midnight, watched him beat a carpet, nor discussed books and silver polish in the dining room. And he knew instinctively that she no longer spent late nights in the library.

———

Insomnia swooped down upon Ambrose that night with a vengeance. It was past midnight when he finally gave up and slipped out from under his quilt. For a while he sat in his chair and stared out at the black night beyond the windowpane, then he grew weary of that and lit a candle. He was without something to read, he realized, and put on his dressing gown and slippers to go downstairs.

The library was dark and empty, as he knew it would be, and he felt a strange pang in his heart because of it. He returned to his room later with a well-worn copy of Benjamin Disraeli's *Coningsby*, a story he'd read twice before. Perhaps words that his eyes could travel by rote would put him to sleep faster than something that required him to think. He was into the fourth chapter when the sentences began melting into one another.

A series of light knocks woke him the next day. Ambrose glanced at the clock upon the chimneypiece. *One-thirty!*

"Yes?" he called out, rubbing sleep from his eyes.

"It's Miss O'Shea, sir."

"Oh." He threw his legs over the side and whipped his dressing gown from the back of a chair. When he was finally presentable, he said in a somewhat calmer voice, "Come in, please."

She bore a tray of tea and sandwiches and looked at him anxiously. "Are you all right, Mr. Clay?"

"Please . . . come in. I overslept, that's all." He moved aside some things from his bedside table to make room for the tray. "I can take this in the sitting room if the maids need to clean."

"No need to do that, sir." She came into the room, leaving the door open. When she'd set the tray down upon a little crisscross table, she turned to him. "If you don't mind, I'll just straighten your bed myself right now while you begin your lunch. And since the dusting was done yesterday, that should do it."

"Yes, of course. May I lend you a hand?"

"No, thank you, sir." She was already picking up pillows and tossing them to the foot of the bed.

He poured himself some tea and sat down in his chair. "Is Mrs. Hollis angry? We had an agreement about my coming down for meals . . ."

"She's not angry—just a mite worried."

"I'm rather ashamed."

"Ashamed, sir?" Miss O'Shea asked, not pausing from her work.

Running a hand through his hair, he said, "Being so blasted weak! Having to be mollycoddled by everyone—like an infant."

She turned to face him again. "Mr. Clay," she said in her calm brogue. "You shouldn't speak of yourself that way."

"Why not?" He laughed bitterly. "It's the truth."

"Well, truth can sometimes be distorted."

"I beg your pardon?"

She looked ready to say something but shook her head. "It's not my place to lecture you."

"Please, Miss O'Shea. I'm drowning. If you've a lifeline, then throw it for mercy's sake."

"It's just that I've given your condition some thought lately," she said after a moment's hesitation.

"Please." He motioned to the other chair. "Have you time to sit?"

"Give me just a minute, sir." After finishing the bed, Miss O'Shea slipped into the facing chair as he'd requested. "May I be blunt, sir?"

"I wish you would."

"It seems to me that you blame yourself when your mood turns despondent, Mr. Clay. Yet how is it that sometimes you are the hap-

191

piest person in the house? What do you do to bring about such a change?"

"Why, nothing," Ambrose answered. "I just wake up feeling full of life some mornings."

Knitting her brow thoughtfully, she continued, "If you don't do anything to cause the good days, then why do you hold yourself responsible for the bad ones?"

"Well, I . . ." He suddenly found himself at a loss for an answer. "I've just always assumed it was some weakness in my character. A man should be able to take care of himself."

"Aye, he should, sir," the housekeeper agreed. "But would you fault a man for not being able to care for himself due to consumption or a crippled leg?"

"Of course not."

"Then, perhaps if you treated yourself more charitably, Mr. Clay, the bad days could be a bit more bearable."

While his initial reaction was to bristle at such simplistic advice, her words brought to mind something he had never considered. Was the self-loathing he felt on his dark days actually adding to their intensity? *It can't be that simple*, he thought, yet what had the plaque above the dining hall door at Saint John's College said? *As a man thinketh in his heart, so is he.*

"Well, I'll leave you to your lunch," she said, starting to rise from the chair.

She looked as if she had more to say, though, and Ambrose wondered if she'd mistaken his silent contemplation for a desire to end the discussion. "Do stay a little longer, please?" he asked her. "What you're saying is quite provoking. And I'm grateful that you would give my condition some thought, when I'm sure you've worries of your own."

"It's nothing, sir," she said and resumed her seat.

"It means something to me—more than you can know. And you've other thoughts on the matter as well, haven't you?"

"I have," she replied right away.

Ambrose found her forthright manner refreshing. The beautiful women he'd known in the past seemed to inevitably be one of two extremes—either tediously coy or fashionably jaded.

"Please, go on."

She nodded. "I don't pretend to ever have suffered from the severe despondency that grips you, sir. But sadness has been no stranger

192

to me. And there are two sources of comfort that have carried me through the sad days."

He was earnestly sorry to hear that she had days that were less than happy, but he couldn't help the wry smile that came to his lips. "You aren't going to attempt to save my soul, are you, Miss O'Shea?"

"I expect that I am, sir," she replied, obviously nonplused. "If knowing the Lord has helped me, then why would I hesitate to tell you so?"

"And you think if I turn to religion, my despondency will vanish"—he snapped a finger—"like that?"

"It's God I'm referring to, Mr. Clay . . . not religion. And I would no more tell you that than tell a blind man his sight will be restored. God's ways are not our ways, Mr. Clay. Sometimes He heals, but sometimes He doesn't."

He admired and even envied her uncomplicated faith, but such talk caused him discomfort and he did not wish to hear any more about it. At least not now. "Miss O'Shea, will you be offended if I ask you to defer any talk about reli—" He nodded agreeably before she could correct him. "About *God* until a later date?"

"As you wish, Mr. Clay." She did not seem offended but made a move to get to her feet again.

Ambrose held out a hand. "Wait . . . please. You said there were *two* things that could help me."

"That I did, sir," she said softly, then took in a deep breath. "It cannot be good for you to spend so much time closeted in your room on your bad days. If you could find something useful to do, sir, it would take your mind away from your troubles for a while. And a good long walk every day would restore your appetite and perhaps even help you to sleep better."

"Useful?" Ambrose thought for a minute and then shrugged. "I'm afraid I'm good for nothing but acting. And I don't do much of that anymore." In spite of the ache inside he was unable to resist teasing. "Do you think Mrs. Hyatt would teach me to do needlework?"

"It would be better than brooding, sir," she replied.

The frankness of her answer surprised him, and he raised an eyebrow. "Miss O'Shea, I asked you once if all Irish were as stubborn as you. Now I wonder if all housekeepers are as outspoken as you are."

A self-conscious smile touched her lips. "That I wouldn't know, Mr. Clay."

"Oh?"

"I've only been employed at two houses in my whole life. Both had butlers instead of housekeepers."

She got to her feet, and Ambrose knew that he could not keep asking her to stay, no matter how refreshing her company. Besides, he was suddenly embarrassed that he'd allowed her to see him this way, with his hair in need of a comb and his chin in want of a shave. But when she got to the door, he couldn't resist saying, "You know, I believe some fresh air and exercise would serve me well."

She turned in the doorway and gave him another little smile. "Absolutely, Mr. Clay."

"And as soon as I've dressed and finished lunch, I plan to give your advice a try."

"Very good, sir."

A pleasant picture drifted across his mind—himself, walking beside Miss O'Shea, conversing easily over little things as did normal, happy people. He did so enjoy her company and making her smile. But dare he ask her to accompany him when she'd made it obvious that she did not care to spend time with him on a social basis?

It can't hurt to ask. "I just hate the thought of going out alone . . ." he finally told her.

Silence stretched between them for several seconds, and then she nodded. "I'll see what I can do about that, sir."

Forty minutes later, he was groomed and fed and just about to go downstairs when another knock sounded. *Why, I'm starting to feel a little better already,* he told himself on the way to the door. He swung it open to find Mrs. Kingston standing in the corridor, stout walking stick in hand.

"Miss O'Shea said you were in need of a walking partner, Mr. Clay. Are you quite ready?"

"Ready?" he said somewhat confused.

"You're not the sort to dillydally about, are you?" the elderly woman asked with a raised eyebrow. "I cannot abide someone who won't keep up."

Ambrose gave a shrug and joined Mrs. Kingston out in the corridor. Offering the crook of his arm, he told her, "Then I'll just have to keep up, won't I?"

*O*n the evening of Monday, September thirteenth, Andrew Phelps peered out the window of the hired coach.

Now fades the glimmering landscape on the sight,
And all the air a solemn stillness holds.

Poet Thomas Gray's words seemed to have been penned for the passing north Shropshire farmland. Though Andrew had lived in cities all of his life, some inexplicable voice out there seemed to be calling to him, telling him that he had come home at last.

"Father?" The voice of Laurel, coming from the seat facing him, brought him out of his reverie. "Are we almost there?"

"Yes, I'm quite certain." Andrew sat back against the seat and gave her a wink. "Excited about our new home, Pet?"

Smiling, she replied that she was anxious to see what Gresham looked like before dark. "Are you sure there will be other children?" she asked, not for the first time during the past month.

"No, Laurel," Elizabeth sighed from beside her. "There are no people living there at all. Father is going to preach to an empty church every Sunday."

"He is *not*."

"Then why must you ask every thirty minutes?"

The strain of the long train ride to Shrewsbury, as well as a half hour of being jolted about in a coach, suddenly caught up with Andrew, and he opened his mouth to snap at his older daughter. The resignation in her expression stopped him. She was simply sitting there, hands folded in her lap, her brown eyes staring dully ahead. *Like a convict on the way to the gallows,* he thought.

He couldn't fault her for that. She was trading the home she'd known for ten years for a place none of them had ever seen. And even though Jonathan Raleigh had returned to Kensington after being awarded his degree, Andrew knew that he still occupied a good deal of her thoughts. "Once we settle in and you make new friends, you'll be happy," he had assured her, hoping that by saying it often enough he could make it come true.

He was about to send a new homily in her direction, but Laurel caught his eye. *This is not a good time,* her expression said, with a slight shake of the head for emphasis. Andrew nodded back. When dealing with her older sister's recent heartache, Laurel had shown herself to possess a maturity beyond her thirteen years. He thanked God for that, for he was aware that his attempts at consolation were feeble, at best. And his mother, who chose to stay in Cambridge, had been too occupied with social obligations to be of much help.

I pray she can forgive me for this one day. But he'd had no choice. He thought about the letter that had come in the post three weeks ago, addressed to him in a familiar bold script. Fortunately, it hadn't reached Elizabeth's eyes. It read:

Dear Reverend Phelps,
    I am returning to Cambridge in two months to join my uncle's legal firm.

Andrew had felt inclined to throw the loathsome scrap of paper in the fireplace immediately, but some morbid curiosity forced him to read on.

    I have pictured a thousand times the look that was in your eyes when I disgraced myself. The only thing worse is imagining the hurt that must have been in Elizabeth's eyes.

If the young man's words had been intended to soften Andrew's feelings, they'd had the opposite effect, but still he'd read on.

    I have always lived an easy life, Reverend Phelps, never having wanted for anything. I can see now that has been a curse, for I never learned to appreciate the things I had. Character can only be developed through hardship, my grandfather used to tell me. Now I understand.
    Is there any way I can earn your forgiveness? I have never felt such pain as I feel now at the thought of possibly never seeing Elizabeth again.
    If only I had known then, how much love . . .

There was more, but it had been then that Andrew balled the letter up in his fist and pitched it into the fireplace. The flames licking around the paper had brought only scant satisfaction, for he knew that even if he continued to forbid Mr. Raleigh entrance into his home, there was no way he would be able to keep the young man and Elizabeth from eventually seeing each other—not if they lived in the same town.

While he realized he couldn't uproot their lives to protect his daughters from every hurt, the memory of how casually Jonathan Raleigh had saluted him was a burr under Andrew's saddle. No man, knowing the hurt that his actions would bring, had the right to treat his daughter in such a spurious manner.

And what infidelities would he commit later, perhaps when they were married with a family? *He would destroy her.*

"Father, what's wrong?"

Andrew relaxed the hands he had inadvertently balled into fists and blinked at Laurel. "Wrong?"

"You've that same look you had when Mrs. Keswick's poodle had an accident on our carpet," the girl said.

"The *second* time, you mean," he corrected, easing into a smile. "I was a bit more understanding the first time."

"Well, I hope she finds some other eligible widower to chase now that you're gone."

"I'll have to remember to say a prayer for that man," Andrew said with a grimace. "And especially for his household furnishings."

In the silence that settled over them once again, Andrew slipped back into his thoughts about the letter. Fortunately, he'd already asked Bishop Myers, an old friend and mentor, to find him a position somewhere away from Cambridge. And blessedly, a dairying village by the name of Gresham was in need of a vicar—its longtime former pastor had been assigned to a drier climate for health reasons. Andrew had gladly accepted the position on the day it was offered.

The first thing that caught Andrew's eye from his window was a red sandstone church tower, rising above rooftops in the distance. *A good omen,* he thought. "This has to be Gresham, all right." Anxious for a view from both sides of the coach, he slid over to the seat on his left to get a glimpse of their new home. Hedgerows, bordered by white clover, encircled lush pastures, where fat black-and-white cows ambled leisurely along the grass. To the west rose a steep wooded hill of some five hundred feet, its summit set ablaze by the setting deep orange sun.

"Look, Father, you can see footpaths," Laurel said, settling back in her seat so that he could see more clearly. "Perhaps we can go hiking soon."

"As soon as possible, Pet." Andrew looked at Elizabeth, hoping for some sign of interest in their surroundings. He was distressed to see her staring down at her hands, both cheeks wet with tears. "Beth. . . ?"

She raised glistening brown eyes to his and whispered, "Yes, Papa?"

Gently, he asked, "Can you understand why we're doing this?"

"I understand."

"You were miserable in Cambridge after . . ." He could not speak the name of Jonathan Raleigh, but he knew that she would understand his meaning.

"Yes," she sighed, her bottom lip trembling. "But the misery is inside of me, so taking me away from Cambridge isn't going to make it go away."

"No, of course not." Reaching across for one of her hands, he held it between both of his. "But it's going to help, with time. I give you my word on that."

He had to believe that. The only damper on Andrew's optimism was that he had not taken the time to seek God's will about the transfer. *Here I am, a minister, not practicing what I preach.* He could only pray that God understood. And as long as God allowed him to stay here, he would serve the people of Gresham to the best of his ability.

———

The setting sun was just dropping behind the Anwyl while Julia Hollis gathered sprigs of mint in the kitchen garden. Red light was thrown over the village and seemed to bathe everything with a beautiful rosy glow. She was savoring the aroma of white jasmine that wafted over from the Worthy sisters' garden—the flower retained its fragrance until October, Jewel had informed her—and humming to herself *Come Thou Fount of Every Blessing* when her ears caught what had become a rare sound in Gresham. *Coach's wheels,* she thought. Straightening, she took a couple of steps down the carriage drive toward Market Lane. Sure enough, four horses were coming up the lane, drawing a black coach. She could see well enough in the evening

198

twilight to note the absence of a family crest upon the door. *A hired one—must be the new vicar.*

In spite of the reasonable attitude she'd encouraged within herself since Vicar Wilson left, she now found herself fighting back a decidedly unreasonable tinge of resentment. It wasn't the new vicar's fault that Reverend Wilson had been transferred.

In the fleeting second before the vehicle turned onto Church Street, she imagined she could see a couple of faces at the window peering at her from the interior. She lifted a hand to wave, just in case her imagination was not playing tricks on her. When the carriage could no longer be seen, she picked three more sprigs of mint and went back around to the courtyard door. "Here's some garnish for the quince pudding," she told Mrs. Herrick on her way over to the scullery to rinse the leaves.

"Thank you, missus," Mrs. Herrick nodded from the step stool she was standing upon at the worktable. "But I could ha' asked Karl to fetch it."

"No need to do that." Julia brought the mint leaves over to the table, where Mrs. Herrick carefully ladled *Northseas Crimped Cod and Oyster Sauce* from a copper pot into a serving platter. "Besides, I believe he's fixing up a box in the lamp room for the kittens."

That brought a smile to the cook's face. "I'll warrant he's got someone helpin' him too," she replied, scraping the pot for the last of the sauce.

Julia had to admit she was right. Grace had scarcely left the kittens' side since they were discovered yesterday morning.

Mildred came from the dining room wearing her usual anxious expression. "I wonder if Mrs. Hyatt is feeling poorly today?" she said to Julia on her way to the worktable.

"Why do you think that?"

"She usually comes down to help me lay out napkins and silver, but I haven't seen her all evening."

"That's odd, all right." No one would have dreamed of asking a lodger to help set the table, but Mrs. Hyatt had generously insisted upon doing so since her second day at the *Larkspur*. The elderly woman enjoyed being in the dining room early enough to greet the others as they arrived for meals and had no qualms about being seen performing servants' work. "Would you like me to help you set the table?" Julia offered.

"Thank you, ma'am, but it's already done." Mildred began sticking mint sprigs into the individual dishes of quince pudding. "It's just that I'm a bit worried about Mrs. Hyatt."

"Well, everyone loses track of time now and then," Julia told her, using two folded dish towels to pick up a tureen of mulligatawny soup. "I'll take this on to the dining room. And don't worry about Mrs. Hyatt. She'll most likely be down with the others."

The others consisted of the lodgers, as well as Philip, Aleda, and Grace. The adults actually seemed to enjoy her children's company at the long table, very likely because Julia did her part in insisting that the children keep silent during meals unless spoken to. As a child, she had gleaned much information about the world by listening to the conversations of adults and felt it would also be good for her own children.

At five minutes of seven, the dining room began filling. At five minutes past, Mrs. Hyatt still had not presented herself.

"Perhaps I should run upstairs and knock on her door?" Mr. Durwin offered.

Julia eyed the side tables, groaning with dishes of chicken-and-leek pie, boiled beef and carrots, pickled onions, swedes, tomatoes, and Yorkshire pudding. Mildred, her cheeks glowing from the heat of the kitchen, waited to dish up bowls of mulligatawny soup at the sideboard. Meals were served *à la Russe*, with each person responsible for filling his or her own plate. It was likely that she could be downstairs with Mrs. Hyatt before the chairs were filled. "Thank you, but I'll go. Mr. Durwin, if you would be so kind as to ask the blessing. . . ."

"We shan't mind waiting," spoke up Miss Rawlins.

Mr. Clay echoed her sentiments. "We don't mind at all."

"I'll try to hurry, then," Julia said gratefully. Three minutes later, she stepped from the first floor landing and stopped at the second door to her left. "Mrs. Hyatt?" she called, giving a gentle rap on the oak wood.

There was no answer, though she imagined she heard a footstep. Julia was lifting her hand to knock again when the knob gave a faint creak. She took a step back as the door edged open wide enough to reveal a serious gray eye.

"Is that you, Mrs. Hollis?" came a voice barely above a whisper.

Puzzled, Julia nodded and whispered back. "Everyone is in the dining room now."

"Oh, dear. Would you mind sending up a tray?"

"A tray, Mrs. Hyatt?"

"Yes." The eye blinked. "I'm afraid I'm rather stiff from the hike today."

Narrowing her eyes suspiciously, Julia peered down at the fragment of face before her. "You've been up and down the Anwyl dozens of times, Mrs. Hyatt."

There was a pause, and then, "I suppose my age is catching up with me." The door opened another inch, exposing half of an apologetic smile. "Actually, I've a huge apple on my dresser that will make a lovely supper. Do run on down and join the others, dear."

Julia couldn't fathom what was going on, but not for a moment did she believe that Mrs. Hyatt was feeling her age. Why, two months ago, the spry woman had turned her ankle against a loose stone on one of the footpaths that crisscrossed the Anwyl. Regardless of the pain, she'd still limped up and down the stairs afterward, in direct disobedience to Dr. Rhodes' orders, and against the admonitions of practically everyone in the house.

The need for a bit of solitude was something that Julia could understand, what with so many people living under one roof. But Mrs. Hyatt, bashful as she was, seemed to thrive upon the company of others. Remembering the appetites downstairs that were presently being held in rein by good manners, Julia leaned closer to the door. "May I come in, Mrs. Hyatt?"

The eye blinked three times in rapid succession. "Come in? But the others . . ."

" . . . are only too glad to wait for you," Julia finished, applying firm pressure to the door with the tips of her fingers. "May I?"

She could hear a sigh from the other side as Mrs. Hyatt stepped back to allow her entrance. When they were face-to-face, the petite woman looked up at her with the expression of a young schoolchild who was about to be scolded for not completing an assignment. A slight tremor had even taken hold of her lips. Assuming her most non-threatening smile, Julia said, "If you truly wish to be alone, I understand. But I shan't enjoy my meal for worrying about you."

"I'm simply tired," Mrs. Hyatt replied, but her doe eyes lowered to focus somewhere in the vicinity of Julia's chin. "You needn't worry."

"Are you sure that's all?"

"Yes."

"Well, I'll send up a tray, then. An apple won't hold you until morning." Julia was about to turn and leave when a face flashed across her mind—one that wore a decided frown. *Could it be* . . . She reached out a hand to touch Mrs. Hyatt's shoulder. "Has Mrs. Kingston said something to you?"

Footsteps sounded in the hall. Julia turned to find Georgette framed by the doorway, her spectacles magnifying the confusion in her eyes. "Mrs. Hollis?"

"Please ask the others to go ahead with their supper," Julia told the girl. When they were alone again, she turned back to Mrs. Hyatt and lowered her voice. "Has Mrs. Kingston hurt your feelings?"

"Perhaps it wasn't intentional," Mrs. Hyatt murmured with typical charity.

Oh, I doubt that, Julia thought, tightening her lips to keep the words from escaping from them.

Before Julia could advise her that the best way to handle the occasional nips from Mrs. Kingston's tongue was to ignore them, Mrs. Hyatt looked up at her and blurted out, "Do *you* think I'm throwing myself at Mr. Durwin and making a spectacle of myself?"

"She told you *that*?"

Mrs. Hyatt's soft cheeks turned pink. "She didn't refer directly to me . . . but after our hike she said, 'Isn't it ridiculous the way *some* old heifers are so afraid to be alone that they follow any available man around.' "

Julia felt her own cheeks grow warm. "And so that's why you won't come down for supper."

"What must the others think of me?" the older woman glanced at the door and wrung her hands. "And Mr. Durwin . . . why, I feel such a fool."

Sighing inwardly, Julia reminded herself of Mrs. Kingston's good qualities—how she'd kept her word about being agreeable, for the most part anyway. Why, the woman had become almost like a mother to poor Mr. Clay. *She's considerate of the servants and doesn't complain about my children making noise outside or walking through the garden.* And she was even a faithful member of the Women's Charity Society, which met weekly to knit woolens for needy families. Why then, Julia wondered, did she feel the need to make so many negative comments to dear Mrs. Hyatt, who wouldn't purposely hurt a soul?

In an instant the answer came. *Of course!* Had she been too busy to notice what was going on under her own roof? Julia eyed Mrs. Hyatt seriously. "And why do you suppose Mrs. Kingston would say such a thing?"

"Mr. Durwin was the one who initiated the conversation," came out in a defensive tone, as if Mrs. Hyatt feared that Mrs. Kingston wasn't the *only* one who believed her to be an aging coquette. "While Mrs. Kingston and I were strolling back down the Anwyl, Mr. Durwin caught up with us. He wanted us to see some herbs he'd collected among the ruins. Mr. Durwin believes that very type of herb was used by the Romans for toothaches."

Julia nodded thoughtfully. "And he didn't show them to Mrs. Kingston, did he?"

"Well, he was just about to. She was on my other side, you see, and Mr. Durwin to my left. But before he could hand the basket across to her, she began muttering something about not having the time to waste on a handful of weeds and took off ahead."

"Yes, I can imagine." In fact, Julia actually could visualize the whole scene in her mind—Mrs. Kingston's formidable figure bustling down the path, her expression as foreboding as March thunder. "And then later she accused you of pursuing Mr. Durwin."

Before Mrs. Hyatt could answer, Julia went on. "Have you asked yourself *why* Mrs. Kingston would say such a thing?"

"Why?" the older woman echoed pensively. It was obvious from her tone of voice that she had not. "Perhaps she didn't feel well?"

Julia shook her head. "I suspect there is some jealously at play here."

"*Jealousy?*"

"Haven't you noticed that Mrs. Kingston seems to have some affection for Mr. Durwin herself?"

"Why, I never noticed." After a long moment's thought, though, she nodded sadly. "But I believe you're right, Mrs. Hollis. She does seem to light up at times when he's around."

"And so when Mr. Durwin gave you some attention first . . ."

"The poor dear!" Mrs. Hyatt exclaimed, raising a hand to her soft cheek.

"Jealousy is a painful thing to suffer, Mrs. Hyatt."

"Why, I'll have to reassure her that I have no intention of coming between the two of them."

At first Julia was satisfied with Mrs. Hyatt's change of mood, until the true meaning of her words took hold. Folding her arms, she said, "But, Mrs. Hyatt, if *you're* fond of Mr. Durwin, you shouldn't have to step aside to spare Mrs. Kingston's feelings."

Mrs. Hyatt just stood there, her flush deepening to a bright crimson.

"There is nothing ridiculous about having affection for someone, no matter what your age," Julia went on gently.

"But what if *he* suspects how I feel about him?"

Julia smiled. "Why, I imagine he would feel flattered."

"And Mrs. Kingston. . . ?"

"Isn't betrothed to Mr. Durwin. You have as much of a right to enjoy his company as she has."

"Won't she be terribly hurt if—"

"If it becomes apparent that he prefers your company to hers?" The gray eyes lowered again. "Yes."

"Possibly so," Julia answered. "But that will have been his decision. And your stepping aside won't make Mr. Durwin any more or less fond of Mrs. Kingston."

Mrs. Hyatt's brow knitted together as she considered this for a moment. "Things were so much simpler with my Adam," she said in a voice colored with remembrance. "We were third cousins, and my family had taken it for granted ever since we were children that we would marry one day."

"A woman never forgets her first love, I suppose," Julia said, and for a brief minute an image of Philip smiling lovingly at her brought a hollow ache to her heart. It was the first time she'd thought of him in weeks, and she forced the image from her mind.

"I do so enjoy Mr. Durwin's company," Mrs. Hyatt went on to admit, her voice dropping to a near whisper again. "The things he has to say about herbs and nutrition. Well, I don't understand some of it, but it's very interesting."

Julia had to smile again. "Of course it is." Then linking her arm through the older woman's, she said, "Now, why don't we go downstairs? I'm sure you don't really want to have supper alone."

"No, I don't," Mrs. Hyatt smiled back. "Thank you, Mrs. Hollis. It is so reassuring to live in a house with such a capable person in charge."

The usual mealtime voices and clicks of silver upon china drifted from the dining room, muffled by the double doors. As Julia opened the one on the right, Mrs. Kingston's voice could be heard above the rest.

"Well, I don't care how much education he has. His sermons will never hold a candle to Vicar Wilson's . . . you just wait and see. There are some things that can't be taught in ivory towers!"

Julia felt ashamed of the resentment she'd felt in the kitchen garden toward the new vicar.

"Pay her no mind," Julia whispered to Mrs. Hyatt and received a grateful nod in return.

"Why, we were afraid you weren't coming," Mrs. Dearing beamed from the table, while Mr. Durwin and then Mr. Clay rose to stand behind their chairs until Mrs. Hyatt and Julia could serve themselves.

When everyone was finally seated, Mr. Durwin asked from behind his platter of boiled vegetables and fresh fruit, "Everything is all right, I trust?"

Julia caught the meaningful glance he directed at Mrs. Hyatt and wondered if he had always looked at her in such a manner—right under her own unobservant nose.

"Everything is quite all right," Julia answered to deflect attention away from Mrs. Hyatt, who would likely need some time to settle into the table conversation. "Thank you for asking."

She glanced over at Mrs. Kingston, seated adjacent to Miss Dearing, but there was no expression on her face as she busied herself with her meal.

"We were just saying that the new vicar should be moving in today," Miss Rawlins said. "Reverend Phelps is his name. Degree from Cambridge." To the "humph!" that came from farther down the table she cut her eyes to Mrs. Kingston and said, "It's *only* the most prestigious university in the world!"

Speculation about the new vicar continued as every meager morsel of information was chewed over thoroughly. Julia was curious about the new vicar too, as she was of any new face in Gresham, but after a while she found her thoughts drifting to the compliment Mrs. Hyatt had given her upstairs.

She said I was capable! Julia had been too busy since arriving in Gresham to pause and take inventory of her skills . . . but could it be so? Mistakes she'd made, but none of them major. *And everyone seems to feel at home here—even Mrs. Kingston.* From the head of the table she looked at Philip and Grace to her left and at Aleda to her right. They were so caught up in listening to the adult conversation around them that only Aleda caught her eye and smiled. Julia smiled back. *And most importantly, the children are thriving.*

Capability had crept up upon her unawares, it seemed, while she was laboring over linen inventories and choosing wall coverings. And it had come from God, she was certain, for He answered most of her prayers that way. Unobtrusively. Quietly.

She smiled again, to herself this time. Six months ago, on her first night in the *Larkspur,* she had determined to learn to be content one day. She had naively assumed back then that one particular day would arrive hand in hand with the absence of any troubles. Now she realized that there would likely never be a trouble-free time in her life.

For one thing, it was difficult raising children without a father, and trying to manage a business at the same time made it even more so. And Philip still seemed to distance himself from her at times, even though when asked he would insist that there was nothing wrong. *Still, I'm more content now than I have ever been in my life.* Perhaps it was because she had seen the hand of God mightily at work in her life, and now she knew she could trust Him with her present concerns as well. It was a safe, comfortable feeling, and one she prayed she would never take for granted.

*P*hilip's vow to graduate from Gresham School as top student had not diminished over the summer months. Three weeks into a fresh school year, he found himself studying harder than ever and easily performing better than the other students in the sixth standard. Success was becoming such a habit that he felt no concern when the new vicar's daughter, Laurel Phelps, walked into the classroom for the first time.

The only impression that struck him was that she was pretty, with straight blond hair tied in a blue ribbon and dark brown eyes. Not that her appearance mattered, for with studying, fishing, and cricket taking up the bulk of his time, he had none left to think about girls. Philip glanced around at Jeremiah and Ben. Both faces watched with slackened jaws as she made her way down the row of desks on the opposite side of the classroom. *I suppose they'll be fighting over her now,* he thought wryly.

He heard a clunk and looked over at the girl again. She'd dropped a book on the floor beside her new desk, and just before kneeling to retrieve it, she happened to look over at him. A dimple appeared in her cheek as she gave him a quick bashful smile.

Philip smiled back, and a strange warmth filled his heart. In fact, he found himself wanting to bound over there and pick up the book for her. He touched the crown of his head and wished he'd bought another jar of pomade after Grace used it all. His stubborn cowlick was again asserting its right to stand apart from the other hairs.

That's all right, he consoled himself. Hadn't he overheard Miss Rawlins say to Mrs. Dearing just last week that women were more attracted to a man's intelligence than his appearance? It wouldn't take this Laurel Phelps long to discover who was the most upstanding student in the whole school.

Captain Powell's authoritative voice snapped him out of his reverie and brought his attention to the front of the classroom.

"Students in sixth standard, clear your desks and prepare pens and paper," he was saying.

Philip obeyed, confidently looking forward to the first history test. Mr. Durwin had called out dates and events that occurred during the classical era for over two hours yesterday evening, drilling him until he'd had dreams last night of Diocletian dividing the Roman Empire and Vandals capturing Carthage. After filling his pen from the inkwell upon his desk, he scripted his name at the top of the page and waited for the first question.

Captain Powell's first question, as it turned out, was directed to the new girl. "Miss Phelps," he said. "Would you prefer to delay your examination for a week? You've not had the advantage of preparing for it."

You should wait, Philip urged silently, watching her face from the corner of his eye. *Captain Powell's examinations are beastly hard.* He could even offer to help her study. And of course she would see the advantage of having him do so, for the top scorer would probably be announced by the end of the day. Captain Powell was inclined to use every hour of daylight available to him, so he often graded papers during break while seated on the school steps.

But Laurel Phelps surprised him by shaking her head. "No, thank you, sir," she said shyly. "I studied the classical world last year. I believe I can remember most of it."

Philip felt sorry for her, for he was aware of what she was doing. It was better to risk making a poor score than to set yourself apart from the other students on your first day. With a quiet sigh, he turned his attention back to the examination, answering the first question by writing, *The cause of the Punic Wars was commercial rivalry over the Mediterranean Sea between Rome and Carthage.* Captain Powell insisted that answers be given in the form of whole sentences. He didn't recall the headmaster informing Laurel Phelps as such and hoped she would instinctively figure that out.

During the break, Philip, Ben, and Jeremiah joined several other boys for a game of marbles around a circle they'd scratched in the dirt under an elder tree. They played with more animation than ever, congratulating themselves loudly for good plays, but so many glances were directed to the girls' side of the school yard that points were few and far between. And sure enough, Captain Powell graded papers on the steps. Hopefully he would allow the new girl to take a makeup examination in a few days. Philip wished he had the boldness to sidle up to the schoolmaster and suggest that he do so. Wouldn't *that* make him a hero in her eyes!

It was not until the closing minutes of the day that Captain Powell handed out the graded examinations. Even though he'd received a twenty-nine out of a possible thirty points, Philip sat silent amidst the low groans and self-congratulatory remarks. His near perfect scores had always made the former unnecessary, and as far as the latter . . . well, praise was always sweeter coming from someone else's lips. Casually leaning back in his desk chair, he pretended to study a blister on his thumb and waited for the announcement of the top score. He would accept the congratulations of his teacher with his usual modest composure, so that no one could accuse him of conceit.

His body went rigid when the captain called out Laurel Phelps's name.

———

"Hey, Philip, what do you think of the new vicar's girl?" Ben asked as the two walked down Church Street together after school. Jeremiah, who lived on the squire's property, had already gone off in the opposite direction with his two younger brothers. Aleda and Grace dawdled several feet behind with Helen Johnson, the baker's daughter, and the six-year-old Peterson twins from the infant school.

Philip shifted *The Oxford Study of Mathematics* and lunch pail to his other arm. The examination on multiplying and dividing compound fractions wasn't until Friday, but he reckoned that studying ahead never hurt anybody. "She seems intelligent enough." His answer was truthful, for after the shock of being beaten by a new student, he'd reasoned with himself. Why shouldn't she be allowed that small victory on her first day of school? Even though his marks averaged out to be the highest in his standard, there were occasional times when Ben scored a point or two higher on an exam.

"Hey, *Phil*-ip!" came a singsong voice from behind them. Philip ignored it, as was his usual rule. Helen Johnson was a pest to end all pests, and her favorite hobby, besides giggling, was giggling while cuffing him on the arm and sprinting away in the hopes that he would chase her.

"*Phil*-up!" the irritating voice called again. "I wonder if the trophy's going to go to a *girl* again this year?"

Loyal Ben slowed his steps long enough to throw over his shoulder, "Fernie Sanders was looking for you yesterday, Helen. He wants to ask you to marry him."

"He does *not*!"

"Just ask him! I'll go fetch him if you like."

"I'll go fe-*etch* him if you li-*ike*," Helen sang out for lack of a more witty retort, causing her female companions to break out in giggles.

The boys hastened their steps until they were out of hearing range, then Philip asked if his friend wanted to go to *Trumbles* for some peppermint sticks. "Mr. Clay insisted I take sixpence for fetching one of his coats from the tailor's. I just have to nip inside and get it from my room."

"If you've a mind to share," Ben replied. "Odd chap, your Mr. Clay, isn't he? Always looks like he's just been invited to his own funeral."

"He's just moody, that's all," said Philip. "But always pleasant enough. And sometimes he's quite good company."

They crossed Market Lane to head for the carriage drive—Mother insisted that lunch pails be brought directly to the kitchen. To his right, over the low stone wall in front of the inn, Philip could see Mrs. Kingston, a commanding figure in black moving about in the flower garden. Even though most of the early blooming flowers were fading with the approach of autumn, late blooming dahlias, delphiniums, marigolds, and pinks were coming into their own, and she still spent most of her time fussing over them.

And that's just fine with me, Philip thought as he and Ben returned the waves of the Worthy sisters. He had once supposed that lodgers, especially elderly ones, would be inclined toward sitting around idle, but the very opposite was true. Just as Mrs. Kingston busied herself in the garden, Mrs. Hyatt and Mrs. Dearing went through skeins of wool to make hangings for the *Larkspur*'s walls, Mr. Durwin collected and catalogued medicinal herbs, and Miss Rawlins wrote stories. And even Mr. Clay now accompanied Mrs. Kingston on her daily walk and spent a good deal of time rebinding some of the older books in the library.

Philip was glad of all that for his mother's sake. She had enough to do without attempting to keep six people from being bored. He reckoned that the lodgers' activities were to them what fishing was to him. Since moving to Gresham, he'd discovered some sort of hobby was necessary to most lives. Except for perhaps the Sanders brothers, unless bullying could be considered a hobby.

The air that greeted them when Philip opened the kitchen door was warm and fragrant with cinnamon. All thoughts of Mr. Trumble's peppermint sticks vanished from his mind as he ushered Ben through the doorway. Mother turned to smile at him from the kitchen table, where she sat with Fiona, Mrs. Herrick, Mildred, and Gertie over mugs of tea.

"Good day, boys. Where are the girls?"

"They're dawdling with their friends." Philip set his lunch pail on a cupboard shelf. To his relief, Mother did not get out of her chair and kiss him in front of Ben. His eye caught a large towel-covered pan at the center of the table. "What smells so good?"

"Apple strudel," Mrs. Herrick answered from the head of the table, then added with a mock scowl, "And we're all doin' just fine, thank you."

Philip winced. "That was to be my next question."

Moving the towel from the pan of pastries, Mother asked Ben, "Why don't you join us?"

"If you're sure there's enough," Ben answered with a timid eye turned toward the cook. "I've never tasted strudel."

"Aye," Mrs. Herrick replied, then winked at Fiona. "More than enough, and with another pan over there on the stove. Everyone's been served but you and the girls."

Mildred got up to pour the boys some milk, and Philip took the empty chair next to his mother's. Ben went straightway around the table to sit next to Fiona. While she served up generous portions of the pastry, Mother told them that today was the Herricks' twentieth wedding anniversary.

"It's my Karl's favorite, so I always bake strudel on our anniversary," Mrs. Herrick said, as if any explanation was necessary for the wonderful, flaky confection that now melted away on Philip's tongue. He did manage to take his mind off his taste buds long enough to feel grateful that Mrs. Herrick had had the foresight to marry a German.

Suddenly there was the sound of a man clearing his throat, and then, "Excuse us, ladies." All heads turned to the corridor doorway, where Mr. Clay and Mr. Durwin were now standing.

"May we come in?" the actor asked with eyebrows raised pleadingly.

The four servants at the table made moves to get to their feet, but

Mr. Clay advanced to the table and held up a restraining hand. "Please—do keep your seats."

Mr. Durwin, looking quite self-conscious, walked over to stand at Mr. Clay's elbow. "We would just like to say how much we enjoyed the apple strudel. Our sincere compliments to the cook."

"Yes," agreed Mr. Clay. "And I personally would like to ask for her hand in marriage."

Philip chuckled, and Ben covered a shocked grin with his hand. Mrs. Herrick, however, took in the proposal with aplomb. "And you happen to know that you're safe in saying your fancy words, Mr. Clay. But I do thank you gentlemen for the compliment. How about if we send you out another tray?"

"No need to go to the trouble, if you can stand our company."

"Please, gentlemen . . . take a chair."

The offer did not have to be repeated. Mr. Durwin walked over to the chair next to Philip, and Mr. Clay went around to sit across from him, next to Ben.

"Why, hullo, Mr. Mayhew," the actor said to Philip's friend. "My eyes were so full of strudel that I didn't notice you there. Tell me, gentlemen, what did you learn in school today?"

"That we're not as bright as we thought we were," Ben answered right away, causing Philip to shoot him a warning look and everyone else at the table to smile.

"Well then, I've always maintained that the beginning of true knowledge is when we realize we don't know everything," Mr. Clay said.

"That's a fact, boys," Mr. Durwin nodded. He studied Ben for a second and then said, "Your father works for the squire, doesn't he?"

"No, sir," Philip answered for him. "That's Jeremiah's father. Ben's father is a wheelwright."

"Is that so?"

Ben spoke this time. "Yes, sir. His shop is on Worton Lane, attached to our house."

"Past that old abandoned mill?" asked Mr. Clay.

"You've seen our place?"

"I've seen practically every cottage in Gresham," Mr. Clay answered, feigning a sigh. "Mrs. Kingston insists upon changing the route of our walk every few days. Isn't there a family of basket weavers at the end of the lane?"

"The Keegans," Philip replied.

"Indeed?" Mr. Clay looked past Ben to Fiona. "Miss O'Shea, were you aware that you aren't the only person in Gresham of Irish heritage?"

Philip wondered if he were the only person to notice how Mr. Clay's voice softened just a bit whenever he said "Miss O'Shea." And how the man's eyes seemed to follow her whenever she came through a room. He supposed that Mr. Clay must be in love with Fiona—after all, she was the prettiest, kindest woman in England . . . next to Mother. The thought occurred to him that perhaps they would marry one day. That was quite all right, as long as neither moved away from the *Larkspur*. Perhaps Mr. Clay wouldn't have so many sad moods if he had a good wife.

But then another thought followed, and he shook his head at his own ignorance. If Mr. Clay *did* indeed love Fiona, that wasn't enough for marriage. She had to feel the same way about him too, just as Mother and Father had loved each other. And while she was certainly kind to Mr. Clay, she did not treat him any differently than anyone else.

"Yes, I've met the Keegans," the housekeeper replied to Mr. Clay's question. Her smile seemed pasted on and the violet eyes took on a worried cast. "They've made baskets and mats for us."

"Were you acquainted with them in Ireland?" Mr. Durwin asked.

"I'm afraid not, sir. They hail from Dublin, and I'm from Kilkenny."

"We gave them some fish once," Ben said in an obvious effort to impress her. "They were very happy to have them. And we'll likely do it again soon."

Curiously, Fiona's lips pressed together as if she were angry. "How kind of you," she said at length in her soft brogue but then pushed out her chair and stood. Mr. Clay reached her before anyone else could think to move and put a hand upon her shoulder.

"Please . . . don't leave, Miss O'Shea. What's wrong?"

Philip watched as his mother hurried around the table. "Fiona? Are you ill?"

"Why don't you have her sit down?" Mildred suggested.

Philip met Ben's curious look with a blank stare. He couldn't recall ever seeing Fiona upset, even when Georgette walked into a table once and caused a lamp to break.

"I've the marketing list to prepare," Fiona insisted, but Mother and Mr. Clay coaxed her back into the chair. She sighed and apologized again. "So silly of me . . ." .

"Well, nothing to be embarrassed about, dear," said Mrs. Herrick. "You just rest there until you feel better."

Mr. Durwin nodded. "Is there something any of us can help you with, Miss O'Shea?"

"It's kind of you to ask, but I don't think so."

"Surely it would help to talk about it," Mildred suggested.

Fiona pressed her lips together in an effort to compose herself, but a second or two later sighed. "It's that family. They're just so helpless."

"Who, Fiona?" asked Mother, taking the chair that Ben vacated for her, while Mr. Clay stood just behind Fiona's other shoulder.

"I believe she means the Keegans," said Mr. Durwin. "Is that correct, Miss O'Shea?"

She nodded. "Yes, sir. I went over there just this mornin' to see about some baskets for the pantry. Someone has been playing tricks on them."

"Playing tricks?" Mother asked. "What do you mean?"

Taking a deep breath, Fiona explained that the Keegans went to Shrewsbury almost every Saturday to sell baskets and spend the night, something Philip and Ben already knew. "They've a wooden shed that they store finished baskets in. Every Sunday afternoon when they return from Shrewsbury, they find the shed tipped over."

"But why?" asked Gertie.

"I haven't the foggiest," Fiona sighed. "And I suppose it sounds like a small matter. But they've never felt welcome in this village, so this has them feeling even more . . ."

"Alienated?" Ben offered.

"Yes. Alienated."

Philip raised an eyebrow at Ben and received a slight nod in return. He could tell that one particular surname had crossed his friend's mind as well as his own. Should he mention their shared suspicion yet? He turned his face toward Fiona—for a brief instant, his eyes locked with Mr. Clay's.

"Well, it's a small matter to fetch the constable right away!" Mr. Durwin huffed indignantly. "Malicious mischief is still against the law in this country."

Fiona shook her head. "Please don't, sir. I offered to go with them to see Constable Reed, but the Keegans insisted that they're afraid of angering whoever is doing this."

"It can't be just one person," said Gertie. "Would take at least two to push over a shed."

"Do they know who it is?" Mother asked.

"I've a feeling they suspect someone, ma'am. But they wouldn't share it with me."

"Afraid to *anger* vandals?" Mr. Durwin sputtered. "And who gives a tinker's curse if they become angry? Spending a few weeks in the lockup would cool some tempers."

But Philip understood. If indeed some of the Sanders boys were up to this, it was still apparently in the prank stage. If they saw that their nocturnal activities were causing no stirs, after a while they would probably give them up and move on to greener pastures. But allow the law to become involved, and the whole clan would consider it a matter of family honor to exact revenge in as many sneaky ways as possible.

He'd once read something about elephants, how those majestic-looking creatures were really quite petty and could nurse grudges for years and years. That description seemed to fit the Sanders perfectly.

"Please." Finally assuming her usual composure, Fiona said to Mr. Durwin, "That is so kind of you to offer, sir, but we must consider the Keegans' wishes."

"Well, I don't know how it was in Ireland, but here in England people have the right to expect the law to protect their property."

"But it's a small matter to set the shed upright every week, compared with having to replace broken windows or worse. Besides, they've no *proof* of who's doing this."

She pushed her chair out again and rose from the table. First giving Mother and Mr. Clay an appreciative look, she apologized to everyone for becoming upset. "If you'll excuse me, I'll see to that marketing list now."

A thoughtful silence settled over the group for a second or two after Fiona left the kitchen. It was broken when the kitchen door swung open. "What smells so good?" Aleda exclaimed, flanked by Grace and Helen. Deciding it a perfect time to leave, Philip motioned to Ben, thanked Mrs. Herrick for the strudel, and asked Mother to be excused. Permission was granted, and Philip and his friend went out the back door as the chattering girls found places at the table.

"Do you still want to go to *Trumbles*?" Philip asked half-heartedly as they ambled across the courtyard.

Ben patted his stomach and belched. "May we tomorrow instead? Besides, I've chores waiting, so I'll have to leave soon."

"All right." He kicked a loose stone. "What do you think of what Fiona said in there?"

"I think the same thing you do. Should we have told?"

"I don't know. Mr. Durwin sounded ready to jump up and fetch the constable." Philip sighed and kicked another stone. "Surely they'll tire of their little game one day." Changing the subject, he said, "Have you time for a game of horseshoes?"

"Just one."

The spike was set in the ground just outside the courtyard. Ben had just tossed the first shoe, a miss, when the courtyard door opened and Mr. Clay came outside and strolled over to them with both hands in his pockets.

"Would you like a turn?" Philip asked.

Mr. Clay smiled, but his slate gray eyes studied both of them. "Some other time, thank you." He nodded back toward the benches under the giant oak tree. "Why don't we sit and have a chat?"

"A chat?"

"Just for a bit. I've a feeling you two have an interesting tale to share."

Philip did not need much coaxing to tell everything he knew about the Sanders brothers once they were settled upon the benches. Indeed, it was a relief to get the matter off his chest, and Ben appeared to feel likewise. "But Fiona . . . Miss O'Shea . . . doesn't want us to go to the constable, so what can we do about it?"

Mr. Clay nodded, tapping the cleft of his chin absently with a finger. "Surely there's a way to right this wrong."

"You mean, you want to do something about it?" Philip asked, surprised. Even in his best moods, Mr. Clay had few dealings with people not attached to the *Larkspur*. But then he remembered the way the actor looked at Fiona and understood.

"I wouldn't mind. It would require some creative thought, though."

"We could hide behind a tree or in the bushes one Saturday night and catch them," Ben offered.

"And then do what with them once we've caught them?" Philip asked.

"Threaten to tell Constable Reed. They can't hold it against the

Keegans if we're the ones who report them."

"But they can hold it against *us*. And I don't care to have to hide from the Sanders for the rest of my life."

Ben frowned. "That's something to think about, sir," he told Mr. Clay. "They give us enough grief as it is, and they're not even *angry* at us."

"I don't want to put either of you in jeopardy," the actor said. Seconds later, his lips curved into a half smile. "But perhaps there is another way."

*T*he vicarage was a snug two-story cottage of the same red sandstone as Saint Jude's. It roosted on a grassy knoll a stone's throw from the church, and its wooden gate opened up to a neat little flower garden. Cheery multicolored woven rugs softened the oak plank flooring, and odd pieces of furniture, though none of it matching, appeared polished and well cared for.

The servants, Luke, Dora, and Mrs. Paget, had greeted Andrew and his family the previous evening with some uncertainty showing through their smiles. Andrew could understand this—he'd been informed by Bishop Myers that the vicar he was replacing, Reverend Wilson, had been much loved by the community. No doubt the servants felt the loss even more keenly than did the villagers. Their reserve melted a bit when Andrew warmly expressed his gratitude for the kettle of chicken and leek soup Mrs. Paget had kept simmering for them and indicated his appreciation of the garden and tidy rooms.

He had been pleased to discover that a river, the Bryce, flowed just north of the vicarage. Perhaps there would be a little time for fishing once a routine was established. Even more pleasing was the little book-lined study just off the parlor. Andrew had spent his first full afternoon in Gresham—after inspecting Saint Jude's and lunching with Elizabeth at the home of the churchwarden, Mr. Sykes—thumbing through a clothbound notebook that Vicar Wilson had left upon the desk with a letter of welcome. *You may find this helpful,* his predecessor had accurately written, for within its pages were thoughtful descriptions of every family in the parish—occupations, births and names of children, conversions and baptisms, deaths, and even facts that would aid a pastor in serving, such as:

Mrs. Ramsey (a seamstress living on Thatcher Lane, so the notebook said) *tends to her ailing mother and cannot attend church. They both look forward to Monday morning visits for prayer and hearing details of the previous day's service.*

Another entry told of a Mr. Kerns, a cheese factory worker: *He is a decent man, but occasionally struggles with the temptation of the bottle. If Mr. Kerns should be spotted entering or leaving the Bow and Fiddle at any time, it would be beneficial to deliver a stern lecture against allowing his nine children to live in want while he wastes money on strong drink. The effects of such admonition will last three months, perhaps even four, before needing to be repeated.*

"Bless you, Vicar Wilson," Andrew said aloud, for how long would it have taken him to learn such things on his own? He made a mental note to write a letter of appreciation to the good reverend and turned his attention to the notebook again. Next came a warning that while patronizing Mr. McFarley, the barber, conversation should be gently steered away from politics lest an uneven haircut result.

And if anyone even mentions the phrase "Scottish Reform Bill," it would behoove you to remove yourself from the premises immediately. Andrew smiled and glanced up at the chimneypiece clock—then winced at the time. *Half past four.* He hadn't intended to cloister himself away for so long. Laurel had likely returned from school by now, and Elizabeth, who'd gone upstairs after lunch with a book, would need to be encouraged to spend some time with the family.

He wondered as he placed a folded sheet of writing paper inside the notebook to mark his stopping place if he should have been patient and waited for a city assignment. Perhaps he could have persuaded her to attend a women's college as a day student. It wasn't good for her to have so much time to brood.

But was more education the answer? Had he encouraged his daughters to fill their heads with knowledge to the neglect of their character development? He had always been so secure and just a little proud of the fact that he'd led them both to faith in Christ at early ages, but shouldn't he have encouraged them upon a journey of spiritual growth, just as he would have done for any of his other parishioners?

The painful realization hit him that, because his daughters were raised in a minister's home, he had assumed they would automatically absorb the spiritual principle that had taken him decades to glean. But, as Bishop Myers was fond of saying, *God has no grandchildren.*

Forgive me for being a stumbling block to my own children, he prayed, sighing. *And please give each a stronger sense of purpose for*

219

their lives . . . especially Elizabeth now.

The search for his daughters ended in the kitchen. It was a pleasant room, with a clean flagstone floor and savory aromas. A black-leaded range shone beneath a fringe of utensils hanging from the chimney-piece, where Mrs. Paget stood tending a kettle. Both girls were seated at a well-scrubbed oak worktable over cups and biscuits and looked up when he entered the room.

Andrew pulled out the chair at the head of the table, adjacent to both girls. "Good afternoon, my two favorite daughters."

Six or seven years ago, this greeting never failed to elicit either a giggle or at least a correction of his context, but it had become a little worn with time. Now all he received were indulgent smiles. Elizabeth's half-hearted attempt did not match Laurel's in intensity, but he was nonetheless encouraged that it wasn't a frown.

"Hello, Papa," they said, almost in unison.

"Would you be wantin' some tea now, vicar?" asked Mrs. Paget from the stove. She appeared at least fifty years of age, with graying blond hair and fine wrinkles webbing her eyes. She carried her thick figure with a grace that any dancer would envy. The cook had been in service at the vicarage for thirty-two years, she'd told Andrew yesterday evening, and her husband, Daniel Paget, had held Luke's position until his passing on ten years ago.

"Tea would be nice, thank you," Andrew replied. After the cook poured, he asked Laurel about her day at school.

"It went very well," she said, her brown eyes sparkling. "I scored the highest mark in the class on a history examination."

"Wonderful! And how did you get on with your classmates?"

"They were quite friendly."

"I trust you didn't gloat about the exam, Laurel," Elizabeth said in a tone filled with elder-sister-admonition. "You have a tendency to do that, you know, but the others won't like you if they think you're conceited."

"I didn't gloat," Laurel assured her. "And some of the girls even congratulated me over it." She excused herself then, saying she had a composition assignment that was due the next day.

After the sound of her footsteps had faded away, Elizabeth gave Andrew a wry smile and remarked, "She'll be ordering the headmaster about before too long."

He sipped his tea and smiled back at her, pleased at this glimmer of her old sense of humor. If only that faint shadow of reproach would leave her eyes. He could see it lurking there every time she spoke to him. "She's just a bit competitive, that's all."

"A bit? And from where did she inherit that, I wonder?"

Andrew put a hand up to his chest. "You aren't implying that *I*..."

"All I'm saying is, I noticed you managed to find time to hang your old rowing paddle in your study less than twenty-four hours after our arrival here. And what did your teammates nickname you at Trinity College?"

"Clipper," he mumbled, unable to offer any argument in his own defense. And he *had* felt a flush of pride when Laurel announced her victory at school. But women did not have the same aggressive tendencies as men—the need to prove themselves against others. He felt quite certain that Laurel had been happy about the score on her examination for its own sake, not because it put her ahead of her fellow classmates for the day.

Changing the subject, he asked Elizabeth if she would care to accompany him on a walk. "Just to the river," he added when she appeared about to decline. It hurt him that she showed no interest in learning anything about Gresham or its people. He'd had to practically order her to accompany him for lunch at the home of the church-warden's today. She'd sat mute at the table, unless to respond to a question from Mr. or Mrs. Sykes.

But to his relief she accepted, however unenthusiastically, and fetched a wrap from upstairs. He pulled two golden pears from the tree just outside the back gate and handed one to her on the way. The Bryce stretched out north of the vicarage, and for a long time they stood on the upper bank between two willows and watched the activity at the cheese factory on the other side. It appeared that several red-and-white carrier wagons had returned from the train station in Shrewsbury with empty barrels, which were being hauled up by a pulley into the overhanging gable. Each barrel nosed open the trap door and fell with a loud *clap!* behind them.

"The cheeses are delivered to nearly all parts of England, according to Mr. Sykes," Andrew said by way of starting conversation, as if she hadn't been seated at the same table and heard the same information herself.

"Is that so?" she said with no hint of sarcasm.

Andrew realized her thoughts had been occupied elsewhere during dinner. Upon whom, he did not wish to speculate. Deciding to get right to the point, he said, "I should begin paying calls tomorrow. Why don't you consider accompanying me?"

"Accompany you?" She threw her pear core over to a rook sauntering along the lower bank. "But why, Papa? I never did in Cambridge."

"You were occupied with schooling then."

"Are people here expecting me to come with you?"

"I don't know that, Beth, but I wouldn't ask you to do anything just because people are expecting it. I believe it would be good for you to become acquainted with the villagers. And it would give you less time to brood over the past."

When she protested right away that she wasn't brooding, he amended with "*dwelling* upon the past," though in his mind he could see no difference.

"Are you ordering me to come with you, Papa?" she asked.

"Of course not."

"Then I would rather stay at the vicarage." She did not say *at home*. Then, as if concerned that she'd hurt his feelings, she offered him a strained smile. "Perhaps some other time."

Her attention was drawn to three rooks scrutinizing the ground where she'd thrown the pear core earlier, and Andrew studied her. *So like her mother,* he thought, even though she had inherited his blond hair. Would to God that Kathleen were here now. A mother would more fully understand what her daughter was feeling and be able to offer a more soothing consolation.

But you understand loss, a voice reminded him.

"Elizabeth," he began haltingly.

She turned to him. "Yes, Papa?"

How could he put into words the feelings he had held inside for so long? But it seemed he had no choice. "When your mother passed away . . . I wanted to die myself."

Her brown eyes took on a liquid sheen. "You loved her very much, didn't you?"

"More than I can tell you. She was more than a helpmate, Beth. She was my dearest friend."

With a somber nod, she asked, "How did you cope, Papa?"

He shrugged his shoulders. "For a while, I didn't. I blamed God, blamed myself, and blamed anyone else who happened to have the privilege of living. Perhaps I would still be doing so . . . who knows? But I had two daughters to consider and knew I could ill afford the luxury of extended grief. So I asked God to give me some renewed purpose for my life."

"And He did?"

"Not right away. Or more likely, I didn't recognize it right away. But eventually, I found that I had a deeper appreciation of my remaining family and my ministry. When I gave up dwelling upon my own misery and absorbed myself with the lives of those around me, the peace that I was lacking returned."

After a space of silence she threaded her arm through his. "Are you happy, Papa?"

He patted her hand. "Yes, Beth. But don't you see? When we pursue happiness for its own sake, it's like chasing the end of a rainbow. It will always elude us. It is when we're committed to some higher purpose that happiness somehow breaks through and comes to dwell with us."

Giving her a self-conscious smile, he said, "I sound as if I'm in the pulpit, don't I."

"A bit," she smiled back. "It's not the first time."

"Habit of the trade. But do you understand what I'm saying?"

"I do, in my head." Her eyes became liquid again. "But my heart still feels like it's dying."

Reaching into his waistcoat pocket for a handkerchief, he wiped her cheek with it. "And it will continue to feel that way as long as you keep thinking about him."

"I need some time. You had time to grieve over Mother."

"But your mother wasn't a scoundrel," came out of his mouth before he could stop himself. The change in her expression was immediate, for she now stared at him with lips pressed together tightly.

Andrew put a hand upon her shoulder and felt it stiffen. "Beth, I shouldn't have—"

"Yes, Father, Jonathan was a scoundrel. And so that means I've no right to feel hurt?"

"No, of course not." Anger rose in Andrew's chest—at the man who had so smoothly trifled with his daughter's affections, and at Elizabeth, for even having loved him in the first place. The level of his voice rose a fraction. "But I do wish you would have enough self-respect to forget about him and get on with your life."

In the short silence after he spoke, Andrew held his breath and waited for the eruption he knew was coming. Elizabeth worked her crimson-splotched face in a struggle to keep composure, then finally turned and dissolved into tears against his shoulder.

"There, there now." While she wept, he patted her back awkwardly, wishing back the years when his daughters' hurts were the results of less-critical issues such as a failed examination, a misplaced locket, or a blemish on the chin. Those hurts could usually be soothed away by such paternal consolation. He felt utterly helpless now. He could say comforting words from now until Christmas, but none had the power to wrench Jonathan Raleigh out of her wounded heart.

Why are you still so sleepy, Philip?" Julia asked the boy after his third yawn over his plate of bacon and eggs the next morning. On school days they breakfasted at the kitchen table, as in their "pre-lodger" days. The children had to leave early, and there was no sense in making the maids bring food to the dining room twice. "Didn't you sleep well?"

He covered another yawn while replying, "Yes, Mother."

"Perhaps he needs a good strong dose o' liver tonic," Mrs. Herrick suggested from atop her stool at the other end of the table, where she rolled out scones for the lodgers' breakfast. "You can get a pint for sixpence over to Mr. Trumble's. 'Course you'd have to keep it away from Miss Grace, or she'll be pourin' it over her head."

This was said with an affectionate look at the youngest child, for Grace, a frequent visitor to the kitchen, was obviously Mrs. Herrick's favorite. Grace colored a little, but when she realized everyone was smiling at the notion, she ducked her head and smiled.

It took Aleda to break the spell, for she said casually, while toying with her fork and coddled eggs, "I would be sleepy too if I woke up at five o'clock."

"Aleda!" the boy hissed.

"Well, Mother *asked*."

"But she didn't ask *you*."

"That's enough! *Both* of you." Julia took a deep breath to compose herself and turned to Philip again. "And why did you wake so early?"

Letting out a sigh that sounded suspiciously like another yawn, Philip replied, "I had to finish my homework."

"Didn't you finish last night?"

"I did, but I woke up worried that my composition wasn't good enough."

"Wasn't *well* enough, you mean," Grace corrected while tearing her bacon into tiny bits to sprinkle over her eggs. "Miss Hillock says you shouldn't say 'good.' "

"I doubt that very much," said Aleda.

"But she did."

"In what context?" Philip asked, his blue eyes intent upon his youngest sister, as if she'd made the most profound statement he'd ever heard.

Aware that the boy was attempting to keep the conversation steered away from himself, Julia buttered a scone and allowed the grammar lesson to continue.

Grace stopped tearing bacon pieces and stared blankly across at Philip.

"I mean, what was Miss Hillock talking about when she told that to the class?" he asked.

The child screwed up her face for a second, then answered, "She said if someone should ask how you are doing, you should answer, 'I'm quite well, thank you,' and never just 'good.' "

"But that doesn't mean you mustn't ever use the word." Aleda launched into a lecture about the correct usage of good and well, while Philip seized that opportunity to push away his empty plate.

"That was delicious," he said to Mrs. Herrick, then asked Julia if he might be excused. She smiled and shook her head.

"If you will recall, I looked over your composition last night." The subject of the three-page assignment was to be *My Most Interesting Day*, and Philip had penned a lively account of the balloon races at Brighton two years ago. He went even further to explain in succinct terms the workings of a hot-air balloon. "I thought it was a fine paper."

The boy shook his head. "I began too many sentences with dependent clauses. You're supposed to vary your sentence structure, you know."

Julia didn't know how to respond to this. It was good that he cared about maintaining good marks. *Or would that be "well"?* But he seemed to be carrying it a bit too far. How she envied families with fathers intact! Her husband may have been absent most of the time, but he was someone with whom she could share her concerns about the children—even though he had laughed most of them away.

226

It was on her lips to ask if this quest for perfection had anything to do with coming in second behind the new vicar's daughter on an examination yesterday. Aleda and Helen had giggled about it at the kitchen table after school yesterday, until Julia silenced them with a warning look. Philip had a competitive streak, true, but surely a difference of one point on an examination hadn't ruffled his feathers. "Well, you need your sleep, son," she finally told him before granting him permission to leave the table. "So don't be slipping out of bed so early anymore."

"I won't." Looking relieved that the interrogation was over, he left the room to clean his teeth and fetch his book. When the girls had finished breakfast and all three children had left for school, Julia asked Mrs. Herrick if she would have time today to bake something she could bring to the new vicar's family. She thought she would ask Fiona to accompany her to the vicarage after lunch for a brief welcome call. She would never forget how welcome Reverend Wilson and Henrietta had made her family feel when they first moved to Gresham. The vicar would have his church and parishioner responsibilities to occupy his time, but no doubt Mrs. Phelps was feeling a little like a fish out of water.

"The vicarage already has Mrs. Paget, so something sweet would be more appropriate than a meal dish . . . don't you think?" she asked Mrs. Herrick.

"Aye," the cook replied, motioning for Gertie, who had just come in from preparing the dining room for the lodgers' breakfast, to bring over a pan for the scones. "And one of my chocolate and black cherry tortes would be just the thing."

———

"But didn't you hear?" Fiona asked later, when Julia and the housekeeper were halfway down Church Lane. They each held a handle of the basket that enclosed the torte in a loose wrapping of brown paper. From the south a bracing breeze carried a faint aroma of apples from the squire's orchard and sent leaves dancing across the lane. "There isn't any Mrs. Phelps. The vicar's a widower, just like the Reverend Wilson."

"Oh, dear." Julia's steps slowed. "I'm sorry to hear that."

"He's been one for a long time, ma'am."

"Is it proper for us to be paying a call?"

"Proper?"

"You know." Recalling her recent conversation with Mrs. Hyatt, Julia said, "I wouldn't want him to think . . ."

Fiona's violet eyes filled with amusement, but she tactfully refrained from smiling. "He's our pastor now. And you've called on Vicar Wilson before, haven't you?"

"Well, yes. But Henrietta was always there."

"Reverend Phelps has an older daughter at home as well."

"I wasn't aware of that." Julia glanced at the school building as they passed it on their right. "How did you learn all of this?"

This time Fiona smiled. "Mildred went out to the kitchen garden for some basil this morning."

"And the Worthy sisters were outside?"

"Exactly, ma'am."

Julia had to smile, no longer concerned about the propriety of their visit. Besides, they were planning to stay only long enough to welcome the family. When they reached the vicarage gate, they saw the figure of a young woman resting in a wicker garden chair on the opposite side. She apparently was asleep and had not heard their approach. One cheek leaned against the curved back of the chair, and both hands rested upon the pages of the open book in her lap. After unfastening the latch Fiona pushed open the gate slowly, but the hinge let out a squeak and the young woman raised her head and blinked at them.

"We beg your pardon," Julia said and wondered if the girl were ill. Her eyes were swollen underneath, and red splotches stained her face. In her left cheek was etched the crisscross pattern of the chair, adding to her rather pitiful appearance. "Should we come back another time?"

"Why, no," the girl replied, rousing herself to her feet and setting the book on the chair seat. She had obviously been asleep only a short while and had no idea of her appearance. Julia thought that she must ordinarily be a pretty girl. Her dark brown eyes were thickly lashed, and her hair appeared golden in the patch of sunlight.

"I stopped to rest my eyes and must have dozed off," she said. "Please, do come in."

"Are you all right?" Julia couldn't refrain from asking as she went through the gate and walked over to extend her hand.

"Oh." The splotches on the girl's face grew redder, but she shook Julia's and then Fiona's hand. "I . . . must have sat in the sun too long. Are you here to see my father?"

"If he's available. I'm Julia Hollis, and this is Fiona O'Shea."

"I'm Elizabeth Phelps." She gave them a feeble attempt at a smile. "I'm sorry, but my father is out making calls."

"Then we'll just wait and make his acquaintance on Sunday." Julia lifted the basket in her hand. "We've brought you a torte. Welcome to Gresham, Miss Phelps."

"How kind of you. I'll run it in to Mrs. Paget and return with your basket." A hand went up to her lips. "Oh, forgive me. Would you care to come inside for some lemonade?"

"Thank you, but we didn't intend to stay long anyway," Julia replied. She couldn't help but notice the relief that came to the girl's eyes. *Perhaps it's homesickness that has her so miserable.* "And I'll send one of my children to collect the basket in a day or two."

She and Fiona bade the vicar's daughter good-day and turned to leave. When they reached the gate Julia glanced back over her shoulder. The girl was still standing in the same spot, one hand holding the basket and the other lifted in farewell. It was such a poignant picture that Julia felt compelled to turn and give her a reassuring smile. "Sometimes it takes a while for the newness of a place to wear off, Miss Phelps. A little homesickness is natural."

"Yes . . . thank you," Miss Phelps said in a small voice, then turned abruptly and fled into the house. Julia could only stare at the closed door. A second later she felt a touch on her sleeve and turned to Fiona at her side.

"I didn't mean to upset the poor girl."

Fiona nodded. "I don't think you did, ma'am. It looked like she was feelin' that way before she ever set eyes on us."

"Should I go back and ask to speak with her?"

"I don't know. Do you think it might upset her more?"

Julia decided that Fiona had brought up a good point and turned regretfully to leave. "Perhaps we should look in on her in a few days, when she's had more time to adjust to the move."

Down the vicarage lane the two started again, neither in the mood for conversation now. They had just turned onto Church Lane when they came upon a gentleman who was obviously the new vicar. He was younger than Julia would have imagined, but then, she had formed a mental picture of someone resembling Vicar Wilson. His frame—only a few inches taller than her own, and thick without being corpulent—was clothed with a gray coat and black trousers.

"Good afternoon, ladies," he said upon reaching them. The lift of his bowler hat revealed wind-disheveled hair the same dark blond color as his neatly trimmed beard. "Were you just at the vicarage?"

Then as if he felt compelled to explain his forwardness, he added right away, "I asked that because I watched you turn from the lane just now."

Julia offered her gloved hand. "We were there but a minute or so. I'm Mrs. Hollis, and this is Miss O'Shea."

"Andrew Phelps," he said. His smile, as he shook both of their hands, crinkled his hazel eyes at the corners and transformed a face that would be described as plain into one filled with good-humored warmth. "Do forgive my being absent—I've been making calls. Would you care to return with me?"

"Thank you, but we just wanted to welcome you to Gresham." With a glance back in the direction of the vicarage, Julia added, "I'm afraid I upset your daughter, Reverend Phelps."

He glanced in the same direction, his eyes saddening. "Elizabeth. And I thought she was better today."

"All Mrs. Hollis did was assure her that her homesickness would pass eventually," Fiona said in a respectful but straightforward tone, as if she felt the need to defend Julia.

"I do appreciate that, Mrs. Hollis. And please don't blame yourself."

"My daughter Aleda was upset about moving here as well," Julia told him. "But she's quite happy now. I'm sure the same will happen for your daughter."

"Would that it could. But it's not just homesickness that's affecting her." He shook his head and sighed. "Her heart was recently broken by a young rogue."

"I'm so sorry," Julia told him, and Fiona murmured the same.

"I appreciate your sympathy. I can only pray that she eventually forgets about the young man."

"I'll pray that too, sir," said Fiona.

"How kind of you." The vicar smiled again warmly. "And here I am neglecting my manners. I don't believe I've asked where either of you live."

"The *Larkspur Inn*, on Market Lane," Julia told him. "We operate a lodging house."

"Yes? But you mentioned your daughter being reluctant to move here, so I take it that it's a new establishment?"

"New to us," Julia smiled. "We've only been there six months, but the building dates back to the 1600s." Then realizing that the vicar must be anxious to see about his daughter, she said, "We'll bid you good day now, Reverend Phelps. Welcome to Gresham."

He thanked them both with another tip of the hat and said he looked forward to seeing them again on Sunday.

"He seems a pleasant person," Fiona said as she and Julia walked back down Church Lane.

"Yes, he does. I just hope he can deliver a decent sermon, or Mrs. Kingston will never let us hear the end of it." The school came into view on their left, and Julia's thoughts turned to her son. "Did you know Philip woke at five this morning to rewrite a school paper?"

"Five? Has he ever done that before?"

"Never. I can't help but wonder if his nose is out of joint because the vicar's other daughter outscored him on an examination yesterday."

"Oh, Philip is too mature for that, ma'am."

"I suppose you're right." She linked arms with the housekeeper. "You know, that chocolate torte smelled terribly good. I wonder if Mrs. Herrick could be persuaded to bake another one some time soon?"

"Only if she's asked." Fiona smiled back.

––––––––––

"A half-pound of sour balls please," Philip said to Mr. Trumble, setting his school books and lunch pail up on the counter.

"Comin' right up, Mr. Hollis," the shopkeeper responded cheerfully. He unscrewed the lid to a two-gallon glass jar filled with candy. "Got these in fresh yesterday."

"Yes?" Philip said, but he hadn't the appetite for anything at the moment. And if not for Ben and Jeremiah eyeing the progress of the candy to the scale, he would just as soon have gone home to lick his wounds. Just the memory of Laurel Phelps's triumph was as grating to his nerves as fingernails on a chalkboard. How was he to have guessed that *anyone* at school would have met Benjamin Disraeli? But apparently her grandmother had headed a ladies fund-raising committee for the Tory party, and the prime minister had accompanied the archbishop of Canterbury to a dinner at her house this past summer.

To make matters worse, the girl had embellished her composition with little tidbits that brought gasps of delight from the class, such as how Mr. Disraeli had popped a cube of sugar into his mouth during after-dinner coffee, and how the handle of his umbrella was a bronze caricature of the Duke of Wellington wearing an eye patch.

My sentence structure was twice as varied as hers, he thought bitterly. But Captain Powell didn't even seem to consider that. It just wasn't fair! How many students had had the privilege of meeting someone famous?

"You boys catch any big fish lately?" Mr. Trumble asked as he handed over the small parcel to Philip.

"Jeremiah caught a four pounder last Saturday," Ben answered, clapping his friend on the shoulder. "Took him a good ten minutes to land it. They both put up a good fight."

"A *whale* of a fight, you say?" the shopkeeper asked, chuckling at his own joke.

"That's a good one, Mr. Trumble," Ben chuckled back. "More like a *trout* of a fight."

I should have written about Mr. Clay's experiences in the theatre, Philip thought.

"Oh, by the way," Mr. Trumble said when the three boys were heading for the door. "I finished sorting today's mail just a while ago, and I seem to recall you've a letter."

"Someone wrote *me?*" asked Philip.

"Actually, I believe it was for your housekeeper, Miss O'Shea." Mr. Trumble went over to the postal counter, transforming himself from shopkeeper to postmaster in seconds. He pulled out a letter from the slots and nodded. "It's for Miss O'Shea, all right. Would you like to take it on now?"

In his current mood, Philip cared less about the letter than he did the candy, but he went over to the counter. Fiona didn't hear from her family often and would be glad to receive it today rather than waiting until Mr. Jones delivered the post tomorrow. He stuck it in his history book and thanked the shopkeeper.

"You're welcome. You've quite a load of books there, Mr. Hollis."

"Oh, well," Philip shrugged. "Homework."

"He has his eyes set on the 'top student' trophy," Jeremiah volunteered, a sour ball bulging from one cheek. Philip shot him a glance as sour as the candy, but Mr. Trumble nodded approval.

"Nothing wrong with having high aspersions, lads."

———

"How did Captain Powell like your composition?" Julia asked after hearing Philip's prayers that night. He'd spent most of the evening studying in his room, emerging only for supper, until Julia had insisted that he go on to bed an hour early. Even now, as he lay looking up at her from his pillow with shadows under his eyes, he still protested that he wasn't sleepy.

"Not as much as he liked Laurel Phelps's," the boy grumbled.

"I'm so sorry." Julia smoothed some hair away from his forehead. "But surely you don't hold that against her . . . do you?"

For a second it looked as if he would cry, but then he shook his head. "I guess not. But it doesn't seem fair."

"What doesn't?"

"That I have to study so hard and it seems so easy for her."

Julia smoothed his hair again. "You're a bright young man, Philip. If you're doing the best you can, you shouldn't have to worry about what other people are accomplishing. You're going to make your way in this world too."

He was looking at her through half-closed lids now, making her think he'd drift into sleep any moment. But instead he asked, "Do you miss Father?"

The question caught her by surprise, and she answered with an evasive, "It's good that the lodging house keeps me so busy. I've hardly time to think sad thoughts."

"Oh."

"Are you lonesome for him, Philip?" she asked gently.

His eyelids dropped a fraction lower as he murmured. "I was always lonesome for him."

"What do you mean?"

"Didn't like to be with me."

Tears welled up in Julia's eyes. So this was what had been troubling Philip, causing the sadness that had lurked behind his smiles. He most likely was only telling her tonight because fatigue had weakened his defenses. She understood now that he'd kept his own grief to himself so as not to be a burden to her.

"Philip, your father loved you. He just didn't realize how little time he had left to show it."

"Yes?" the boy mumbled, barely moving his lips.

"Yes." Bending low to kiss his forehead, she assured him, "What father wouldn't love a son like you?"

Later that evening after the other servants had gone to bed, Fiona decided to have a look at the upstairs water closet before the lodgers left the hall for their bedchambers. It was Willa's responsibility to keep all the water closets stocked with soaps and fresh towels, but the chambermaid was becoming more and more forgetful as her courtship with Danny Toms, one of the squire's footmen, progressed. *Does love always addle the brain?* she wondered. She supposed she should be more stern with the maids, as Mr. Jensen had been back in London, but then the servants there had been notorious for sneaking as much idle time as possible when not directly in his sight. And the four maids under her charge were hard workers, even if Georgette did bump into things and Willa walked about in a daze.

Before going upstairs, she stopped inside the hall, where most of the lodgers were still assembled. "May I bring back anything from upstairs for you?" she asked.

"Oh, do be a love and fetch the *Lloyd's Weekly* from my bedside table on your way down, will you?" Mrs. Dearing asked. "I was just telling Miss Rawlins about an article on a typing machine that has been patented."

Replying that she would be happy to, Fiona was just about to turn toward the corridor and staircase when Mrs. Hyatt lifted a finger meekly. "Miss O'Shea?"

Fiona gave her a smile. "Is there something I can fetch for you, Mrs. Hyatt?"

"My reading spectacles, dear?"

"Of course."

She took to the stairs, looked in on the soap and towel situation and was pleased to see that Willa had taken care of both. She then retrieved the magazine and spectacles from the two bedchambers. In the corridor again, she met Mr. Clay coming out of his room, dressing gown over his arm, and a toothbrush and can of tooth powder in his hand. She had noticed as she went through the hall that he wasn't downstairs with the others, but Mrs. Kingston had told her this morning that Mr. Clay had been in another despondent mood since last night.

"Good evening, Miss O'Shea," he greeted her in a quiet voice.

"Good evening, Mr. Clay," Fiona returned. The sadness in his gray eyes so moved her that she found herself adding reassuringly,

"You'll feel better in a day or two, Mr. Clay."

"I suppose so."

"Well, good evening," she said again, taking a step toward the staircase.

"Miss O'Shea?"

His voice stopped her. Fiona turned. "Yes?"

He passed a hand over his haggard face. "Do you think we could walk together sometime? In the afternoon, perhaps?"

It was at that moment Fiona realized how much affection she felt for the man, affection she had effectively kept buried . . . and must continue to do so.

"I'm sorry, Mr. Clay. We can't."

He didn't appear surprised but seemed to struggle with the corners of his mouth to keep from frowning. "Is it because of my insanity?"

"Don't say that, Mr. Clay. You aren't insane."

"That's debatable."

She gave him a pleading look. "Mr. Clay . . ."

"Then because you're a housekeeper? That doesn't matter to me one whit, Miss O'Shea."

Sheer willpower kept Fiona from giving vent to the tears that threatened to form. *You have to tell him. And now.* "Mr. Clay," she said softly, in case her voice should drift downstairs.

"Yes?"

The words stuck in her throat like a wad of cotton. "I'm . . . married."

He looked as if he'd been slapped. "Married?"

"Yes, Mr. Clay. And now I have to go back downstairs."

Ambrose didn't take his eyes off Fiona until she reached the staircase landing and turned out of his sight. *Why are you surprised?* he asked himself while bitter irony burned in his chest. Although she'd always shown compassion toward him, there had still been a distancing on her part. He'd assumed it was because of his despondent moods or possibly because of her position in the household. He had even wondered if it was because he didn't profess to be a Christian, though he had been reading the Bible Mrs. Kingston had given him every night as of late.

And yet even with the wall that she kept between them, he hadn't been able to keep from thinking about her. The few minutes here and there that he was able to spend time in her company always made his day a little brighter. It was as if the two of them shared a certain kinship that he couldn't fully understand.

But none of that mattered now. Later, when he'd dressed for bed and pulled the covers over his shoulders, Ambrose wondered about the husband. Why wasn't he here with her? Was he in the army or something like that? He sighed, closed his eyes, and waited for the sleep he knew would evade him for hours. *I hope the man knows how fortunate he is,* he thought.

*P*hilip seemed his old self at breakfast Thursday morning, causing Julia to wonder if he even remembered talking with her about his father last night. "Do you think Jeremiah and Ben could stay over Saturday night?" he asked while he buttered his toast.

"Wouldn't Friday be better? We've church the next morning."

"But they could walk with us and join their families there. Please?"

"All right, then," Julia replied after thinking it over for a second. She was so relieved to see the sadness absent from his face that she thought she would have granted any request. "But I don't want the three of you sitting up in your room and whispering all night."

"We won't. Thank you, Mother!"

"May Helen stay with me too?" Aleda asked hopefully.

"I'm sorry, Aleda, but not in the same weekend," Julia told her with a consoling smile. She looked up at the round dial clock on the wall. "You've only five minutes until it's time to leave. Let's finish our breakfasts now, shall we?"

When the children were gone, she went to her bedroom writing table and drafted a cheque to Jensen. "Twenty pounds," she murmured while moving her pen. How wonderful it felt to be just a little closer to having that obligation paid off. She didn't know how her husband had been able to live with the specter of debt continually hanging over his head. Apparently he had managed not to think about it.

She penned a letter to the butler, and after tucking it into an envelope with the cheque, she rifled through the stack of correspondence and receipts in the top drawer. Who could have guessed that operating a lodging house would generate so much paperwork? *I should think about finding space for an office,* she told herself. There were a couple of storage rooms on the ground floor, too small to convert into bedchambers, that would possibly do.

A light knock at the door followed by Fiona's voice interrupted her musings. "Mrs. Hollis?"

"Come in, Fiona."

"Tending to business again?" the housekeeper asked, stepping into the room. She wore a dress Mrs. Hyatt had helped her construct of mauve calico that flattered her porcelain complexion and dark hair. But then, Fiona could wear a tent canvas and still look as though she'd stepped right out of the pages of a Jane Austen novel.

"I'm sending Jensen another twenty quid," Julia replied. "And a letter, of course."

"Please send him my greetings as well."

"I knew you would say that, so I took the liberty of doing so already."

Fiona smiled. "You've a caller in the hall, ma'am. It's Miss Phelps."

"Elizabeth Phelps?"

"She's returning your basket. She caught up with me as I was leaving Mr. Trumble's store and walked with me the rest of the way."

"That sounds encouraging. And how does she seem to you?"

"She seems a mite more cheerful than yesterday."

Rising from the writing table, Julia said, "Then I shouldn't keep her waiting."

The lodgers were having breakfast when she passed the dining room door, and sounds of amiable conversation drifted into the corridor. She found Miss Phelps seated in the wing chair closest to the fireplace, staring at the flames licking the coals.

"Miss Phelps?"

The girl got to her feet and smiled. She wore a dress of periwinkle-blue calico trimmed with straw-colored piping, and a small straw hat trimmed with blue ribbon. The sides of her hair were pulled back into a comb, but the back was left hanging loose in the latest American fashion. With her face clear of splotches, Miss Phelps looked even younger than she had yesterday.

"Mrs. Hollis. I was just enjoying your fireplace. I don't think I've ever seen one so huge."

"It has a lot of space to heat," Julia smiled back, walking over to offer her hand. "High ceilings are interesting, but hardly practical. And how are you this morning?"

"Very well, thank you," she replied.

The assurance seemed just a shade forced to Julia, but she supposed her perception could be influenced by the incident at the vicarage yesterday. "I'm so happy to hear that. Would you care to have a seat?"

"Are you sure I haven't come too early?"

"I'm an early riser myself." Julia motioned to the chair behind the girl. "Please."

"Thank you," Miss Phelps said again. They both settled into chairs, and after a space of awkward silence, the girl said, "We enjoyed the torte very much. I gave the basket to Miss O'Shea, by the way."

"I'm happy that you enjoyed it, but you didn't have to return the basket so soon."

"Oh, I didn't mind. I've been up for hours—or at least it seems so." Giving Julia a humorless smile, she said, "You know how difficult it is, getting used to a strange bed."

"Other than that, are you settling in comfortably in the vicarage?"

"Quite so. But it's rather . . . different, living in the country, isn't it?" She tucked a lose strand of blond hair behind her ear and looked over toward the north wall again. "Your fireplace heats so nicely."

"Thank you." Julia studied the profile in front of her—the uncertain expression, and the way she was knotting her fingers together. Could it be that the girl was trying to work up the courage to speak to her about something other than the efficiency of the fireplace? *It doesn't seem that she came here just to return that basket.*

"I do hope I'm not keeping you from anything important, Mrs. Hollis," the girl said, turning her face from the fireplace again.

"Making new friends is important too, isn't it?"

She relaxed, just a bit. "Yes—thank you."

Obviously this young woman was searching for a sympathetic ear—whether or not she was even aware of it herself. Judging from the tenderness and worry on Vicar Phelps's face when he spoke about his oldest daughter yesterday, Julia imagined that he was only too willing to listen to her. But there were some times when a woman felt the need to pour out her heart to another woman.

Fiona is better at such things than you are, Julia told herself, wondering if she should excuse herself long enough to ask the housekeeper to join them. What experience did she have with counseling young women? But Miss Phelps had had a perfect opportunity to speak with Fiona as they walked from *Trumbles* together. For some reason, probably because she had expressed sympathy to the girl in the vicarage garden yesterday, she was being sought out. She had to show the girl, without frightening her away, that she was willing to listen.

Julia glanced back at the doorway the lodgers would come through any second now. "Miss Phelps?" she said, and the girl turned to her.

"Yes?"

Give me the right words, Father. "I find it terribly difficult to sit and chat surrounded by so much space. There is a sitting room upstairs that's not quite so intimidating. Why don't we continue our visit up there?"

The brown eyes became hopeful, even as the corners of the girl's mouth quirked downward a bit. "It's selfish of me, keeping you from your duties."

"Nonsense." Rising, Julia motioned for the girl to do the same. "I'll send for some tea. Have you had breakfast?"

"Well no, I didn't have much of an appetite earlier . . ."

Julia linked arms with Miss Phelps and ushered her toward the corridor door. "You'll have one once you've caught sight of Mrs. Herrick's egg-in-a-nest."

"Egg-in-a-nest?"

"That's what we call them. She hollows out a slice of bread and fries an egg in the center—in butter of course."

Miss Phelps smiled sheepishly. "Perhaps I am feeling a little hungry now."

After Georgette was dispatched for a tray, Julia kept Miss Phelps occupied with small talk at opposite ends of the sofa while waiting. Whether she could be of any help to the girl was questionable, but at least she would have breakfast. She asked safe questions about the city of Cambridge and the girl's schooling, and answered questions about London. When the food arrived, the girl ate with considerable relish—she dabbed her mouth with a napkin afterward and gave Julia an embarrassed smile.

"I just haven't been able to eat anything since lunch yesterday." Her eyes widened at this slip of the tongue. "I didn't intend to deceive you about the torte, Mrs. Hollis. When I said 'we' enjoyed it, I was referring to my father and sister and the servants. But there is at least half left, and I certainly intend to have some later today. It looked delicious."

Julia took a sip of her tea to cover her smile at this outpouring of youthful insecurity, then said, "That's quite all right, Miss Phelps. One can enjoy the sight of a pastry as well as the taste."

The girl looked relieved. "Thank you for saying that."

During the brief silence that ensued, Julia wondered how she should go about asking if Miss Phelps were in need of a sympathetic ear. She certainly couldn't admit knowing about the young man who'd broken the girl's heart without possibly causing some friction between father and daughter.

Just when Julia was again considering asking Fiona to join them, the girl spoke.

"Mrs. Hollis," she began in a soft, distant voice, staring down at the creamery pitcher on the tea table in front of them. "I didn't come here just because of the basket. Father planned to return it himself until I asked him to allow me instead."

"Yes?"

"Yesterday . . . when you spoke to me in the garden. You seemed so kind and understanding."

With utmost calm, lest she cause the girl's boldness to crumble, Julia said, "Would it help to talk about what is troubling you, Miss Phelps?"

"I need to talk about it or I'll go mad, but . . . it has to do with losing someone I loved. Mrs. Paget told me that your husband passed away less than a year ago. Will it cause you pain to talk of such things, Mrs. Hollis?"

Julia smiled reassuringly. "I appreciate your consideration, but no. I'm sure it will cause me no pain."

"Thank you." The girl took in a deep breath. "My father tries to comfort me, but his opinion is greatly prejudiced against the young man involved, and so he doesn't care to hear anything about him." Turning sad eyes to Julia, she said, "But I can't talk about what's troubling me without talking about him. You see, I was practically engaged to a man in Cambridge—Jonathan Raleigh. He stopped seeing me after my father confronted him one night."

"Why did your father do such a thing?" Julia asked. She could probably venture an accurate guess from Vicar Phelps's previous label of rogue, but she was careful to keep her expression blank.

With flushed cheeks, Miss Phelps told how her beau had been spotted with a married woman of notorious reputation. "I was devastated when Father told me about it."

241

"Do you blame your father?"

"Blame Father?" She shook her head. "He had no choice. That much I understand."

"And what is it that you don't understand, Miss Phelps?" Julia probed gently.

"How he can expect me to pick myself up and carry on as if I had never been in love. Father feels that since Jonathan wronged me, I should be happy to banish him from my mind. But he was . . ." A sob broke her words, and she swallowed before continuing. "He was my whole life, Mrs. Hollis."

Julia nodded sadly and thought back to the days when she was sixteen and being courted by Philip. He was her first thought when she woke in the mornings and her last as she drifted into sleep at night. She only wore gowns in the colors he was fond of, and when he mentioned that she would look more sophisticated without fringe, she began having her hair fastened away from her forehead with combs. She even neglected her friends from childhood, choosing instead to stay at home in case Philip should pay a call. "So now you feel empty inside? And yet there is actual pain in your chest that won't go away."

The girl closed her eyes and nodded. "I just knew you would understand."

It was time to be brutally honest, Julia thought, no matter how much discomfort it would bring—for what good was experience if it couldn't be used to steer someone else around the pitfalls of life? *If only someone had warned me about my obsession with Philip before we married,* she thought. Oh, her parents had voiced misgivings about the age difference and the short length of their courtship, but no one had seemed concerned that she'd practically worshiped him.

The only thing she would not allow herself to discuss was how her husband had failed his family. She would honor his memory as much as possible for the children's sake. Propriety was the other reason— and the only one. Not too long ago she had discovered that the only feelings she had left for her late husband were of pity.

"Miss Phelps," she began tentatively, "I don't pretend to be the wisest woman in the world, but I have learned some things of late. You said that the young man . . . Mr. Raleigh?"

"Yes. Jonathan Raleigh."

Julia nodded. "You said that Mr. Raleigh had been your whole life while you were courting. I understand how you could have allowed yourself to feel that way—but it disturbs me to hear it."

"I know." The girl gave a resigned shrug. "He wasn't worthy of those feelings."

"It's not his worthiness I'm concerned with at present, though I'm glad you found him out before marrying him." She frowned, certain that she wasn't making herself clear. "Don't misunderstand. Worthiness is important too, of course."

"Of course," the girl nodded in agreement, though there seemed to be some incomprehension in her brown eyes.

How can I possibly explain this? Julia thought. Her mind possessed a clear picture of what she wanted to say, but in the process of forming just the right words, she felt like an insect slogging his way through treacle. *Help me, Father,* she prayed again silently. When the words became available, she began again. "I have learned through painful experience, Miss Phelps, that we should never allow another person to become our whole life."

Miss Phelps's eyes widened. "Surely you believe in love, Mrs. Hollis. You were married."

"Of course I do. A wife should love her husband completely, and a betrothed woman her fiancé. But I know now that there is a difference between loving someone and making an idol of him."

With faint umbrage in her voice, the girl said, "I don't quite think I made an idol of Jonathan."

"And yet you said he was your whole life at one time." Julia raised a questioning eyebrow. "Isn't idolatry when we put something or someone else ahead of God?"

While her visitor seemed to search for a reply, Julia went on. "Please don't think I'm judging you, Miss Phelps. I was the same way—in fact, you remind me very much of myself. But when we place someone up on a pedestal, it is impossible to see the flaws. And the flaws can turn out to be devastating, as you've found out yourself."

The girl gave her a curious look. "Did you make an idol of your husband?"

"I did," Julia admitted.

"And was he unfaithful to you?"

"No, Miss Phelps, not in the way Mr. Raleigh was unfaithful to you. But because of my children, I would rather not discuss the specifics of my marriage. Do you understand?"

"Yes." The girl withdrew a handkerchief from her reticule and wiped her eyes. "But I have clearly seen the flaws in Jonathan for weeks now. Why is it still so hard to forget him?"

"Because when we lose someone we've allowed to be our whole life, we find that we have very little left to sustain us. Not only have we distanced ourselves from God, but we've lost something of ourselves in the process. When my husband passed away, I discovered that my relationship with God had been a shallow one at best, and that I had no reservoir of inner strength to draw from."

Miss Phelps's face had assumed the splotches of yesterday, but aside from occasional dabs at her eyes with a handkerchief, she appeared fairly well composed. "Then how did you manage?"

"There was my children's welfare to consider, so I could ill afford to live in the past. And I began building a long neglected relationship with God." Julia reached out to touch the girl's hand. "It has been an interesting journey, Miss Phelps. And it can be so with you as well."

"I don't know if I can stop myself from thinking about the past."

"Then perhaps you should stop trying so hard. The past can eventually fade away on its own if you'll replace it with something else."

"I haven't children to care for, Mrs. Hollis, or a business to manage." She raised both hands in a helpless gesture. "I don't even know what I want to do with my life."

"But God will show you, if you'll allow Him."

"And in the meantime?"

Julia's thoughts carried her back to her first day in the *Larkspur* and the sense of accomplishment that had come over her when she discovered that her hands were indeed capable of worthy labor. "Why not immerse yourself in something else? Find something with which to occupy your time. You'll discover things about yourself you never knew. Then when another young man comes into your life, you can approach the relationship as a whole person."

"You sound like my father now," the girl sighed.

Julia had to smile. "I suppose all parents say the same things. But it must pain him terribly to see you hurting so."

"It does," she nodded. "And I'm afraid I've been rather a martyr lately."

"It isn't a crime to be young, Miss Phelps."

That seemed to comfort the girl, for a corner of her mouth lifted just a bit. Turning her face to Julia again, she said, "I appreciate your spending this time with me, Mrs. Hollis."

"Any time you'd like to talk."

"Would you mind calling me Elizabeth?"

Touched, Julia answered, "I would be honored, Elizabeth."

———

Friday afternoon, Captain Powell announced that Philip scored a near perfect mark on an open-text mathematics test—neglecting to show his computation on the last problem had cost him two points. Ben came in second, having miscalculated a boggling word problem, and Laurel Phelps third because, although she made the same word problem error as Ben, she also misplaced a decimal.

Even though the scores had already been announced, Philip did not relax in his desk until he held his test paper in his hand. He thought he would have kissed it had he been alone. It was tangible proof that he was still the head student. History and composition scores could often be subjective—after all, the headmaster was a human being, prone to be influenced by certain answers that struck his fancy. But mathematics was mathematics . . . one plus one had equaled two since the beginning of time and would continue to do so forever.

While pretending to study the clock on the wall to his right, he glanced over at Laurel. She was staring down at her paper with a look of stunned disbelief. *Serves her right for being so conceited,* he told himself but was immediately ashamed of the thought, for he had never heard her boast about the history examination or composition paper. And how could he fault her for wishing to perform her best at school? By dismissal time he was feeling so generous of spirit that he decided England would still rule the world if all of her students applied themselves as diligently to their studies as did Laurel Phelps and he.

But she's not going to take that trophy from me.

𝒮aturday afternoon found Ambrose in front of his open window, allowing the cool September breezes to bathe his face. This latest despondency had held him in a tight grip for the past three days, but he'd been able to sleep relatively well last night. He was beginning to feel the positive effects of the morning walks with Mrs. Kingston—the bouts with insomnia had lessened somewhat, and his appetite had increased. Steepling his fingers under his chin, he leaned forward to peer at the cottages lining Market Lane. How many villagers had happened to peek from their windows at the two of them last Saturday, he wondered, sloshing purposely up Market Lane through a torrential rainstorm?

"Can't we put it off until this afternoon?" Ambrose had asked the elderly woman when she showed up at his door bearing two umbrellas. "It's raining cats and dogs out there."

She simply gazed down at him with her commanding blue eyes. "Exceptions are dangerous, Mr. Clay. Give them a foothold and they turn into habits."

He could do nothing but follow, shaking his head at her iron will but not daring to argue further. The three miles had turned out to be quite invigorating, with the scent of rain pleasant about them. And today, his usual midafternoon lethargy seemed to be avoiding him, so much so that he decided not to nap in the hopes of sleeping even better tonight.

Bless you, Miss O'Shea, he thought sadly just as a soft knock sounded upon his door. He got up to answer it, hoping in a nice stroke of coincidence that she would be standing there. "It was all a joke," he imagined her saying with a little smile. "I'm not really married. Why do you think I'm called miss?"

But pessimism was another feature of his despondency, so that he was not surprised when it turned out to be Philip Hollis on the threshold instead. Yet his heart still managed to give a little lurch.

"Yes?" Ambrose said politely.

The boy gave him an apologetic look. "I hope I didn't wake you, Mr. Clay."

"Not at all, Mr. Hollis."

After a furtive glance in both directions down the corridor, he asked, "May I come in?"

"Certainly." Ambrose stepped back and watched the boy close the door. "What may I do for you?"

"I just wanted to tell you that my friends Ben and Jeremiah have gotten permission to stay over tonight."

"How nice."

Panic washed across the young face. "But today is Saturday. Don't you remember?"

"That today is Saturday?" As fond as Ambrose was of all the Hollis children, he was beginning to grow just a bit annoyed. Perhaps he would take that nap after all, he thought. "It was kind of you to remind me. Now, if you'll excuse me . . ."

The boy looked stunned but allowed himself to be shepherded back to the door. He turned back around before going through it, however.

"Mr. Clay, don't you remember the plans we made for tonight? The Keegans?"

"What are Keegans?"

"The Irish family. You wanted to help them."

"Indeed?" Ambrose ran a hand through his thick hair while his memory dredged up a conversation in the kitchen having to do with basket weavers. He blew out his cheeks when the plan he had outlined to Philip and his friend came back to him. "Sorry, my young friend, but I don't think I'm up to it today. Let's have a go at it next Saturday."

Disappointment lengthened the young face. "But Ben and Jeremiah probably won't be allowed to sleep over then. Please, Mr. Clay. It's such a splendid plan."

Ambrose sighed again and recalled the satisfaction he'd felt upon crafting his plan. Obviously it had been during one of his good days. Then he remembered how distressed Miss O'Shea had been over the torment the Irish family was having to endure. Even if he had no hope of a future with her, he liked the idea of doing something that would make her happy.

But just the thought of carrying out all of the steps necessary was exhausting. *You manage to walk three miles every morning,* he reminded himself. With a twisted little smile he thought, *Perhaps you should ask Mrs. Kingston along to motivate you.*

"Mr. Clay?"

The boy was watching him expectantly, and Ambrose found he had not the heart to disappoint him. "Very well," he said with a reluctant nod. "But we'll have to wait until the others are abed. Meet me in the courtyard at half past ten."

"Thank you, Mr. Clay!"

"You're welcome," Ambrose said, shooing his young visitor out of the room and closing the door behind him. As he settled back into his chair, he found himself smiling inexplicably. It *was* a splendid plan indeed.

By ten o'clock, Philip was so riddled with anticipation that he could do nothing but pace his room. "You'll wake your mother," Ben warned from the corner in which he sat cross-legged on the floor. A single candle on the bedside table gave the only light. They dared not use the lamp for fear of Philip's mother noticing the glow under the door, should she happen to wake and enter the corridor.

"Then let's go on outside," Philip said.

Jeremiah, seated on the foot of the bed, brightened. "Yes, let's. We can play hide-and-seek while we wait."

But both Philip and Ben shook their heads at that less-than-quiet idea. After creeping through the house, they sat outside on the benches and stared back at the courtyard door like cats watching a butcher's cart. The time seemed to stretch out forever, and Philip began to wonder if Mr. Clay had changed his mind. He was obviously going through one of his dark moods. Perhaps they would have to try again next week after all.

Just as he was opening his mouth to convey his fears to Ben and Jeremiah, the courtyard door opened and a figure emerged. He was clad in tights and a knee-length robe, and in the moonlight that shone through the oak branches, he appeared as gray as a monument from head to foot. As he approached the benches, the color took on a faint unearthly glow.

Even though Philip knew it to be Mr. Clay, he still jumped when the apparition spoke.

"Well, I'm glad to see so many stars out."

Jeremiah leapt to his feet and exclaimed, "You look just like a ghost!" before being hushed by Philip.

"Where did you find such a getup?" Ben asked with awe in his voice.

Mr. Clay brushed a fold from the hem of his robe. "I played the ghost of Hamlet's father in my earlier days onstage. I never could bring myself to discard a costume."

"What makes it glow?"

"Phosphorescent greasepaint on my skin, powder in my hair. And the fabric was soaked in a similar solution. You should see this under stage lights." An arm, swathed in gray cloth, lifted to point out in the direction of the darkened outbuildings.

Murder most foul, as in the best it is,
But this most foul, strange and unnatural . . .

The low mournful voice sent shivers down Philip's spine. *Please don't let the Sanders be there yet*, he prayed under his breath. This was too good to waste. "Shouldn't I fetch something to cover you? What if someone sees you on the way?"

Mr. Clay shook his head. "I don't care to get greasepaint on my cloak, and it's doubtful your mother would react too favorably to my ruining a blanket. I'll just have to duck behind a tree if we hear someone coming."

The four of them started up Market Lane and were fortunate that Gresham seemed to be settled in for the night. Patches of moonlight between trees illuminated Mr. Clay as he stepped into them. He took the occasions to glower menacingly at Philip and his friends, causing them to cover their mouths with their hands to keep from laughing out loud. As they passed one cottage, a small mongrel dog raced out of the yard to yip at them—it slunk away like a pariah when Jeremiah brandished a stick.

They slowed their steps and moved to the far side of Worton Lane while passing Ben's house. At the end of the lane, the Keegans' cottage windows were dark, and their wagon and two mules absent. Only the incessant chirping of crickets and an occasional low croak of a frog reminded them that they weren't the only living beings stirring on the property. Philip was relieved to see the shed still upright. It was obvious why the Sanders brothers had chosen this particular outbuilding to tip, because it was the only one not constructed of the same weathered stone as the cottage. Mr. Clay looked thoughtfully about the place, then motioned toward the birch Mr. Keegan had been sitting under the day Philip and his friends had brought the fish.

"Do you think the bridge can be seen from the top of that tree?"

Ben squinted back in the direction of the bridge and answered, "I would think so. And Jeremiah's the best climber."

Jeremiah looked pleased at the compliment, even while cuffing Philip on the arm for adding, "He's a regular ape, he is."

"Then climb on up there and keep a lookout," said Mr. Clay. "I don't care to crouch behind a bush all night, so give us a signal when you see the boys coming."

"What kind of signal?" asked Jeremiah.

"I don't know—any signal will do. An owl?"

"Try it out now before you climb," Ben suggested.

Jeremiah nodded and cupped his hands to his lips. "Who-o-?" he called, but the sound that issued was more human than fowl-like. After another attempt proved futile, he hung his head. "I'm sorry."

"That's all right, old chap," Mr. Clay assured him. "Just call down to us as softly as you can. I'm sure you won't be heard."

Jeremiah took a step toward Mr. Keegan's bench underneath the lowest limb. He turned before reaching it, though, his expression considerably brighter. "I can do a goldfinch."

After a puzzled ghostly look, Mr. Clay replied, "You mean, you can make the sound of a goldfinch?"

"Yes, sir." Cupping his hands on both sides of his mouth, he closed his eyes in concentration. Five or six seconds passed, then Jeremiah whistled a fluid, perfectly finchlike *switt-witt-witt-witt!*

Even the crickets joined in the awestruck silence that followed, which was finally broken by Ben. "That was perfect, Jeremiah."

"Better than perfect," Philip agreed.

"Well now, there you have it," Mr. Clay said to Jeremiah. "Let's scramble on up there, shall we?"

"Yes, sir!" The boy jumped up on Mr. Keegan's work bench, wrapped both arms around the closest limb, and was swallowed up by the dark foliage within seconds. Philip, Mr. Clay, and Ben took a few steps back and stared up, unable to see the boy, but hearing the rustle of leaves and branches.

Mr. Clay's ghostly face assumed a concerned expression. "I didn't realize it would be so dark up there. Do you think he'll be safe?"

"Don't worry," Ben assured him. "He could climb a tree blind-folded. It's the only way he has any privacy at home."

"He has two younger brothers," Philip explained.

Some five minutes later, Jeremiah called down in a low voice, "I can see the bridge now! The lane too."

"Can you see anyone coming?" Mr. Clay called back.

"Not yet."

"Good lad! Latch on to something sturdy and remember the signal."

With the lookout established, Mr. Clay stepped back over to the bench, brushed away the twigs that had fallen, and sat down. His shoulders sagged as he closed his eyes and propped his back against the tree trunk. Aware that Mr. Clay tired easily when the dark moods took hold of him, Philip felt a renewed appreciation for the effort the actor was putting forth tonight. He put a finger up to his lips when Ben looked on the verge of asking a question. They stood there and listened to the night sounds for what seemed like half an hour. Finally Ben could stand it no longer.

"He's asleep, Philip."

Philip shook his head. "He's just resting."

"He's snoring."

They both took a step closer. Sure enough, the actor's ghostly mouth was gaped open, and faint sonorous sounds were issuing forth. As if some inner signal warned him that he was being stared at, Mr. Clay opened his eyes.

"No visitors yet?" he yawned.

"Not yet." Philip sat down on the bench beside him. "Where should we hide?"

The actor pointed to a thick yew tree between the cottage and shed. "Plenty of room behind there. But you two need to find a place as well."

"We thought we'd be hiding with you," Ben told him hopefully.

"Sorry, son. I don't like to share a call." He looked around for a few seconds, then back up into the tree. "How about up there?"

"In the tree?" Philip asked, disappointed.

"You can settle on low limbs out of sight. Why, it's like having orchestra seats at the theatre."

There was nothing to do but agree, and Philip conceded in his mind that he would feel a mite safer not standing on the same ground as the Sanders brothers. "Should we climb up there now?"

251

"You'll have time when the signal comes," Mr. Clay replied. Seconds later a perfect *switt-witt-witt-witt!* drifted down from the tree. He stood and brushed his hands together. "Well then, shall we get a move on?"

Philip's heart rose to his throat. Now that the plan they had spent hours chuckling over was being set into motion, the seriousness of it sank in. At least two Sanders brothers were walking the dark lane, every second bringing them closer. If anything went wrong, the bullies would dedicate themselves to hunting them out. Mr. Clay they would leave alone simply because he was an adult, but he and Ben and Jeremiah would have to make sure they never went anywhere unaccompanied for the rest of their lives.

"Philip?" Mr. Clay was looking at him with an odd expression. "Are you all right?"

Philip nodded and realized that Ben was already pulling himself up into the tree. He jumped up on the bench and waited his turn. When he had secured himself next to Ben on a stout limb well into the tree, he looked down and noticed that Mr. Clay was no longer standing underneath. A shiver ran through him. Peering up into the branches overhead, he could see no sign of Jeremiah either. He was thankful that Ben was there beside him. The suspense would be unbearable if he'd had to wait alone. It was the perfect hiding place, however, for the shed stood only about eight feet away.

"I hear them coming!" Ben whispered. It was obvious from the strain in his voice that he was just as nervous. Philip held his breath and listened—the sound of muffled conversation met his ears. He gave Ben a solemn nod.

Soon footsteps rustled the grass behind them. Philip didn't dare turn to watch for fear of making a noise and drawing attention to Ben and himself. The conversation, just a bit louder now, was jovial and unsuspecting. Finally two shapes came into view on Philip's left. Ben, farthest out on the branch, moved his head back a bit to give him a better view.

The two on the ground didn't go straight for the shed but went over to the cottage and peered in the darkened windows. They were close enough now to be told apart. Fernie chuckled softly at some private joke, mumbled something, and Oram joined in. Then both turned toward the shed. Philip held his breath again and watched the yew tree. The actor had managed to conceal himself totally, for not a scrap of luminous gray was visible. In fact, Oram and Fernie passed right by the tree with not even a glance in that direction. Silently they went around to the side of the shed—they'd had weeks of experience, so no verbal collaboration was necessary. They braced their shoulders against the wall and grunted with the exertion of pushing.

Pulse racing, Philip looked over at the tree again. "Come on, Mr. Clay!" he urged under his breath, but he saw no movement in that direction. A mental picture flashed into his head of the actor leaning back against the tree with his eyes closed and mouth gaping. Had he fallen asleep in his hiding place?

"Where is he?" Ben whispered.

"I don't know."

They watched the shed begin to rise and tilt. When the side was about two feet off the ground, first Oram, then Fernie dropped down to catch the soleplate with both hands. Their grunts grew louder as the gap between building and ground widened. One mighty heave and it would be upon its side, but where was Mr. Clay?

And then it happened. A ghostly gray figure stepped from the back of the shed to stand behind the Sanders brothers. Philip motioned to Ben and held his breath while waiting for Mr. Clay to growl in some macabre manner, but the actor simply tapped Oram's back.

"Huh?" said Oram, peering over his shoulder as much as was possible with a building in his hands.

"I say there . . . could you use some help?"

"AH-H-H!" Oram screamed and jumped back, and with only one person left holding the shed, it thudded to the ground. The cry that came from Fernie's lips was more out of pain than fright, but his brother hadn't noticed, for Oram had already passed the tree on his way out of the yard.

"It's on my foot!" Fernie wailed, his cheek against the wall of the shed. Both arms were spread open against the side, as if he would press himself through the wood if humanly possible.

"Hold on—I'll lift it," Mr. Clay told him and immediately began pushing at the wall with his shoulder. A second later, Fernie was loose. He took one look at his rescuer, let out a yelp of terror, and followed his brother's tracks—his fleeing was made difficult by a severe limp, but he made admirable distance nonetheless.

"I'm terribly sorry!" Mr. Clay called out, following across the yard in a brisk pace. "Won't you allow me to assist you home?"

Fernie's limping gait accelerated, and soon he was gone. The plot had worked, but it was a somber trio that climbed down the tree.

"I didn't think his brother would let go of the building like that," the actor said regretfully when the boys caught up with him in the lane.

"It's not your fault, Mr. Clay," said Ben. "They shouldn't have been over here causing mischief."

"I know," Mr. Clay sighed half-heartedly, then started for home. Exchanging worried glances with his two friends, Philip hurried over to Mr. Clay's side. A lantern now illuminated a window of the Hopper family's cottage, but Philip was too preoccupied with the events of the night to give it more than a passing glance as they hurried home.

By the time the *Larkspur* came into view, silhouetted against the night sky, Philip felt he had to say something. He touched Mr. Clay's sleeve. "Fernie's foot can't be too bad if he was able to run like that."

"You think so?"

"Yes, of course."

Ben and Jeremiah nodded agreement as well. "And you did give them both a good scare," Ben said admiringly.

"I did at that," the actor said, then shrugged. "Let's just hope the lesson sticks. I'll not be frightening children in this getup again."

*T*he *Larkspur*'s lodgers attended Sunday services at Saint Jude's faithfully, save Mr. Clay, who stayed home, and Mrs. Dearing, who accompanied the Herricks to the Baptist chapel. Though they often strolled to church with Julia, her children, and servants, they chose to occupy a pew farther back toward the vestibule.

Julia glanced back at the lodgers present while worshipers filled the nave that morning. She was dismayed to see that Mrs. Kingston was not seated with the others but was instead across the aisle with Mrs. Perkins, another widow in her charity sewing group. Was Mrs. Kingston still angry at Mrs. Hyatt over the herb incident on the Anwyl? But there seemed to be no spite on the elderly woman's face as she listened to the organ strains of the *Gloria Patri* with closed eyes. Could it be that Mrs. Kingston had given up on Mr. Durwin after all?

Movement out the corner of her eye caught her attention several seconds later. Elizabeth Phelps was walking up the aisle to the first pew—she sent a quick smile to Julia. Beside her was a younger girl with the same blond hair visible beneath the brim of a velvet and lace hat—obviously her sister, Laurel. Though she was in Philip's standard at school, the younger girl did not glance at him as she passed. Not that Philip would have noticed if she had. He was seated between Grace and Fiona with eyes drooping. Julia had had to wake him and his friends twice this morning, and all three had sat at the breakfast table in a lethargic stupor.

They must have whispered all night, Julia thought, remembering how it was when she used to spend the night with friends as a child. *I shouldn't have allowed night company on a Saturday.* No doubt Ben and Jeremiah, seated with their families, were having the same trouble staying upright in their pews.

Reverend Phelps's first sermon at Saint Jude's centered around the parable of the workers in the vineyard from Saint Matthew. While he seemed more reserved than Reverend Wilson, the new vicar projected an attitude of caring that seemed to surprise the parishioners who'd not yet met him. In fact, after the service Mrs. Pool from the *Bow and Fiddle* murmured to Julia as they moved down the aisle toward the door, "He ain't so snooty as you'd think someone from—" Remembering to whom she was speaking, she paled a little and did not add the obvious "from the city," substituting instead, "from the north." Julia smiled agreement and did not point out that Cambridge lay southeast of Gresham.

Vicar Phelps stood just outside the door, bidding the exiting congregation farewell and thanking those who welcomed him to Gresham. His eyes were warm as he caught Julia's hand. "Thank you, Mrs. Hollis."

He did not elaborate because of the people about, but Julia knew instinctively that he was referring to her chat with Elizabeth. *I hope that means she's feeling better.*

"You're welcome, Vicar Phelps," she replied, then moved on so as not to monopolize his time at the door. Mrs. Rhodes motioned Fiona and her aside while the children visited with friends.

"I just want to warn you there seems to be another ghost rumor floating about," Mrs. Rhodes said, her moss-green eyes anxious. "And I did hear Jake Pitt's name mentioned."

Julia put a hand up to her throat. "Please say you're joking."

"I'm afraid not."

"What happened?" asked Fiona, distress evident on her face as well.

Mrs. Rhodes nodded toward a small circle of women engaged in conversation several feet away. "Mrs. Hopper there," she said, indicating a middle-aged woman in brown poplin. "She lives on Worton Lane. It seems that her husband heard a ruckus sometime after midnight. He went to a window and saw a ghost. It gave him such a fright that they both dashed to their larder and hid for a couple of hours afterward."

"A ghost?" Julia didn't know what to think. "Obviously they were mistaken."

"Of course they were. But the Hoppers have always lived rather quiet lives here. It's not like them to fabricate something like this for attention."

"Then what do you think happened?"

"Well, she said her husband lit a lamp before going to the window, so he couldn't have seen very well out into the darkness. It could have been an owl."

"Well, there you have it," said Fiona, letting out a relieved sigh. "Some owls can grow quite large, can't they?"

"They can. And when we're afraid, things always look larger than life. But what's even more perplexing is that Mr. Hopper claims to have spotted three boys as well."

"With the ghost?" asked Julia. "And at the same time?"

"That's what his wife says. And they seemed to be in no peril from their companion."

Three boys . . . Julia thought, but then dismissed the idea. Philip's room was at the end of the family corridor. She would surely have heard them had they stirred from the room, and anyway, what reason would they have had to walk about town at night? *And with a ghost?* She shook her head. She wasn't acquainted with the Hoppers other than recognizing their faces. It crossed her mind to wonder if Mr. Hopper had consumed any alcoholic beverage last night. Immediately she was ashamed for judging someone she didn't know without just cause.

"Why would anyone presume this vision to be Jake Pitt?" she asked. "Isn't Jake supposed to haunt the *Larkspur* exclusively?"

"I suppose he's a convenient source of blame," Mrs. Rhodes shrugged. "He's Gresham's only ghost, you know. But I didn't want you to be taken by surprise."

"And I appreciate that," Julia said, easing into a smile. "You've been a good friend to us."

"Ah, well . . . so have you. And now I shall excuse myself and see about my husband at home."

"I hope Dr. Rhodes isn't ill," said Fiona.

He was a faithful churchgoer, and Julia felt a little embarrassed that she was just now noticing his absence.

"Not at all. But he was up most of the night delivering the Givens baby across the river—a healthy boy, by the way. And he no sooner arrived at home in the wee hours of the morning when he was called back out across the river to see about a broken foot." She clucked her tongue. "Everyone looks down on the Sanders boys, but at least one seems to have his heart in the right place. The poor lad found himself unable to sleep early this morning and decided to have a head start on the chores. He was carrying a full pail of water to a trough when it fell on his foot."

Julia expressed sympathy for the boy while trying to place the name. *Sanders?*

Mrs. Rhodes left then, sending a wave after she'd gone a few steps. Returning the wave, Julia sensed someone's eyes upon her and turned to see Elizabeth Phelps approaching from the front of the church. Quietly, Fiona excused herself, saying she would accompany Mrs. Kingston home.

"Mrs. Hollis," Elizabeth said. "Have you a minute?"

"Of course," Julia smiled, taking the girl's hand. "I believe everyone was impressed with your father's sermon."

There were still faint circles under the brown eyes, but the expression in them was refreshingly calmer than it had been just two days ago. "I could tell Father was worried about it. He doesn't want people to think he's flaunting his education, but at the same time he doesn't want to give less than his best."

"And how are you, Elizabeth?"

The girl smiled at this use of her given name. "Better, Mrs. Hollis, though to be truthful, Jonathan still occupies a great deal of my thoughts. But I told Father I would go with him to make his calls starting Monday. So you see, I'm taking your advice about finding something to keep myself busy."

"I'm so glad. And I hope you'll come to visit me again soon."

Giving Julia a quick embrace, Elizabeth said, "I would like that very much."

Aleda appeared at Julia's side. "This is my oldest daughter, Aleda," she said to the vicar's daughter. "And this is Miss Phelps."

"Why, my sister, Laurel, mentioned you yesterday," Elizabeth said to the girl. "She said you play the piano quite well."

"She did?" Aleda beamed.

"I took lessons for five years, but I still find myself disheartened if there are too many sharps or flats." They chatted about music for a minute longer, then Elizabeth bade them good-day and joined her father at the church door. When she was gone, Aleda turned to Julia with a worried expression.

"Helen says some people said they saw the ghost last night."

"Do you believe them?"

The girl's forehead creased. "Why no, Mother."

"Are you sure? Because if it has you worried . . ."

258

"I'm not worried about the ghost being real. I just wonder if people blame us, since everyone thinks he lives in our house."

The thought had crossed Julia's mind, but she couldn't burden her daughter by admitting it. Putting an arm across her shoulders, Julia drew her close. "I know it's difficult, but the best thing to do is change the subject whenever anyone mentions anything about it."

"Do you think that will stop them from talking?"

"To be honest, I doubt it. But they'll get the message eventually that it's not something you wish to discuss. And I'm sure the talk will fade away like it did last time."

"I hope so." As they ambled on together to gather the rest of the family, Aleda said, "Miss Phelps is nice, isn't she?"

"Yes, she is," Julia said.

"Why was she hugging you when I came up?"

"Oh, I gave her some advice recently and she was grateful."

"Advice about what?"

Julia looked at her sideways and raised an eyebrow. "Curious, aren't we?"

"I'm going to be a writer," Aleda answered. "Miss Rawlins says they're supposed to be curious. And you don't have to worry about my telling anyone. Writers are supposed to keep secrets too."

"Well, I trust your discretion, but I'm afraid I can't betray a confidence. You understand that, don't you?"

The narrow shoulders shrugged. "It must have been about love, then."

"Why do you say that?"

"Oh, most problems seem to be about love," she said with a deep sigh. "It seems to work better in stories than in real life." She shook her head before Julia could ask the question her mind was framing.

"I haven't been reading Miss Rawlins' books, Mother."

Julia suppressed a smile and glanced over at Mrs. Hyatt and Mr. Durwin, lost in conversation as they strolled slowly across the green. She felt a slight pang for the way they enjoyed each other's companionship. "Oh, I don't know. Sometimes it works out quite well."

"Did you hear what everybody's saying?" Philip asked Ben and Jeremiah in the school yard Monday morning as soon as he was out of earshot of his sisters.

Jeremiah looked over his shoulder and broke out into a grin. "Jake Pitt."

"It's not funny, Jeremiah. My mother asked me if I knew anything about it."

"She did?" asked Ben, his blue eyes growing wide. "What did you tell her?"

"I had to lie." Philip mashed down on a clod of dirt with the toe of his shoe and wondered if his conscience could hurt any worse than it had for the past twenty-four hours. Lying to one's mother was especially wrong, in his opinion, because it combined two major sins . . . lying, and dishonoring a parent. He didn't even blame God for being displeased with him at the moment, but in an effort to ease his aching conscience, he added, "Partially, I mean."

"How do you tell part of a lie?"

"I told her that I didn't know anything about three boys walking around with a ghost Saturday night."

"But we *did* walk around with—" Jeremiah began until his brown eyes lit with understanding. "Oh, but Mr. Clay wasn't a real ghost. So you told the truth, then."

Philip shook his head. "The truth doesn't upset your stomach. I almost told her the whole thing this morning."

"You can't do that!" Ben exclaimed, then glanced at the boys playing marbles just a few feet away and lowered his voice. "Fernie Sanders' foot is broken. Did you know that?"

"No—how did you find out?"

"Dr. Rhodes' cook has a brother who works for my father. She told him that one of the Sanders boys broke two bones in his foot."

"They're going to kill us," Jeremiah said, peering fearfully out toward the green, as if he expected to see an army of Sanders materialize as he spoke.

"Not if they never find out," Ben reassured him. To Philip, he said, "You can't *ever* tell your mother, because then she'll feel obliged to let our parents know. I don't mind getting a strapping from my father, but the more people who hear about it, the greater chance it has of reaching the Sanders' ears."

"We can't tell anybody," Jeremiah agreed. "Ever."

Miss Hillock came to the steps to ring the school bell, bringing an end to the conversation. Later, Philip was in the middle of penning neat rows of *It is better to light one candle than to curse the darkness* in his copybook when he remembered Mr. Clay. The actor had felt wretched about causing the shed to drop on Fernie's foot. If he found out that the foot was broken, who knew what he would do? Perhaps even march over to the Sanders and apologize! Even if Mr. Clay claimed sole responsibility for the act—which would likely be the case—word was all over Gresham that three boys were involved as well. It wouldn't take a genius to figure out the identity of the three.

But Mr. Clay seldom left the house save his morning walks with Mrs. Kingston. And everyone who knew him tended to shield him from unpleasant news, so there was still a chance. *Oh, Lord, please don't let him find out,* Philip prayed, then shuddered at his nerve for trying to involve God in his own misdeeds.

As the school day moved on with leaden feet, Philip didn't even think of his academic rivalry with Laurel Phelps. When lightning could possibly come out of the sky and strike him on his way home, the matter of a trophy seemed small indeed.

———

"I don't know. Maybe they just don't like the water around the bridge anymore," Jeremiah said that Saturday as the three boys carried their rods and tackle along the Bryce toward their second-favorite fishing spot in the north edge of Gipsy Woods.

"It's the same water," Philip told him. "Why would that matter?"

"Well, we breathe the same air," said Ben. "But *we* like some places more than others."

There was no arguing that logic, so Philip switched his fishing pole to his other shoulder and said, "All I know is . . . I told Mrs. Herrick I'd try for a string of perch today." And he hoped that by bringing home a string of fish and thereby saving his mother some money he could lessen the guilt he'd carried around all week. Perhaps God would even look down from heaven and form the opinion that a boy who provided food for his family should be absolved just this once.

"What are you looking at?" Ben asked Jeremiah, nudging Philip out of his reverie.

Jeremiah pointed past the steeple of Saint Jude's to a place up the river just north of the vicarage. "Isn't that the vicar?"

Philip could only see willow trees along the bank. "How can you tell?"

"I saw him walk from the vicarage."

They indeed came upon the sight of Vicar Phelps among the willows of the bank, staring out upon the water with both hands in his pockets. He appeared to be deep in thought but turned to greet them as they drew closer.

"Good morning, young men."

"Good mornin'," they chorused in return. Ben, the only one wearing a cap, reached up for it, but the vicar shook his head.

"That isn't necessary, thank you. Going fishing, eh?" Before anyone could reply to this obvious question, the vicar's smile broadened. "But of course you are, aren't you? You aren't exactly outfitted for cricket."

Philip, unable to resist the opportunity for a quip, darted a hand into his tackle basket and brought out the jar of chirping insects he'd caught behind the stables just this morning. "We're outfitted *with* cricket, sir."

The effect upon the minister was immediate, for he gave a great laugh that seemed to come from somewhere deep in his chest. Caught up in the moment, the three boys joined in.

"That's a good one," Vicar Phelps said, wiping his eyes when the laughter had subsided into grins.

In spite of his wish that Laurel Phelps had never enrolled at Gresham School, Philip's opinion of her father increased threefold during that exchange of levity. He had learned that some adults appreciated humor more than others. Miss Rawlins, as pleasant as she was, always seemed to assume a blank expression whenever Mr. Clay said something witty that left everyone else laughing.

"Forgive me for asking, because your faces do look familiar to me from Sunday, but what are your names?" Vicar Phelps was saying, and it seemed from the expression in his hazel eyes that he wasn't just being polite. After Ben made introductions, the man nodded. "And I'm keeping you from your fishing, aren't I? No doubt your families will be pleased to have fish on the platter this evening."

"We hope so, sir," said Jeremiah.

Ben nodded. "But we've spent an hour at the bridge with barely a nibble."

"We're especially hoping for some perch today," was Philip's comment.

"And with crickets, you say? Do you catch many perch with them, ordinarily?"

"Sometimes." Ben cocked his head at the vicar, but respectfully so. "You know how to fish, Vicar Phelps?"

"Not when I was young like yourselves. But one of my parishioners in Cambridge taught me to fish the backs—the River Cam. It flows behind the colleges, you see. We had trouble bringing in perch as well, until someone lent me a very helpful book."

"A book?" Jeremiah blinked, looking a bit crestfallen. "There's a *book* about fishing?"

The vicar smiled again. "*The Compleat Angler,* by Isaak Walton. It's actually quite popular, I've since discovered. I wish I had a copy to show you."

"What does it say about perch?" Philip asked, intrigued.

"Minnows."

"Minnows?" Ben and Jeremiah said at the same time.

"They work like a charm, most of the time. Keep your crickets for the graylings, and trout, mind you . . . but why don't you catch up some minnows as well?"

They thanked him, assuring him that they would heed his advice. He waved farewell and started for the vicarage. When he was out of earshot, Ben said, "Do you think we should have asked him to come along?"

Philip looked at him askew. "Ask the vicar?"

"Well, why not? You could tell he's fond of fishing."

"Oh, I don't know. I'm sure he's terribly busy." He had other thoughts on the matter too but did not care to share them. As likable as the vicar appeared to be, he was still Laurel Phelps's father. Let Laurel find out, as she would, that he'd fished with her father, and she would assume that her attempts to usurp his position as head of the class were just a trivial matter. Perhaps that would be so if he hadn't already imagined a certain trophy occupying a place of honor on the chimneypiece in the *Larkspur*'s hall.

*W*ant t'see the pig, vicar?" Mr. Towly asked around the clay pipe stuck in the center of his stubbled cheeks. He owned a small dairy farm to the far east of Gresham, past the manor house and along the edge of Gipsy Woods. Like the other dairy farmers in the village, he sold most of his herd's output to the cheese factory.

"Why, yes . . . thank you," Andrew replied, aware of the honor being bestowed upon him. He'd learned much about the rural folk of his parish during the three weeks since he'd moved his family here. Even the poorest cottage usually had a sty in the backyard, and the enclosed animal was treated as an important member of the family. Children on their way home from school filled their lunch pails with sow thistle and dandelions to supplement the pig's diet of kitchen scraps, and they often roamed along the hedgerows on wet evenings collecting snails for the animal's supper. In late autumn, the creature repaid such solicitous treatment by providing his keepers with bacon, hams, sausages, lard, and other parts . . . "nothing wasted except the squeal" was a saying Andrew had heard more than once.

He got up from his rush-bottomed chair and followed the man from the cottage, leaving Elizabeth listening intently as Mrs. Towly explained how to braid a rag rug. The pig, brown like its owner's thatched roof, was one of the largest he'd seen yet. Andrew made sure to comment on his great size, which brought a flush of pleasure to his host's stubbled cheeks.

"The little ones—they lets him run loose in the woods every so often." A faint look of alarm crossed the man's face. "Ye ain't gonter tell the squire, are ye?"

"Why, no," Andrew replied. He had become aware that Squire Bartley owned most of the land in Gresham, including Gipsy Woods, but surely he would have no objection to a pig rooting about in the shrubs for sloes and snails.

And if he did, well, Andrew was a guest in the Towlys' home, bound under the same constraints of civility as any other guest. And he'd learned years ago to save most of his spiritual ammunition for the deadly sins that dishonored God and destroyed lives. But in that Mr. Towly's confession had involved him in the matter, Andrew did feel compelled by conscience to add, "Just remember, Mr. Towly, there are no secrets from God."

Later, as Rusty, the blue roan from the vicarage stable, pulled the trap bearing Andrew and his daughter down the tree-shaded Church Lane, he thought about how Elizabeth had kept her word about accompanying him on his calls. What made him especially grateful was that he was aware the visits bored her, no matter how adept she was at pretending interest in such things as rag rugs.

Immerse yourself in something else, Mrs. Hollis, the owner of the lodging house, had advised her. Good counsel it was, for Elizabeth had a greater chance of finding something that interested her while out making calls than by sitting at home absorbed in memories.

The *Larkspur* happened to come into view on his right. Had he ever thanked Mrs. Hollis, he wondered? He certainly had intended to, but it was hard to recall what he said to people at the door of the church. And he'd not yet made a call at the lodging house.

Tomorrow, he told himself. "I appreciate you coming with me, Elizabeth," he said to his daughter. "I find it much less intimidating to have someone at my side when I knock on a door."

His daughter drew her wool shawl closer about her shoulders, then looked askew at him. It was good to see a trace of her old humor returning, even though the haunted expression in her eyes still cropped up often.

"I never knew making calls intimidated you."

"They never have before. Well, not counting my earlier days in the ministry. But I still feel a bit out of place here."

"Like a fish out of water?"

"Yes," Andrew said, smiling. "Or like a piano in the pantry."

She thought for a second. "Like a mouse in the soup."

"Good one." Now he had to think. "Like a cabbage in a rose garden."

"How about like a deck of cards in a church pew?" Elizabeth of-

265

fered, but then put a quick hand up to her mouth. "Was that sacrilegious?"

"Why, I don't think so," Andrew told her. "Don't you think God has a sense of humor?"

"I never thought about that."

"Well, He made *me*, didn't He?"

"Papa!" she exclaimed, giving him an indulgent smile while at the same time shaking her head in a reproving manner. "You're quite handsome."

"Now you're going to make me vain."

They rode in silence for a while, Andrew greatly encouraged by the lightness of their exchange. *Why, in another week or so she won't even remember his name.*

"Do you regret moving us here?"

Andrew's shoulders fell slightly at the flatness of her voice. "Moving *us*," she had said, not even looking at him. Was there accusation in her tone, or was he just extra sensitive to her moods lately?

"No regrets, Beth," he said in answer to her question. Her face was still turned toward the lane ahead, but he caught the tremble of her lip. *How can she be laughing one minute and ready to weep the next?*

"I'm trying, Father."

Patience, Andrew reminded himself. "I know that. And I do appreciate it." Taking a hand from the rein, he touched her cheek lightly. "You're going to discover one day that you're stronger than you think, Elizabeth Phelps." At least he prayed that would happen.

Their last morning call would be to the Burrell cottage, south of the village on Short Lane. Mr. Burrell had been a skilled carpenter at one time, so said Reverend Wilson's helpful notebook. But the bottle had ruined him, and now he kept himself supplied with drink by taking on odd jobs here and there. By poaching too, it was rumored. His poor wife kept their seven children clothed and fed by working at the cheese factory and shame-facedly accepting parish assistance when the rent could not be met.

Andrew had paid a call one evening last week, when Mrs. Burrell was home and her husband out, to reassure the overworked woman that he would continue to see about her family, as his predecessor had done. He now wanted to meet the man face-to-face. With the memory of Mrs. Burrell crying on his shoulder still fresh in his mind, he felt compelled to admonish the man for abandoning his role as provider and nurturer of his family. Likely it would bring no change.

Vicar Wilson had made heroic attempts at the same for years . . . but he had to try.

He had almost decided to make this call at a time when Elizabeth wasn't along. Drunkards were not pretty sights. But during his morning prayers, a strong impression came over him that she should be with him.

It was obvious that Jonathan Raleigh still occupied a great deal of her thoughts. She'd led too sheltered a life and could not grasp the severity of what happens to a wife when a husband hands his life over to the devil. Oh, he'd cited examples to her—keeping the names private—of sad cases he'd seen during his years in the ministry, but the lessons that made the deepest impressions were those that could be experienced firsthand.

He pulled Rusty to a halt in front of the Burrell cottage—a hovel, actually, of wattle and daub, showing numerous chinks and cracks. The first thing that caught Andrew's eye was a small child of about three trying to lift the end of a large stick.

"Dear me, no!" Elizabeth exclaimed, quickly moving herself out of the trap. Andrew's heart skipped a beat with the realization that the stick was an ax. He dropped the reins and jumped out on his side, but his daughter reached the child first.

"Here now, you mustn't play with that," she was saying, prying the little fingers away from the handle. The child gaped up at her with eyes that seemed extraordinarily blue in a small face begrimed with dirt. Her light brown curls were matted and uncombed, her gown— likely a sleeping garment—dirty, and there were no shoes on her feet despite the briskness of the early October air.

"Tha's ack," the child said and pointed to the ax that now lay on the ground.

"Yes, but it's dangerous." Elizabeth shook her head. "It'll hurt you."

"Is hot?"

"Yes, hot."

The child nodded somberly. "Hot."

Elizabeth looked up at Andrew, her eyes tearing. "How can a mother . . . ?"

Giving her a sad smile, he said, "The mother leaves for work before the sun comes up."

Now his daughter's eyes shot to the cottage. "Who watches the child?"

Andrew recalled what had been written in Vicar Wilson's note-book and what he had seen for himself last week. "One or another of the older children stays home from school when the father's not around," he replied. His lips tightened at the sight of the door hanging crookedly on its hinges. "But I suppose he's here today."

The inside was as desperate as the outside—a packed earth floor and mismatched pieces of furniture that had apparently been castoffs. Still, there were heart-rending attempts at beauty—hand-sewn curtains of cheap but colorful gingham in the windows and some blue mist flowers in a jar at the center of the crude trestle table. A partially open curtain sagging from a rope formed the only other room. The foot of a rusty iron bedstead was visible, and a grating sound came from that direction. It was snoring, Andrew realized. *At eleven in the morning!*

He was on his way across the room when movement caught his eye. In a wooden box on the floor, obviously a makeshift crib, a child lay on a folded blanket. Andrew walked over to it and crouched down. The child appeared to be a boy, quite younger than his sister, and was so still that Andrew worried that he might not be breathing. Gently, he touched a soft cheek and let out a relieved breath when he stirred slightly.

Surely babies don't sleep this late, he thought. And while he couldn't recall most of the particulars of his daughters' infancy, he thought it was a bit too early for a nap.

"What's wrong?" asked Elizabeth, standing behind him. She still had the other child in hand.

"I'm not sure." He saw a glint of metal, partially hidden by a fold in the blanket, and picked it up. It was a tin spoon. "This is an odd thing to put in a child's bed."

"Perhaps he's ill. There is some medicine out."

He peered up at her over his left shoulder. "Where?"

"Right beside you," she said, pointing. "The cupboard."

Andrew turned his head to the right, then got to his feet immediately. Against the wall sat a massive old cupboard with one door wide open, and on its ledge was an uncorked amber bottle. He picked it up and sniffed. *Gin!* While setting it back on the ledge, the side of his hand brushed against something grainy. It was sugar, he realized, and it had come from a crock on the upper shelf, exposed by the open door.

"What is it, Father?" asked Elizabeth. The child at her side murmured something unintelligible and pointed to the curtain, apparently thinking she'd been asked the location of her own father.

"I hate to say out loud what I'm thinking." Andrew still held the spoon in his left hand—he brought it up to his nose and sniffed. The odor of gin still clung to the metal. "Why, that good-for-nothing!" he muttered, turning on his heel.

"Father?"

There was alarm in his daughter's voice, but Andrew was not in the state of mind to answer. He went through the open space in the curtain and over to the sunken bed where its occupant lay on his shirtless back, oblivious to the goings-on in his own cottage. Mr. Randy Burrell was a bull of a man, with greasy brown hair and a mustache as thick as a paintbrush curling over his upper lip. Stained teeth looked like a row of crooked headstones in the gaping mouth, from which came drafts of foul breath. Andrew grabbed a shoulder and shook him roughly.

"Mr. Burrell!"

A snort, and then "ugh?" came from the reclining figure.

"Wake up, Mr. Burrell!"

This time the man opened both bloodshot eyes, blinked several times, then raised his head to squint at Andrew. "Who are you?" he demanded.

Andrew returned his scowl threefold. "I'm Andrew Phelps, the new vicar. Now, get out of that bed and put on a shirt. I want to talk to you."

But Mr. Burrell's eyes glazed over, and his head fell back to the pillow. Andrew watched in stunned fury as the mouth gaped open and snoring sounds resumed. He seized the bare shoulder again, this time allowing his fingers to dig into the flesh.

"Get out of bed, Mr. Burrell."

"Go 'way," the man grumbled.

"You will abandon that bed immediately, Mr. Burrell, or I shall thrash you on the spot."

"Father!" Elizabeth exclaimed, now standing wide-eyed in the gap of the curtain.

In his anger he had forgotten that she was in the cottage, and the shock in her expression sobered him. *You're a minister of God!* he reminded himself. But then Andrew looked down at the child still attached to his daughter's hand. There was no surprise on that round face, only the acceptance of one who has seen all too many rows in that little cottage. Seized by anger again, Andrew waved them both away.

"Wait outside until Mr. Burrell is dressed, Elizabeth. Then I want you to see what a piece of human trash looks like."

"Wha?" came from the man in the bed, now roused enough to lift himself to a sitting position. Fixing Andrew with a menacing look, he growled, "Get out o' my house!"

Andrew glanced down at the fists Mr. Burrell had balled at his sides and wished the man would get up and swing at him. He couldn't recall ever being possessed by such raw fury, not even when he'd confronted Jonathan Raleigh. He could picture the whole scenario now—the child in the box had cried upon awakening, and Mr. Burrell, not ready to greet the light of day, had dragged himself from his bed long enough to administer a dose or two of gin and sugar. Probably the reason the older sister hadn't received the same treatment was that she played quietly and did not wake her father. He felt the cords in his neck tighten as he glared at the man through narrowed eyelids. "How dare you drug a child like that!"

"Huh?"

"You gave that baby gin . . . didn't you!"

"What's it ter you?" Mr. Burrell glared back. "Ain't yours."

"And it's a pity that he's yours, Mr. Burrell. Is sleep so precious to you that you're willing to turn your children into drunkards like yourself?" Taking a step closer to the mattress, he said, "Now . . . you will get up and dress, or so help me, I'll tie you up in that blanket and toss you in the Bryce!"

It was shock that gaped Mr. Burrell's mouth this time. But after a second or two he swung his legs—swathed in an incredibly wrinkled pair of brown trousers—over the side of the bed. Not taking his eyes off of Andrew, he pointed to a stained shirt hanging from the back of a chair. Andrew handed it to him.

"You're the *vicar*?" the man asked warily while fumbling with buttons.

"I am. And I must tell you . . . people like you make me ashamed to be a man."

"Where's Vicar Wilson?"

"Gone. And I'm glad he doesn't have to see this."

The last button was giving Mr. Burrell some difficulty, and he lowered his head to concentrate on it. "Vicar Wilson ne'er talked ter me like thet. He were a gentleman."

"Well, I'm not."

When Mr. Burrell was finally decently covered, Andrew motioned for him to go through the curtain to the front part of the cottage. He was surprised when the big man obeyed so meekly, but then the sway to his steps gave evidence that the effects of the gin in his system hadn't worn away. *He likely took a nip from the bottle himself while he was drugging the child.*

Andrew bent down to scoop up the sleeping child and realized the napkin was sodden. To Mr. Burrell, who had planted himself at the table and now sat there with hands cradling his head, Andrew said, "Where are the child's nappies?" A shrug was the only reply he received. He looked around the cottage, noting the clothes hanging from pegs on the walls. The cupboard was the only piece of furniture capable of storage. He went over to it and pulled out one of the deep bottom drawers. Stockings, flannels, and other cloth items were in surprisingly neat stacks. Among them he found a stack of eight cotton napkins, rough and gray but clean. There were a couple of small garments that obviously belonged to the baby. Andrew took them as well.

"Elizabeth," he called. She came through the door right away. The older child, now carried in Elizabeth's arms, rested her head against his daughter's neck in a touching manner.

"Yes, Father?" After one curious glance toward Mr. Burrell slumped at the table, Elizabeth avoided looking at him. *This is what happens to a woman's children when she marries a scoundrel!* Andrew was tempted to say to her, but when she looked straight at him, he could see tears on her face. She had absorbed the lesson, all right.

"Look on those pegs and see if you can find something clean for that child."

"What are you doin'?" the man at the table mumbled.

Andrew didn't answer until he'd gone over to the cupboard, picked up the bottle of gin, and emptied it outside. Back in the cottage, he set the empty bottle on the table in front of Mr. Burrell. "We are taking your two children home with us today. We'll bring them back when your other children are here to watch them."

Mr. Burrell fixed doleful eyes upon the empty bottle and raked a hand through his greasy hair. "But I don't know . . ."

"And you will stay here and sober up so you can watch them decently tomorrow. A drunkard is a danger to his children, Mr. Burrell. The older one was playing with an ax while you were sleeping."

271

"Vicar Wilson ne'er poured out—"

"I am talking about your children, Mr. Burrell," Andrew cut in, then shook his head. He'd forgotten that it was useless to reason with a drunk.

"Did you find some clothing?" he asked Elizabeth.

"Yes. Some little cloth slippers too."

"Good." He bent down over the box again, a clean napkin in hand. It suddenly occurred to him that he had never changed a nappie before—had never even witnessed such a duty being performed.

"Mr. Burrell," he said over his shoulder. "Have you any pins in the house?" Receiving no answer, he turned and saw that the man was asleep again, his head resting upon the tabletop.

"He's asleep, Father," Elizabeth said, coming to peer down at the box.

"I know." Andrew sighed, then sent her up a pleading look. "I don't suppose you've ever changed a nappie . . . have you?"

She took a step backwards. "Never."

He imagined as much. "Well, will you look about for some pins? I didn't see any in the drawer."

"Won't there be pins in the one he's wearing?"

Of course! Andrew thought. Gently he rolled the child onto his back. The boy whimpered and opened his eyes. He appeared older than Andrew had initially thought, perhaps even a year old. "Hey, little fellow," Andrew soothed.

The boy stared up at him while Andrew studied the way the napkin was fastened at each side with a pin. Then realizing he was stalling the inevitable, he unfastened the pins and pulled the sodden cloth away with two fingers. He set it on the floor next to the box—surely one of the older children would know what to do with it. Arranging the clean napkin on the baby was much more difficult than he had imagined it would be, but finally he managed to accomplish the task in a slipshod way.

"Aren't the other children going to wonder where they are?" Elizabeth asked.

Andrew listened to the snores coming from the table and wondered if Mr. Burrell would even remember that he'd had company. Lifting the boy up against his shoulder, he said, "We'll make sure to return before school is over."

They gathered the clothes and went back outside to the trap. The

272

older child smiled while being lifted into Elizabeth's arms and pointed to Rusty. "Tha's horse."

"Yes, that's a horse," she cooed back while Andrew went around to his side. Elizabeth had offered to hold both children, but he thought he could hold the boy and manage the reins at the same time. His daughter sat wrapped in a thoughtful silence until they were half-way home, and then she turned to him.

"I've never seen you so angry as you were back there."

Andrew knew that he would eventually apologize for his display of temper, but the rage inside him had not cooled enough for him to do so quite yet. He glanced down at the baby leaning against his chest and clutching the lapel of his coat. "I can't stomach men who won't take care of their families, Elizabeth. The Bible calls them worse than infidels, and I wholeheartedly agree."

"Aren't there women who are just as bad?"

"There are." He'd seen more than he cared to recall during the twenty years of his ministry. But he took the case of men more per-sonally—in his eyes, their failings tainted the institution of father-hood, reflecting even upon himself.

"And isn't there hope for redemption?" his daughter probed.

"Yes, Beth . . . of course there is." How could he explain his feel-ings to her without sounding like the biggest hypocrite who ever lived? He preached faith every Sunday, and yet his faith in humankind was at times terribly weak.

I can't explain it, he thought. In order for her to understand, she would have had to accompany him on calls for two decades and watch him try to stretch parish assistance to the victims of the likes of Mr. Burrell as far as it could go. She would have needed to see his attempts to claim for Christ the erring fathers or mothers . . . to pray with them, lead them to an understanding of the Gospel from the Scrip-tures, clean the vomit from their faces, use his own funds to purchase clean clothes, and find them jobs. In almost every case, the person he'd poured his heart into would joyously accept Christ and the fam-ily would be restored. A row of new faces would beam up at him from a pew in church, and it would warm his heart to pay a call at a dwelling and find family harmony therein.

But then—perhaps in as many as half of the cases—a face would begin to turn up missing from the Sunday pew, and later, the whole family. Slowly, or sometimes quite rapidly, the erring parent would return to his old ways. And children would suffer again. *Always the*

273

children, he thought, absently rubbing the back of the little one in his lap.

Many times lately he'd confessed his cynical lack of faith . . . but still found himself wondering, on the occasion of leading someone to faith in Christ, if the person had truly committed his life or if he would fall by the wayside. *The half who keep the faith are worth not giving up,* he thought. And of course, so was Mr. Burrell.

"Father?"

He looked at Elizabeth again. Mercifully, she did not pursue the subject that so troubled his thoughts but said instead, "We don't even know their names."

"Know dare names," the girl in her arms echoed, matching Elizabeth's serious tone. Andrew couldn't help but smile.

"Why, I didn't think to ask." The child in his lap watched the landscape move by with wide-eyed wonder. *I doubt if they've ever ridden in a carriage before.*

"He Dabid."

Andrew and Elizabeth both looked at the girl, who was pointing now at her younger brother.

"His name is David?" asked Elizabeth.

"He name Dabid. Dabid."

"Well, what is your name?" Andrew asked her, smiling again. He'd forgotten how pleasantly whimsical small children could be. He didn't really expect her to answer, but she did.

"Mol-yee."

Mol-yee? he mouthed to Elizabeth, who looked puzzled but then nodded.

"She's saying Molly."

"Name Mol-yee," the child nodded back. She pointed to her brother again. "He name Dabid."

*T*hey brought the children into the vicarage, where Dora clucked over them and Mrs. Paget dished out bowls of vegetable soup. She soaked pieces of soft bread into the liquid to give it body and make it easier to spoon into the small mouths. Molly was able to sit at the table with the aid of an upside-down kettle in her chair, and Elizabeth held David in her lap for the feeding. The children ate hungrily, opening their mouths like robin nestlings, and Andrew couldn't help but wonder if Mr. Burrell would have prepared any food at all for them.

"You can go ahead and make your afternoon calls," Elizabeth told him after he'd had his own lunch. "I'll stay and watch the children."

"I'm sure Dora won't mind watchin' them," Mrs. Paget said from the stove, but Elizabeth shook her head.

"She has enough to do. And they're used to me now." She gave Andrew a worried look. "You don't mind going alone, do you, Papa?"

"Of course not," Andrew replied, then warned, "But you won't have me here to change nappies." They exchanged smiles at that, for as soon as they brought the children into the vicarage, Dora had had to undo his handiwork and reapply little David's napkin. "I'll be back in time to carry them home."

He made three calls and returned to find the children in the parlor with Elizabeth, Dora, and Luke. The children had been bathed, and now with clean clothes and hair and shining faces, they'd lost some of their waifish looks. It did Andrew's heart good to see Elizabeth read to Molly from one of Laurel's old picture books, and to watch little David chuckle until he hiccuped at the faces Luke would mug for him. But the afternoon was drawing to a close, and he didn't want the other Burrell children to be concerned about their sister and brother.

"Will you help me return them?" he asked Elizabeth. She looked up at him as if surprised that he would have to ask.

"Of course, Father. And Mrs. Paget made a shepherd's pie to bring to the Burrells."

Luke and Dora handed Molly and David up to them once they were in the trap and put the towel-wrapped shepherd's pie in the boot— along with a dozen apples Mrs. Paget had added as an afterthought.

"Do you think their father will be there?" Elizabeth asked once the carriage turned from the vicarage lane onto Church Lane.

"I hope so," Andrew replied and was indeed relieved to find Mr. Burrell sitting on the stoop when the trap came to a halt outside the cottage. Elbows propped upon knees and hands cradling his chin, he appeared to have been crying.

Andrew climbed down from the seat with the boy in his arms. "Mr. Burrell?"

"My babies," the man whimpered. "You took my babies?"

A begrudging compassion found its way to Andrew's heart as he walked closer and caught sight of the reddened eyes and the lip trembling under the mustache. "Considering the state they were in this morning, Mr. Burrell, we dared not leave them here."

Mr. Burrell wiped his nose with his sleeve. "I loves my babies, mister."

Andrew did not argue with that, having learned a long time ago that there were different levels of love. Why, even a stable rat was capable of loving her brood . . . until they were replaced by another litter. Handing the boy over into his father's arms, he turned back and helped Elizabeth and little Molly from the carriage.

"Do you remember who I am?" he asked back at the stoop again. The man clutched both children against his chest as if they'd been gone for days. "New vicar, ain't you?"

"I'm glad you remembered. My name is Andrew Phelps."

Unaccountably, Mr. Burrell burst into a fresh spate of tears, causing little David to open his mouth and cry as well. Andrew lifted him from his father's arms and lightly bounced the boy until the weeping stopped.

"I ain't no good a'tall," the man on the stoop blubbered, resting his chin on top of Molly's freshly washed curls. "Just no good."

"Now, Mr. Burrell. God can change any man."

"That's what Vicar Wilson used t'say. But just look at me."

"Vicar Wilson was right. And don't your children deserve—?"

"My children!" Mr. Burrell sobbed. He was working himself up

276

into such a state that Andrew thought it best they leave so he could calm himself.

"Mr. Burrell?" he said, leaning down to return David to the man's arms. "We have to go now. But I'll be back in the morning with some breakfast to help you start the day."

Mr. Burrell blinked up at him. "You're goin' away?"

"Just until morning. And we'll talk some more then."

"Ain't gonter drink no more, vicar."

"I'm glad to hear it, Mr. Burrell." Leaning forward again, Andrew patted the man's shoulder. "Now, you take good care of those babies."

"No more gin. You'll see."

When Rusty had pulled the carriage out of earshot, Elizabeth turned a somber face to Andrew again.

"Do you think he means it?"

"We can only pray so," Andrew answered, but his heart felt heavy.

———

Elizabeth was reflectively quiet for the rest of the evening—not any more so than she had been since moving to Gresham, but there was something different about her. This time, instead of acting annoyed when Laurel attempted to involve her in a conversation, Elizabeth gave her an absent nod and participated to some degree. Andrew could tell the Burrell children occupied many of her thoughts and expressed no surprise when she asked to come along with him the next morning.

They were both dismayed upon reaching the Burrell cottage to find the two children in the care of their older brother Mark, a nine-year-old. He was admirably a more competent caretaker than was his father—the children had been changed from their nightclothes, and David's nappie appeared to be dry. However, feeding time seemed to have been more than the lad could handle, for both children held chunks of brown bread in their hands as they played on the floor of the cottage.

"He went away last night," Mark answered when queried about his father.

"Where did he go?" Andrew asked and received a shrug of the shoulders in reply. "Well, do you know when he'll return?"

"Don't know, sir. He didn't tell us he was goin'." There was acceptance in the boy's expression, and Andrew suspected this wasn't the first time Mr. Burrell had disappeared.

"Has he done this before?"

"Yes, sir."

Andrew shook his head and half wished he'd thrashed Mr. Burrell while he'd had the opportunity.

"Father?" Elizabeth said from the corner.

He turned and found her seated on a stool by the fireplace with both children in her lap. "Yes, Beth?"

"It's a pity that Mark has to miss school. Why don't we take the children home with us again?"

It was a good idea, but Andrew had to make sure she understood the implications of what she was suggesting. "I can't neglect my calls, Beth," he told her. "And we can't expect the servants to shoulder the extra responsibility."

"I'll take care of them. You don't mind, do you?"

"Mine, do you?" Molly echoed from his daughter's lap, tilting her little head inquisitively at him and bringing a smile to his lips.

"Of course not."

They gathered the children's things while Mark ate two of the Scotch eggs and an apple tart that Mrs. Paget had sent. Andrew stashed the rest of the food in the cupboard, explaining to Elizabeth that since the little ones took much longer to eat, she could feed them something at home if they were still hungry. He wanted to make sure the boy was present at school for at least some of the morning lessons.

Mr. Sykes was at the vicarage when they alighted from the trap. The churchwarden gave a curious look at the children in Andrew's and Elizabeth's arms but did not voice the question in his eyes. "It's the Sheltons over on Walnut Tree Lane. The grandmother passed on in her sleep last night."

"I'll leave at once," Andrew told him, handing David over to the startled man. As he went back around to his side of the chaise, he said over Rusty's back, "Would you mind helping Elizabeth take the children inside?"

The churchwarden apparently could stand it no longer. Peering down at the boy in his arms, who studied his face with rapt concentration, he asked, "Who are they?"

Andrew swung himself into the seat and picked up the reins. "The Burrells' youngest."

"He's took off again?"

There was no use denying the truth. "I was too rough on him yesterday, Mr. Sykes. I should have tried harder to help him."

The churchwarden snorted. "Don't blame yourself, Reverend. Vicar Wilson tried for years, and you see how much good it did. Well, let's just hope he stays gone this time and gives that poor woman some relief."

In spite of his low opinion of Mr. Burrell's actions, Andrew felt the shock that was now registering on Elizabeth's face. "How can you say that?"

The man did not back down. "They're better off without his dipping into her wages for gin and slappin' her about when the money's gone. Some people make the world a better place by leavin' it."

———

Andrew spent the rest of the day with the Sheltons, consoling the grieving family, thanking on their behalf the neighbors who brought food, and listening when one or the other spoke about the life she'd lived. He'd only met the elderly Mrs. Shelton once—not counting greetings at the church door. There was something cold-hearted about speaking words over the coffin of a virtual stranger, so he wanted to know as much as possible about her before he performed the burial ceremony. He found that family members were almost always willing to relate tales about their deceased loved ones. Perhaps it helped their grief—he wasn't sure. He wondered if he would have healed more quickly after Kathleen's death if he'd allowed himself to talk about her.

The sun was setting behind the Anwyl's crest as he drove Rusty down Church Lane back to the vicarage. Passing the *Larkspur,* this time from the south side, he remembered again his intention to call upon Mrs. Hollis. The funeral was to be on Thursday, so he decided to call tomorrow if possible.

He knew why he'd put off the call, though admitting it to himself was difficult. He'd found the young widow immensely attractive upon their first meeting just outside the vicarage lane. The day had been blustery, bringing roses to her cheeks. The scattering of freckles across her nose conflicted with the maturity in her face in an interesting way, and the auburn hair beneath the brim of her hat was as warm as a sunset. But it was her voice that had impressed him the most, filled with a grace that would be impossible to feign by someone who did not possess that quality.

It wasn't until he arrived back at the vicarage that he realized he hadn't compared Mrs. Hollis to Kathleen, as he did other women. The thought was unsettling, for what must Mrs. Hollis think of him? Had he stared at her like some infatuated schoolboy? There he was, the new vicar on his second day in Gresham and trying to charm the ladies like some slick Don Juan?

I'll ask Elizabeth along, he thought. Surely Mr. Burrell would have returned by then, and his daughter would be free to accompany him. And he would be as cordial as was befitting a minister—but not so much as to be considered flirtatious.

Laurel was alone in the parlor when he walked into the vicarage. His youngest daughter had discovered that the most comfortable place to study was in a high-backed, old leather chair with a soft padded footstool. On the wall overhead hung a portrait of Kathleen as a young bride. Though she had yet to bear two daughters, there was a maternal warmth to her expression that the artist had captured perfectly.

"Hello, Papa," she greeted, looking up from her homework. "Did you have a good day?"

He went over to kiss the top of her head. "Good . . . and long, Pet."

"Mrs. Paget has some supper for you in the kitchen. And Elizabeth left with Luke just a little while ago to bring the babies back home."

"How could they? I had the carriage."

"Luke borrowed Mr. Sykes's horse and trap."

"Then I shouldn't keep Mrs. Paget waiting." He paused at the parlor door, though, realizing that he hadn't asked Laurel about her day. He was aware that he'd spent more time with Elizabeth than with her lately—and that couldn't be helped, what with her sister being home all day while she was at school. But equally aware was' he that he'd spent an inordinate amount of time concerned about his older daughter's emotional state, neglecting Laurel in the process.

Turning back to face her, he said, "I'm sorry, Pet. I didn't even ask about your day."

She brightened and smiled, making him glad he'd asked. "I made a perfect mark on a geography assignment. We had to draw a map of Canada, with the rivers and lakes and mountain ranges."

"Outstanding! And I didn't even know you were interested in maps."

"I still find them boring, to be truthful," Laurel shrugged. "But I like scoring high marks."

He didn't want to leave her company but also didn't care to endure another lecture from Mrs. Paget about how having meals at irregular hours would impede his digestion and put him at risk for gout. "My grandpappa lived to be ninety-five," the cook had told him, waving a wooden spoon at him when he attempted to skip breakfast last Sunday morning. "And folk could set their watches by his mealtimes, if they'd a mind to."

As it was, Mrs. Paget grumbled because he was an hour late, but her humor was quickly restored when Andrew complimented her new apron. And she didn't give so much as a frown when he asked if he might take his supper to the parlor on a tray. He chatted with Laurel as he ate his supper and was finishing up his blackberry cobbler when Elizabeth returned. She went straight to Andrew and knelt down at his side, resting her arms upon the arm of his chair.

"I met Mrs. Burrell this evening," she said, her cheeks flushed with the night air. "That poor woman works so hard to keep her family from starving."

"It's a sad case," said Andrew.

"Has her husband returned?" Laurel asked from her chair.

Elizabeth turned to shake her head and answer, "Not yet. Mrs. Burrell said sometimes he's gone for days." When she turned back to Andrew, the flush upon her face had deepened.

"Please don't be angry, Father, but I offered to keep Molly and David on school days in the meantime. Then none of the older children would have to miss their lessons." She was rushing her words, as if fearful that he would interrupt with a negative reply. "They're all quite bright, the older children, and it would be a shame to have their education suffer. And they could bring the babies here before school and fetch them afterward, so you wouldn't have to worry about being away in the carriage. They walk both ways anyway, and it would just be a little farther."

Finally she paused for breath, giving Laurel an imploring look at the same time, as though trying to enlist her particular negotiating skills. Laurel came through immediately, declaring, "They *were* awfully sweet babies, Father."

"Terribly sweet," Elizabeth agreed, sending her sister a grateful smile.

This encouraged Laurel to add, "And you know what Jesus said about doing for the least of our brethren."

Now both daughters watched him, waiting for his answer. Andrew ran a hand through his hair and recalled other projects that Elizabeth had taken up with gusto, only to abandon them when the excitement wore off. And far more was at stake here than watercoloring and archery lessons.

He sighed and wondered why no one had ever warned him how hard parenting would become as the girls grew older. Not that he could have done anything to change that, but at least he wouldn't have been blindsided.

"That's quite a responsibility," he felt compelled to warn her. "What if Mr. Burrell stays away for weeks this time? It would be cruel to encourage the family to become dependent upon you if you don't plan to carry through for that long."

To her credit, Elizabeth did not argue but appeared to think his words over. "Yes," she said at length, quite calmly. "That would be cruel. And those children have had enough cruelty in their lives."

"More than enough," Andrew agreed.

"I know I've been flighty in the past, Father. But what if I gave you my word that I'll tend to those children through the rest of the school year, if it comes to that. And without complaining."

He admired her willingness to help the Burrells but had to make certain it wasn't just a passing fancy. "Why do you want to do this, Elizabeth?"

Tears gathered in the corners of her eyes. "It's been nice to feel . . . well, needed, these past few days. Oh, I know you appreciated my making calls with you, but you're quite capable of making them just as well without me. But those children . . . they're so little and helpless. I can make a difference in their lives."

Touched by her compassion, Andrew felt compelled to go along with the plan. He feigned a stern face, though, and said, "I suppose I shall have to make a stop at Mr. Trumble's tomorrow."

His daughters exchanged glances, and then Laurel asked, "Mr. Trumble's?"

"We should keep our own supply of nappies here."

Elizabeth jumped up to wrap her arms around his neck and plant kisses in his beard. Later, as he read *The Shrewsbury Chronicle* and Laurel continued to study, Elizabeth sat in a semireclining position on the sofa and pored over a book she'd found in the vicarage library, *The Care and Feeding of Infants* by Mrs. Wright. And occasionally Andrew looked up from his newspaper, savoring the welcome peace that permeated the room. *It's been a long time,* he thought.

*W*onderful sermon you preached Sunday, Vicar," the tall elderly woman said from the garden in front of the *Larkspur* Wednesday morning. Beaming, she brushed her right hand against the skirt of her ebony gown and then thrust it at him. "I must admit that I wasn't prepared to like you, what with Vicar Wilson being so special and all."

"I can understand that," Andrew smiled back at her while shaking her hand and mentally making a frantic search through his list of parishioners. *Mrs. Princeton, was it?* Why hadn't he reviewed Vicar Wilson's notebook before setting out this morning?

The blue eyes that studied him were sharp, yet there was an odd amusement in her expression. "You're trying to remember who I am, aren't you?"

"Ah . . . I'm afraid so. Will you forgive me?"

"Of course, Vicar. I wouldn't expect you to memorize everyone's name so soon. It's Mrs. Kingston."

"Kingston!" Andrew said, snapping his fingers. "I *knew* it had something to do with royalty."

She chuckled at this, and he relaxed a bit. Glancing at the short spade in her left hand, he asked, "Are you planting more flowers?"

"Oh, heavens no. Preparing the ground for next spring is more like it. I wasn't here to do it last winter, and the garden wasn't nearly as splendid as it could have been. But you just wait 'til spring, Reverend. And be prepared to preach a good strong message on coveting, because that's what all of Gresham will be doing when I win the ribbon for roses at the flower show this June."

"You know what the Scripture says about pride, now, Mrs. Kingston," he teased. "Besides, I hear Squire Bartley's garden is a sight to behold."

He'd never seen it himself, because his introductory call at the manor last week had been so unpleasant that he'd been in no mood to dally around the premises. The squire had subjected him to a litany of Vicar Wilson's faults, which all seemed to boil down to the notion that the vicar hadn't given him the respect he was due.

"My great-great-grandfather founded this town!" the old man had snorted. After listening to some ranting and ravings, Andrew concluded that this bitterness had developed when Vicar Wilson refused to recommend the squire's nephew to Saint John's college. "One of the finest boys who ever walked the earth!" the squire had declared. "And it discouraged poor Donald so much that he gave up all hopes of going into the ministry!"

"But if the boy was truly called by God, he wouldn't allow something like that to alter his life's plans," Andrew had said as tactfully as possible. The squire's eyes had seemed to bulge then, so much that Andrew feared an imminent stroke. That was when he bade his host good-day and left the manor.

"Ah, but the squire will have no chance this year." Mrs. Kingston interrupted his thoughts, speaking in a conspiratorial voice after sending a glance down each side of the lane and to the door of the *Lark-spur*.

"Do tell?"

"If I ask you to keep something to yourself, you're obligated do so . . . isn't that correct?"

"That is correct, Mrs. Kingston. Unless you've gone and buried the squire in your garden, that is."

"Now, there's a thought," she chuckled. "But come see what we discovered behind the inn this spring." Dropping the spade, she led him over to a bush about two feet high. The leaves were sparse and darkening with the season, and it appeared to be more twigs and thorns than anything else. Yet she had mulched around the base with oak leaves and what appeared to be rabbit pellets.

"Is it a rose?" Andrew asked, though he could only see the reddish-brown remains of five or six flowers.

The blue eyes were sparkling. "Not just any rose, Vicar. It's the rare *Rosa Allea*, the oldest rose on record in Great Britain."

"This bush?"

"No, of course not *this* particular bush. But this one began as a cutting from an older bush, which began as a cutting . . . and so on back through the ages. Would you care to hear more of its history?"

284

Andrew had never been particularly interested in flowers except to admire their colors and scents, but he had a fondness for history. While manners would have dictated that he answer in the affirmative anyway, he found himself genuinely wishing to know the story. "Do tell me, Mrs. Kingston."

She smiled indulgently down upon the bush, as a mother would her sleeping child. "The *Rosa Allea* was chosen by the House of York as its emblem in the fifteenth century, Vicar. If you remember your schooling, Henry VII was struggling for the throne of England."

"The War of the Roses," Andrew nodded. He studied the rather pitiful-looking plant again. The trappings of royalty were surely missing. "Forgive me for asking, but how can anyone be absolutely certain that it was this particular kind? Are you an expert on roses?"

"Oh, ye of little faith!" she chided, but with good humor. "A botanist by the name of Mr. MacQuarrie stayed at the *Bow and Fiddle* for a week or so back in late July—he was traveling about Shropshire, cataloguing the flora and fauna, you see. When I found out about the young man, I asked him to look at the garden and give me some advice regarding some spotting on the begonia leaves. He was so startled to find what appeared to be a *Rosa Allea* here, that when he returned to the University of Edinburgh, he looked up records and sent me verification that it was indeed so."

"Amazing. Part of history growing right here in your garden."

Mrs. Kingston beamed at his interest, her high opinion of him obviously having gone up a notch. "But you must keep it to yourself, Vicar. I've only told one other person—Karl Herrick—the caretaker here. Even Mrs. Hollis isn't yet aware of the significance of this particular bush. The squire is going to receive the shock of his life!"

"Undoubtedly!" Andrew looked at the bush with new respect, then remembered the reason for his call. Warmly, he said, "Thank you for allowing me into your confidence, Mrs. Kingston. Rest assured, your secret is safe with me."

"Thank you, Vicar Phelps. And now would you like me to show you into the house?"

When she ushered him into the hall, Andrew was glad he'd not delayed his visit until later in the day, for it became apparent that he would be spending some time here. Three other familiar faces from his congregation offered greetings, and Mrs. Kingston kindly introduced them as Mrs. Hyatt and Mr. Durwin. Miss O'Shea he remembered from his meeting with Mrs. Hollis and her on the vicarage lane, and a Mrs. Dearing was introduced as being a Baptist. Miss Rawlins, he was told, another member of Saint Jude's, was upstairs penning a novel, and there was a lodger named Mr. Clay, an actor, who was resting in his bedchamber.

Mrs. Hollis, he was told, was in her office. He was glad of this, for he couldn't very well tell her of the recent changes in Elizabeth's attitude in front of an audience. "Please don't disturb her now," he told Miss O'Shea as he handed over his hat. "But perhaps you could show me the way there after I've had a chance to visit in here for a little while?"

The housekeeper smiled and asked if he would care for some tea. He accepted gratefully, then spent some time becoming better acquainted with the people gathered in the hall. Mr. Durwin asked if he could divulge the subject of this Sunday's coming sermon. Always happy to talk about his ministry, Andrew replied that he would like to contrast Nehemiah's rebuilding the wall around Jerusalem with personal holiness in a Christian's life. They seemed to find this intriguing and spent some twenty minutes discussing biblical themes related to the subject. Mrs. Dearing, though not Church of England, had an impressive command of Scripture, and even brought out a point that he made a mental note to include in his sermon.

When he had decided that he could politely take his leave, he stood and asked Miss O'Shea, standing silently in the background, if she would mind showing him to Mrs. Hollis's office. "I've enjoyed the stimulating conversation," he smiled at the group.

"You come visit us again, Reverend," Mr. Durwin said to a chorus of agreement.

As the Irish housekeeper led him down a corridor, Andrew complimented her on the two cups of tea he'd consumed in the hall. "Delightful blend. Was it purchased here in Gresham?"

"I'm afraid not, sir," she replied. "Mrs. Herrick orders a special blend through a company in London. She wouldn't dream of serving anything else. Would you like me to ask for the address?"

"That would be very kind—" he told her, but a second thought brought him pause. "Do you think Mrs. Paget would take offense? She rather prides herself on the tea she serves."

Miss O'Shea bit her lip. "Well, sir, I'm not well acquainted with her. But cooks do seem to take any suggestion for change a bit personally."

"That's been my experience as well. Perhaps it's better to have a happy cook than the best tea, don't you think?"

"I agree, sir," she said, smiling, and Andrew liked the calm manner in which she conversed with him—respectful, but not subservient.

"Forgive the obvious question," he said. "But you're from Ireland, aren't you?"

"Kilkenny, sir. I came over when I was eighteen."

"By yourself?"

"By myself."

"I suspect there is an interesting story there."

Her smile did not alter, but the violet-colored eyes were serious. "Interesting perhaps, sir, but best forgotten."

"I understand," he told her and received a look of appreciation in return.

"Here is Mrs. Hollis's office," she said, leading him to an open door on their right. Inside, Mrs. Hollis was seated at a desk that took up about a third of the small room. She looked up from a ledger in which she was writing and got to her feet.

"Why, good morning, Reverend Phelps," she said, offering her hand over the desk. He stepped forward to take it.

"Miss O'Shea was kind enough to show me here. I hope this isn't an inconvenient time."

"Not at all." Nodding toward a chair against the wall and adjacent to the front of her desk, she said, "Please, make yourself comfortable."

"Thank you." Andrew waited until Mrs. Hollis had taken her own chair again before sitting down himself. From the doorway the housekeeper asked if she could bring a tray.

"Would you care for some refreshment, Reverend?" Mrs. Hollis asked.

Andrew shook his head. "No thank you. I've already had two excellent cups of tea."

Miss O'Shea left then, and Mrs. Hollis asked how he liked Gresham after so many years in Cambridge.

"Very much. I'm finding myself, little by little, learning to relax and adjust to the slower pace. Was it the same way with you when you moved from London?"

"Actually, life here was a bit frantic until we settled into a routine," she replied, smiling. "But I've learned to enjoy the pace as well. And the quietness. I had never realized nights could be so quiet."

"Nor so dark, without the streetlamps," Andrew said. "But that's rather nice too. My daughters and I enjoy sitting out in the garden some evenings and noticing how much brighter the stars seem."

There was an awkward silence for just a fraction of a second. At least it was awkward for Andrew, for he suddenly found himself feeling an inexplicable bashfulness. Mrs. Hollis looked even more attractive than she had in the vicarage lane. The hair that had been covered with a bonnet that day was now drawn back into a loose knot. Rich auburn it was and provided quite a contrast to her emerald eyes. And the black gown, plain and adorned only with jet buttons, only heightened the color in her cheeks.

You've seen attractive women before, he scolded himself silently. Some had been just as beautiful as Mrs. Hollis, if not more so. Why, now, were emotions stirring that he'd assumed to be dead?

"Would you rather we visit in the hall with the others, Reverend?" Mrs. Hollis asked, emptying her pen back into the jar. There were blue ink stains upon the thumb and forefinger of her right hand, but she seemed not to be aware of them. "I'm afraid my office is rather confined. It was a broom closet just last week, you see."

Was I staring? he wondered uneasily. "No, this is fine. It's good to have a place to keep your work separate, isn't it?"

Smiling again, she said, "Truthfully, most of my duties seem to be outside my office."

"And mine as well."

"But I do enjoy having papers gathered in one place and not scattered about in the living quarters."

"And you can close the door to it whenever you wish." *She's too busy for small talk*, he reminded himself. *Don't take advantage of her hospitality.*

Andrew cleared his throat and got right to the purpose of his call. "I wanted to tell you how grateful I am for the encouragement you gave my daughter, Mrs. Hollis. It was very kind of you." He told her how Elizabeth had started accompanying him on his calls in response to her advice to busy herself with something worthwhile.

"And as a result, she's found something else to do that she seems to enjoy very much. She's going to be tending two small children so their mother can support the family. I don't know how long her enthusiasm will last, but she's given her word to see it through until summer."

"I'm so happy to hear that," she smiled back. "And I enjoyed talking with her. Elizabeth is an intelligent young woman."

"Thank you, Mrs. Hollis. Lately I've wondered if I should have told her so more often. If she'd any idea of her own worth, surely she wouldn't have allowed someone like Mr. Raleigh to trifle with her heart."

"You mustn't blame yourself. Elizabeth's barely out of childhood. It's difficult for most women her age to see past a charming exterior."

"He even had *me* fooled for a while," Andrew admitted. "He was so personable, so bright and witty. Any father would have wanted a son-in-law like him . . . or so I thought."

For a brief instant Mrs. Hollis's green eyes took on a faraway look, and then she said, "It seems that many people who are deficient in character have an overabundance of charm. I wonder why that is?"

"I've noticed that too. Could be that people devote most of their energies to developing that charm and ignore the building of character." He shook his head. "I never told Elizabeth, but my greatest fear was that she would elope with the young man."

"I'm glad it didn't happen. You know, I'm beginning to suspect childrearing becomes more difficult as they grow older."

Andrew gave a little chuckle. "At least you're learning that while your children are still young, Mrs. Hollis. I was completely blindsided."

She seemed amused by this, and Andrew wondered if anyone had ever told her she had a graceful smile. *Probably her husband, God rest his soul.* No doubt the poor man had adored her.

"I've kept you from your duties long enough, Mrs. Hollis," he told her with reluctance. To his surprise, she seemed genuinely disappointed at his imminent departure.

"Can you stay a little longer?" she asked. "To be honest, I was hoping you would call soon. I'm afraid I'm in need of your counsel."

"But of course." Andrew lowered himself back into his chair and raised a solicitous eyebrow. "What is troubling you, Mrs. Hollis?"

"It's concerning a ghost that is rumored to haunt this house and now is supposedly walking the streets . . . Jake Pitt. I don't suppose you've lived here long enough to have heard about him. . . ."

"Actually, I have."

She sighed heavily at this, making him sorry that his answer caused her some discomfort. "I trust you've met the Worthy sisters, Reverend Phelps?"

"Yes, but I must tell you that they weren't the first to inform me about the situation. And someone recently asked me to conduct a ceremony consecrating the road in front of his house. He claims to have spotted a ghost there."

"That would have to be Mr. Hopper."

Alarm must have registered on Andrew's face, for she raised a reassuring hand from the desktop. "Everyone in Gresham has heard about it, so you haven't betrayed a confidence. But may I ask—whatever did you tell him?"

"I'm afraid I was rather abrupt," Andrew replied. "I said that the things of God were not to be used as superstitious rituals, and that I would not perform any such ceremony."

"Do you think it did any good?"

"I wish I could say so. But Mr. Hopper refused to back down from what he saw." Rubbing his beard absently, he said, "You know, I have to be careful of appearing to look down on the way of life here. But I can see that a sermon on superstition is needed very soon."

There was little hope in Mrs. Hollis's expression. "That is very kind of you, but I must warn you that Vicar Wilson preached two strong sermons in the same vein during his last months here. The people here are the salt of the earth, Reverend Phelps, but I've learned that most were practically weaned upon fables and superstitions."

"I must try, though. Faith is of little use if everything is easy."

"Forgive me," she said with a self-effacing little smile. "I obviously forgot that."

"Oh, I wasn't preaching at you, Mrs. Hollis. I can understand your frustration." He became curious then. "How did it affect your children—moving into a house with such a dubious reputation?"

"Fortunately, I was able to warn them of the ghost story before they heard it from anyone else. I'm afraid my son, Philip, enjoyed the attention, but to the girls it was simply a nuisance."

Resting her elbows upon her desk, she leaned forward slightly. "The rumors started fading a bit, you see, as time passed, and people could see that we were brought to no harm in this house. Now this latest sighting has them all stirred up again. None of us, my lodgers included, can go anywhere without someone asking about Jake Pitt. Mrs. Temple, a widow who lives across from the lending library, stopped me in *Trumbles* to say that she'd heard a knife-grinding wheel just outside her window one night. And yesterday morning one of our maids found scatterings of elder twigs at each outside door."

"Elder twigs? I'm afraid I don't understand."

"They repel ghosts, so the superstition goes. Obviously someone wishes to keep Jake Pitt within the bounds of the *Larkspur*. And the general consensus seems to be that if we had taken care of the matter when we first moved in here, he wouldn't be menacing the streets right now."

Andrew shook his head. "I wasn't aware of that. Then it seems this has gone beyond superstition into mass hysteria. Why, just last Thursday . . ." his voice trailed off as he berated himself for starting to say something that would only add to her worries. "Well, it doesn't matter."

"Does this have to do with Jake Pitt, Reverend Phelps?"

"Just another case of hysteria," he reassured her. "Forgive me for even bringing it up."

Her green eyes became pleading. "Please continue. I can't feel any worse about it than I do now. And I would like to keep the other people who live here informed so they aren't taken by surprise by someone else's revelation."

"Well, if you're certain you want to hear it."

"I am. Please."

Andrew blew out a long breath. "Are you acquainted with Mr. Seaton?"

"Doesn't he pastor a small Wesleyan chapel across the river?"

"He also owns a small dairy farm, like so many others here. I was making calls last Thursday and came across him mending his front gate. We struck up a conversation, and before I knew it I was invited to have lunch with his family." Andrew gave her a little smile. "Even pastors of differing denominational backgrounds love to compare notes, much the same as two schoolmasters or two bakers would do. Anyway, he told me about a member of his congregation, a young woman, who related somewhat of a dilemma to him."

He paused. "Are you quite sure you want to hear this, Mrs. Hollis?"

"Yes . . . please," she nodded. "Go on."

"Well, one of the woman's younger brothers, who recently suffered a broken foot, has been having nightmares having to do with a ghost. After one such incident, the boy asked her to give him her word that she wouldn't tell their father what he was about to confide in her. With some reluctance she gave it, and the young man admitted to being accosted by a ghost while he and another brother were in the process of playing some sort of prank. The only reason I mention this now is that the sighting supposedly took place on Worton Lane."

He noticed then that her scattering of freckles now stood out boldly against a background the color of whey.

"Mrs. Hollis?"

"Do you happen to know the boy's name?" she asked, her lips barely moving.

"Why, Mr. Seaton did not mention it." Andrew moved up to the edge of his chair. "Are you all right, Mrs. Hollis?"

"Yes, it's just . . ." She rubbed her temple with an ink-stained finger, leaving a black smudge. "I have a terrible suspicion about all of this."

"Mrs. Hollis?" Andrew reached out to touch the hand that still rested on the desktop. "Please forgive me—I've upset you."

"Upset me?" Mrs. Hollis blinked once and looked up at him again. "Oh, please don't think that, Vicar. You've been a tremendous help." Again she rubbed the temple. "But I've developed a headache, I'm afraid. Would you mind if. . . ?"

Getting to his feet, Andrew said, "Of course not. I'll show myself out. But may I ask Miss O'Shea to see about you?"

"If you wish . . . thank you. And again, I do appreciate your visit."

How can you help it, with all the cheer I've spread about in here? Andrew thought miserably as he moved up the corridor toward the hall in search of the housekeeper.

*B*ut I just need to close my eyes for a moment," Julia said when Fiona insisted that she leave her office. "I can do that right here. It's just a headache."

The housekeeper's will prevailed, though, and Julia allowed herself to be led like an invalid down the corridor to her room. She balked at going to bed, however, and insisted upon settling in a chair. After helping her prop her feet on the footstool, Fiona said, "Now, missus, you rest, and I'll bring you some tea.

Mr. Hopper claims to have seen three boys that night, Julia thought when she had privacy again. *Three boys in addition to the ghost.* Her memory carried her back to a gathering at the kitchen table around a platter of apple strudel. Fiona was disturbed about some pranksters who were tipping over the Keegans' shed. *And there were two men present—Mr. Durwin and Mr. Clay.*

Immediately she ruled out Mr. Durwin. True, he had seemed the most upset at the news, but she could not imagine him stooping to such behavior. And Mr. Clay . . . well, it was true that the actor could be quite playful during his good days, but she distinctly remembered that he'd suffered depression that whole weekend. And while Mrs. Kingston was able to coax him into daily walks even during the bouts of depression, she doubted that three boys could have persuaded him to dress up in a sheet and walk the lanes at midnight.

"Here we are, missus," Fiona said, coming through the doorway again with a tray. "But I'm afraid Mr. Durwin met me on my way to the kitchen and insisted upon brewin' you some of his herbal remedy. He says not to mind the bitterness. It'll cure your headache almost right away."

"What is it?" Julia asked as the cup and saucer were handed to her.

"I believe he said feverfew." The housekeeper stood there with hands pressed together while Julia took a tentative sip.

"Oh, this is more than bitter," Julia choked, making a face. "It's vile."

"I'm sorry," Fiona said, bending to reach for the cup. "Here, I'll just have to tell Mr. Durwin that you can't drink it."

Julia waved her hand away. "No, don't do that. I suppose if he went to the trouble of brewing it, I should force it down." She took it in a single unlady-like tip of the cup, holding her breath the whole time. "Thank you," she croaked, handing the cup over.

Giving her a sympathetic look, Fiona reached into her apron pocket and produced two chocolate biscuits wrapped in a clean dish towel. "Mrs. Herrick took pity on you when she saw what Mr. Durwin was up to. She slipped this to me and said to tell you it would rid your mouth of the taste."

It would take a dozen chocolate biscuits to get rid of the bitterness that lingered, Julia thought, but she broke one and popped a half piece into her mouth. "I'll have to thank her at lunch," she said after chewing and swallowing it. Recalling the matter that had brought on the headache, she motioned to the bench at her dressing table. "Fiona, would you mind sitting for a little while?"

"Of course not, missus," the housekeeper replied and pulled the bench over to her chair.

Julia popped in another biscuit half. Indeed her taste buds were returning to normal. "Would you like this other one?"

"No, thank you."

"Then, I'll ask you something. Do you remember when Philip had Jeremiah and Ben here to stay over?"

Fiona smiled. "Judging from their faces the next morning, little sleeping was done."

"Tell me, do you recall any sheet or blanket missing the next day? Or perhaps that turned up in the washing with anything unusual on it?"

"Unusual, missus?"

"Such as dirt?"

"Not that I can recall. Of course, Willa takes the washing over to Mrs. Moore. Would you like me to ask her?"

"I don't know. It may not be necessary." Julia's thoughts were drawn like a magnet to Mr. Clay again. "Fiona, didn't Mr. Clay arrive here with two trunks?"

"Yes, ma'am. One for his clothes and the other for his costumes."

"His costumes?"

"You know . . . theatre costumes. That's what he told Ruth when she offered to unpack the trunk. He said it didn't need unpacking, that he would just push it against a wall." Fiona eyed her curiously. "Is there something wrong?"

"I would say that," Julia nodded. Strangely, her headache was beginning to abate just as her temper was rising. "But I would rather tell you later, Fiona. I want to talk with Mr. Clay as soon as possible."

"I'm afraid he's up in his room, ma'am. Mrs. Kingston says he's having a bad day."

Julia got up from her chair, swayed a bit from the effects of the herbal tea, and took a step toward the door. "Well, I believe his day is about to become a little worse."

"Come in," she heard from the other side of Mr. Clay's door three minutes later. She eased the door open. He was seated in his chair facing the window and rose upon seeing that it was her. "Good morning, Mrs. Hollis."

"Have you a few minutes to spare, Mr. Clay?" Julia asked. She had come to think of the actor as a tragic older brother but swallowed her sympathy and nodded toward his extra chair. "I believe we have something to discuss."

"Am I behind with my rent?" he asked as he turned his chair to face hers, then waited until she had taken a seat.

"Not at all, Mr. Clay. And I don't wish to offend you, but I must ask you a question you may find blunt."

"Well, blunt away Mrs. Hollis," he said with a humorless little smile.

Julia drew in a deep breath and thought, *Why can't he be in one of his good moods today?* It would be much easier to accuse someone with a face not quite so long. "Did you dress up as a ghost to frighten the Sanders brothers three Saturday nights ago?"

"Dress up as a ghost?" His slate gray eyes widened for the fraction of a second. "I beg your pardon?"

You have it all wrong! she told herself miserably. *And now you've insulted him.* With a voice gone flat, she said, "You've no idea what I'm talking about, have you?"

In spite of Mr. Clay's dark mood, a corner of his mouth twitched. "Actually, I have."

"You have? Then, why . . ."

"It's a technique called 'stalling for time,' Mrs. Hollis. You caught me unawares, and I wasn't quite ready to admit my guilt, yet I couldn't bring myself to lie to you. Hence, the manufactured look of surprise. It was childish of me, and I do apologize for it."

It was frustrating to be furious with someone so *likable*, Julia thought. But she had a right to her anger and wouldn't allow herself to be charmed out of it.

"Mr. Clay, you've spent most of the past fortnight up here in your room insulated from what's going on outside these walls. Are you aware that the whole village believes Jake Pitt is taking tea with us during the day and stalking the roads by night?"

He looked genuinely perplexed. "They do?"

"Have you any concept of how difficult it is for all of us to have to endure such a reputation? Why, Sarah had to be talked out of handing in her notice yesterday. She's convinced that Jake Pitt has been scratching on the garret windows while she's sleeping."

"I'm so sorry," he said, hanging his head like a chastised schoolboy. "If it's any consolation at all, Mrs. Hollis, I regretted the stunt as soon as I pulled it."

But Julia was not to be appeased so easily. "You're an adult, Mr. Clay. Adults are supposed to set examples for children, not slip out of the house with them to do mischief."

"You know about—"

"That the boys were with you? Well, I know that for *sure* now, don't I?"

He winced. "Please don't blame them. It was my idea."

"Oh, I've enough blame to hand out four ways, Mr. Clay." The misery on his face was beginning to soften her anger in spite of her defenses. Sighing, she said, "I admire that all of you wanted to help the Keegans. But this was an extreme way to go about it. Why, it's fortunate that the boy's foot was only broken and not severed."

Mr. Clay straightened in his chair. "Broken?"

"Didn't you know?"

"Why, no. True, the building fell on him, but then he managed to run away with admirable speed."

"Well, it's broken. In two places."

"Terrible," the actor mumbled. "I had no idea!" He gave a pleading look to Julia. "I'll have to call on the boy right away and apologize. And the doctor's fee. Do you know—?"

"How much?" Julia shook her head. "I'm sure Dr. Rhodes would, be happy to tell you. But I must ask that you delay your call until Philip is home from school. He will want to accompany you."

To her surprise, the schoolboy expression vanished from Mr. Clay's face. "Mrs. Hollis, that is not a good idea. I'm the one who frightened those boys."

"And what was Philip's part in this?"

"Basically, he sat in a tree and watched."

"I suspect there's more to it than that."

"Very little more. As you pointed out, Mrs. Hollis, I'm the adult. I'll bear the responsibility."

Julia didn't know how to respond to this. It was so difficult making decisions on her own that could affect the childrens' lives forever. If she didn't insist that Philip apologize, would he take for granted that there were no consequences to be paid for any of his actions? Was that how anarchists and hedonists started out? Before she could muster a reply, Mr. Clay shook his head firmly.

"Women grow up sheltered, Mrs. Hollis. You've no idea how difficult it is for a young boy to be tormented by bullies. There is no guarantee that the Sanders will be forgiving, and I'll simply not put Philip in that situation."

During the long silence that followed, Julia thought of the rumors she had heard about the Sanders brothers' bullying. The thought of her son being battered was more than she could bear. Finally she asked, "Are you sure this is the right thing to do?"

"Your son did nothing at all to the Sanders boys. If you want to punish him for slipping out, you've every right as a parent." He gave her a little smile, though the gray eyes were serious. "But let's not throw him to the wolves, shall we?"

"I wish to remind the students in the sixth standard of the importance of listening to instructions," Captain Powell said as he returned papers to the seven students involved.

Philip smiled at this, holding out his hand for his scored grammar examination. During the almost two weeks since the "ghost" prank, he had allowed himself to put the matter out of his mind . . . save the stabs of guilt over his lying whenever his mother prayed with him at night. Ben's report that the Keegans had come home last Sunday afternoon to find their shed upright for the third week in a row had helped a great deal. Why, Mother would likely be proud of him for

297

participating in such a benevolent effort, he told himself.

And so as his rationalizations took effect on his conscience, his desire to win the "top student" trophy returned in full force. Which was why when he looked down at the score of seventy-three at the top of his page, he clinched both sides of the paper so tightly that he almost tore it. Never in his life had he made such a poor mark! He glared at the *Listen to instructions before beginning* comment Captain Powell had penned under the score. He *had* listened, he thought, and most attentively. Actually, he was writing the answer to the first question as the instructions were explained . . . but that had never hindered him *before*.

A glance at the desk beside Philip told him that even Jeremiah, who had no pretensions of being a scholar, had scored an eighty-five! And of course, Laurel Phelps had turned in a perfect paper, receiving Captain Powell's congratulations.

He was determined not to look over at the high and mighty Miss Phelps. Why give her the satisfaction of seeing the disappointment on his face? But then some inexplicable impulse took over—such as the one that would compel him to curl his big toe in his shoe, despite the pain, for days after he'd jammed it on the bedpost—and he dragged his eyes over to her side of the room. She was staring down at her examination paper with an infuriating little smile on her face.

Why, she knows I'm looking at her! he realized, jerking his head to the front again. He fumed, clinching his hands together on top of the wretched paper. It would have been better had she scowled at him, then he could have scowled back. But to sit there with a pleased-as-punch-but-too-modest-to-gloat expression, knowing full well that he was looking, was almost more than he could bear. *Why did she have to move here?* Philip thought. While he rather liked Vicar Phelps and especially appreciated the advice about catching perch—which happened to work very nicely—weren't there other villages in need of ministers?

He passed up an after-school cricket match, brushing off Ben and Jeremiah with an "I'm not in the mood to play." As he slunk home ahead of his sisters, he wondered why he'd even bothered to get out of bed this morning. This day couldn't possibly get any worse.

His melancholy fog accompanied him to the kitchen door. When he opened it, he discovered his mother sitting alone at the table. There was no refreshment or cup of tea in front of her—in fact, it seemed as if she were waiting just for him, for she got to her feet right away. "Philip?" she said, folding her arms.

He set his lunch box on the cupboard ledge. "Yes, Mother?"

"Let's go to your room. We have something to discuss."

———

As angry as his mother was with him for slipping out of the house that Saturday night, Philip could see in her eyes that it was his lying about it afterward that had hurt her the most. "I'm sorry, Mother," he told her, aware of how feeble his apology sounded.

She only frowned. "Are you, Philip? How many other times have you lied to me?"

"This was the only time, Mother. And I'll never do it again." He meant it too. She'd had enough grief in her life, what with Father dying. Never again did he want to cause her sadness.

"I hope so, Philip."

His punishment, she told him, would be to come straight home from school for the next month, and to stay home those Saturdays as well. Philip didn't argue. After having deceived the person whom he loved more than anyone on earth, he almost looked forward to paying some penance.

He apologized again, tears burning his eyes, and Mother moved forward to kiss his forehead. "Forgiven," she said, smiling. "But you understand that the punishment still stands, don't you?"

"Yes, Mother."

As Philip went back to the kitchen for his books, he thought that at least one good thing had come from his dubious action. He would have more time to study.

*A*mbrose Clay's first errand of the next day, after his walk with Mrs. Kingston, was one he did not relish. The directions he'd asked of Mr. Jones, the postman, led him across the Bryce, a mile past the cheese factory, and then east on a winding dirt road. It was called Nettle Lane, he had been told, even though there was no signpost to identify it. Thick hedgerows flanked both sides of the lane, behind which sat the occasional thatched-roof cottage with barn, pig sty, gardens, and outbuildings.

I should have taken Mr. Herrick up on his offer of the carriage after all, Ambrose thought another mile later when none of the cottages he had passed fit Mr. Jones' description. But before he could talk himself into giving up, the next bend in the lane revealed a large but nondescript half-timbered cottage with the peak of a stone barn rising up from behind it.

At least two dozen cattle stared at him curiously from a field to the left of the cottage. *Perhaps the doctor's fee was no hardship.* That thought gave him a little comfort. Even though he would insist on reimbursing the Sanders, it was good to see that no meals were likely missed because of it.

Now all he had to do was figure out exactly what words a grown man should use to confess to skulking the roads of Gresham dressed as a ghost. For once he regretted that he'd awakened this morning in a decent mood. If he were in the grip of despondency, the situation would probably have overwhelmed him too much to do anything but sit by his window and watch life go on in the streets below.

Well, get it over with, he thought and stopped at a wooden gate set in the hedgerow. He did not see the boy on the other side until he heard a voice.

"What d'you want?"

Ambrose looked up, startled by the hostility in the tone. "Do you live here?"

"Mayhap. Who wants t'know?" The boy looked to be about thirteen years of age, with a shock of thick hair the color of straw over a tanned face. Ambrose could recall hearing a similar voice while hiding behind a yew tree in the Keegans' yard. *This must be the brother that ran,* he told himself. He could see no cane or crutch under the boy's arm.

"My name is Ambrose Clay. I would like to speak with your father."

"You ain't from the school, are you?"

"The school? Why, no."

"You sure look like one o' those school people. Like my papa told you folk, my little brothers don't wanter go. And it ain't against the law—"

"I'm not from the school." Ambrose let out a sigh and reached out for the latch. "Look, it's been delightful chatting with you, but I would like to see your father now."

"You!" The one word spoke it all—surprise, recognition, and anger, and the boy's face flushed crimson. "You talk just like that ghost!"

"Guilty, I must confess, though it pains me to do so. And you are. . . ?"

"You don't need to know," the boy scowled. "You hurt my brother."

"Most unforgivable of me," Ambrose said with a shake of the head. "And I've come to apologize and possibly make amends. I know it won't make up for the terror you suffered or cause your brother's foot to—"

Ambrose stopped, puzzled by the change in the boy's expression, for the redness in his cheeks had bleached to the color of chalk.

"It's all right, mister," the boy said, glancing furtively back over his shoulder at the cottage.

"But I want to—"

"Just go away!"

In the brief moment that it took the boy to send another glance at the cottage, Ambrose understood. The brothers had apparently manufactured a story in relation to the injury. He folded his arms and leaned against the gate. "So . . . if I apologize to your father, he'll find out that you both lied to him?"

"Please, mister. Go away!"

"I gather your father is rather unreasonable about that sort of thing."

"I'm beggin' you, mister. He'll take a strap to us!"

No matter what the boy had done in the past, it would take a heart of stone not to be moved by the pleading in his voice. But instead of leaving, Ambrose stepped back into the lane, allowing a plum tree leaning over the hedgerow to shield him from the cottage. He could still see the boy clearly. "But that leaves me with some problems."

"Problems?"

"Well, for one, I had my heart set on paying Dr. Rhodes' fee."

"Then just give it to the doctor, mister. It ain't been paid yet."

"Won't your father wonder. . . ?"

"My sister's the only one who can read, and she pays the bills. She won't tell Papa."

Pulling absently at his chin, Ambrose thought this over. While it was wrong of the two hooligans to deceive their father, was it his duty to burst into the cottage and inform him of such? Judging from what little he knew about the sons, he wasn't quite sure he wanted to spend a lot of time in the company of the father.

You came here to take care of the doctor's fee and to apologize, he reminded himself. And if the first could be taken care of as soon as he got back to town, then all that was left was to apologize. Which he had done only two minutes ago and could assume that the boy would relate his message to his brother.

"Is that all right, mister?"

The meekness in the lad's tone did not match the flash of memory that came back to Ambrose, of the two trying their best to tip over a helpless family's shed. And the fear that came into Philip Hollis's eyes when he spoke of the Sanders brothers. He stroked his chin again and studied the boy through narrowed eyes. *Some assurances for the future should be in order.*

"*Please*, mister?"

Ambrose smiled. "What is your name, son?"

"Oram," the boy replied, then added as an afterthought, "Sir."

"I would like to take you up on your suggestion and continue on home now. But I just can't do that until we've made an agreement."

"An agreement," the boy echoed, bobbing his head like someone dunking for apples. "Yes, that's fine."

"I won't tell your father—"

"Thank you, sir!"

". . . and you and your brother will leave the Keegans alone forever."

The bobbing paused. "The Keegans?"

"The Irish family. The basket weavers."

"We'll leave 'em alone," Oram declared, resuming nodding.

"I don't even want to hear that you've been *talking* to them. Or going anywhere near them or their place. Do you understand?"

The boy was starting to look drained but relieved. "Mister, you don't have t'worry about that. We'll never go near 'em. Ever."

Now Ambrose had to be careful, for he was determined not to implicate the three lads who had accompanied him on that night. But while the boy was in such an agreeable mood, he might as well get all he could out of it. "And there are some other boys in Gresham that you bully. It disturbs me to hear of it. Some are my friends."

"Just tell me who your friends are and we'll leave 'em alone."

"H-m-m," Ambrose said, tapping his forehead thoughtfully. "The names escape me at the moment. . . ."

"Then we won't bother nobody. Just please stay away from our papa."

"Very well, then." Ambrose touched the brim of his bowler hat. "Have a good day now, son."

The boy mopped his brow with his sleeve. "Yes, thank you. Sir."

———

By the time Ambrose crossed the Bryce again, it was past time for lunch. While an occasional rumble from his stomach reminded him of that fact, it seemed far more pressing that he attempt to undo the rest of the harm his prank had caused. *There has to be a way,* he thought, though for the life of him, he could not see it at the moment. And then a name crossed his mind, and instead of continuing down Market Lane, he found himself crossing the green.

"My father's conducting a funeral service at the church," the vicar's daughter, who introduced herself as Elizabeth Phelps, told Ambrose at the door of the vicarage. He had heard table talk about the family but hadn't realized any daughter was married. She seemed too young to be mother to the wide-eyed boy in her arms and the girl clutching her skirt at her side. "The servants are there as well, but I was afraid the children would make noise, so I kept them here."

"Then I'll come back at a more convenient time," Ambrose told her, hat in hand.

"Actually, he should be home any minute." Miss Phelps smiled and hefted the boy up a bit. "You may come in and wait if you like."

Propriety forbade him to accept the invitation, even though there were two small chaperones present. "I believe I would enjoy waiting out in your garden," he told her politely. "Would that be all right?"

"Of course."

He had just arranged his limbs into a wicker chair when voices drifted over from the direction of Saint Jude's. He stretched his neck and caught sight of four figures, two male and two female, coming his way from the churchyard. Ambrose supposed the man wearing the black suit to be the vicar. He was a little surprised. His acquaintance with men of the cloth had been limited, but he carried a preconceived notion that they were all required to be tall and lean, clean-shaven and scholarly looking, and of equal importance, slightly stoop-shouldered with hair graying at the temples. Spectacles were optional.

The man who'd just lifted a hand to wave at him looked as if he'd just unhooked a team of oxen from a plow. Broad-shouldered he was, with a blond beard and comfortable gait that was almost Nordic. Ambrose got to his feet and raised a hand in return, then studied his own shoes and wondered for the fourth time since setting out from the *Larkspur* exactly what he had hoped to accomplish here. He found himself more nervous than he had been while approaching the Sanders' place.

When he looked up again, the three servants had veered off toward the back of the cottage and the black-suited man was only six feet from the gate. "Reverend Phelps?" Ambrose said.

"Yes?"

"Ambrose Clay." They shook hands over the gate. "I lodge at the *Larkspur*."

"Ah," the vicar nodded. "You must be the actor."

"How could you tell?"

"I knew there were two men lodging there, and I met Mr. Durwin just yesterday and learned a little about him." He tilted his head a bit. "Besides . . . you look like an actor."

Ambrose took a step backward as the man let himself in the gate. "You don't look like a vicar, if you'll forgive my saying so. The beard and all."

Reverend Phelps laughed at this. "Well, you know what Shakespeare wrote about beards, don't you?"

"I'm afraid I don't," Ambrose admitted after a moment's thought.

" 'He that hath no beard is less than a man.' " The vicar's hazel eyes crinkled at the corners. "No insult intended. Just quoting the Bard."

"From *Much Ado About Nothing*! I believe it was Beatrice who made the observation."

"You are correct, Mr. Clay."

Now it was Ambrose who laughed as they ambled up the stone walk together. "Touché, reverend. I take it you're fond of Shakespeare?"

"Extremely so. And while I'm happy in my called profession, I can't help but envy you a little."

"Me?"

"As exciting as it is to read his works, it must be thrilling to live them on the stage."

"It has its moments," Ambrose said but could not discuss his career without being painfully reminded of his weakness, so he changed the subject. "I wonder if I might have a few minutes of your time, Reverend Phelps."

The vicar paused with his hand on the doorknob. "But of course, Mr. Clay."

Ambrose was reintroduced to the older daughter, now reading to the children in the parlor, and was somewhat relieved to learn that the two children belonged to a family in the village. Still, Miss Phelps seemed to have great affection for them, and likewise on their part, for they had settled in her lap like robins in a nest. The vicar's younger daughter, he was told and had already assumed, was at school.

"We'll visit in the study," the vicar said after asking a maid he called Dora to send some tea. Ambrose was led down a short corridor to a small room lined with shelves of books and took the chair the reverend offered facing the desk.

"Very comfortable room," Ambrose remarked, looking about him. Only one wall, the one the door opened from, did not contain shelves groaning with books, but instead, a framed Constable landscape hung between a long-case clock and a rowing paddle. A small cast-iron coal stove gave off heat in a corner. He wasn't quite sure what he had expected from a minister's house—stark, austere walls and rows of pews, perhaps?

Vicar Phelps pulled out the chair on the opposite side of his desk. "Thank you. I realize it's a bit formal in here for guests, but I always assume most people who visit would rather talk in private."

"That's certainly my case."

"Yes? What may I do for you, Mr. Clay?"

"Well, I've caused a bit of trouble and can't seem to find a way to undo it. And since I've learned that Mrs. Hollis—my landlady—spoke with you yesterday, shortly before having a serious discussion with me, I must assume that you're aware of what I've done."

After several seconds of silence, the vicar shook his head. "I'm afraid you have me at a loss, Mr. Clay. Mrs. Hollis never mentioned your name."

"She didn't?" Ambrose chewed on his lip. "But then how did she know I was the ghost?"

Now the vicar's blond eyebrows shot up. "You?"

"You know about the ghost?"

"Along with half the village. But I assumed it was a hallucination."

"If only that were the case." Ambrose passed a hand over his face. "I supposed I've obligated myself to explain."

"Please. I'm intrigued."

The maid came in with tea and shortbread, poured, and then left. After taking a sip from his cup, Ambrose pulled in a deep breath and began with the afternoon in the kitchen of the *Larkspur*, when he'd heard about the Irish family's troubles. *And you wanted to make Fiona O'Shea happy,* he thought but did not say. When he had gone through the following Saturday night in every detail, he sat back in his chair and waited for the censure that was sure to come.

Instead the vicar appeared to be struggling to rein in a smile. "That's quite a story, Mr. Clay."

"Go ahead and laugh, if you wish. I would too if I weren't the principal character and hadn't involved three boys." Ambrose took a longer drink of the tea, *almost* wishing it were something more potent. "And now Mrs. Hollis is unhappy because new fuel has been added to the Jake Pitt rumor."

"I gathered that yesterday." The vicar steepled his fingers and pressed them against his chin. "And now you wish to make amends, Mr. Clay?"

Ambrose nodded. "If at all possible. I've already spoken with one of the Sanders boys involved, so things seem to be taken care of in that regard. But it's the ghost rumor that I would like to nip in the bud. I don't know quite how to go about doing that, and I fear it may be a lost cause."

Leaning forward in his chair, he continued, "I realize I haven't the right to ask you this, not being a member of your congregation, but is there any way you could help me?"

*Y*ou're all invited for punch and cake in the town hall after the evensong service," Vicar Phelps announced from the pulpit three days later after the closing prayer of the morning worship. "And some very special entertainment, so please plan to attend if at all possible."

"What do you think that was about?" Mrs. Kingston asked Julia and Fiona as the congregation milled around outside the church doors. "Why the secrecy? Is he going to sing?"

"Why, I don't know," Julia replied. She thought about the way the vicar had smiled at her when he shook her hand at the door. Had she imagined a conspiratorial glint in his eyes? But what would punch and cake and entertainment in the town hall have to do with her? "But no doubt it's going to be a lovely evening."

"And surprises are nice, don't you think?" Fiona added.

Mrs. Kingston glanced back at the church door and frowned. "Well, I do like the young man. But he just *winked* at me when I asked him what was going on."

"Did you wink back?" Julia teased.

"Not on your life!" she snorted.

Julia looked beyond Mrs. Kingston at a woman and group of children gathered around Elizabeth Phelps. The vicar's daughter held one of the children, a small girl, in her arms, and appeared to be enjoying the company of the whole group. It was encouraging to Julia to see some calm in the girl's expression.

"You've become friends with his elder daughter, haven't you?" asked Mrs. Kingston, noticing the object of her attention. "Why don't you go over there and ask her about tonight?"

"I would rather be surprised," Julia told her firmly but smiling. "And so would you, I'm sure." She dropped the subject to compliment Mrs. Kingston's gown, a navy silk trimmed with ruching of the same color. Just yesterday, the woman had abruptly declared herself weary of wearing black after three years and asked Willa to air and press some gowns that had been consigned to the bottom of her trunk. Though the gown was cut in a Pompadour pattern of the last decade, it was of good quality cloth and softened the woman's imperial appearance considerably. And instead of the usual black bonnet, she wore one of taupe-colored velvet bedecked with tiny silk flowers. "Why, you look absolutely stunning."

"Like Cinderella on her way to the ball," Fiona said.

"Nonsense," Mrs. Kingston muttered but could not hide the pleasure in her expression. It became even more pronounced when Mr. Durwin came by to remind Julia and Fiona that he would not be in attendance for Sunday dinner. He had recently discovered that a half-dozen other village men possessed some skill with wind instruments—Mr. Durwin played the baritone himself—and had approached each with the idea of forming a brass band.

"Captain Powell has invited us to lunch at his house so we can plan our practice sessions," Mr. Durwin explained, though he had already given Fiona the same information yesterday.

"It's going to be so nice having a band in the village," Mrs. Kingston gushed in a most uncharacteristic manner. "Will you be performing concerts, Mr. Durwin?"

"We hope to in the future," Mr. Durwin replied, seeming not to notice anything unusual. "I daresay most of us are a bit rusty at present."

That information squelched the notion forming in Julia's mind that the meeting in the town hall had something to do with Mr. Durwin's brass band. "I'll be sure to inform Mrs. Herrick," she told the gentleman. As he thanked her and walked away, Julia noticed that Mrs. Kingston's blue eyes followed.

"I just know she's going to be hurt one day," Julia told Fiona later in the day as they enjoyed a rare visit, with feet propped up on footstools in the housekeeper's tiny parlor.

"But you can't shield her from that, ma'am," Fiona said tactfully from one of the overstuffed chairs. "She's an adult and old enough to manage her own affairs."

"I know," Julia sighed, resting her head against the back of her chair. "And at least her family situation seems to be improving, judging from the letters that go back and forth to Sheffield."

"Do you think we'll be looking for another lodger one day soon?"

Julia raised an eyebrow. That possibility hadn't crossed her mind. "I hope not *too* soon. I'm rather fond of the crusty old soul."

"So am I," Fiona agreed. "And I can't see her leaving just yet. She has high hopes for the garden come spring."

"It does her good to have Mr. Clay to fuss over as well."

Fiona's face clouded at the mention of the actor's name. "Aye, missus."

"What's wrong, Fiona?" Julia asked. At the same time a light seemed to go on inside her head. *Why are you the last person to notice what goes on around you?* she asked herself. "Mr. Clay cares for you, doesn't he?"

A somber nod was Fiona's answer.

"And how do you feel about him?"

"It doesn't matter how I feel."

The fact that Julia had managed to push Fiona's cruel sham of a marriage from her mind didn't mean that it had ceased to exist. She felt an acute sense of loss for her friend, for she now knew the answer to her question. "I'm so sorry, Fiona."

Fiona stared, unblinking, down at the slippers she had propped up on the footstool. "Thank you, missus."

"Have you told him about your husband?"

"Just last week."

"You poor, poor dear. How did Mr. Clay take it?"

"It happened to be one of his bad days, missus, so he was already feeling despondent before I told him. But he seems to have accepted the matter, so perhaps that affection was just a notion in my head."

"I don't know about that," Julia responded doubtfully. "But I'm relieved to hear he's acting the gentleman and not pressuring you. I would hate to have to ask him to leave. Everyone rather likes him."

"Yes," Fiona sighed. "He has that way about him, hasn't he?"

Vicar Phelps's evensong sermon on Jacob and Esau was shorter than usual. Which was wise, Julia thought, considering the anticipatory mood of the congregation. She was learning that in Gresham special occasions were not taken for granted but were cherished and talked about for years. After the closing hymn, no one dawdled outside the door of the church as usual but hurried on over to the town hall. Chairs were set up facing the platform, and just inside to the right, Elizabeth and Laurel Phelps, along with Mrs. Paget and Dora from the vicarage, handed out servings of cake and punch in the crockery dishes and cups used at church functions.

"Please find a seat as soon as you've been served," said Vicar Phelps, closing the doors against the night chill when the last person had entered. The massive cast-iron stove in the left corner, huge as it was, would take an hour to warm the room again, but the ninety or so people present didn't seem to mind keeping their wraps on as they settled into chairs.

Cake and punch cups in hand, Julia and the girls filed into seats in the sixth row with Fiona, Miss Rawlins, and Mrs. Kingston. Mr. Durwin and Mrs. Hyatt had taken places elsewhere, and Philip was in the front row with Ben and Jeremiah. All conversation died down when Vicar Phelps walked up to the platform.

"Thank you for your presence here this evening," he said, smiling. Julia had the idle thought that the minister looked more at ease tonight than he had on his first Sunday in Gresham back in late September. Perhaps the country was growing on him, as it had on her family. "We're going to dim some of the lamps, but we'll keep these on the platform burning, so don't be alarmed."

The hum of conversation returned now as Luke extinguished the four lamps hanging from posts on either side of the hall, and Julia could hear Mrs. Kingston's, "Well, I certainly have no idea what's going on" above it. She felt Grace move a little closer and put an arm around her shoulder.

"You aren't afraid, are you?" Julia asked her.

"They aren't going to put out all the lights, are they?"

"Not all of them."

"You'll see presently why we've done this," Vicar Phelps said, his face assuming a serious expression in the glow of the lamps at the foot of the platform. "But first, I wish to thank you good people for being so patient with me. I have learned many things from you since moving to Gresham and still have much more to learn. You have been kind to my daughters and have not resented my humble attempts to follow in the footsteps of your beloved Reverend Wilson."

He smiled then and clasped both hands behind his back. "I found myself wishing, recently, for a way to repay you for your kindness. And an opportunity was handed to me that very same day. No doubt you are all aware that an esteemed actor, Mr. Ambrose Clay, resides at the *Larkspur*."

A low murmur ran through the assemblage and then died. Julia met Fiona's puzzled eyes over the tops of Grace's and Aleda's heads. *I don't know,* Julia mouthed.

"Mr. Clay approached me only days ago, concerned that he had caused a misunderstanding in the community. I suggested that he tell you about it himself, and since his acting has been acclaimed throughout Great Britain and even as far as New York and Canada, I asked that he give us a demonstration of his talent as well."

Now there were murmurs of what appeared to be surprise mingled with delight.

"I must warn those with children that Mr. Clay is in costume. While his appearance is in no way fierce, it is, well, different. You may wish to take a minute to reassure them not to be alarmed."

"You hear that, don't you?" Mrs. Kingston said, leaning forward to peer past Miss Rawlins and Fiona at Grace and Aleda. "It's just going to be Mr. Clay. There is no cause for fright."

"Yes, ma'am," Aleda told her.

"And now I present to you, Mr. Ambrose Clay," the vicar said before taking a seat on the front row. Forewarned as everyone was, there were still gasps when Mr. Clay came through the storage room door and stepped up on the platform. He had the appearance of a moving marble statue in his gray wig, tights, and robe. And through the greasepaint that gave his skin an unearthly glow, Julia could see a sheepish expression lurking. Mr. Clay gave a bow and then spoke.

"It has been my great pleasure through the years to perform various parts in William Shakespeare's *Hamlet of Denmark*. One of my earlier roles onstage was of Prince Hamlet's father—who was murdered and returns as a ghost. But before I perform some lines from the play, I've a confession to make."

At the word "confession" Julia sensed a collective holding of breath.

"No doubt many of you have noticed Mrs. Kingston and me walking the lanes of this fair village. We participate in this activity every morning, no matter what the weather."

Some turned to their neighbors with knowing nods, as if to say, *That's true, I've seen them.*

"On the Saturday of September twenty-sixth, I happened to take two walks. The first was my usual appointment with Mrs. Kingston, and the second was down Worton Lane. It was near midnight, and I was wearing this same costume."

Murmurs broke out all around, and several faces turned to the left. Julia followed the line of vision to see Mr. and Mrs. Hopper seated across the aisle with stunned expressions. Turning back to the front, Julia could only see the backs of Philip's and his companions' heads, but they sat there as rigid as three gateposts in a row.

"No doubt you're asking yourself why a grown man would act in such a bizarre manner," Mr. Clay went on, and it was clear from his tone that he would rather be anywhere than on that platform. "Unfortunately, I am not at liberty to tell you, but let me assure you my actions were neither illegal nor immoral. And will never be repeated."

That matter closed, he allowed a smile to relax his face. "From William Shakespeare's *Hamlet*. In this scene from Act I, the ghost, Prince Hamlet's father, is telling Hamlet that he was murdered by his own brother, who has now married his wife and ascended to the throne."

"Is Mr. Clay going to sing now?" Grace whispered up at Julia.

"Not sing . . . act," Julia whispered back. "I'll explain at home."

An awesome transformation came over Mr. Clay's face. He raised an arm slowly and spoke with such conviction that Julia could almost see Prince Hamlet standing onstage with him:

. . . I am thy father's spirit'
Doom'd for a certain term to walk the night,
And for the day confined to fast in fires,
Till the foul crimes done in my days of nature,
Are burnt and purged away. But that I am forbid
To tell the secrets of my prison-house,
I would harrow up thy soul, freeze thy young blood . . .

Applause rippled through the room when the actor paused to take a breath, but he held up a restraining hand before it could escalate.

. . . Now, Hamlet, hear:
'T is given out that, sleeping in mine orchard,
A serpent stung me' so the whole ear of Denmark
Is by a forged process of my death
Rankly abused; but know, thou noble youth,
The serpent that did sting thy father's life
Now wears his crown.

And he was only just beginning, for while even the children sat spellbound, Mr. Clay performed bits from several scenes in the play—

sometimes as the ghost, sometimes as Hamlet—and even received a complimentary jeer or two during his portrayal of the evil murderer, Claudius. As he moved from one scene or character to another, he took the time to inform his audience what was taking place, and they appeared to love him for it. Julia smiled to herself, aware that any eccentricity Mr. Clay had confessed had been forgiven.

And hopefully, Jake Pitt could finally be laid to rest, for even the villagers not present would hear all about this tomorrow in the shops and factory and at the common pump. *Bless you, Mr. Clay!* And Vicar Phelps too, she thought, for his part in this.

After the last scene there was an almost reverent silence, until Mr. Sykes rose and began pounding his hands together and was quickly joined by others. Mr. Clay gave an incredible encore, though streams of sweat now mingled with the greasepaint on his face. It was a quick-as-lightning comedy sketch between a gravedigger and Hamlet, using faint differences of voice and posture to signify which character was which. When he finally stepped down from the platform, dozens of villagers of all ages surged into the aisle to be among the first at the front to shake his hand. Among those was Mrs. Rhodes, who stopped long enough to greet Julia as well.

"I have an idea about what happened that night," the veterinary doctor whispered as she leaned over to give Julia a quick embrace. "Fernie Sanders breaks his foot about the same time? Perhaps someone thought he needed a good scare."

While Julia gaped at her, the veterinarian gave her a knowing smile. "But I'll keep any such notions to myself, you can be sure."

"I would appreciate that," Julia said, returning her smile. After Mrs. Rhodes had moved on up the aisle, Julia turned to her right and caught the bleakness in Fiona's expression.

"Are you all right?"

"Yes, ma'am," Fiona replied, but her eyes said differently.

She loves him, Julia thought. She put a hand on her friend's arm. "I'm so sorry, Fiona."

"It's all right, ma'am," Fiona replied with a forced little smile. "I would like to go on home now. Do you mind?"

"Of course not. The children and I will walk with you."

Miss Rawlins and Gertie joined them as they attempted to keep up with Mrs. Kingston's pace across the green under a cobalt October sky. A slice of harvest moon stood poised over the Anwyl ahead while night breezes eddied about them. "That was something, wasn't it?" Miss Rawlins declared, smiling.

"Maybe you could write a book about it," Gertie suggested shyly.

To her credit, Miss Rawlins cocked her head and pretended to consider the suggestion. Or perhaps she actually *was* considering it—Julia could never be sure about Miss Rawlins' plots.

"Interesting . . ." the writer said.

"What I can't understand," Mrs. Kingston began, resignedly slowing her steps so the group could catch up. "is why Mr. Clay wouldn't tell us his reason for wandering about in that getup."

Julia looked over at Philip, who was walking with both hands in his pockets just behind the rest of the group. No doubt he had suffered during Mr. Clay's confession, wondering exactly how much the actor was going to reveal. She veered over to him and put a hand on his shoulder. "I'm sure he had good reasons," Julia said to the others. The boy shot her a grateful smile.

It was after they arrived at the *Larkspur* that Julia remembered with some chagrin that she hadn't thanked Mr. Clay and Vicar Phelps. After tucking the children in bed, she decided to write a note of appreciation to the vicar, to be sent tomorrow, and wait to thank Mr. Clay in person. She penned the note, then chatted with the other lodgers in the hall while waiting for Mr. Clay. When he hadn't shown up an hour later, she decided it would keep until tomorrow and went on to bed.

*A*mbrose wasn't quite sure how he ended up standing at the riverbank with Vicar Phelps. They had both stayed in the town hall until every last villager had returned home, including the vicar's daughters and servants. Then Ambrose changed from his costume, wiping what was left of his greasepaint on a towel. He was a little surprised to see the vicar waiting for him when he came out of the makeshift dressing area in the storage room, but then of course the lamps had to be extinguished.

The two ended up spending a good half hour on the stoop engaged in conversation about the stage. Ambrose was amused at the way the vicar's eyes lit up while listening to his stories about mishaps that had taken place in the course of touring and about occasions when actors sometimes were forced to improvise onstage after forgetting lines they'd known for months.

And then without either man suggesting that they do so, they began walking north across the green. Living out of a trunk for most of his thirty-six years had given Ambrose scant opportunities to cultivate friendships with other men. He had never truly realized what a vacancy this had left in his life until tonight. And it was good to talk, to keep his mind occupied so that it wouldn't stray to the person he no longer had the right to think about.

But if anyone had told me a year ago that I'd be comfortable chatting with a minister, I wouldn't have believed him.

" . . . and so, that was the extent of my acting experience," the minister was saying as he threw a stone through a gap between two willows to skip over the Bryce's surface. "A student production of *A Midsummer Night's Dream*."

"You certainly don't fit my idea of Puck," Ambrose told him.

"Ah, but you must remember these were my preparatory school

days. I was two inches shorter then and lighter by a good three stone."

"And now you perform on a different type of stage," Ambrose said without thinking, then grew horrified at his own words. Even he, who had rarely been inside a church—and then only for the occasional wedding or funeral—realized he had just insulted the man.

But the vicar picked up another stone and threw it at an angle toward the water. "You know, sometimes I become full of myself and do just that. Perform, I mean. But God has a way of reminding me that I'm just His messenger." He turned to grin at Ambrose. "A postman, if you will."

Ambrose had to chuckle. "Doesn't anything perturb you, Reverend?"

"You wouldn't have to ask that if you had a grown daughter, Mr. Clay."

They started walking to the west, and after a space of companionable silence, Ambrose thought of the myriad of questions his mind had accumulated during his nightly readings in the Bible Mrs. Kingston had pressed upon him. He had not been able to ask anyone at the *Larkspur*, not even Mrs. Hollis, for fear of encouraging discussions about his mortal soul—discussions that made him uncomfortable on his best days.

But he didn't have to live in the same house with the vicar, he told himself, and as much as he was beginning to like the man, he could brush him off quite easily if he had to. *Go ahead and ask*, some inner voice urged. He cleared his throat and turned his face toward the man. "There are some things that have confused me of late. If I pose a couple of theological questions to you, will you give me your word you'll just answer them and not try to convert me?"

"Hmm, that's a tough one," the vicar replied. "You don't mean . . . not ever, do you?"

"I suppose just for this evening will do," Ambrose sighed. He should have known it wouldn't be as simple as he'd proposed.

"Then I will give you my word. For this evening. But if I lapse into preaching you'll have to remind me. It's as much a part of me as my arm."

"Fair enough." Ambrose chewed on his lip and tried to decide upon the first question, finally coming up with, "Why is it we're not supposed to wear clothes woven from linen and wool together?"

"What?" The vicar said, halting in his tracks. An indulgent smile spread across his face. "Tell me, Mr. Clay, how long have you been reading the Bible?"

"Who said I'm—"

"You recently picked it up and started at the first page, didn't you? And you've gotten yourself bogged down in the book of Leviticus."

"I normally begin books from the first page, vicar," Ambrose bristled. "What's wrong with that?"

"Well, the Bible isn't a novel, Mr. Clay. It must be spiritually discerned. And frankly, you cannot obtain that discernment until you've met the Author."

"Met the author?"

"You've asked me not to try to convert you this evening, and I'll keep my word. But I strongly recommend you first read the book of Saint John, and then Saint Paul's letter to the Romans. Then I'd like to talk with you about what you've read."

Things were moving too fast for Ambrose, and he was starting to feel great discomfort. Holding up a hand, he said, "Perhaps we'll talk about it. I don't know yet."

"As long as you're reading anyway, will you at least start with Saint John?"

"All right," Ambrose shrugged, and they resumed their walk. Presently, he grumbled, "I don't see why you can't just tell me about the wool and linen."

"I'll be happy to," the vicar chuckled. "Forgive me for being so vague. Since you've read past Exodus, you know that the Israelites were a people God wanted to set apart. He gave them several laws meant to instill a reverence for order that was set by Him—such as the law forbidding two varieties of seeds to be mixed together while sowing. I don't pretend to understand many of them, Mr. Clay, but then I don't have to, since they were addressed to the Israelites, and under the old covenant."

"The old covenant? Well, what's the new covenant then?"

"The new covenant, my talented friend, is the blood atonement of Jesus Christ. You did ask. And it would be a lie to give you any other answer."

"And . . . I believe I'm feeling a little worn from the performance," Ambrose told him. "Your daughters will be wondering about you as well."

"Then I suppose it's time to bid you farewell," Vicar Phelps said, causing Ambrose to appreciate the fact that he did not attempt to pressure him. They shook hands and the vicar turned to head back toward the vicarage.

Ambrose had gone about twelve feet when a fish jumped in the water to his right. It was a lonely sound in the still darkness, but it gave him comfort in a way that he couldn't fathom. He turned and looked at the retreating back of the minister, barely visible in the darkness, and impulsively called out, "Saint John, you said?"

Slowing his pace only a little, the vicar looked over his shoulder and waved a hand. "Let me know when you're ready to talk."

———————

Darcy Knight's tiny nostrils flared with fury, her iridescent green eyes clawing across the handsome dragoon's face like talons. "Just because you've beaten General Bonaparte, Colonel Jefferies, doesn't mean you can march back up here to Keld and expect me to fall at your feet like the rest of England! If the moors couldn't tame me in six years, what makes you assume you can in three weeks?"

Fiona rubbed sleep from her eyes, the words briefly running together on the page. *Is it possible to be a heroine without having a willful streak, pouting lips, and wild mane of hair?* she asked herself. *And must every hero be tall, with an aquiline nose and strong square chin?*

She didn't know why she didn't put the novel down and go to sleep, but then that would require the routine necessary for dressing for bed. It seemed easier just to lie across her coverlet and stare at an increasingly predictable plot. *But it was kind of her to lend it to me*, Fiona reminded herself.

The trouble had started when Miss Rawlins recently learned that she was an avid reader and had generously insisted upon lending Fiona eight of her published novelettes. "You may take your time reading them, Miss O'Shea," she had said, beaming as would a mother holding out her brood for a neighbor to admire. "But I would appreciate hearing your opinion as you finish each one. A reader's insight is so valuable."

That was the most difficult part, trying to think of something complimentary to say after she finished the first book, *The Marquis' Daughter*, without being dishonest. And pointing out that the spelling was flawless didn't seem to be the kind of observation the novelist was seeking. But it turned out to be no problem—once Fiona mentioned, truthfully, that she enjoyed the description of Venice, Miss Rawlins smiled appreciatively and took over the conversation.

"I'm so happy to hear that, Miss O'Shea, because the setting is almost as important as the plot itself," she'd said, pushing her reading spectacles up the bridge of her nose.

"And just how many books have *you* written, Fiona O'Shea?" Fiona murmured as she turned another page. It was easy to criticize someone else's work, particularly when it was something she'd never attempted. *But eight books!*

A second dying ember snapped in her fireplace . . . or so she thought until the realization hit her that both sounds had come from her window. She closed the book, got up from the bed, and went over to press her face against the glass. There was Mr. Clay, standing in the courtyard, waving a hand at her. She opened the casement and leaned out a bit.

"Mr. Clay?" she whispered loudly, lest she wake up the others.

"Forgive me, Miss O'Shea," he whispered back, "but your light is the only one burning. My key must have dropped from my pocket as I was changing at the town hall. I went back there to look, but the door's locked."

"I'll be right there."

She padded quietly down the corridor, aware in the circle of candlelight that her dress was terribly wrinkled from where she'd lain across the bed to read. She did not bother to brush out some of the wrinkles, for what did it matter? At the courtyard door she raised the latch and allowed him in.

"Thank you," he said, rubbing his shirt sleeves. "It's turned a bit nippy out."

"Where is your costume?"

"Back at the hall . . . with my key, I presume. Sorry to disturb you."

"It's all right, Mr. Clay." She found that she could avoid looking directly into his eyes by focusing just a shade to the right of each one. Pushing open the door to the lantern room, she said, "If you wouldn't mind holding my candle, I'll get another for you."

"Thank you."

Fiona stepped into the room, with Mr. Clay holding the candle aloft behind her. She could feel his eyes upon her back, but he did not step through the open doorway. Soon she'd fitted another candle upon a holder. Back in the corridor, she lit it from the one Mr. Clay still held.

"Well, thank you for rescuing me," he told her in a friendly but not particularly intimate tone.

She wondered if she had presumed wrongly about his feelings for her. That should have caused her some relief, but it did not. "Good night, sir. And thank you for what you did tonight."

"You mean, locking myself out like an idiot?"

"Trying to put an end to the Jake Pitt rumor. And especially for what you did for the Keegans."

He did not answer until she finally was forced to look him in the eyes. "I did nothing for the Keegans."

"But their shed hasn't been distur—"

"I did it for you, Miss O'Shea. And now I bid you good-night."

On her way back to her room, Fiona didn't realize she was crying until a cold tear dropped from the side of her chin to the bodice of her gown. She wiped her face with the back of her hand and went over to the mirror above her chest of drawers. The woman who stared back at her looked ghastly in the candlelight, with hooded eyes set into an amber-palled face.

You look just like an adulteress, she thought and wiped another tear from her face. For it was nothing short of adultery for a married woman to love a man who was not her husband. *You must leave this place at once.*

It was the only way. *And as soon as possible.* If she stayed long enough to give notice or even say good-bye, Mrs. Hollis would ask Mr. Clay to leave instead. As much as her heart ached at the thought of leaving the family she had come to love, she could not do that to him. He'd found a harbor here in Gresham, a safe place that would encourage him to collect the strength to allow him to return to the stage one day.

And who knew? There seemed to be a rapport between Mr. Clay and Vicar Phelps, judging by what she had observed in the town hall tonight. Perhaps a friendship would develop that would ultimately cause the actor to come to faith.

A picture of the mistress and children standing dumbfounded in the hall upon their first arrival at the *Larkspur* floated into her mind, but she shook it away. *Sentiment will weaken your nerve,* she warned herself. The *Larkspur* was providing a good living for the Hollises, so she didn't have to worry about looking out for them anymore. And the servants were used to their routines, so they could do without a housekeeper for as long as it took to hire another.

She would go back to London, she decided. Surely Mr. Jensen, who turned out to have a kind heart after all, could be persuaded to give her a good character reference. A housekeeper with the experience she now possessed could easily find a position through one of the domestic agencies. Early tomorrow morning she would pack whatever she could fit into a gripsack and wave down a ride to Shrewsbury with one of the cheese factory carriers. They rumbled past the *Larkspur* daily before the sun appeared and often rented out extra space on their wagon seats for travelers wishing to spare the expense of a coach.

Father, forgive me for being so underhanded, she prayed. *But please give me the strength to carry through with it.*

First snow of the season, and on Christmas day, Julia thought early that morning, padding over to her bedroom window in her slippers. She drew her wrapper more tightly about her and touched the cold glass. Light, powdery flakes danced this way and that and had already started collecting in the corners of the windowsill.

"Are you thinking about us, Fiona?" she murmured. Her friend had been gone for over two months now, but Julia often thought she could sense her presence across the miles, could even feel the prayers she knew were being lifted up for her family. Selfishly, she realized, she had assumed Fiona would always be part of their lives. A lump welled up in her throat, and at that moment she could imagine Fiona looking at her with that straightforward expression, saying, *It's time to get on with your life, missus, as I've gotten on with mine.*

And Fiona had gotten on quite well, according to her first letter from London, finding a housekeeping position in the home of Mr. Harold Leighton, a member of Parliament. Her letters asked about everyone at the *Larkspur,* including the lodgers, but she did not mention any particular lodger by name.

Nor did Mr. Clay ask about her anymore, but some relief had come to his face when Julia volunteered at the dinner table that she was safe and sound in her new location. Afterward she had been tempted to tell Mr. Clay privately the full particulars of Fiona's marriage, but fortunately thought better of it and held her tongue. If he became aware of the past cruelty of her husband, any romantic notions he still had would be fueled—perhaps he would feel the need to rescue her. But the marriage was as binding as if her husband were a saint. Some things couldn't change, no matter how badly one wished they could.

Mr. Clay had to have suspected that she had left because of him. He had volunteered, even insisted upon moving away himself in the hopes that she would return. But the note Fiona had left behind on her night table had let it be known that no set of circumstances would cause her to change her mind. *And so she sacrificed everything she was familiar with so he would stay.*

Julia sighed and turned away from the window. *It's Christmas, and here you are moping.* And with a hundred things yet to do. She must get dressed, and there were the children to wake, if they hadn't already slipped out to prod and poke among the packages under the decorated tree in the hall.

She had just taken a gown from her wardrobe when a light knocking sounded upon her door.

"Come in," she said softly, and Mrs. Beemish, the new housekeeper, stepped into the room. After the shock of Fiona's departure had lessened, Julia sent letters of inquiry to the two domestic agencies in Shrewsbury. Mrs. Beemish was the first applicant sent up to Gresham for an interview, and Julia had liked her so much that they saw no need to interview any other applicants. She was a soft, rounded woman of average height, fifty-one years old, and with brown doe eyes and graying dark hair drawn back into a bun. Since starting out in service at age eleven, Mrs. Beemish had worked at every position possible in a well-run house, including that of cook. But she wisely allowed Mrs. Herrick total command over the kitchen, just as Fiona had, and so the two got on quite well.

Yet the best thing about her, in Julia's opinion, was her voice, as soothing as a warm cup of tea. And soothing was what she had needed after Fiona left.

"Merry Christmas, Mrs. Hollis!" the housekeeper said, smiling.

"And the same to you, Mrs. Beemish. Did you sleep well?"

"I'm afraid not, missus. You'd think that after fifty years, Christmas wouldn't excite me so much anymore."

Julia smiled. "I don't think that's such a bad thing."

"Thank you, missus. I just thought you might want to know that the children are in the hall, eyeing the stockings. They said they didn't want to wake you, but I suspect they were hoping I would."

"Then I should hurry before eyeing leads to touching." With the housekeeper's assistance she dressed quickly. On her way down the corridor, she thought with a touch of melancholy, *Our first Christmas without their father.*

On second thought, she recalled that he wasn't at home last Christmas, either, but then she had understood, because medical

323

emergencies had no consideration for the calendar. And surely it *had* been an emergency, for no decent father would bow out of Christmas with the family to gamble. At least she chose to believe that.

Reaching the hall, she paused for a minute in the doorway to drink in the sight before her. Philip sat in a chair in pajamas and slippers, and the girls were still clad in nightgowns on the sofa. All three sipped from mugs that likely contained hot chocolate, knowing Mrs. Beemish. Hanging from the chimneypiece were three bulging stockings, and in a corner stood the eight-foot fir tree that Mr. Durwin and Mr. Clay had hauled down from the Anwyl. Its branches were bedecked with little baskets and trays filled with candies, fruits, fancy cakes, and gilded gingerbread figures tied with colored ribbons. There were wax candles on the ends of the branches as well, to be lit after the church service when guests arrived for dinner and merrymaking.

Aleda caught sight of her and leaned forward to set her mug on the tea table. "Mother, you're awake!"

"Merry Christmas, children," Julia said, walking into the room. She bent to kiss each forehead, then squeezed in between the girls. "How long have you been in here?"

"Oh, ages and ages," Grace answered, sliding toward the edge of the sofa.

"May we take down our stockings now?" asked Philip. The children were already aware that the packages would have to wait until the lodgers were up and had breakfasted.

"Well . . ." Julia pretended to think this over.

"Oh, please, Mother," Grace pressed. "We can't wait another minute."

"Then of course you may."

With the aid of a chair, Philip took down all three stockings. They spent the time remaining before having to dress admiring their own and each other's gifts. Grace's favorite was a tiny tea set made of bone china, Aleda's, a silver flute, and Philip's, a folding pocket knife with a carved ivory handle. After breakfast, packages were opened from under the tree, with even the servants joining in. Julia and the three older women lodgers had bought or made something for each of them as well. The children reaped the greatest bounty, each receiving not only a gift from Julia—dolls for the girls, and a set of small tin soldiers for Philip—but something from every lodger, and even from Fiona via the post. This caused Julia a bit of concern, for she didn't want them growing up to associate Christmas with gifts alone.

What a far cry from what worried me back in March, she thought. Back then, her concern had been whether she would be able to provide the basic necessities for the children. *You're so good to us, Father.*

Snow was falling steadily as Mr. Herrick drove the members of Saint Jude's to church in the new landau behind Donny and Pete, two Welsh cob horses purchased in Woverhampton from an acquaintance of Doctor Rhodes. He had already delivered Mrs. Herrick, Mrs. Dearing, and Ruth to the Baptist chapel and would be joining them shortly. Saint Jude's seemed like a forest; there was so much holly about that members of the congregation seemed to be sprouting it. The organist and chancel choir performed at least a dozen Christmas carols, asking the congregation to accompany them, and Vicar Phelps's sermon about that holy night in Bethlehem was nothing short of moving.

Afterward, Vicar Phelps and his daughters, Dr. and Mrs. Rhodes, Captain and Mrs. Powell, the Worthy sisters, and Miss Hillock joined the occupants of the *Larkspur* for a dinner of roast goose with all the trimmings and plum pudding for dessert.

There would have been even more people present if the Keegans weren't spending the day with family in Shrewsbury—Julia had walked up to Worton Lane last week with a batch of Mrs. Herrick's almond-sugar cookies and, after being received so graciously, had extended an impulsive invitation. She wasn't quite sure if it had come from the goodness of her heart or from a longing to hear an Irish accent again.

After carols around the pianoforte with Aleda playing accompaniment, Julia took a brief respite from hostessing to stand by the tree and watch the gathering. Guests and lodgers alike were obviously enjoying one another's company. Even Mrs. Hyatt and Mrs. Kingston stood near the fireplace, their heads together while admiring the workmanship in Elizabeth Phelps's cranberry velvet dress. Apparently Mrs. Kingston had decided that Christmas was not a time for competing for the affections of a certain man, or better yet, no longer had an interest in him. The garden had most likely helped that along, giving Mrs. Kingston a project to keep her hands and mind busy. Even though she couldn't be out there working in it now, she pored over gardening books, making plans for spring. She was as determined to win a prize in the garden show as Philip was to win the school trophy.

And Philip . . . she watched the boy showing his new knife to Doctor and Mrs. Rhodes. Though not aggressively rude, he had practically ignored Laurel Phelps when he sat across from her at dinner. She didn't want to spoil his Christmas by scolding him, but in a day or two they would need to have a long talk about his resentment of the girl.

"My parents would never allow me to have a knife," came a voice at her right elbow, and she turned to smile at Vicar Phelps.

"Did you want one?"

"Oh, terribly."

"Do you think it was foolish of me?"

The vicar shook his head. "He seems a responsible boy."

Julia glanced over at the draughts table, where Laurel and Aleda were absorbed in a game. "I just wish he were more sociable toward your daughter, Vicar. I'm afraid he's become single-minded about this school competition."

"Well, I have to tell you that Laurel hasn't been a saint about it. I'm not sure now if she wants the trophy for its own sake or to prove that she can best him." He gave her a reassuring smile. "They'll grow out of it, Mrs. Hollis. You know what the Scripture says . . . 'When I was a child, I spake as a child.' "

She was indeed reassured and told him so. Since his first call in early October, Vicar Phelps had managed to pay a brief visit every week. Julia would join the lodgers in the hall and, like the others, appreciated his warm wit and kind nature. *And it's been over a month since I've heard Jake Pitt's name,* she thought.

"Mrs. Hollis," the vicar said from her side, interrupting her reverie. "Has Elizabeth visited you lately?"

"Why, not since early November. I suppose the children still keep her quite busy."

"They do indeed, but she hasn't complained. And the little girl, Molly, has taken to addressing her as Aunt Beth."

He glanced at the nearest chairs, where Jewel Worthy sat chatting with Miss Rawlins, then leaned closer and lowered his voice to a conspiratorial tone. "Another thing that's keeping her busy is . . . she has a beau."

Julia smiled and raised an eyebrow. "Yes?"

"His name is Paul Treves, a curate assigned to Alveley. He seems a decent fellow."

"But of course he is, if . . ."

He gave her a wry little smile. "Unfortunately, some men embrace the ministry for other reasons than a desire to preach the Gospel, Mrs. Hollis. But I'm impressed with what I've seen in him so far."

"I'm glad to hear it." Lowering her voice, Julia said, "Perhaps she's forgotten about Mr. Raleigh after all."

"Perhaps," he replied with a little less than total conviction in his voice.

"The aftermath was far worse than the amputation itself," Philip overheard Captain Powell say to Mr. Clay as he was passing by the two men. Suddenly his feet took root on the carpet beneath them.

"I felt 'ghost' pains for weeks afterward," Captain Powell went on, "and would often forget the arm was missing and reach out for things."

Did he just say how he lost it? Philip wondered, pretending to be absorbed in his knife as he stood just behind Mr. Clay's left elbow. Surely it had happened in the midst of some heated exchange of gunfire between Boer resistance and the British army. Or had it been the result of desperate hand-to-hand fighting with bayonets? He stepped a little closer to Mr. Clay, who surely must know that an eavesdropper lurked nearby, and listened intently.

"Were you right-handed before the amputation?" the actor asked.

"Left-handed, fortunately, so at least I didn't have to learn how to write all over again."

That would be hard to do, Philip thought, then happened to glance in the direction of the Christmas tree. His mother and Vicar Phelps caught his eye, standing close and smiling at each other as they chatted, as if no one else were in the same room, or even the same house. Philip blinked and studied the vicar a little closer, forgetting all about the arm Captain Powell may have left on the plains of South Africa. He had seen that look many times before on Mr. Clay's face when Fiona was still here.

But he's the vicar . . . and Mother just lost father.

In February, he reminded himself. Ten months ago. And as for Vicar Phelps being a minister, they were certainly allowed to marry, or Elizabeth and Laurel wouldn't be here.

Laurel, he thought, grinding his teeth a little. He turned his attention to the draughts board. As if sensing his eyes upon her, the vicar's daughter looked up and sent him a decided smirk. He returned the smirk, and then a horrid thought struck him. If his mother were to marry the vicar . . .

"Did you have a nice Christmas?" Julia asked as she tucked Philip's blankets over his shoulders. The children had been allowed to stay awake until the guests left at ten, and the effect of too much activity and too many rich foods was evident upon their faces. The girls had barely been able to stay awake during prayers, yawning incessantly as they held their new dolls.

"It was nice," he answered, but a bit of the old haunted look came back into his blue eyes.

"What's wrong, Philip?"

"Do you ever think about Father anymore?"

"Of course I do," she answered truthfully. *Not very often, but . . .*

"Will you ever get married again?"

"Married?" The question was so incongruent with the activities of the day that she had to take a second or two to absorb it. "Why do you ask?"

"Just wondering."

She had wondered that herself on occasion. Her earlier bitterness toward the whole institution had been tempered with time, and she missed the companionship, however shallow, she'd shared with her husband. And it did concern her that the children had no father. *Perhaps it would be nice . . . one day.* But she had no immediate plans along that line, which was appropriate because she was still officially in mourning and had no romantic feelings for any man of her acquaintance.

Before she could answer, the boy said, "I saw you and Vicar Phelps." His tone was almost accusing, and Julia looked at him askew.

"I beg your pardon?"

"Over by the Christmas tree. You were standing close together."

So that's why he asked, Julia thought. Did he honestly think she and the vicar were courting? "Philip, Vicar Phelps was telling me something that he would like to keep private for now."

"About what?"

"About something that wouldn't interest you. And I'm sure you'll find out soon enough." And giving him a reassuring smile, she added, "Men and women can enjoy each other's company, just as you enjoy being with Ben and Jeremiah. That doesn't mean they're courting."

"Is that so?"

"Quite so, young man. And believe it or not, you'll feel the same way when you're older."

He looked a little more peaceful now, and she leaned over to kiss his cheek. "Now, let's try to be more cheerful, shall we? It's Christmas, after all."

Christmas, Ambrose grumbled, punching his pillow into shape for the fourth time. Was he the only person in England to feel that the day had betrayed him? Why had he allowed his expectations to be raised once again?

You were hoping she would come, weren't you? he thought mockingly. It had been an irrational hope, but one he had clung to until the last candle was snuffed. And, of course, that hope had failed him.

And if she were to come back—what then? She was married. And even if she were not, what could he offer her? A lifetime of emotional instability? He wouldn't even be able to give her a family. It would be cruel to subject children to the same childhood he and his siblings had suffered.

And so the curtain closes. With no encores. She's stepped out of your life, and that's that.

After at least another hour of tossing and turning, he groaned, sat up in bed, and lit the lamp on his bedside table. The air was frigid, but he dashed out from under the bedclothes to tuck his top sheet back in under the foot of his mattress. As he moved back to the side of the bed, his eye caught the Bible in the seat of his chair. Since Vicar Phelps had suggested he begin with the New Testament, he had done so with vigor, perusing every text from Saint Matthew to the mysterious Revelation. But while he was finding himself extremely interested in the concept of a God who loved sinners so much that He would sacrifice His own Son, he could not help but wonder if this Jesus Christ was nothing more than a skilled actor. Perhaps the most talented to walk the face of the earth.

After reading accounts of the crucifixion, he had no doubts that Jesus had died on that cross, but it was the aftermath that gave him trouble.

"How do we know He rose again on the third day?" he'd recently asked Vicar Phelps over tea in the vicarage parlor.

"Because it's written in the Scriptures," was the vicar's answer.

"And who wrote them?"

"The New Testament? Why, most were written by the disciples, Mr. Clay. Under the inspiration of the Holy Spirit."

"And how do we know that they didn't perpetrate a fraud?"

"You mean, hide the body?"

"Yes. Does it shock you that I would ask?"

With a shake of the head the vicar had replied, "You aren't the first person to ask such a question. But let me tell you what happened to those men afterward. Excluding Judas Iscariot, of course. All but John were martyred—and he himself was banished for several years."

"Martyred?" Ambrose had heard of the disciples all of his life but had never thought to wonder how they had died.

"And in insidiously cruel ways. Most were crucified, and some were killed by other means. Bartholomew was flayed alive, James sawed to pieces, and Thomas was speared to death. Do you believe those men would give up their lives like that for a fraud of their own making?"

"They had no way of knowing they would be martyred."

"After what happened to their leader? They knew, Mr. Clay."

Ambrose went over to the chair and picked up the Bible, bringing it back to bed with him. He couldn't sleep anyway, he thought, so he might as well read. There was something in those pages that had eluded him thus far, something that could be clearly seen in such people as Fiona O'Shea, Mrs. Hollis, and Vicar Phelps. He envied their simple trust.

Where do I go now? he wondered, staring down at the book on his pillow as he lay on his side, his head propped up with his left arm. The thought of trying to understand the Old Testament just yet was a little overwhelming, so he decided to start with Saint Matthew again. An hour later, he came across something he had scarcely noticed during his first reading. *They deserted Him in the garden!*

It was right there in front of him. *Then all the disciples forsook him and fled.* These were the same men who later preached so boldly, not fearing execution?

He reread the passage, tracing the words with a finger. *Why did they run?* he asked himself. If they truly believed Jesus Christ was God's Son, wouldn't they have trusted Him with their lives?

"Could it be that they had doubts too?" he murmured.

*O*n the Wednesday afternoon of January nineteenth, Andrew Phelps sat in the vicarage parlor savoring a post-lunch cup of coffee and *The Shrewsbury Chronicle*. He seldom drank coffee, preferring tea instead, but there were some days that seemed made-to-order for the stronger drink. On and off for over a week now, winds from the northwest had brought freezing rains across the whole of Shropshire, crusting the drifts of the earlier Christmas snow with ice. Noses of the villagers were perpetually red, and incessant sniffles had provided accompaniment to his sermon last Sunday.

But today, finally, the sun beamed down on Gresham through a cloudless sky, and the air, though chilly, did not cut through one's clothes like a knife. Andrew had managed to pay a half-dozen calls to parishioners along Walnut Tree Lane today and planned to make more after his newspaper and coffee were finished. His first call would be to the *Larkspur*, for Ambrose Clay had been in his thoughts all morning.

He was beginning to feel like a failure as far as the actor was concerned, in that his witness to the man seemed to be bearing no fruit. *It's because I've attempted to convert him solely through reason.* And what was reasonable about salvation? How could the human intellect alone understand that a man must become as a little child to enter the kingdom of heaven? That the blood shed on a Roman cross centuries ago still had the power to cleanse the vilest sinner?

I know you're drawing him to you, Father, he prayed, staring blankly at the newsprint in front of him. Why else would Mr. Clay continue to seek out Scripture with such diligence? *Please send your Spirit to soften his heart and make him more receptive to the Gospel.*

He sensed a presence, as he often did when he prayed, but this time it was inexplicably different. Lowering his newspaper, he scanned the room with his eyes. There was a flash of motion as a little head darted back behind an upholstered chair in the corner.

"Have you seen Molly?" Elizabeth asked from the doorway, where she stood with little David tucked under her arm, wrapped in a bath flannel. The children's father had not yet returned to his family, and there was now some speculation as to whether he was dead or alive. Though Andrew grieved for Mr. Burrell's soul, he had to admit that Mr. Sykes had been correct in his view that his family fared better when he was absent.

"Have I seen Molly?" Andrew echoed, a little louder than necessary.

Her brow furrowing, Elizabeth shifted the child to her other hip. From his perch he stared down at Andrew with blue eyes as wide as his sister's. "David rubbed treacle in his hair, so I had to give him a bath. And when I turned around Molly was gone. It's time for their naps."

"*Gone*, you say?" Andrew glanced at the chair again. "But wherever can she be?"

His daughter gave him a puzzled look. "Why are you talking that way, Papa?"

"What way?"

"Answering everything I say with a question."

"Why, I'm just concerned about little Molly."

Elizabeth frowned and glanced down the corridor. "I suppose she went in the kitchen. Mrs. Paget gives them pieces of dough when—"

"Have you tried the ash bin?" Andrew cut in.

"Papa . . ."

"Because I do believe that's where you'll find our Molly. Up to her nose in the ash bin. Why, you'll have to scrub her from now 'til tomorrow—"

"I not in ash bin."

They both looked in the direction of the corner, where somber-faced little Molly was easing herself out from behind the chair.

"See what I mean?" Andrew winked at Elizabeth, who only rolled her eyes. "Why, she's covered with soot from head to toe."

"No soot. I not in ash bin."

"That certainly looks like soot to me. And it's a pity, too, because I had hoped to read aloud to someone. But I can't risk getting soot on my clothes now, can I?"

The three-year-old pressed a palm to her cheek, stared down at it with a perplexed expression, then approached Andrew's chair with hand outstretched. "See? Not soot."

Andrew took her little hand and pretended to study it. "Well, I suppose you're right after all, Miss Molly. Does this mean you wish me to read to you?"

Her answer was to hurry over to the rosewood console table against the far wall, where Laurel's and Elizabeth's old storybooks were now stored in the bottom drawer. While Elizabeth brought David back upstairs to clothe him, Molly knelt in front of the open drawer and rifled through the dozen or so books. She returned to Andrew with *The Butterfly's Ball* in both hands. Her blue eyes stared at him as he lifted her up on one knee.

Though the children had come to the vicarage every school day now for four months, and Andrew could cause David to chuckle with just one bounce of the knee, he had yet to receive a smile from Molly. That she was capable of the expression wasn't in question. He had seen her smile at every other person under his roof. He would never admit it to anyone, but it hurt him a little.

"Let's wait for your brother, shall we?" Andrew said to her.

She looked over at the door and nodded. "Dabid come to read book."

Some twenty minutes later, both children were sound asleep against his chest. Andrew carried them upstairs and helped Elizabeth tuck them into her bed.

"They look like little angels, don't they?" he whispered as they stood over them.

She smiled. "And you must seem like a big angel to them."

"Me? Why, unless I have a book in my hands, they hardly notice me."

"That's because they're in awe of you, Papa. You're likely the first man who's ever treated them decently."

The thought hadn't occurred to Andrew, and while it pained him that their lots in life had to be so hard, he couldn't help but be comforted.

"Perhaps you should rest a while too," he told Elizabeth.

Elizabeth shook her head and tucked a strand of blond hair back over her ear. "I'm not tired, Papa. I plan to write a letter while they're asleep."

"Oh? To anyone in particular?"

She actually blushed now. "Perhaps."

He patted her shoulder. "Well, I'll leave you to it. I've a call to make at the *Larkspur*."

"Oh? To see anyone in particular?"

Andrew turned back to face her. "Why, to see Mr. Clay."

"I *see*," she replied. "And there's no one else you'd be interested in seeing?"

Andrew knew exactly of whom she was referring, and he wondered if his cheeks were reddening now. Thank heaven for the beard. "Ministers are obligated to make calls, you know," he told her flatly. That only brought on a maddening smile from her, so he gave up and bade her farewell.

So I'm that obvious! he thought on his way down the staircase. Did anyone else suspect the feelings he had for Mrs. Hollis—feelings that he'd prided himself on keeping well hidden? He could definitely feel his cheeks burning now. How absurd it suddenly seemed to him—a vicar past his prime, harboring romantic thoughts again! *There is no fool like an old fool!* his father had been fond of saying, perhaps as a warning to his sons not to make themselves look ridiculous in their later years.

You're only forty-five! some part of him that didn't want to give up cried in protest. He fastened the buttons to his wool greatcoat and sighed. *And still as plain as an old shoe.* It was time to stop acting like a schoolboy, he sadly decided while searching his pockets for his gloves. If men of the cloth could not conduct themselves with dignity, how could they ask the same of their parishioners?

He gave up and walked down to the kitchen to ask Dora and Mrs. Paget if they'd seen his gloves. He couldn't help but wish that he would at least have the opportunity of a minute or two in the company of Mrs. Hollis when he reached the *Larkspur*. If one had to settle for crumbs, one should at least be allowed to savor them.

"Too much ice out there, *Frau* Hollis," Karl Herrick warned Julia in the kitchen while Mrs. Herrick, Mrs. Beemish, and Mildred bobbed heads in agreement.

"You'll catch cold, missus," Mildred added.

"And you've little enough flesh on your bones to fight it off," was Mrs. Herrick's admonition.

"I'll bundle up," Julia said, determined not to give in. The first clear skies in over a week were out there waiting, and she was weary of wood fires and lantern light. Besides, if her three children could walk to school and back, she should be able to make it to *Trumbles* without the whole household worrying that a blizzard would come along and snatch her away. "Now, just tell me what we need."

"I've a list in my parlor," the housekeeper said resignedly and went to fetch it.

Mr. Herrick disappeared at the same time but came back seconds later with a huge pair of Wellington boots that were almost as long as his short legs.

"I find these over the stables some time ago," he said. "Your feet they vill keep varm und dry."

"But they're too big, Mr. Herrick."

"So your shoes you keep on inside them, *ja*?"

Reluctantly she took them. They were heavy as flatirons, but she had to admit to herself that even her heaviest leather slippers wouldn't do for sloshing through the ice that had accumulated in the lanes. It hadn't occurred to her when she'd ordered the children's boots from Mr. Derby, the cobbler, that she would need some for herself. *I still forget that the city ways won't do here,* she thought.

"You'll wear them?" Mrs. Herrick asked, as Mrs. Beemish returned with her list.

Julia smiled at all four faces and thought that it was rather nice to be fussed over once in a while. "I'll slip them on at the front door, thank you. I want to see if the lodgers need anything." She went to her room for her cloak and gloves, then on to the hall. All the lodgers but Mr. Clay, who had been in a dark mood since yesterday, were on sofas and chairs pushed a little closer to the cavernous fireplace.

"Would any of you care for something from *Trumbles*?" Julia asked, pulling on her gloves.

"Nothing for me, thank you," Mrs. Kingston said from one of the sofas.

From a chair, Mrs. Hyatt lowered her reading spectacles. "Do you think it wise to be going out in the cold, dear?"

"I'll be quite toasty, thank you," Julia said, lifting the boots to prove her point. She made a mental note to speak with Mrs. Hyatt privately later. The dear lady seemed preoccupied lately, and Julia just wanted to make sure there was nothing serious troubling her.

"If you're determined to go, would you see if Mr. Trumble has a skein of wool in either heliotrope or pistachio?" asked Mrs. Dearing.

Purple or green wool, Julia thought, adding that to the mental note about Mrs. Hyatt. She did not want to take off her gloves to write on the list.

"And a ream of paper?" Miss Rawlins said apologetically.

Ream of paper.

———

". . . and a stove brush," Julia read to Mr. Trumble.

"What style?" the shopkeeper asked.

Julia looked up from Mrs. Beemish's list. "Style?"

"Yes'm." Turning his back to her, he stepped up on the stool and reached up to the top shelf. He brought down two black wire brushes and set them on the counter before her.

"I've sold this here oval-shaped one for years, but I'm told this new convex style is better for scrubbing."

They looked almost the same to Julia. After picking up and study-ing one and then the other, she asked, "Which do you recommend, Mr. Trumble?"

A smile widened the handlebar mustache. "I lean toward progress meself, Mrs. Hollis. We'd still be cooking over open fires if it wasn't for invocations."

"Then I'll take the newer one."

"Will that be all?"

"Not quite." She ordered the wool and paper for Mrs. Dearing and Miss Rawlins, then pulled back up the hood of her clock. "Good afternoon, Mr. Trumble."

"And a good afternoon to you, Mrs. Hollis. I'll send it all round before close o'day."

After leaving the shop, Julia slogged up Market Lane in the heavy boots, swinging her arms for ballast, trying to avoid puddles of ice in the cobblestones. Fortunately, few people were outside to notice her swaggering like the captain of the Queen's Guard. Even the Worthy sisters had consigned their lace-making operation to the indoors weeks ago. She found herself thinking about Mrs. Hyatt again as she labored along. *I haven't noticed her spending time with Mr. Durwin for the past couple of days,* she realized. *Have they parted company?* She hoped not. Mrs. Hyatt was a gentle soul and didn't deserve to be hurt.

The next thing she knew, one of her encumbered feet hit a patch of ice at the crossroads and slid out from under her. She performed an awkward little dance, windmilling her arms at the same time, but the ground rushed up to claim her before she could balance herself.

On her backside she landed with a jarring *thud*. Fortunately, her thick outer clothes absorbed most of the impact, but uprighting herself proved more difficult than she had imagined. The patch of ice seemed to be directly under her now, and her unyielding boot refused to take hold.

"MRS. HOLLIS!" A male voice off to her right pierced the snow-numbed air. Wincing at this proof that her performance had indeed had an audience, she turned her head and squinted at the figure hurrying down Church Lane in her direction. Vicar Phelps it was.

"BACON MADE THE WELL BLUE!" he called, waving an arm.

Bacon made the. . .? On second thought, Julia realized he was saying, "Wait and let me help you!" That sounded like good advice, no matter how embarrassed she was. He was still several yards away—too far away for her to be screeching back an answer, so she swallowed her pride and occupied herself with pulling her gloves away from the sticky ice.

She'd managed to get to her knees when he was about twenty feet away and closing in, puffing white vapor like a locomotive. "You should slow down," Julia warned, but he continued to quicken his pace.

"You just have to avoid those icy—" he began. Suddenly both legs flew up into the air and sent him crashing to the frozen ground. He did not stop there, but kept sliding until coming within inches of Julia. In fact, she was able to catch his bowler hat as it attempted to fly past her.

For a second or two he simply sat there gaping up at her, for she was still upon her knees and therefore taller than him by several inches.

"Vicar?" Julia said, resisting with Herculean effort the impulse to burst into laughter.

He blinked, then sighed as he pulled one of his gloved hands from the ice. "I cannot begin to tell you how completely mortified I am."

"Well, it certainly wasn't your fault. Are you injured?"

"Only my dignity." Narrowing his eyes to study her for a moment, he said, "Why, Mrs. Hollis, you're struggling to keep from laughing, aren't you?"

"Certainly not!"

He was attempting to get to his feet now, first rising slowly to a crouched position. "It isn't healthy to suppress a laugh, Mrs. Hollis. Unless you're in church, of course."

"That wouldn't be fair, Vicar. You didn't laugh when I fell."

A mischievous glint came to his eyes. "Well, actually . . ."

"You *laughed* at me?"

Finally on his feet, he leaned down toward her. "Now, I'm going to take your arms."

"But your hat."

"Yes, thank you." Vicar Phelps took it from her hands and set it back on his blond head. He then caught her arms just below the elbows to brace her while he pulled. "I may have chuckled a bit," he admitted when she was finally vertical again. "And laughter is good medicine, the Scripture says."

Julia pretended to scowl. "Then I suppose I should have broken an arm so you could have even stronger medicine."

"Oh, come now," he teased. "You aren't angry, are you, Mrs. Hollis?"

She couldn't resist the humor in his eyes and found herself laughing. He joined in, chuckling so hard that he almost lost his balance again. Which made them both laugh even harder. Finally Julia remembered that they were standing at the village crossroads, then looked around and brushed some snow from her cloak. "At least no one was around to witness our performances."

A bell chimed, and both she and the vicar automatically turned their heads to look at the school building in the distance. He turned to her again and, after what appeared to be some hesitation on his part, said, "That won't be the case if either of us slips again. Why don't you allow me to escort you the rest of the way? We can keep each other from falling."

"Thank you," she said, taking the arm he offered. For several minutes the only sounds were those made by boots crunching against the frozen lane—Julia's louder than the vicar's. Julia listened to the distant cries of children escaping academic captivity for the day and thought about how pleasant it was to be able to banter with Vicar Phelps . . . or just to be quiet with him. She had never had a male friend before—not even her husband had assumed that role. And having been raised an only child, she'd also missed out on the opportunity to have a brother. It seemed she had both now, and in the same person.

"Are you out making calls?" she finally asked.

"Actually, Mrs. Hollis, I thought I would visit with Mr. Clay, if he's up to company. He's been on my mind all day for some reason."

Julia thought about the actor's reclusiveness for the past two days and offered, "I should warn you that he's suffering with one of his dark moods, so if he declines your company, you'll know it's nothing personal."

"Of course." He absently patted her gloved hand, his brow furrowed in thought. "But I can't help wondering if it's God who keeps shoving him to the forefront of my thoughts. I don't think I could sleep tonight if I didn't try to talk with him."

"You've been good for him, Vicar."

"I don't know about that. Perhaps if I were more forceful—"

"He would turn a deaf ear, just as he does to Mrs. Kingston when she lapses into preaching at him. I suppose some people must be led gently if they are to be led at all."

"Yes, it does seem that way." After a short silence he looked down, his brow creasing once again.

"What's wrong?" Julia asked him.

He looked up again. "Wrong? Oh, nothing."

"It's a sin to lie, Vicar."

"Touché, Mrs. Hollis," he replied after a chuckle. "If you must know, I was wondering . . . wherever did you get those boots?"

"Hey, isn't that Vicar Phelps with your mother?" Ben asked Philip as they walked toward Church Lane.

Philip slowed his steps, his lips tightening at the sight at the crossroads some two hundred feet away. While he liked and respected Vicar Phelps personally, he couldn't look at the man without being reminded of his younger daughter. Fresh in his mind was the memory of the older girls during the break indoors, singing out quietly the spelling of *collaborate* to the tune of *Here We Go 'Round the Mulberry Bush*. It was an amateurish effort, and some letters had to be squeezed together so that all the syllables would fit, producing verses that sounded like:

see-oh el-el ay bee

oh ARR AY tee ee!

And on and on *ad nauseam,* until Mr. Powell raised himself at the head of the classroom.

For *collaborate* had happened to be Philip's undoing during the morning spelling drill between the fifth and sixth standard boys and

339

girls, when he and the vicar's daughter had been the only two left standing for a good ten minutes.

And while he never noticed her actually joining in the chorus that ensued, she had managed to look pleased with herself every time he stole a glance at her. *I can't believe I ever thought she was pretty,* he told himself during the break. Whoever said that character was more important than appearance was completely right. It was easy to see what kind of character Laurel Phelps had. Prideful. And the last time he looked in his Bible, pride was listed as a sin.

And it ought to count against you double if your father's a vicar. After all, ministers' children grew up with a constant reminder of how a good Christian should behave.

The worst part was that he couldn't tell her what he thought of her. Mother had scolded him soundly after Christmas, promising to take away his fishing privileges for weeks if she learned that he'd treated her rudely. So he was forced to sulk in silence, with only Ben and Jeremiah aware of the depths of his dislike for her.

"Philip?" Ben said, jarring him back to the immediate present.

Philip blinked. "What?"

"I just wondered if that was the vicar with your mother, but I can see that it is. They're moving along awfully slow, aren't they?"

They were indeed walking slowly, but of course there were patches of ice here and there, and even the children's steps were measured. Recalling what his mother had told him on Christmas night, he said a little testily, "A gentleman and a lady can enjoy each other's company without everyone thinking they're courting."

Giving him a curious sidelong look, Ben said, "Who said they were courting?"

"Well, just in case you were thinking it, Mother says they're not."

"Fine with me," his friend shrugged, but after a couple of steps added, "But what if she hasn't told that to the vicar?"

———

"Would you be wantin' some tea, gentlemen?" the chambermaid Andrew recognized as Willa asked after showing him up to Mr. Clay's room.

Standing in front of his chair, the actor reminded him, "You're terribly fond of Mrs. Herrick's tea, Vicar Phelps."

"Tea would be nice, thank you," Andrew replied.

"And some for me as well, please," said Mr. Clay. He attempted

340

a smile in the maid's direction, but when taken in with the bags under his eyes and bearded shadow across his cheeks, it appeared more grimace-like than grateful. Still, the girl seemed to find nothing unusual about this and gave a quick bob before exiting the room.

"Please have a seat, Vicar," Mr. Clay said, nodding toward the empty chair facing his. "I suppose you've heard I'm in one of my sulking moods."

Andrew took the chair and, when the actor had settled back into his, said, "I've never heard it described as sulking, Mr. Clay. Perhaps you could manage a little more charity toward yourself?"

The actor's expression clouded even more so. "Someone else once said almost those exact words to me."

"Indeed? And who was this other sage?"

"Just an acquaintance," he answered somewhat evasively, considering how the words had seemed to affect him.

Andrew knew not to press any further. "Actually, Mr. Clay, I had no idea you were in a bad way until I reached the house a little while ago. But you've been in my thoughts since early this morning."

"Yes?"

"And when God puts someone so heavily on my mind, it is always for a reason. Would you happen to know what that reason is, Mr. Clay?"

"You're asking me to guess the motives of God?" The actor raised an eyebrow. "Wouldn't that be more in line with your occupation, Vicar?"

"I just hoped you could make it a little easier for me in this circumstance," Andrew quipped lightly. *And I'm positive now that You wanted me to be here today,* he prayed under his breath. *Please help him to open up to me.*

———

When Philip arrived at home, wiping his feet before entering through the courtyard door, he gave his lunch pail to Mildred in the kitchen and hurried through the house to find Mother. To his relief she was sitting in a chair in the hall, listening to Mrs. Kingston tell of her plans for the garden come spring. The vicar was nowhere to be seen. *He was just helping her home . . . probably from Trumbles.* After all, the lanes *were* slippery. Any gentleman would have done the same, coming across a lady outside under those conditions.

341

"Why, hello, Philip," she said, smiling up in his direction. "How was your day at school?"

"Fine, Mother. Good afternoon, Mrs. Kingston."

"And the same to you, Philip," the older woman said. "My, I believe you've grown another inch when I wasn't looking."

Philip found himself straightening appreciatively. He had turned fourteen just last week and expected that he would launch into a growth spurt any day now, as quite a few of the adults in the house had predicted he would.

On his way back to the kitchen to hint for a snack, he thought again of the vicar, who must be upstairs visiting Mr. Clay. *You can't blame him for liking Mother.*

He had given his mother's situation much thought since Christmas and had come to conclude, painfully, that it was selfish to expect her to stay alone the rest of her life. In less than a year he would be enrolled in the Josiah Smith Preparatory Academy in Worchester with his visits home limited to one weekend every month. How could he keep watch over the family and attend school at the same time? Women needed husbands, even bright women like Mother. He didn't want her ending up alone like Mrs. Kingston. And even though he was practically grown himself and had no need for another father, Aleda and Grace should have one.

But not one who already has children. For no matter how kind and good the man happened to be, wouldn't he favor his own? He couldn't stand the thought of his sisters being treated like Cinderella in their own home!

Reason took over, and after he'd thanked Mrs. Herrick for the shortbread square she'd handed him, he started back toward his room to study. It was ludicrous to assume someone as kind as Vicar Phelps would ever turn into the male equivalent of a wicked stepmother. If only he didn't have that one liability! For even though in another nine months Philip would only be home for short visits, the thought of calling Laurel Phelps sister for even two days out of thirty was a horror to him. There seemed to be no reason to expect her to change her superior, condescending ways, so how could there be any family harmony?

A bit of conscience pricked him, suggesting that he was being enormously selfish. Mother's happiness should be the most important thing. *But how could she be happy with children who couldn't get along?* Hadn't the vicar just mentioned something like that in the pulpit recently, that the family who lives in harmony has a little of heaven on earth?

Please, God, he prayed, squeezing his eyes shut as a bit of shortbread melted away in his right cheek, *Send the right person to marry Mother one day. Someone like Mr. Trumble. Amen.*

He would have prayed specifically that Mr. Trumble himself be that person, but word had gotten out that the shopkeeper and Miss Hillock were fond of each other. His conscience caused another twinge, so he closed his eyes to add, *And please let Vicar Phelps find a nice wife too.*

"Nothing out of the ordinary has happened since our last little chat," Mr. Clay was saying, rubbing his stubbled chin. "Except . . ."

Andrew leaned forward a little. "Yes?"

"I've come to believe that Jesus Christ actually did come back to life after the cross."

Andrew's breath caught in his throat. "And you say nothing extraordinary happened?"

"Extraordinary would be my coming to faith, Vicar Phelps. I'm afraid that has not occurred, nor do I see the likelihood of it happening in the near future."

"But why? If you believe—"

"With my head, Vicar," the actor said poignantly. He raised a hand to tap the center of his chest. "There is nothing happening here."

Willa returned with a tray, and another chambermaid followed with a folded crisscross table. For once, Andrew was grateful for the interruption. He needed time to send up another prayer. *I know you've been drawing Mr. Clay to you, or else he wouldn't feel compelled to search the Scriptures so faithfully. But why is he afraid to give himself over to you? Please show me, Father.*

After the maids left the room, the only sound was the delicate clinking of silver against bone china, then silence as each man took a sip from his cup.

"So, Mr. Clay, how did you come to the conclusion that Christ did actually come to life again?" Andrew asked in a dispassionate tone, while fighting the urge to get on his knees and plead that the actor believe this very minute. And he might very well be doing so, were he dealing with someone with a more suppliant temperament.

343

Mr. Clay balanced his saucer and cup on his crossed knee, steadying them with both hands. "It was the only logical conclusion I could make."

"Logical?"

"Do you recall telling me that most of the disciples were martyred because of their bold preaching of the Gospel? And yet earlier they deserted Jesus in the garden, when surely He needed friends at His side."

"They were fallible men, Mr. Clay. Perhaps I would have done the same thing myself."

"Then after the burial, they shut themselves up in a house for fear of the same mob that had crucified their leader. It must have been a long three days for them. When did their courage come?"

Andrew opened his mouth, but Mr. Clay held up a silencing hand and continued. "It came after they actually saw and spoke with the risen Christ. And for the first time, they had absolutely no doubts that He was God's Son. Even Thomas became convinced."

"And He gave them the Holy Spirit, Mr. Clay," Andrew added, smiling. "To comfort them and give them power to become mighty witnesses."

Mr. Clay nodded soberly. "They became almost suicidal maniacs, then, in their quest to spread the Gospel. Could they have done that, knowing the ultimate consequences, if they weren't totally convinced that Jesus had come back to life?"

Unable to stand it any longer, Andrew leaned to set his cup and saucer on the tray before him with more enthusiasm than necessary, causing tea to slosh over his fingers. Forgotten was his earlier resolve to restrain from being too forceful. "For mercy's sake, man, I couldn't have preached it better myself! It's time to trust in Christ yourself!"

"It's not that simple, Vicar."

"It's the simplest act in the world, Mr. Clay. Don't be a King Agrippa!"

"King Agri—" Mr. Clay stopped himself and nodded. "That fellow who told Paul the apostle that he was almost persuaded to become a Christian."

His pulse jumping, Andrew said, "And unless he changed his mind, he's had centuries in hell to regret those words."

When the actor did not respond to this, Andrew sat back in his chair, ran his hands through his hair, and sighed. "Just how many times have you read through the New Testament?"

The actor thought for a minute. "Four, actually. And I've started on the Old again. I just finished the book of Joshua yesterday."

"How can you read so much and not find anything that moves you?"

"Who said I haven't been—"

Tapping his own chest, Andrew told him, "You said there was nothing there."

Mr. Clay's face turned a shade paler. "Don't you think I *want* to feel something, Vicar?"

He's afraid, Andrew realized suddenly. *But of what?* Mr. Clay did not seem to be the sort of man who would reject Christ because of fear of ridicule of others. And Christians weren't burnt at the stake anymore in their part of the world, so what would prevent him from embracing the Gospel as the lifeline that it was? Who wouldn't wish for the love and guidance of a heavenly Father?

Father . . .

He frowned, chewing on his lip. *Is that it?* Was it the very parenthood of God that compelled the actor to keep his distance? Mr. Clay had once confided in him that his father had been a highly unstable influence in his children's lives, and his later suicide had shattered the family. Was he afraid to put his trust in another Father who might also fail him?

Too simple. Mr. Clay's too intelligent for that, he reasoned. But didn't emotions often act independently of intellect? *They certainly do for me,* he thought, briefly thinking back to how pleasant it had been to walk arm in arm with Mrs. Hollis.

"Mr. Clay," Andrew said finally.

Mr. Clay, who had turned his face to stare over at the window, turned to look at him again. "Yes?" came out with a weary sigh.

With all the compassion that he felt for the man coming out in his voice, Andrew continued, "Mr. Clay, why don't you leave your Bible closed tonight?"

His friend blinked. "I'm surprised to hear you recommend that."

"You can be sure this is the first time," Andrew smiled back. "But the Scriptures also instruct us to 'be still and know that He is God.' I believe it's time to take pause from your frantic intellectual searching and allow His Holy Spirit to speak to your heart."

There was clear misery in the man's gray eyes. "And how do I do that, Vicar?"

"Just meditate on the things you've already read about Him, Mr. Clay. That He is a faithful Father, merciful, loving and just. That He loved you so much He sent His only Son to the cross so that you could have salvation. That He is ready to forgive your sin and take you into His bosom as one of His children, if you'll only ask in the name of the risen Christ."

Now Mr. Clay's cup trembled visibly in his hand, and he set it down on the table. "I can't think now, Vicar," he said, avoiding Andrew's eyes. "And I'm fatigued. I must ask you to leave."

"All right." Andrew got to his feet, but before leaving, he stepped around the tea table to put a hand on the man's shoulder. "You don't have to be afraid, my friend. He is one Father who'll never disappoint you."

The actor nodded but did not look up at him. With a final squeeze of Mr. Clay's shoulder, Andrew turned and left the room.

Downstairs in the hall, Andrew again returned the well-wishes of the lodgers, who pressed him to stay for a visit. His heart was not in it, though, for it was heavy for his friend upstairs. He was aware that Mrs. Hollis, seated on one of the chairs, was searching his face for any hopeful sign from their visit, and he shook his head slightly.

It's a shame to have to watch your own body fall apart, Mrs. Kingston thought that same night, squinting through the empty amber bottle of *Dr. Miles' Miracle Liniment For Aching Joints.* Her daily walking routine usually kept the rheumatism in her knees manageable, but she'd been housebound for the past week because of the icy lanes. Tonight, age and inactivity had caught up with her, propelling her over to her mahogany chest of drawers to seek relief from Dr. Miles. She turned the bottle over and bumped the open neck against her cupped palm—only a teaspoon or two of the kerosene-smelling liquid dripped out.

"Now, why didn't I ask Mrs. Hollis to get me another bottle at *Trumbles* today?" she muttered to herself, even while knowing the answer. It was one thing to endure the inconveniences of advancing years, but quite another to admit to them in front of a room full of people.

Mrs. Hyatt uses the same liniment on her hands, Mrs. Kingston remembered. She had never actually discussed her aches and pains with Mrs. Hyatt, who in her opinion was a bit insipid, but the odor of the medicine was hard to mask. And surely she wasn't asleep yet, for the lodgers, except for poor Mr. Clay, who'd confined himself to his room for most of the day, had retired from the hall less than an hour ago.

She slipped on a thick wool wrapper and slippers and stepped out into the corridor, lit by a single low wall lamp. Mrs. Hyatt's door was only four steps from her own, but there was no light shining from underneath, and she considered giving up and going back to bed. Just then a dull pain throbbed through her right knee. She raised her hand to rap softly upon the door. *At least she still has several hours left to sleep the night,* Mrs. Kingston told herself.

Immediately she heard a low, "Who's there?"

Well, perhaps she wasn't asleep yet. "It's Mrs. Kingston," she answered as quietly as possible so as not to wake any of the other lodgers. There was a silence of about ten seconds, and just when Mrs. Kingston was beginning to wonder if she'd been heard, the knob turned in front of her. The room that was exposed when the door opened several inches was dark, and Mrs. Hyatt was wearing a flannel nightgown and cap, so she had indeed been abed.

"Yes?" the other lodger said in the wedge of dim light coming through the door from the corridor.

There was something strange about the tone of the single word—it came out thickly. A humorous notion passed through her head that perhaps Mrs. Hyatt had been *drinking* the liniment instead of rubbing it on her hands. In spite of her lack of great warmth for the other woman, Mrs. Kingston felt immediately ashamed for the thought.

"Pardon me for disturbing you, Mrs. Hyatt," Mrs. Kingston whispered. "But have you any liniment to spare for the night?"

"Why, yes, I've an extra bottle in my chest of drawers," Mrs. Hyatt nodded but did not open the door any wider. Again the voice was thick. "Is it your knees?"

How did she know that? Swallowing her pride, she confessed, "I'm afraid so."

After a moment's hesitation, Mrs. Hyatt said, "I'll leave the bottle outside your door in five minutes. Is that all right?"

"Leave it outside my door?" Mrs. Kingston had to remember to lower her voice again. "But why can't you just give it to me now?"

"Now?"

Another wickedly humorous thought came into Mrs. Kingston's mind, and before she could block its way to her mouth, she found herself blurting out, "What's wrong? You haven't Mr. Durwin in there, have you?"

"Mrs. Kingston!" the woman gasped, the whites of her eyes showing.

She gulped, horrified at her own audacity. She was painfully aware that she had a tendency to be blunt, but there was a limit. "I'm sorry, Mrs. Hyatt!"

A sob was the only reply as Mrs. Hyatt started backing away from the door.

"Oh, dear . . . please forgive me!" Mrs. Kingston pushed the door open wider and entered the room. "Never did I actually think that Mr. Durwin was in here."

"I know that," Mrs. Hyatt sniffed as she walked over to her chest of drawers. "I have the liniment right here."

Why, she was crying before I even came here, Mrs. Kingston realized, for the thickness of the voice was the same. Unable to stand it any longer, she walked over to the night table, felt for a match from the tin in the drawer, and lit the lamp. When she turned around, Mrs. Hyatt was rifling through an open drawer.

"Here it is," she said in a now small voice, avoiding Mrs. Kingston's eyes as she held out a bottle.

The older woman moved a step closer and took it from her hand. "Mrs. Hyatt, I can see you've been crying . . . what is wrong?"

"Nothing." She turned briefly to take a handkerchief from the open drawer and blew her nose.

Mrs. Kingston had scant patience with people who forced others to drag conversation out of them, but she couldn't help being moved by the misery in her voice. "There, there now," she found herself soothing, stepping forward to set the bottle on the chest and take Mrs. Hyatt by the hand. "Why don't you tell me all about it. . . ." After a fraction of a second's hesitation she added, "Dear?"

Mrs. Hyatt wiped her face again but allowed herself to be led over to her bed. Mrs. Kingston helped her sit up on the pillows, tucked the covers up under her elbows, and sat down on the side of the bed.

"You'll take cold," Mrs. Hyatt sniffed.

"My wrapper is nice and warm."

"You think I'm a child, don't you?"

The nightcap ruffle framing Mrs. Hyatt's pink cheeks actually did give her a rather infantile appearance, but Mrs. Kingston shook her head. "Everyone weeps now and then."

"Even you?"

Mrs. Kingston folded her arms and thought, *This is getting a bit too personal.* "On occasion. Now, why don't you tell me what's wrong?"

Her lip trembling, Mrs. Hyatt replied in a still smaller voice, "It's Mr. Durwin."

I thought so! "So the old coot has broken your heart, has he?"

The red-rimmed eyes went wide again. "Why, no. He's asked me to marry him."

"Marry him?" Even though she'd resigned herself long ago to the futility of wishing for any sort of future with Mr. Durwin, she still found herself surprised and more than a little annoyed at the news. "And you're upset about that?"

"I know," Mrs. Hyatt sniffed, tears running down her soft face. "He's such a good man, and I do miss not having a husband. . . ."

"And you're practically inseparable," Mrs. Kingston was forced to admit. "So why can't you . . ." She stopped herself, eased her feet back down to the floor, and went over to the open drawer for another handkerchief. After handing it to Mrs. Hyatt, who mumbled a sodden "thank you," and wiped her eyes, she resumed her place at the bedside. "Now, go on."

"He doesn't know my maiden name."

Mrs. Kingston blinked. "Excuse me?"

"My maiden name. He's never asked." Mrs. Hyatt wiped her eyes again. "Or my favorite hymn, for that matter. Or color, or flower."

"Why don't you just *tell* him those things, if you want him to know them?" *Instead of weeping over something so simple to repair,* she thought to herself. "Mr. Durwin can't read minds, you know."

Mrs. Hyatt's lips trembled. "Don't you see, Mrs. Kingston? I know almost everything concerning Mr. Durwin, because that's all we talk about. *His* children and grandchildren . . . *his* interest in herbs . . . how *he* founded *Durwin Stoves.* Am I so uninteresting that. . . ?"

"There, there now, dear," Mrs. Kingston cut in, reaching down to pat the lump that was Mrs. Hyatt's knee. She didn't want to be backed into a corner with *that* question. Her lips tightened. But even though Mrs. Hyatt wasn't the most fascinating person on this earth, Mr. Durwin had no right to use her as merely an audience. It would be torture to be married to a man whose only idea of conversation involved litanies of his own accomplishments. She began to feel a great relief that Mr. Durwin had shown no interest in her. "So you refused his hand, did you?"

"Refused his hand?" Her voice wavered unsteadily. "I don't know how to go about doing that, Mrs. Kingston."

"Why, it's simple," the older widow declared, though she couldn't recall ever having had to break any hearts herself, even in her finishing-school years. "You tell him you don't care to be his wife, but that you'll always think of him with affection."

"I can't do that," Mrs. Hyatt gasped, horror filling her gray eyes.

"Well, I know it's going to take some courage. . . ."

Mrs. Hyatt shrank a little into the covers. "I've never possessed a lot of courage, Mrs. Kingston. I wish I could be as brave as you are."

Suddenly her opinion of Mrs. Hyatt went up a notch. "Oh, I don't know about that," she said modestly.

"Oh, you don't know how many times I've wished to be like you. You're not afraid of saying what you think. I'm always terrified of offending."

"That's because you're so tender-hearted, Mrs. Hyatt," Mrs. Kingston said, wondering why she had neglected to appreciate that fact before.

"It's kind of you to say that, Mrs. Kingston." Mrs. Hyatt wiped her eyes and blew her nose again. "I'm so thankful you came in here tonight. I was beside myself!"

"There, there," Mrs. Kingston soothed, patting the knee again.

There were several seconds of companionable silence until Mrs. Hyatt spoke in a tentative voice, "Mrs. Kingston?"

"Yes?"

"Do you think you could tell Mr. Durwin for me?"

Mrs. Kingston started. "Me?"

"Oh, please . . . I just don't think I can face him."

"But you'll have to face him *sometime*."

"I know. But I'm sure I'll say the wrong words if I turn down his proposal. Please, Mrs. Kingston?"

She finally gave in, fearing that this could go on all night if she didn't reassure the poor soul. "Oh, if you absolutely *must* involve me in this."

Relief and gratitude lit Mrs. Hyatt's ruffle-framed face. "Oh, Mrs. Kingston! I don't know what to say! Bless you!"

"Just lend me some liniment, that's all." Mrs. Kingston got to her feet again. "And go to sleep now, will you? I shan't be able to rest if I know you're in here tossing and turning."

After accepting Mrs. Hyatt's effusive thanks again, she took the liniment from the chest, closed the open drawer, and went back to her own room. *Better to leave the romance in Miss Rawlins' books,* she thought as she rubbed liniment on her right knee. Now it would be *she* who would toss and turn, for what sane person could look forward to the task she had agreed to undertake?

She paused from rubbing her knee and looked at the clock. *Quarter past eleven.* Why not get it over with immediately? Sure, she would have to wake Mr. Durwin, but wouldn't he appreciate several hours to recover before having to face Mrs. Hyatt at breakfast in the morning? *And I would surely sleep better.*

Getting out of bed again, she pushed her feet back into her slippers and retied the sash to her wrapper. The two men's chambers were located in the shorter corridor, past the water closet and sitting room. She knocked softly on Mr. Durwin's door. When she heard a sleep-laden "yes?" from the other side, she decided she didn't care to announce her name out here in the corridor, lest poor Mr. Clay assume the wrong idea, so she just knocked again.

Finally the door opened and Mr. Durwin stood there clad in nightshirt and dressing gown. A lamp burned behind him on a table.

"Mrs. Kingston?" he blinked.

"May I come in, Mr. Durwin?" she whispered.

"I beg your pardon?"

Mrs. Kingston frowned. "I've something to tell you that I don't think you would care to have announced in the corridor. And I've seen men's dressing gowns before, so you don't have to be so modest."

He backed away and allowed her in, his mouth gaping as he did. "What is the meaning of this, Mrs. Kingston?" he whispered when she'd turned from easing the door closed.

"It's concerning Mrs. Hyatt, Mr. Durwin. It is my sad duty to inform you that she must decline your proposal but will continue to think of you with affection."

"Wha—?" He cleared his throat. "What do you mean?"

"Mrs. Hyatt has come to realize that marriage would be a mistake at this time." Tactfully she restrained herself from adding, *because you're a bore.* And with the dubious duty behind her, she bade him good-night and turned to leave.

But Mr. Durwin would have nothing of it. "Wait!" he said, reaching the door at the same time. He put a hand on the knob to prevent her from taking it. "Are you serious about this, Mrs. Kingston?"

"I'm afraid so. But don't despair, Mr. Durwin. You can still be friends."

"But what is her reason? Surely she gave you a reason!"

"I told you . . . because she's come to realize that marriage would be . . ."

His face seemed to have aged ten years. "That's not a specific reason, Mrs. Kingston. What are you keeping from me?"

Why did I ever involve myself in this? she now wondered. This was much more difficult than she had imagined it would be. She had expected that someone of Mr. Durwin's years would take the news a bit

352

more stoically. Could it be that he sincerely *cared* about Mrs. Hyatt, and not just because she possessed a set of ears? "Well . . ." she hedged.

Mr. Durwin's expression became pleading. "Please, I beg of you."

Mrs. Kingston sighed and folded her arms akimbo across her chest. "Very well, then. Tell me, Mr. Durwin, what color are Mrs. Hyatt's eyes?"

"Her . . . I beg your pardon?"

"Her eyes. You look at them every day. What color are they?"

He thought for a minute. "Hazel?"

"Gray, Mr. Durwin. How about her maiden name? Or her favorite flower, or hymn?"

He stared at her for a few seconds, his mind obviously hard at work, before shaking his head. "Why, I'm afraid I have no idea. Is that why she's angry?"

"Not angry. Afraid."

"Afraid, you say? Of what?"

There was no way to soft-soap this, so Mrs. Kingston plunged on ahead. "Of finding herself married to an old man who can only talk about himself, Mr. Durwin."

Mr. Durwin looked as if she'd slapped him. "I didn't realize . . ." he mumbled, but his words trailed off into the chill air of the room.

Compassion stirred in Mrs. Kingston's ample bosom. "But it's quite obvious to me that she cares for you, Mr. Durwin," she said gently.

He simply stared at her, ashen-faced, and Mrs. Kingston figured the best action for her to take now was to leave the room. She'd spread enough gloom and doom for one night and reckoned that the sleep she so craved would certainly evade her. "Well, good night, Mr.—"

But Mr. Durwin seized the doorknob again. "Do you think it possible for me to win her back?"

"Win her back?" Mrs. Kingston reached out and patted his arm. "As I said, I do believe she still cares for you, Mr. Durwin. I suppose that depends on whether or not an old dog can learn new tricks."

I'll never meddle again, Lord, she prayed as she limped her way back down the corridor. At Mrs. Hyatt's door she paused, wondering if she should inform her that the deed had been done. She sighed and continued to her own room. *Beginning this very moment.*

———

353

The murmur of voices from the room next door ceased drifting through the wall, much to Ambrose's regret as he lay in his bed. Even though he had not been able to discern any of the words, nor even the identity of the speakers—but one would *have* to have been Mr. Durwin—the sound had provided some comfort, proof that he wasn't all alone on this earth.

But I am all alone.

You have friends, he reminded himself in an attempt to soften the ache in his chest. *Mrs. Hollis, Mrs. Kingston, Vicar Phelps . . .*

"Vicar," he mumbled in the darkness. How determined the man was to see him come to faith! And if the truth were to be known, Ambrose felt a longing to do so, a longing that he had not been able to admit to the good reverend because the intensity of it frightened him.

He thinks it's because I'm afraid God will fail me as my father did, Ambrose thought, his mind going over Vicar Phelps's parting words again. *Why didn't I tell him he was mistaken?*

Because then I would have been compelled to explain the real reason. And actors were a superstitious lot. Admitting one's fears aloud often ensured that what one feared would come to pass. He had just recently come to understand the basis of his fears, the reason he couldn't allow himself to surrender completely.

What if nothing changed?

Oh, he had chafed at Miss O'Shea . . . *dear, dear Miss O'Shea . . .* once asking her mockingly if becoming a Christian would banish the emotional ball and chain that was his lot in life. What had been her reply?

"God's ways are not our ways, Mr. Clay. Sometimes He heals, sometimes He doesn't."

Ambrose wiped his eyes with a corner of his sheet. He hadn't even realized that he was weeping. During the course of reading the Scriptures, he had begun to harbor a feeble hope that perhaps he could be cured of his despondency after all. Jesus had healed lepers, hadn't He? Even brought people back to life! How much trouble could it be to touch one man's addled mind? He knew from his reading that if he became a believer, he would have the right to make that request of God. Hadn't he read that the Father's children were allowed to approach the throne boldly?

"God's ways are not our ways." He could still hear the calm faith in Miss O'Shea's voice. If only he could speak with her now!

Because I don't think I could bear it if everything turned out to be the same.

Suddenly a picture came into his mind, sharp and clear. Three crosses. A mob jeering. Intense pain and suffering. One of the thieves calling out "If thou be Christ, save thyself and us!" The other addressing Jesus as Lord, asking nothing but that he be remembered in the Father's kingdom.

The first man would only accept Jesus as the Christ if certain conditions were met, Ambrose thought, his eyes widening in spite of the darkness. *Am I guilty of the same?*

He got out of bed, feeling around on the carpet with his feet for his slippers. Once they were secure, he pulled the quilt from the top of his covers, wrapped it around his shoulders, and edged his way over to a chair. For a long while he sat there in the darkness and listened to the quiet. Then he leaned the back of his head against the top of the chair and stared at the dark ceiling. *Why are you fighting so hard?* he asked himself.

Suddenly he was filled with a hunger to know the Father, to really know Him as only one of His children could. The same hunger that had been the impetus for his search through the Scriptures.

The words of a song came to him. Where before had he heard it? *Just as I am, without one plea . . .*

It was when Fred Russell was buried, he recalled now. Ambrose had shared a friendly acquaintance with the prop manager, who'd succumbed to consumption, and had attended the funeral at a small Methodist chapel. Strange that he could still remember the words and even the tune some five years later.

But that Thy blood was shed for me . . .

There could be no prior conditions to accepting Christ, Ambrose understood now with startling clarity. No *if You'll first agree to mend my tortured mind . . .*

And that Thou bidd'st me come to thee . . .

And Ambrose did feel the bidding, so strong that it seemed almost palatable.

Oh Lamb of God . . .

Ambrose closed his eyes.

"I come," he whispered.

*D*id *everyone have trouble sleeping last night?* Julia wondered after she'd exchanged greetings with Mr. Durwin in the corridor just outside the dining room the next morning. Mrs. Kingston and Mrs. Hyatt had come downstairs several minutes earlier, looking no more well rested than had Mr. Durwin.

Hearing footsteps on the stairs again, Julia turned in time to receive a sunny smile from Mrs. Dearing, her long white braid draped over one shoulder. *At least someone seems to have slept.*

"Good morning!" the elderly woman said as she reached the bottom step.

Julia smiled back and returned the greeting. "You look very nice, as usual."

"Why, thank you, dear." She tilted her head at Julia. "You're joining us for breakfast?"

"Yes, just this morning," Julia smiled back and was relieved when Mrs. Dearing simply replied, "How nice," and went on into the dining room. She wasn't certain if she should tell the reason she'd altered her usual morning routine of working in her office after breakfasting with the children. The note Mr. Clay sent her, via Georgette, had only asked that she be present at breakfast. As best as she could imagine, she assumed he was going to make some sort of announcement. Did that mean the dark mood that had held him for the past few days had lifted? *Surely he's not planning to leave here.*

"Good morning, Mrs. Hollis!" So deep had she been in her thoughts that she hadn't heard Miss Rawlins' feet on the staircase.

"Good morning, Miss Rawlins," Julia replied, smiling. "And how did you sleep?"

"Fine, thank you. Like a drugged princess." The writer paused, her brown eyes growing thoughtful behind her spectacles. "Why, I should use that sometime, shouldn't I? A book can never have too many good similes."

"They do seem to add to a story."

Looking reluctantly back at the staircase, Miss Rawlins said, "I suppose I should run back upstairs and write it down. I'm quite forgetful."

"My office is only a few steps away," Julia offered. "Why not write it down in there and collect it after breakfast?"

Miss Rawlins thanked her and accompanied her to the family corridor. By the time they reached the dining room again, Mr. Clay had presented himself, and the lodgers were queued up at the sideboard with plates. Julia noticed that purple shadows were still under the actor's eyes, a sign that his mood had not lifted. Yet when he turned his head and saw her watching him, he gave her an indulgent wink.

Whatever Mr. Clay's announcement would be, she thought when everyone finally sat at the table with their filled plates, she could only pray that it wouldn't add to the tension in the room—it was so thick that not even the aroma of bacon and hot scones could dispel it. Mr. Durwin and Mrs. Hyatt, while seated in their usual places across from each other, seemed to be having a contest at avoiding each other's eyes. And Mrs. Kingston's attention seemed to flit back and forth between the two.

Have they argued? Julia didn't think dear Mrs. Hyatt had the disposition to argue with anyone. And was that why Mrs. Kingston sent so many glances in their direction? Had she sensed that perhaps there was an opportunity for her after all?

I think I'm going to need a nap today, Julia thought, absently stirring her tea longer than necessary. The only conversation—besides asking to have salt or sugar passed—was between Miss Rawlins and Mrs. Dearing, and even that died out as the mood of the room prevailed.

Presently Mr. Clay rose from his chair and cleared his throat. "If you would be so kind as to indulge me with your attention," he said, sending a smile all around the table, "I would like to make an announcement."

There were expressions of surprise, a straightening of postures, and muffled clicks as the lodgers set their cutlery temporarily back on the tablecloth.

"Yes, Mr. Clay?" Mrs. Kingston asked when the activity had ceased.

357

His face was almost radiant now, in spite of the shadows under his eyes. "Because many of you have been concerned about the state of my immortal soul, this morning I would like to put your fears to rest.... ."

The following Wednesday, Julia took a cup of tea and secluded herself in her little office and began to pen a letter.

Dear Fiona,

I pray this finds you well and content. Mrs. Beemish is a dear soul and performs her duties as housekeeper quite competently, but she will never replace you in our hearts. I have promised the children that, if the Lord wills it, we will visit you this summer. We will take the train on a Monday so that we can wring the most of every minute of your Tuesday off, then return the following day after a visit with Mr. Jensen.

She stopped to fill her pen. Even though the ice was finally beginning to thaw a little outdoors, summer seemed like an eternity from now. How good it would be to see her dear friend again! But she could now fully understand the wisdom in Fiona's not wanting Mr. Clay to move from the *Larkspur*.

You will be happy to know that Mr. Clay has come to faith in Christ! He is quite elated about it, as we all are. Mrs. Kingston wept tears when Mr. Clay made the announcement at breakfast last week, and Vicar Phelps visits almost every morning for an hour or so to disciple him and encourage him in his newfound faith. Mr. Clay even attended church services with us on Sunday. I can see the hand you had in his conversion, my friend. Would that I had the liberty to tell him of the sacrifice you made toward that end!

Unfortunately, not all the events of the past week have been happy ones. Mrs. Hyatt and Mr. Durwin no longer sit together in church, nor do they accompany each other on walks. It is obvious that they are both miserable. Mr. Durwin has taken supper at the Bow and Fiddle every night this past week. Odd, when you consider how fond he is of Mrs. Herrick's cooking. Neither has spoken about what led to the cessation of their courtship, but interestingly enough, Mrs. Hyatt seems to have taken Mrs. Kingston into her confidence.

You are the only person on earth I can admit this to, Fiona, but I can only pray Mrs. Kingston is not using her position as confidant to exploit the situation. You can recall, I am certain, when she was interested in Mr. Durwin.

Two more pages flowed from Julia's pen describing the latest activities of the children, news of the servants, and other lodgers. She even wrote of Buff and her three almost-grown kittens that kept the stables free of mice and were often slipped into the kitchen by Mrs. Herrick and Mildred for feasts of meat trimmings and fish heads. Julia was just about to close and sign her name, when two more subjects came to her mind.

Karl Herrick crafted a fine sled from that old one in the stables, and the children have spent the last three Saturdays joining other village children at the east slope of the Anwyl. You will be happy to know that Philip and his friends have successfully persuaded the Keegan children to join them.

And lastly, Miss Rawlins has asked me to inform you that she will be sending you a copy of her very latest novel, The Duchess of Ramsgate, and asks if you would be so kind as to critique it for her. I considered telling her that you had run away to France, but honesty prevailed, and I reluctantly agreed to give you the message. "Forewarned is forearmed," as dear Vicar Wilson once advised me.

After giving Mr. Herrick Fiona's letter to post late that morning, Julia stepped out of the kitchen and almost ran into Mr. Durwin in the corridor. "Excuse me, Mr. Durwin," she said, automatically taking a step backward.

"My fault entirely," he replied. "May I speak with you, Mrs. Hollis?"

Julia smiled at him and wondered if she were imagining a bit of hope mixed with some of the sadness his face had worn for the past week. "Shall we walk down to my office?"

He peered down the corridor with uncertainty, then shook his head. "I don't suppose that is necessary. I would like to inform Mrs. Herrick that I'll be taking supper out again and ask you if I may bring the members of our brass band here this evening."

"Of course," Julia replied. She fought the temptation to ask why

359

he'd taken so many suppers away from the *Larkspur* lately. If he were doing so out of discomfort in Mrs. Hyatt's presence, why did he make appearances at breakfast and dinner? "You could practice in the library, if you'd like. But will there be enough room?"

Shifting on his feet and with another glance down the corridor, the elderly man lowered his voice. "It isn't for practice, Mrs. Hollis. We would like to perform a song in the hall."

"Just one?"

He cleared his throat. "Yes, just one."

This has something to do with Mrs. Hyatt, Julia thought but managed to keep her expression blank. "Why, I think that would be delightful, Mr. Durwin."

"I hope so," he said, blowing out his cheeks. "We're still rather green at this, you know. But we've practiced almost every evening in a room at the *Bow and Fiddle*. That's why I've had meals away. I've felt obliged to compensate the other members of the band for their participation."

"I *have* rather wondered."

"You can be certain it wasn't the cooking. No one can hold a candle to Mrs. Herrick's."

"I'll be sure to tell her that."

He looked a little worried at this. "But please don't mention the ensemble coming here this evening. It's to be a surprise, you see."

A surprise for whom? Julia thought, knowing the answer. Still, she played her part. "Is there anyone in particular I should ask into the hall after supper?"

He gave her an enigmatic little smile. "Thank you, but that will not be necessary."

When he had turned to leave, Julia went back into the kitchen to inform Mrs. Herrick that there would be one less person at supper and that it wasn't her cooking that had driven Mr. Durwin from the table. "His brass band has had several practices lately."

"I'm glad to hear that," the cook declared, cutting dough into a lattice for apple pies.

Mildred came out of the scullery after having helped Gertie wash the breakfast dishes.

"It was dismal around the breakfast table this morning," she told Julia while drying her hands upon her apron.

"Oh, dear. You mean Mrs. Hyatt and Mr. Durwin?"

Mildred shook her head and sent a glance up to the ceiling. "Mr.

Clay. He ate barely enough to keep one of Buff's kittens alive and went back upstairs with scarcely a 'how do you do' to anyone else."

Julia's heart sank. She'd had such hope, along with everyone else who knew him, that Mr. Clay's despondency was a thing of the past. Knowing that it would be a waste of time to see if he were with the rest of the lodgers in the hall, she took the back staircase up to the chamber floor.

"Mr. Clay?" she said with a soft knock at his door.

There was no response, and she was wondering if she had knocked too softly when she heard, "Yes?" from the other side.

"It's Mrs. Hollis, Mr. Clay."

"Come in, please."

He was seated in his chair by the window, as she expected. The haggard face he turned to her brought a lump to her throat.

"Oh, Mr. Clay!" Impulsively she crossed the room to kneel at the side of his chair. She pressed one of his hands between both of hers and looked up into his melancholy gray eyes. "I'm so sorry."

"There, there now," he told her, reaching over with his other hand to pat the top of her head as if she were a fretful child.

"I just hoped . . ."

"I know, Mrs. Hollis. So did I."

They were quiet for a few moments, Julia continuing to hold his hand and stare at the frosted window glass with him. *You've been so good to me,* she prayed silently, *Couldn't You remove this affliction from Mr. Clay? I'm so afraid this will discourage him.*

She felt another touch at the top of her head and looked back up at him. Mr. Clay gave her a weak little smile. "You mustn't be discouraged, Mrs. Hollis."

Julia gaped at him. "But aren't you?"

After some hesitation he replied, "Disappointed, of course. Discouraged? Not at all. I'm sure you understand that God's ways are not our ways."

"Then, you don't regret becoming a believer?"

"Regret? But of course not." He seemed to search for words and then told her, "It's different, this time."

"Different?"

"I've a comfort inside of me, Mrs. Hollis, reminding me that I'm not alone. And assuring me that the joy will return. Haven't you ever felt that comfort?"

"Many times," she whispered, nodding. "It's what has sustained me for almost a year now."

The smile returned, a little stronger this time. "Then you understand."

————

She had left the room some twenty minutes later and met Mrs. Kingston at the staircase landing. "I was just coming to see if Mr. Clay was up to a walk. The ice is melting in the lanes, and it should do him some good to get a little air. He looked rather peaked at breakfast."

Julia nodded soberly. "He's in a bad way again, Mrs. Kingston. One of his dark moods."

"Oh, dear." Mrs. Kingston put a hand up to her wrinkled cheek. "Do you think I should disturb him?"

How can she be so concerned about Mr. Clay and not feel compassion for what Mrs. Hyatt's going through? "I think he would enjoy your company. But he mentioned taking a nap as I was leaving—he had trouble sleeping last night. Perhaps the walk could wait until later?"

"But of course, dear. Should you send notice to the vicar to postpone his visit?"

"I hadn't thought of that," Julia admitted. She went back down to the kitchen, only to find that Karl Herrick had already left to post the letters. Julia was considering walking down to the vicarage herself when Georgette came into the kitchen and announced that Vicar Phelps was in the hall.

362

*M*r. Clay and I discussed that this could conceivably happen," Vicar Phelps said to Julia after expressing his regrets that the actor was abed with depression. He was seated opposite her on one of the horsehair sofas with a tray on the table in front of them. Perhaps sensing that the subject of their conversation would be Mr. Clay's condition, Mrs. Dearing, Mrs. Hyatt, and Miss Rawlins had abandoned the hall for the upstairs sitting room after exchanging pleasantries with the vicar.

"That must be why he's taking it so pragmatically," Julia said after stirring milk into a cup of tea and handing it over to him.

"I hope so." Vicar Phelps took a sip from the cup. "And we should remember that Mr. Clay studied more Scripture before his conversion than most people do afterward. God's Word, hidden in the heart, is a powerful force."

"But I still think it would do him good to visit with you. Would you mind . . ."

"Calling again later today? But of course, Mrs. Hollis. I already plan to do so." After another sip of tea, he eased into a smile that made his hazel eyes seem even kinder. "If I may say so, you seem to feel somewhat protective of Mr. Clay."

Julia returned his smile. "I don't know, Vicar. Mrs. Kingston mothers him far more than I do. But I try to help him as much as I can."

"That's very kind of you. Especially considering that you're going through a valley yourself."

"A valley?" She had to think for a second before realizing he was referring to the fact that she was in mourning. A wave of guilt swept over her. *If you only knew.* Here she was, a tragic figure in black, bravely raising her children alone while accepting the unspoken pity of those around her. *What kind of wife forgets her husband so soon after his death, no matter what he did?* She didn't even attempt to keep his memory alive to the children, unless one happened to say something about him to her. And in those instances she was usually as brief as possible.

I have no right to do that. They deserve to have some good memories to treasure about their father.

With difficulty she made a silent resolve to amend this situation. Her thoughts on the matter had only taken three or four seconds, but the pause was long enough to bring panic to Vicar Phelps's hazel eyes.

"I—I'm so sorry," he stammered. "Did I say the wrong thing?"

"No, I just—"

"I find I am constantly making an idiot of myself in front of you, Mrs. Hollis," he said, a slight flush appearing just above his blond beard. The misery in his expression reminded her so much of her son when she'd scolded him about the ghost caper that Julia couldn't help but smile.

"Vicar, whatever are you talking about?"

"I'm referring to what a comic figure I must seem to you."

"But that's not true."

"Why, then, are you smiling?"

Julia made a futile gesture while groping for words. It would mortify him to learn that he had briefly reminded her of a fourteen-year-old boy. But she could still be truthful in replying, "Because you make me smile, Vicar Phelps. I enjoy your company."

He seemed much startled by this. "You do, Mrs. Hollis?"

"But of course," she reassured him.

"Oh." He opened his mouth to say something else, stared at her for a second, and then closed it again. Setting his empty cup on the tray, he said, "Well, thank you for saying that. I should make my other calls now. I'll show myself to the door."

"Very well, Vicar." Julia said, offering her hand. When he was gone, Julia curled her legs up under her skirt and poured herself another cup of tea.

Mrs. Beemish came through the room some time later and stopped upon seeing Julia. "Is everything all right, Mrs. Hollis?"

Julia smiled up at her. "Yes, of course. I'm just woolgathering."

"Why don't I take that tray?"

"Thank you." Julia handed over her empty cup and, with a glance toward the empty corridor doorway, lowered her voice and said, "Oh, Mrs. Beemish, Mr. Durwin is bringing his brass band here after supper. It's to be a secret until then, but I believe the servants would enjoy the performance. After he arrives would you please quietly usher them into the hall?"

The housekeeper's eyes sparkled with shared intrigue. "I will indeed, Mrs. Hollis—thank you. But I've already been spoken to about it. I'm to allow Mr. Durwin and his friends into the hall while everyone else is at supper, you see?"

"You are? Mr. Durwin didn't mention . . ."

"Oh, it wasn't Mr. Durwin who asked me to do it."

"It wasn't?"

"No, missus. It was Mrs. Kingston."

Julia shook her head, uncomprehending. "But that would mean that Mrs. Kingston and Mr. Durwin are planning this together."

"It does at that, missus. Mrs. Kingston is tryin' to help Mr. Durwin win back Mrs. Hyatt."

"Win her back? You mean, it was Mrs. Hyatt who stopped the courtship?"

Side curls quivered with the housekeeper's nod. "Yes, missus."

So I've misjudged Mrs. Kingston, she thought with a mixture of guilt and relief. "Well, it should be an interesting evening."

"It should at that, missus."

When the housekeeper was gone, Julia leaned her head against the back of the sofa and stared at the high ceiling. *Is it possible that the vicar's attracted to me?* It would hardly seem so. Almost a year of clothing herself in black had caused her to feel like a shadow who moved about in the background. Someone less than feminine and certainly not appealing to the opposite sex.

But why, then, was he often so self-conscious in her presence? Did men sometimes worry about the impressions they made, the way women did? The notion had never occurred to Julia—she supposed it was because Philip had accepted her adoration with aplomb in their courting days, as if it were his due.

She chewed the tip of a fingernail and hoped she was wrong about the vicar. The thought of such a kind, dear person having romantic feelings about her was a little sad, because she could not reciprocate them. He was her pastor, her friend, and almost a brother figure. True, she enjoyed his company immensely, but she could never think of him in a romantic way. Her heart did not race when he spoke to her, as it had with Philip, nor did she entertain fanciful daydreams about him.

Of course, her infatuation with Philip had led her to overlook his faults, so a woman would be foolish to judge the possibility of a courtship by feelings alone. But surely there had to be something beyond friendship, however comforting that friendship may be.

Please help him to get over this, if indeed it's true, she prayed. As an afterthought, she added, *And please help him find a woman who can give him the love he deserves.* She felt some confidence that her prayer would be answered. After all, Vicar Phelps was a man who'd dedicated his life to serving God. And God would want only what was best for him.

"But I've still some studying to do," Philip protested to Julia after supper as she guided her children out of the dining room.

"This should only take a few minutes."

"*What* should?" Grace asked from her other side.

"Sh-h-h!" Julia looked ahead at Mrs. Hyatt, walking arm in arm with Mrs. Kingston down the corridor toward the hall. "I can't tell you right now, Gracie. Just wait and see."

"I'll wager this has something to do with Mr. Durwin," Aleda whispered from behind. Julia turned to gape at her.

"We don't wager, Aleda."

"But it's just a saying, Mother. Everyone says it."

"Well, I don't want to hear it in this house again. Do you understand?"

Aleda lowered her green eyes, so like her own. "Yes, Mother."

You're overreacting! She isn't going to turn out like her father just because she said wager. Julia turned around to wrap an arm around the girl's shoulder. "I can tell you this," she whispered in her ear. "I'm not completely sure of everything that is to happen, but you're absolutely right about this having to do with Mr. Durwin."

"I knew it!" she whispered back, her face brightening. Julia squeezed her hand, and when she turned around again, Mrs. Kingston and Mrs. Hyatt were standing framed by the hall doorway, peering off to their right. Mrs. Kingston's face wore a delighted smile, while Mrs. Hyatt looked to be in shock with her mouth partly open.

"Come now, Mrs. Hyatt. We must allow the others in," Mrs. Kingston was urging when Julia and her children had caught up with them.

"But I don't think—"

"It's only Mr. Durwin's little orchestra. Perhaps they came here to practice."

"It's Mr. Durwin's band!" Grace exclaimed when the two women had moved from the doorway. Julia looked over at the west wall, where

Mr. Durwin stood wearing a black suit and clutching a shiny baritone. With him, and looking just a bit sheepish, were Mr. Clark from the iron foundry with a trombone, Captain Powell with his cornet in hand, Mr. Sway the greengrocer holding a flugelhorn, and Mr. Putnam and Mr. Jones, both with horns. Mr. Summers, a cartier, and the only member without a wind instrument, had a large bass drum suspended from his shoulders. Mrs. Kingston was leading a befuddled Mrs. Hyatt to the sofa while Mrs. Beemish stood by with flushed excitement on her face.

"What have we here?" asked Mrs. Dearing with genuine surprise when she, Miss Rawlins, and Mr. Clay had entered the room. "Are you going to play for us, Mr. Durwin?"

With an exaggerated tilt of the chin, Mr. Durwin appeared to think this over, as if the seven musicians had just happened to be standing against the west wall for some other reason. His eyes seemed to be working hard to keep from straying over in Mrs. Hyatt's direction. "Why, we would consider it an honor," he finally replied.

"What are they going to play?" Philip whispered.

"I don't know," Julia whispered back.

Mrs. Beemish left the room as the men spent three or four minutes tuning their instruments. She returned shortly with the other servants in tow.

"Everyone, have a seat," Mrs. Kingston commanded over the inharmonious sounds of the instruments from her place next to Mrs. Hyatt. The knowing authority in her voice caused Mrs. Hyatt to peer at her curiously, but Mrs. Kingston simply smiled and patted her hand. "After all, since we're all here, we might as well be comfortable."

When everyone had settled into seats and the hall was quiet, Mr. Durwin lifted his baritone to his mouth again. As one, the musicians blew into their mouthpieces. Mr. Summers kept time with subdued blows on his drum. The melody that issued forth was a bit on the bleating side, and an occasional sour note made itself known, but it wasn't every day that one had the opportunity to listen to a brass band, so there were smiles coming from all directions of the room. After three or four measures, Julia recognized the familiar strains of *Now Thank We All Our God*.

"*Now Thank We All Our God*," Grace whispered into her ear.

"Yes, it is," Julia whispered back. And one look at Mrs. Hyatt gave her a clue as to why that particular song had been chosen. The elderly woman sat there with her hand up to her heart, her face filled with some undefinable emotion.

"Do you think we could sing along?"

It was Grace again, and Julia whispered back, "Perhaps we shouldn't." But when the first stanza and chorus were finished, Mr. Durwin raised a hand to silence the scattered applause that had just begun. His cheeks were flushed, and now he looked over at Mrs. Hyatt as he took a step forward.

"We've chosen this particular hymn to play because it is the favorite of a person very dear to us all. Now would you be so kind as to accompany us with your voices?"

There were awkward clearings of throats and exchanges of self-conscious looks as the musicians lifted their instruments again, but every voice joined in, from Grace's soft trill to Karl Herrick's rich accented baritone.

Now thank we all our God, with heart and hands and voices,
Who wondrous things hath done, in whom His world rejoices;

Every voice except for Mr. Clay's, Julia then noticed with a curious glance at a chair to her left, for she was aware that he knew no hymns. He didn't seem uncomfortable but simply sat with closed eyes and a little smile.

Who, from our mother's arms, hath blest us on our way
With countless gifts of love, and still is ours today.

As she continued singing into the second verse, Julia found herself unable to resist a covert glance at Mrs. Hyatt again. She need not have been so careful. Mrs. Hyatt's shining gray eyes were beaming across the room at Mr. Durwin.

There was a hushed silence after the third and final stanza had trailed off to a close, then enthusiastic applause broke out. "Again, please?" Karl Herrick called out. But clearly, the musicians were worn out from the effort.

"Thank you, but some other time," replied Mr. Durwin with a smile after the musicians had given bows over their instruments. "We appreciate your kind attention and participation and now must bid you good evening."

But why is he leaving? Julia wondered as Sarah and Georgette brought the men their wraps. The romantic side of her that she'd forgotten even existed had hoped that Mr. Durwin would fall on his knees at Mrs. Hyatt's feet when the song was finished and plead her hand in marriage. Just the mental picture the scene evoked was enough to make Julia remember that the couple were of another generation. He would not care to make a spectacle of himself, nor would Mrs. Hyatt appreciate being included in such a show.

But still, Mr. Durwin lived at the *Larkspur*. Where was there to go at this hour?

This hour, Julia thought. As chatting servants left the room to clean the supper dishes, she put her left hand on Philip's shoulder. "Bedtime soon. Why don't you see to—"

"My studying," he finished for her and was gone. Grace and Aleda, who had finished their homework, went to their room to see if the glue on their latest batch of valentines was dry. With just over two weeks remaining until Valentine's day, the girls had an ambitious plan to hand out valentines to every person at school as well as every person with whom they were even remotely acquainted. When they were gone, Julia looked across at Mrs. Hyatt again.

"But I don't *feel* overtired," Mrs. Hyatt was telling Mrs. Kingston. "And how did Mr. Durwin know that my favorite song was—" She became silent then, apparently aware that all eyes remaining in the room were focused on her.

But Mrs. Kingston sent a forgiving smile around the room. "I was just telling Mrs. Hyatt that she could stand some rest after all the excitement. Wouldn't you agree?"

There was more command than question in her voice, and Julia found that her head was nodding in unison with all of the others. She probably wouldn't have noticed without it being pointed out, but Mrs. Hyatt did look somewhat peaked.

"But—"

"Just a quarter of an hour or so with your eyes closed and feet propped up . . . you'll see, dear. It'll feel like a tonic."

When they were gone from the room, Julia studied the door for three or four minutes. There was something not quite right here. If Mrs. Kingston had kindly helped arrange the concert, why was she then ordering Mrs. Hyatt to her room? "I should see if she needs anything," she finally said, standing.

"A good idea," Miss Rawlins said, and Mrs. Dearing nodded agreement.

"Curiosity killed the cat," was Mr. Clay's wry input.

"Satisfaction brought it back," Mrs. Dearing told him. "You go on ahead, Mrs. Hollis."

As Julia left the upstairs landing, she heard more than two female voices coming from the room. She hurried to the open doorway and looked in to see Mrs. Hyatt standing in the middle of the carpet with both hands up to her cheeks. In an instant, Julia discovered the source of her amazement, for at least a dozen vases and even tumblers of pink and white dianthus bedecked every surface. Mrs. Kingston stood to the side with a delighted grin, as did Mrs. Beemish, Ruth, and Willa.

"But how did he know about my favorite hymn and flower?" Mrs. Hyatt was saying, rotating slowly to take it all in.

"I suppose he decided he cared enough to find out," Mrs. Kingston said with a nod toward Julia in the doorway, beckoning her inside.

"Where did he get flowers at this time of year?" was what Julia wanted to know.

"The squire's conservatory," Mrs. Kingston replied. "Mr. Durwin plays chess with the old blister occasionally and managed to talk him into selling some."

Julia couldn't imagine Squire Bartley contributing anything for the benefit of anyone who lived under the *Larkspur*'s roof. *He must have charged Mr. Durwin a dear penny.*

"We brought them up here while you were all at supper," Willa volunteered, clasping her hands together. "It's so romantic!"

Julia agreed. Not only was the gesture romantic, but effective, for she caught some of the words that Mrs. Hyatt was murmuring as she buried her face in the tops of some dianthus. "The dear, dear man!"

———

Mrs. Hyatt and Mr. Durwin drew Julia aside five days later to tell her that a wedding date had been tentatively set for late summer, perhaps even September. One of Mr. Durwin's sons, an engineer building a bridge in India, would not return to England until then.

A long time for people in their golden years to wait, but it was important to Mrs. Hyatt that all of the family on both sides be in attendance. That was one of the things Mr. Durwin had recently discovered about Mrs. Hyatt. And that her maiden name was Middleton.

London
February 3, 1870

"A letter for you, Miss O'Shea," said Anne, the under-parlor-maid, from the doorway of the pantry.

"Thank you, Anne," Fiona said, setting her inventory of kitchen supplies in an empty space on one of the shelves. When the girl was gone, she broke the red wax seal stamped with the familiar image of a spray of larkspur blossoms. The date penned at the top of the first page in Mrs. Hollis's even script was January twenty-sixth, eight days ago. Fiona perched herself on the edge of an oaken flour barrel and read all three pages, drinking in every word. By the time she had returned to her inventory with the letter folded in her apron pocket, she could not stop smiling.

She didn't mind being asked to critique another of Miss Rawlins' books . . . she wouldn't mind being asked to do anything in her present state of euphoria. *Mr. Clay . . . a believer!* How she had prayed for that to happen!

A knock sounded on the door. But before Fiona could say, "Come in, please," it swung open and Mrs. Leighton charged through it, waving a piece of paper in front of her.

"This is the invoice from the butcher," her mistress said in her usual thin voice, which grated upon the ears like a file across tin. "Why did you allow Cook to order ten pounds extra of beef last week?"

When her wits had returned to her, Fiona replied, "The dinner party last week, Mrs. Leighton. Remember?" She *hated* being barged in upon like this! It was as if her employer expected to catch her slipping chocolate up her sleeve or some other dishonest act as the last housekeeper to the Italianate-style estate on Kensington Road was reputed to have done. Having been in the employ of the Leightons for almost four months now, Fiona had come to learn that Mrs. Leighton either suspected that every servant under her roof was in the process of pilfering, *planning* to pilfer, or hiding away ill-gotten gains from having pilfered in the past. Her social acquaintances were hardly esteemed in a better light, for silverware and even table napkins were regularly counted as soon as the last dinner guests' footsteps faded from the portico.

And sadly, years of assuming the worst of her servants and even her peers had worked its way into her facial features—though only in her late thirties, she bore very little resemblance to the beautiful young woman in the portrait hanging in the sitting room. The sea green eyes in the portrait, luminescent even captured with oils, now wore a constant ferretlike expression, and anxiety lines were etched into her brow and at the corners of her mouth. Her constant negativity even seemed to have affected her mahogany-colored hair. It no longer had any shine, though it was brushed one hundred strokes every morning and evening by a maid.

But I have to work somewhere, Fiona reminded herself. She had been only half truthful in describing her new situation to Mrs. Hollis, lest she cause her friend and former employer to worry. Mr. Leighton was indeed a Member of Parliament. What she did not say was that he was hardly ever home, preferring to spend most of his nonparliamentary hours at his club.

"Ah, but just look at this invoice!" Mrs. Leighton commanded, holding the paper out for Fiona to take. "I was charged threepence extra for each pound. Cook assumes I never look at the mail, so she feels the liberty to make arrangements with the butcher to cheat me!"

And that's why you've had four cooks in the past three years, Fiona thought, pressing her lips together. She studied the invoice for a second and looked back up at her mistress.

"Brisket has gone up threepence a pound, missus," she said in a calm voice.

The ferret eyes narrowed a bit. "It has?"

"I'll accompany you to Mr. Frith's shop if you'd care to see for yourself."

"Of course you will, after you give him warning. . . ."

"We can go right away, ma'am."

That took some more wind from the woman's sails. The ferret eyes shifted from the paper in Fiona's hand to her face and back again. "Well, I was certain . . ."

"Mrs. Bryant is a good Christian woman, ma'am," Fiona gently insisted. "She's not stealing from you and the mister."

Mrs. Leighton stared back at her, the frown deepening as if she were almost disappointed her suspicion had been proven wrong. "Well then," she sniffed, "I want you to inform her that the salmon was overcooked last night. Overcooked and underseasoned! Food is too expensive to be ruined by unimaginative cooking!"

With that, she turned on her heel and left the room. Fiona sighed, and before returning to her work, she touched the edge of the envelope in her pocket. She would not have time to read it again until this evening, but it would be a comfort all day to know it was there. A reminder, it was, that there was still a place where people cared about one another and about her. A place where she had lived for less than a year but would always consider home.

———

" . . . and thank you for providing for us so abundantly over this past year," Julia prayed at the girls' bedside. She didn't know if the children had realized the significance of the date, February eighth, in the midst of the activities of school and scissoring and pasting valentines. And it hadn't seemed appropriate to wave them out of the door this morning with, "Have a wonderful day at school, and by the way, your father died on this day last year."

But she had carried around the determination all day to give them an opportunity to unburden their hearts if they felt the need to do so. And they did seem to have that need, for after the girls' prayers were finished and Julia had gently reminded them of the anniversary of their father's passing, Grace asked, "Do you think Father would have liked living here if he hadn't died?"

"I'm sure he would have loved it," Julia answered with a squeeze of her little hand.

"But we wouldn't have had to move here if Father hadn't died," Aleda said.

"Are you still sorry we left London?"

"Oh, no. I'm just saying that we wouldn't have run out of money."

That latter part wasn't true, but Julia let it be and leaned over to plant kisses on both foreheads.

Philip's question took Julia a little longer to answer.

"Is it a sin that I'm happier the way things are now?"

His blue eyes had a sheen in the lamplight, and Julia could tell he had struggled with this for some time. Wishing for some Solomon-like wisdom, she said, "Being happy isn't a sin, Philip. I don't think you're saying that you're glad your father died."

"No, of course not," he hastened to assure her, then chewed pensively on his lip. "But when Father was alive, I was hurt so many times. Like when he missed my birthday. And when you had to send for another doctor when Aleda and I had the ague. But now, instead of wondering why he doesn't spend more time at home, I can imagine him watching us from heaven. So you see? He's with us more now than he ever was."

So this is the consolation he's worked up for himself, Julia thought, concealing with a smile the effect his poignant words had upon her. *Now there is a valid reason for his father being absent, one that a boy can understand. And much easier to accept than the idea that his father had some control over his comings and goings and chose not to be with his son.*

She recalled the days of their courtship. That Dr. Hollis was handsome, educated, courteous, and charming were the qualities that attracted her to him. Never once, as a seventeen-year-old girl, had she wondered if he would be a nurturing father to the children they would eventually have together. And even if the question had somehow presented itself to her mind, just how long would she have pondered it? Weren't all handsome, charming men also kind to children . . . especially their own?

Our decisions are like stones thrown into a pool, she thought while tucking the covers over her son's shoulders. An impetuous decision, made by an infatuated young girl with no notion of the seriousness of pledging her life away, was still sending out ripples. She could no longer blame her husband for the troubled waters they had had to navigate, she now realized, when it was she who had tossed in the stone.

———

Julia waited almost two weeks before bringing her regular clothing out of her trunk to be aired and pressed. Somehow, it didn't seem proper to put away her black gowns on the exact date of Philip's death, as if she had been just waiting for the opportunity to forget about their marriage.

When the day came, she chose a dove gray cashmere with tiny tucks along the bodice and a row of pearl buttons. It was certainly not her most striking gown, but she knew she would feel conspicuous enough for several days. Better to begin with the more subdued colors.

"Oh, isn't it beautiful!" Georgette exclaimed that morning while flouncing out the bustle from behind.

"Thank you, Georgette." Julia sent a smile over her shoulder and brushed an auburn hair from one of the long gathered sleeves. Actually, the gown was almost two years old and out of style by her former standards. Had she still lived in London, she would have probably passed it down to some charity drive by now.

But that doesn't matter here. Not when half the women in Gresham came to church wearing gowns of the wide crinolined style of the fifties and even earlier. They had children to raise and gardens to tend, even labored in the cheese factory, and little spare money for such frivolities as keeping pace with the dictates of *Godey's Lady's Book*.

It seemed the whole household knew of the change in dress she would be making today. A soft knock sounded at the door to Julia's room, and Mrs. Beemish and Sarah let themselves in. "Lovely!" exclaimed Mrs. Beemish.

"Lovely," Sarah echoed.

Aleda and Grace voiced their similar opinions when she went in their room to wake them, which was a relief, because she had worried they would feel she was betraying their father's memory. Only Grace held back briefly from her embrace, but it was as if she needed a moment to assure herself that her mother was still the same as before.

Philip didn't even notice until he'd wiped the sleep from his eyes. "Oh, finally," was his comment. "I was so tired of seeing you in black. It was like having a crow for a mother."

"A crow, Philip?"

"Without feathers and beak," he said with a grin.

Three weeks later, Mr. Clay knocked and stuck his head through the doorway of Julia's office after lunch. "Have you a minute, Mrs. Hollis?"

"Of course, Mr. Clay," Julia smiled, looking up from the letter she was drafting. "Would you care to have a seat?"

He stepped into the office but did not take the chair. "I just wanted to tell you that Mrs. Kingston and I looked in on the Worthy sisters this morning. Mrs. Herrick had asked if we would mind dropping off a loaf of apple bread before our walk. The sisters ask that you pop over sometime today."

"Did they say why?" Julia asked, her pen poised in midair.

"To give you a gift. When you stopped wearing black, they decided to make you some sort of lace decoration to wear. A ruffle or something. I don't know the names of all the latest women's frills. By the way, you look very nice in purple."

Julia had to laugh. "It's lavender, Mr. Clay. And sometimes it's impossible to keep up with your train of conversation."

He did not take offense; in fact, his gray eyes sparkled under their thick fringe of lashes. "Sad but true, Mrs. Hollis. Mrs. Dearing says it's as if when the good moods take hold of me, I feel compelled to talk twice as much to compensate for the times I spend staring out of the window during the bad."

"I'm happy that you're feeling well. And it was kind of the Worthy sisters to make something for me. I'll pay them a call . . ." She started to say, "When I've finished this letter," but thought better of it. In Mr. Clay's garrulous mood, he could possibly ask if she was writing to Fiona, which she was, in reply to the letter she'd received from the former housekeeper yesterday.

" . . . in a little while," she told him instead. "Thank you for telling me."

"You're welcome. I'll leave you to your work." His hand had barely touched the doorknob when he turned back to face her again. "Mrs. Hollis . . ."

"Yes, Mr. Clay?"

"Why don't you take a walk with me after you visit the sisters?"

"But you've already walked with Mrs. Kingston today."

"I don't mean a *walk* walk. I've promised to accompany the vicar on a call, and when I joined them for supper last Tuesday Miss Phelps mentioned how much she admires you. Why don't you keep her company while we're away?"

Puzzled, Julia sat back in her chair. "You're accompanying the vicar?"

"To lend moral support, actually. Our good reverend has intentions of trying to save the souls of a certain hoard of barbarians."

Julia didn't even have to ask of whom he was referring. "Shouldn't you bring Constable Reed along?"

"Now, now, Mrs. Hollis. And just how receptive to the Gospel do you think that would make them? And surely Mr. Sanders has enough paternal integrity not to allow his sons to commit murder on his own property."

"I've never heard Sanders and integrity mentioned in the same sentence, Mr. Clay."

"Worrying will give you wrinkles, Mrs. Hollis," he told her. "Now, what have you going on here that can't wait for an hour or two?"

Casually she allowed her hand to stray over to Fiona's name on the letter. *You've been planning to visit with Elizabeth for weeks now,* she reminded herself. And she certainly couldn't expect the young woman to put forth the effort, not with two small children to tend.

She was aware of why she'd put off calling at the vicarage, and the reason had a blond beard and kind hazel eyes. If it were so that Vicar Phelps did indeed harbor romantic feelings toward her, it would be unfair to raise his hopes by making a call to his house. Wouldn't he assume that she had some interest in him beyond friendship?

For the first time, she could see the fallacy in that assumption. Vicar Phelps clearly had so modest of an opinion of himself that she could stare at him with doe eyes, the way Georgette used to stare at Mr. Clay, and he would torment himself trying to recall what ridiculous thing he'd done lately. The thought of such a polished orator in the pulpit battling such personal insecurities in her presence made him rather endearing to her, in a nonromantic sort of way.

"What are you smiling at, Mrs. Hollis?"

She returned her attention abruptly to the actor. "Just a stray thought, Mr. Clay." *Besides, he'll be away most of the afternoon.* "I would enjoy a visit with Miss Phelps. Thank you for suggesting it."

———

The Worthy sisters' gift to Julia was a beautiful collar of finely woven ecru lace. It was long in front, with one side lapping over the other at her bodice, and ended about three inches above her waist.

"Why, it goes very well with that frock," Iris declared as Julia slipped it on over her gown in their cottage.

"*Children* wear frocks, Iris," Jewel corrected but wore a pleased smile. "Ye do look nice, Mrs. Hollis."

"You've both been so kind to me."

At Iris's urging, Julia stepped over to an oval mirror hanging from the wall above the washstand. The face that stared back at her wore a strange expression of expectancy, and Julia realized she was actually looking forward to the afternoon's outing. And why wouldn't she? Mr. Clay and Vicar Phelps were pleasant company. And as for Elizabeth, any woman would be flattered to have a younger woman look up to her and seek her counsel.

She touched the fine lace of the collar, appreciating the work that went into every square inch. Turning again to the sisters, she went over to kiss both wrinkled cheeks. "It's one of the most beautiful things I've ever owned. Thank you so much."

Iris wore a beatific smile across her face. "You've been a good neighbor, Mrs. Hollis."

"A good neighbor indeed," Jewel echoed, then darted a meaningful glance in Iris's direction. "Even if ye were a mite reckless in the matter of Jake Pitt."

*C*ozy in her wrap and gloves, Julia strolled along Church Lane with Mr. Clay. Though the gardens were just starting to bud the flowers that would form tapestries of color in another month or so, the village still clung to its charm. From a spinny of gray silver aspens between Captain Powell's cottage and Bartley Lane, one of the first woodlarks of the season serenaded them from atop a broken branch. Distinct white markings formed large triangles around the bird's eyes, giving him the appearance of a studious little brown creature in spectacles. Julia pursed her lips and attempted to mimic his trilling *toolooeet!* Clearly unimpressed, the bird took flight from its perch.

"Do you think I offended him?" Julia asked Mr. Clay, who chuckled.

"Obviously he was mortified because your song was superior."

She smiled at the actor. "I believe I prefer your reason."

A dozen steps later, he gave her a quick sidelong look, wearing the expression of a boy who wishes to ask a question but fears what the answer may be.

"Yes, Mr. Clay?" Julia asked after the third such glance in her direction.

"Mildred told me that a letter arrived from Miss O'Shea yesterday."

"Yes, that's so. She writes that she's doing well."

"Do you think she means it?"

Julia had to think about that one. Fiona was too honest to lie, but sometimes there were certain gaps in her letters that she wondered about.

"She would do anything to spare us pain, Mr. Clay."

He frowned and shoved his hands into his pocket. "Yes. And I was a selfish cad for allowing her to leave the way she did."

"How could you have prevented her from doing so?"

"I could have moved away myself when we discovered her absence." Turning a somber face to Julia, he asked, "Do you think she would return if I did so now?"

Julia shook her head. "Fiona knows we've another housekeeper. I'm positive she wouldn't want to take any action that would jeopardize someone else's position." *And she'll do anything to ensure that you stay here where you can have some peace, Mr. Clay.*

Suddenly she grew weary of the conversation. She missed Fiona more now than ever, and such talk served only as a reminder that there was an empty space in her life. But of one thing she was certain—never would she give up hope of Fiona returning to Gresham.

Mr. Clay would be allowed to refuge here as long as he found it necessary, but when the day came that the actor felt strong enough to leave, she intended to write Fiona and beg that she return. Fiona could take the room now being reserved for Jensen, and there would be ample time to fix up the groomsman's apartment over the stables for the butler.

Julia didn't need a new housekeeper—Mrs. Beemish was more than competent. What she wanted back was the friend who was more like a sister to her than anyone she'd ever known.

She glanced at Mr. Clay, who was walking with hands in pockets in a melancholy cloud of self-blame, and felt a surge of pity. How could she find fault with him for loving Fiona? Gently she touched his shoulder. "Mr. Clay."

He started slightly, as if she'd pierced some deep thought. "Yes, Mrs. Hollis?"

"At least we had her with us for a while."

"We did at that, didn't we?"

"Do you regret it?" *After all, if you'd never met her, you wouldn't be suffering the loss right now.*

With a glint in his eyes over a sad little smile, he replied, "Not for one second."

———

Having finished copying and solving the twelve long-division problems Captain Powell had chalked on the blackboard, *and* after checking his work, Philip looked over to the girls' side of the classroom. Laurel Phelps's eyes still looked from blackboard to paper, and then back again, which meant she had not even begun to check her computations. She could write all the snooty compositions she wished about Mr. Disraeli, but she could never hold a candle to him in arithmetic.

I should study history now, he thought. No examinations loomed ahead in the near future, but when did it ever hurt to learn something new? *Or in this case, old,* he thought, smiling at his own humor as he took out his copy of *History for Young Scholars.* With the school year advancing rapidly to a close, only a quarter of the book was left unread. He flipped though those pages with interest. Since the text had been published in 1862, the writers had had no idea which side would eventually win the war between the American states, nor even how long it would continue, but the advantage seemed to be with the Confederate states. *If they would have just put off finishing the book for a couple of years . . .*

Something wedged between two of the latter pages caught his attention. An envelope, he realized right away. *How did that get there?*

As soon as he saw the name on the outside, he felt a little queasy. Clearly now he could recall Mr. Trumble entrusting him with the delivery of a letter to the *Larkspur.* When had that been? His discomfort increased with the realization it had been sometime in late September or early October. *Six months ago!*

———

Vicar Phelps himself met them at the door carrying a girl of about three years of age up on a broad shoulder. Julia remembered seeing her outside the church with her family.

"I was just about to bring little Molly upstairs," he informed Julia after warmly welcoming them into the vestibule. "It's time for the children's naps, so Elizabeth will be happy for your company. Would you care to wait in the parlor?"

Julia smiled at the girl, who only regarded her gravely. "Why don't I bring her up there myself so you two can go on ahead?"

"Thank you, but I'm afraid Dora's visiting her sister in Stone, so I would need to show you the way anyway."

"Yes?" She lifted an eyebrow. "And just how many people are wandering around lost up there, Vicar?"

After a brief startled look at her, he joined Mr. Clay in a chuckle, his eyes crinkling at the corners. "I see your point, Mrs. Hollis." After

381

he'd lifted the child from his shoulders to the floor, he crouched down and said in a gentle tone, "Mrs. Hollis will bring you upstairs to Aunt Beth now."

But Molly tugged at his sleeve while pointing at the doorway leading to the rest of the vicarage. "Read book?"

"We've already read two, Molly. It's time to sleep."

"Dabid sleep. Moll-yee read book." Another jab at the doorway with a little finger. "Sit down in chair."

"Looks as if she's used to giving you orders," Mr. Clay observed, smiling.

"As is every other female in this house," the reverend responded good-naturedly, causing the actor and Julia to exchange amused glances. To the child, Vicar Phelps said with gentle firmness, "Another time, Molly. Now, please take Mrs. Hollis's hand and show her where to find Aunt Beth."

Julia realized she had been holding her breath, expecting a scene that a three-year-old would be fully capable of delivering. But Molly simply allowed her to take her by the hand.

When the two men had left on their evangelistic mission—*just like Paul and Silas going to the heathens,* Julia thought—she smiled down at the child again. "Can you climb the stairs, or shall I carry you?"

The girl pointed again to the vestibule doorway, but instead of asking for a story, she said, "Moll-yee walk uptairs."

They made their way slowly, because Molly could not ascend one step until both feet were planted on the one below it. Julia held her hand and kept the pace patiently. Halfway up the staircase, she heard a muffled childish chuckle from someone on the next floor. Molly turned her small face to her, finally wearing something resembling a smile. "Dabid laff, huh?"

"He did indeed," Julia smiled back. Upon reaching the landing, Molly walked slightly ahead of Julia and pulled her hand down the passage.

"Come in," came Elizabeth Phelps's voice from behind the third door after Julia's soft knock. She opened the door, and inside, the vicar's daughter was sitting on the side of a tester bed, patting the back of a boy much younger than the child still attached to Julia's hand.

"Why, I thought you were Papa!" Elizabeth said with a welcoming smile. "And don't you look stunning! I love seeing you in colors now."

"You're too kind." Julia walked over to give the young woman a quick embrace. "Your father and Mr. Clay left for the Sanders'."

"Ah, yes. Well, how good of you to come."

The vicar's daughter took charge of Molly then, leaving Julia with the boy while she led the girl to a water closet in another part of the house. "So, you like to have your back patted, little David?" Julia asked when she noticed the child staring up at her from his pillow. Taking up Miss Phelps's place on the side of the bed, she gently began patting his back. Patting led to humming, which led to looking around the room. It was a typical young woman's room, one that Julia might have had at one time. Though the wall covering—stripes of mauve, eggshell, and marigold—was faded somewhat with age, it did not detract from the rose and green-leaf pattern on the dimity bed coverings, curtains, and tester.

Julia turned her attention back to the child in the bed. The visible right side of his face was the very picture of an angel in repose. Fair, wispy lashes rested against his cheek, and his small shoulders rose and fell with his breathing. Her heart went out to the little fatherless cherub. *How good of Elizabeth to tend to them like this. She has such a tender heart . . . just like her father.*

Miss Phelps returned with Molly, and after tucking her in next to her sleeping brother, she took a heavy velvet bolster from the foot of the bed and placed it alongside the girl to prevent her from rolling to the carpet. She turned to Julia and whispered, "There is a tiny sitting room at the end of the corridor. Would you mind if we visited in there? I don't want to leave them up here alone."

Julia said she didn't mind at all, and just minutes later they sat in front of a wood fire on an ancient sofa of burgundy plush that sagged in all the right places.

"As you may recall, I'm fond of fireplaces," the young woman said with a hint of her father's self-effacing humor.

"I certainly remember," Julia told her. "And I thought you were charming that day."

"Thank you for saying that. But I'm afraid I'm not a good hostess. Would you care for something to drink? Mrs. Paget made some lemonade just this morning."

"Why don't we just visit?"

"That would be nice." They chatted about everyday things, Molly and David in particular.

With brown eyes shining, Elizabeth said, "You know, they exhaust me sometimes, but I find myself missing them in the evenings."

"Little ones can capture your heart, can't they?" Julia smiled.

"Absolutely. Papa warned me, though, that as much as I love them, I should always bear in mind that they have a mother who loves them even more so. He's afraid I'll be devastated when the time comes that they no longer need me."

"I'm sure you'll always be Aunt Beth to them. But I agree with your father's advice. And one day you'll have children of your own to love without reserve."

Just a hint of color stained the girl's cheeks. "I suppose you've heard about Mr. Treves."

"I have," Julia admitted while darting a glance down at Elizabeth's hands. She was knotting her fingers together the way she had on her first visit to the *Larkspur*. Touching the girl's shoulder, she said, "What is wrong, Elizabeth?"

"Wrong?" Elizabeth looked at Julia curiously. "Why, nothing, Mrs. Hollis."

"Are you quite sure?"

The smile that came to her lips seemed genuine enough, but not quite in harmony with the doubt that shadowed her brown eyes for just an instant and was gone. "It's just a major decision, becoming engaged."

Julia's eyes widened. "You're going to marry—"

Now the girl gave a soft giggle. If it sounded a trifle forced to Julia's ears, she reckoned it was because the doubt she'd seen in the girl's face just seconds ago had prejudiced her to be suspicious.

"I'm sorry, Mrs. Hollis, but you looked so shocked just now. It's nothing official yet, but Paul—that's his name, Paul Treves—will likely be promoted to the vicar of Alveley this time next year. If indeed that is the case, he will be asking Papa for my hand. Paul would like to prove to Papa that he can afford to take care of a wife, you see, and he cannot do that on a curate's salary."

"And so you're happy about this?"

"Very happy, Mrs. Hollis," Elizabeth assured her. "Why, tending the children has strengthened my desire to be a mother. And Paul is an upstanding man who'll make a fine husband."

The question had to be asked, for the girl's sake, though Julia was not comfortable with its bluntness. "Elizabeth . . ."

"Yes?"

"Forgive me for asking, but have you completely gotten over Mr. Raleigh?"

"Completely, Mrs. Hollis."

Julia saw no doubt in the girl's expression this time, but then Elizabeth wasn't quite looking her in the eyes. "Well, at least you have another year to be sure. As you said, becoming engaged is a major decision."

"Yes." Elizabeth leaned over to touch her hand. "I do appreciate you asking the questions my mother would be asking right now. But please don't worry. I shall be very happy as Paul's wife."

Before Julia could say anything else, the girl brightened and said, "Would you like to see a photograph of my mother?"

"I'd like that very much," Julia replied, smiling. "She must have been very special to have such a dear family."

"Very special . . . and thank you." Elizabeth got to her feet. "If you don't mind my leaving you alone for a few minutes, I'll peek in on the children too."

"Take all the time you need." As the door closed behind the girl, Julia found herself praying silently, *She's still so young, Father. Please help her to understand in the coming year the seriousness of the commitment she's making.* As an afterthought, she added, *And if this young curate is the right man for her, please remove all thoughts about Mr. Raleigh completely from her mind.*

"I didn't realize how rutted the lane was when I walked it," Mr. Clay told Andrew, raising his voice over the rattle of the trap's wheels and Rusty's hoofbeats.

"Is it much farther?" Andrew practically shouted back.

"Just around that next curve, I believe. Yes, that's it."

Andrew pulled Rusty to a stop as far to the side of Nettle Lane as he could, in front of a wide gate set in a hedgerow. He took his hat from his head and beat the dust from the brim, then replaced it. "Well, it's now or never."

"*Never* sounds rather appealing at the moment," the actor said with a wry smile as he shook the dust from his own hat.

"Oh, come now. What can they do to us?"

Mr. Clay looked over at the house and then back at Andrew. "I suppose we're about to find out."

The noise of the trap apparently had drawn some attention, for by the time Andrew and Mr. Clay had stepped down and walked over to the gate, they noticed a man walking from the barn in their direction. He could have been any age, but his tanned, leathery skin gave him the appearance of someone older than either of them. He wore corded pants and a brown coat, a battered cap, and boots that were dusty.

Stopping about twelve feet from the gate, the man put both hands on his hips and said, "What do ye want?"

Andrew raised a hand in greeting. "Mr. Sanders?"

"Mayhap."

"Now I can see where the boy got his knack for conversation," Mr. Clay whispered at Andrew's side."

"Sh-h!" To the man with hands still on hips, Andrew called, "I'm Vicar Phelps, Mr. Sanders, and this is Mr. Clay. We realize you're busy but wonder if you might spare us a few minutes?"

Some motion caught Andrew's eye back in the direction of the barn. A couple of boys who appeared to be younger than Laurel had just started in their direction, but Mr. Sanders turned and waved them back to work. To Andrew and Mr. Clay, he simply said, "I don't talk ter no preachers. Go away!"

"Would you just consider attending church this Sunday? You would be most welcome."

"No."

Andrew took a deep breath and gave one last try. "Your children should be brought up to know the Lord, Mr. Sanders."

The man did not answer but bent down. At first, Andrew thought it was to tie a boot lace, but then Mr. Clay pulled at his arm.

"He's picking up a rock!"

———

"What are you going to do?" Ben asked Philip after school was dismissed, his back propped against one of the walnut trees.

"I'll just have to tell my mother." He *hated* the thought of doing so. Was this how a fourteen-year-old man of the house managed his responsibilities? *But you were thirteen when you put the letter aside*, he reminded himself in a futile attempt at comfort.

"Why don't you just throw it away?" suggested Jeremiah. "I mean, Miss O'Shea doesn't even live here anymore, and the news is old now."

"What if it's important?"

Ben was thoughtful for a second, and then said, "Perhaps you should open it and see. There's no imprint on the wax, so you could reseal it with a little heat."

"Yes?" Philip said, but then shook his head. "It just doesn't seem right, reading someone's mail."

"I'd let everyone read *my* mail," Jeremiah shrugged. "If I ever got any, I mean."

Recalling the shame he'd felt when his mother found out about his deception in the ghost prank, Philip shook his head again. "I'm just going to have to face this head on."

But upon arriving at the *Larkspur* and finding that Mother was away, he came up with another idea. What if he took the letter out of the original envelope, readdressed and posted it? Mother had envelopes in her office, along with a small leather-covered book of addresses. Fiona's would be in there. If she wondered, on the receiving end, why the envelope did not match the letter inside, it wouldn't be like her to mention it. *And that's all Mother would do anyway . . . post it. Why shouldn't I go ahead and save her the trouble?*

Keeping a lookout for his sisters, Philip hurried down the corridor to his mother's office. He eased himself through the door and felt for a candle, for there were no windows. After addressing another envelope, he opened the original envelope with trembling fingers and withdrew the letter. Curiously, the folded page appeared to be blank. There were no signs of ink having blended through from the other side. *Why would someone send her a blank sheet of paper?* Some perverse notion took hold of him then, and hating himself for doing so, he unfolded it.

The letter was composed of two lines:

Dear Fiona,

> *Your husbund has past away affer a fall frum a horse whiles hunting. Maye God have mercy on his soul.*

> > > > *Breanna*

*I*t was taken on their fifth anniversary," Elizabeth told Julia as they both stared down at a photograph set in a silver oval frame. The subjects, Vicar Phelps at about thirty years of age, and a dark-eyed woman in possibly her middle twenties, were captured from the waists up as they stood beside each other. Julia hadn't noticed at first glance, but there was a hint of mischief to both sets of eyes, though the faces were arranged in the sober expressions that could be seen in any family gallery of photographs.

"Why does it seem as if they're both on the verge of laughing?" she asked.

"Because Papa is balancing himself on a copy of *War and Peace*," Elizabeth explained. "Mother was the same height as Papa, you see, so he brought the book from his library to the photographer's."

Julia had to smile. "Your father doesn't strike me as being self-conscious about his height."

"Actually, he isn't. But he says he didn't want future generations referring to him as 'the short Grandfather Phelps.' Yet he tells everyone who sees the photograph that he's perched upon a book."

"They must have been very happy together."

"It was something I took for granted. I was twelve when Mother died. I wasn't old enough to realize that not *all* mothers and fathers were the best of friends."

There were tears clinging to her lashes as she said this, and Julia took her hand. "I lost my mother eleven years ago, Elizabeth, and I still miss her. But it's so much greater a loss when you're young."

"Just like your children with their father."

"Yes, like that." Julia turned her attention back to the woman in the photograph, Kathleen Phelps. In addition to the laughing eyes, there was an aura of security in her youthful face, the kind of security a woman feels when she knows she is cherished. *And you were cherished, weren't you?* she thought. She couldn't imagine Vicar Phelps *not* cherishing a wife. *How he must have grieved when you passed away!*

Just for a moment, Julia allowed her thoughts to drift to what it would be like to be married to someone like the man in the photograph. Someone who would consider his wife his best friend and not just an accessory to the house. A man who didn't feel it beneath his dignity to carry a three-year-old around on his shoulders. And who concerned himself with the happiness of his children. Why hadn't someone told her how important those qualities would be fifteen years ago?

"Mrs. Hollis?"

"Oh . . . I'm sorry," Julia said, realizing she'd forgotten all about the young woman beside her. She handed back the photograph. "Your mother is a lovely woman. I wish I could have known her."

Elizabeth gave her a grateful smile. "Thank you for saying that."

From outside came the sound of a horse and carriage. Elizabeth set the photograph down beside her and went to the window. "Why, Papa's back already." Leaning closer to the glass, she added, "But where is Mr. Clay?"

Julia and Elizabeth had just reached the front door when Vicar Phelps came through in a gust of cold air. "I dropped Mr. Clay off at Dr. Rhodes'," he said upon seeing their anxious expressions.

Julia's knees went weak. "Dr. Rhodes?"

"He's fine," Vicar Phelps assured her. "His forehead just requires some stitching. Mr. Sanders tossed a rock at us, and unfortunately, Mr. Clay caught it."

"Did you tell the constable?" Elizabeth asked through the hand still covering her mouth.

"No, Beth. The man was on his own property. And he *did* warn us to leave." To Julia, he said, "I'll look in on Mr. Clay again after I deliver you back home, Mrs. Hollis."

"May I go with you to see about him?"

"But of course," he answered.

————

"I should have never allowed him to come with me," Vicar Phelps said as he drove the trap up Church Lane a short time later.

"Mr. Clay is a grown man," Julia reminded him.

"But as his minister, I bore the greater responsibility."

"I'm positive he isn't blaming you."

That clearly brought him no comfort, for he blew out a long breath. "Mr. Clay isn't the blaming sort. But I should have known better than to expose a new believer to—"

She reached over and touched his sleeve. "Vicar?"

"Yes?" he said with a puzzled sidelong look.

"Hush."

After a second or two the puzzlement in his face eased into a smile, and he sat back at the reins again. "Very well, Mrs. Hollis. Thank you."

"You're welcome, Vicar."

They found Mr. Clay only a little worse for the wear, perched on a stool in the surgery across from the front parlor. As it turned out, Dr. Rhodes was away, and it was Mrs. Rhodes who administered the eight stitches required to close the actor's forehead. The swollen area behind the wound was already beginning to discolor.

"You aren't going to treat me for distemper, are you?" Mr. Clay quipped after Julia and the vicar had arrived.

Mrs. Rhodes smiled as she tied off the last stitch holding together the two-inch gash. "No, but if you should feel the urge to give chase to a cat within the next day or so, do send for me."

After a round of laughter, Mr. Clay waved away her offer of some laudanum to help him sleep, should the wound start to throb. "I'll just tough it out, thank you."

Julia knew it was because he had once had trouble with alcohol and feared sedating himself. Her respect for the actor grew. *Why did I ever think him a weak man?*

"We'll keep a watch out for him," she told Mrs. Rhodes. "And I'm sure Mrs. Kingston will hover over him like Florence Nightingale."

When they had delivered Mr. Clay to his room at the *Larkspur* and Mrs. Kingston indeed took up the duty of seeing that he took in some warm broth, Julia walked Vicar Phelps to the door.

"I hope you aren't still blaming yourself," she told him as he buttoned his coat. "Why, he acts as if it's all been a lark."

The vicar smiled and looked up at her. "He does have a certain resilience about him."

"And your friendship has been good for him."

"Actually, it's been good for both of us," he said, taking his gloves from his pockets. "I hadn't realized how lacking my life had become in close friendships until Mr. Clay came along." He cocked his head thoughtfully. "It's strange how one always thinks of children needing friends, but I don't suppose we ever outgrow that need."

Julia thought of Fiona and felt a pang. "I believe you're right. I still find myself talking to Miss O'Shea, the former housekeeper here."

"I'm sorry. You must miss her terribly."

"Well, as you said, vicar, we never outgrow that need."

As Andrew allowed Rusty to pull the trap back to the vicarage, he thought back to the brief conversation at the *Larkspur*'s door. He was aware, from sharing conversation with Mr. Clay, that his friend sorely missed Miss O'Shea. Andrew had not lived in Gresham long enough before the housekeeper's leaving to realize how close she and Mrs. Hollis had been.

I wonder why she didn't mention her husband? he thought. No matter how deep a friendship she shared with Miss O'Shea, surely her recently departed husband would be foremost in her mind.

Perhaps the pain is too fresh to speak of him, he thought, and mumbled, "I could barely speak of you for years, Kathleen."

Rusty quickened his pace at the sight of the turnoff to the vicarage lane. Holding the reins more tightly, Andrew was again overcome with shame for the affection he felt for Julia Hollis. Not because of Kathleen, for she had been a practical woman and would have been distressed at the thought of his spending the rest of his days alone, just as he would have wanted her to marry again had she outlived him. But that he'd allowed himself fanciful daydreams about a woman still mourning her husband seemed a self-serving act—like carrion moving in immediately after a relationship had died.

At least she doesn't seem to know how I feel about her, he thought, sighing. And who knew what the future held? Perhaps one day, as the years passed by, Mrs. Hollis would feel some affection for him. They did get along very well. Wasn't that how Kathleen's and his love had developed, from a mutual comfort in each other's company?

But you've been without a wife long enough, and our daughters long enough without a mother, he could almost hear Kathleen say. "What am I to do? Sweep her off her feet?" he argued to no one's ears but Rusty's. The horse merely stood in the harness outside of the stable and snorted his impatience to be at his oats.

391

Feeling sheepish now for having said such intimate thoughts aloud, he climbed down from the trap and waved a greeting at Luke, who was thankfully out of earshot and coming in his direction from the back of the vicarage.

"Did you have a good drive, vicar?" Luke asked.

Andrew gave him a wistful smile. "It was an eventful one."

———————

"And does it hurt terribly, Mr. Clay?" Mrs. Dearing asked at the supper table.

Aware that all eyes were upon him, Mr. Clay played up to his audience. "Only when I laugh, Mrs. Dearing. So I must ask that you refrain yourself from saying anything even remotely amusing within my hearing."

"Really?" asked Grace, her eyes wide.

Julia smiled with the others at her question. Even though the children were expected to be silent at the table, the young girl understood a lapse when the occasion warranted. And it wasn't every day that someone came to the table sporting a bandaged forehead.

Mr. Clay smiled, too, from his place three chairs away. "Actually, Miss Grace, it hurts the same whether I laugh or cry. But not so much as to justify my carrying on about it. Why don't you tell us what you learned in school today?"

After receiving a permissive nod from her mother, Grace described the old hornet's nest that Miss Hillock showed to the class. Everyone seemed interested except for Philip, who paid scant attention to his supper plate as well.

Is he thinking about his father again? Julia wondered. When she could catch his eye, she smiled and raised her eyebrows questioningly. He gave her back a half-hearted smile that must have required some effort. Not wishing to draw embarrassing attention to him, Julia wondered if she should take him aside privately after the meal and see what was the matter.

But as it turned out, it was Philip who sought her out as she was coming out of her bedroom after exchanging her short Balmoral boots for some comfortable suede slippers. "I've done something horrible," he said, his expression grim.

———————

"Ouch! Mrs. Kingston! Have some pity!" Ambrose exclaimed

from his chair as the bandage was pulled from his wound.

"Now, now, Mr. Clay," she clucked, leaning over him with Mrs. Beemish at her side. "Just a little dried blood sticking to it. Mrs. Rhodes gave implicit instructions that the bandage was to be changed before you retire for the night."

"But it's *hours* before bedtime."

"Not before *mine*. With all the excitement I neglected my afternoon nap today. If you expect me to stay up and greet the sun as is your custom—"

"Greet the sun, Mrs. Kingston?" He flinched away from the wet flannel she'd pressed against his skin. "Ouch! What is that!"

"Just a little soap and water. I must say, Mr. Clay, you're being rather childish about this." She exchanged a knowing look with the woman at her elbow. "I daresay there wouldn't be a dozen people left on earth if men bore the children, eh, Mrs. Beemish?"

The housekeeper covered a grin with her hand, and before Ambrose could respond to the insults regarding his maturity and tolerance for pain, a knock sounded at the door. Mrs. Beemish walked over to allow Mrs. Hollis into the room.

"You're just in time to rescue me, Mrs. Hollis," Ambrose told her.

"She must have heard your bloodcurdling screams," Mrs. Kingston muttered while winding a fresh bandage around his head.

Mrs. Hollis smiled at the exchange but seemed preoccupied in her manner. "I'm sure Mrs. Kingston is a capable nurse." When the task was finished, she said to the two women, "May I speak with Mr. Clay privately?"

Julia walked Mrs. Kingston and the housekeeper to the door, then turned back to face him. Mr. Clay stared back at her with a mixture of curiosity and anxiety in his expression.

"What is wrong, Mrs. Hollis?" the actor asked. His eyes dropped to the envelope in her hand. "This isn't about Fiona . . . Miss O'Shea . . . ?"

"She's quite all right, Mr. Clay. May I sit?"

He got to his feet and motioned to the second chair. "Please."

When they had both settled into chairs—Julia sitting back in hers, and Mr. Clay leaning forward—she took in a deep breath and wondered if the interfering she planned to do would come back to haunt her one day. *But it's too late to back out now.* "Mr. Clay, I've a letter from Fiona's sister in Ireland."

It seemed that he raised his eyebrows, for the bandage moved up a bit. "Her sister?"

"Her name is Breanna." Julia stretched out her arm to hand over the envelope. "Here, see for yourself. It arrived in Gresham about six months ago, but Philip misplaced it."

She thought about the tears that had come to her son's eyes as he made his confession. It had been a long time since she'd seen him cry. And though she'd had to scold him—not as much for the thoughtless misplacement of the letter as for the plan he had almost carried out to conceal his mistake—she now felt pride in him for having had the courage to approach her with the truth. The fact that he could be so torn up over his own near deception gave her great hope that he would not follow in his father's footsteps.

There was a rustling of paper as Mr. Clay opened up the page. When he'd finished reading the two lines, he looked up at her again. "Does this mean that Miss O'Shea has no idea that her husband is dead?"

"I believe that to be so. Breanna only writes about once a year. I plan to send this on to Fiona tomorrow with a letter asking her to return to us. I wonder if there is any message you would care to enclose?"

Mr. Clay appeared startled at her question. "Me? But I should think she would be too distraught about her husband—"

"There is something else you should know."

"Please . . . tell me."

Don't hate me for this, Fiona. "Her husband mistreated her, Mr. Clay. She did not love him. She ran away from him and came to England several years ago, yet she was too good a person to betray her marriage vows."

"He mistreated her?" Mr. Clay looked stricken, and a hand moved to his chest as if propelled by its own will. "But why?"

"Because some people are just content to be evil, Mr. Clay. I know I should be saddened over the loss of a life, but I must confess to a great relief for my dear friend's sake."

He stared absently into space for several seconds, until Julia said, "Mr. Clay?"

"Forgive me. I was just—" The actor stopped himself. "Mrs. Hollis, is it possible that I could hire Mr. Herrick to deliver me to Shrewsbury early in the morning?"

"To Shrews—?" Realization hit her then, and it was now Julia's hand that went to her heart. "Mr. Clay."

"Yes?"

"You *aren't* planning to go to London."

"I am indeed, Mrs. Hollis." He sprang from his chair and moved toward his wardrobe, rubbing his hands together. "Let's see . . . a valise should be enough. One extra set of clothes, my toiletries, and I can purchase other clothing if necessary."

"But—"

"One thing you can say for London, Mrs. Hollis. There are more than enough places where one can buy clothes."

"Please, Mr. Clay. You're acting . . ."

He stopped in the center of the floor and turned to her with a sad smile. "Irrational? Crazy?" Coming back over to her chair, he got down on one knee and took Julia's hand. "And you're afraid that when my present euphoria is dispelled by another dark mood—which will indeed happen—I'll regret any impulsive action I've undertaken."

"You have to consider that, Mr. Clay. Why don't you write to her first? Give this a little time. Perhaps she'll even give her notice in London and come back here."

Mr. Clay's slate gray eyes grew tender. "Because I have loved Fiona O'Shea for months, Mrs. Hollis, during dark times and good times. And I believe she feels the same for me."

London
March 16, 1870

"But if you were to *speak* to Mrs. Bryant, ma'am," Fiona said, following Mrs. Leighton down the staircase of the Kensington Road house the next afternoon.

"About what, may I ask?" her mistress replied. The click of heels upon marble did not slacken.

"Perhaps she would withdraw her notice if you'd only—"

At the bottom of the staircase, Mrs. Leighton turned around to flash a patronizing smile. "Beg her forgiveness? After she insulted me the way she did?"

Anger, an emotion she usually managed to keep in check, rose in Fiona's chest. Why was it that some people assumed it beneath them to grant common courtesy to those of lower stations in life? After the silver meat platter the cook was accused of stealing was discovered to have slipped behind a cupboard shelf, one would think an apology would be of paramount importance. "Mrs. Leighton," she said, keeping her voice as steady as possible, "she was accused wrongly."

"Well, that's no excuse to raise one's voice to one's betters." Mrs. Leighton turned and continued on toward the front door, straightening a glove on the way. "Besides, I'm rather weary of her habit of overcooking every dish. Send Charles to the agency with a note saying we would like to schedule some interviews for a new cook. Monday morning would be fine. And have Nellie tighten the button to this glove when I return. It'll keep for now, but you know what they say about a stitch in time."

An hour later, Fiona was in the dining room polishing the rosewood Windsor chairs. It was a tedious chore, and one she could have easily assigned to one of the maids, but she needed the physical activity to keep herself from brooding. As she worked, she smiled a little at the memory of having dispensed advice to Mr. Clay regarding the very same thing. What had he replied? *Do you think Mrs. Hyatt would teach me to do needlework?*

"Miss O'Shea?"

Fiona looked up from the seat of the chair she'd just polished to the maid standing near the foot of the table. She had been so deep in thought that she hadn't heard anyone coming through the door. "Yes, Sarah?"

"You've a visitor in the drawing room, a gentleman. Shall I finish dusting?"

"He must be from the domestic agency. That was fast." *But I suppose they're used to the routine by now*, she thought wryly. In reply to the maid's offer, she said, "Yes, thank you. I've done all but four."

The caller was standing at the fireplace and turned when Fiona came through the doorway. Her heart quickened at the sight of the familiar face, and her breath caught when she saw the bandage on his head. "Mr. Clay?" she said, barely daring to breathe.

"Miss O'Shea," he replied, his expression incomprehensible as he came across the room to her. For a second she feared he would attempt to embrace her—and that she would yield to his embrace—but thankfully he took her hand instead.

She could not take her eyes from the bandage. "You're hurt."

"A minor wound," he said reassuringly. Releasing her hand, he went over to the door and closed it. He came back to her and took her by the elbow. "Would you mind sitting down, Miss O'Shea?"

The solicitous way he was looking at her—as if she were fragile and might break at any moment—alarmed Fiona. She put a hand up to her chest. "Mrs. Hollis and the children . . ."

"Are fine." He motioned toward the nearest chair. "Please."

After she had allowed Mr. Clay to assist her in taking a seat, Fiona watched with a growing sense of foreboding as he got down on one knee beside the chair's arm. *If not the Hollises, then who?*

"I've a letter here from your sister." He took an envelope from his waistcoat pocket and held it. Regarding her somberly, he said, "I have to tell you that your husband died more than six months ago, Miss O'Shea."

When her breath came again, Fiona held out a shaking hand for the letter. "Please." She read her sister's brief message three times, then dropped the hand bearing the page to her lap and closed her eyes. Even after eight years she could easily picture his face in her mind—brutal and remorseless and, unless some miracle had occurred, still shaking his fist at God until the very moment of his death.

May God have mercy on his soul, she half prayed, echoing her sister's words, yet all the while knowing that it was too late to make that plea once a body has yielded up its spirit.

"The letter was in Philip's possession for all this time," Mr. Clay said softly.

Fiona opened her eyes again. He was staring at her with such solicitude in his gray eyes that the love she'd tried so hard to suppress came to the surface again. Which still brought tremendous guilt, for what sort of woman thinks of love for another man when holding such news in her hand?

"He'd forgotten that he had it. Are you going to be all right?"

"Aye, Mr. Clay," she whispered, collecting herself. "I just wish it could have been different."

"I know. But he chose his path, and you had nothing to do with that. *And*, I suspect, you could not have influenced him to change direction, even as good a person as you are."

"Thank you for saying that, sir."

"Fiona, may I come back tomorrow?" he asked abruptly.

It suddenly dawned upon her that "Fiona" had replaced the "Miss O'Shea" in his speech. Why was he here, she wondered, when the news could have been wired? Brought back sharply into her present situation, she sent an anxious glance toward the door. "I've already had my day off this week, Mr. Clay. And we aren't allowed callers. If Mrs. Leighton knew about your being here now—"

He caught up her hand and held it to his cheek. "Oh, Fiona," he said, his voice thick with emotion. "It grieves me to hear of anyone demeaning you so. I wanted to give you a day to absorb the news of your late husband . . . but would you think me terribly insensitive if I asked you to marry me now?"

"Marry you?" He could have spoken Greek, and her mind would have been just as muddled. "Mr. Clay, this is so—"

"Sudden?" He kissed the hand he held. "You've known how I've felt about you since the night you made me that awful hot chocolate. And please stop calling me Mr. Clay."

You're free now, Fiona realized, understanding fully the change that Breanna's letter had brought about. Custom dictated that at least a year should pass before she allow another man to say such endearing words to her, but in her mind the marriage had died a decade ago. *And I've already mourned.*

And she did know that Mr. Clay—*Ambrose*—loved her, but he was wrong about her being aware of his feelings the whole time. But what did that matter? Fiona found herself unable to contain a smile and reached out to touch his bandaged forehead. "Oh, Ambrose!"

She was lifted to her feet and into his arms. His kisses were as gentle as she had somehow known they would be, but after she had submitted and even returned what surely must have amounted to a score of them, she pushed him away slightly. "I must ask you . . ."

"Yes?"

She forced her voice to become serious now, in spite of the fact that he was smiling down at her as if he would kiss her again. "You told me once that you didn't feel you should father children."

After a second his face went pale. "Oh, Fiona. I didn't even think."

Aware of the reason for the fear in his expression, she shook her head. "I just want to be sure you haven't changed your mind. I'm unable to have children."

"You poor dear." Ambrose caught her up in his arms again. As she rested her head against his shoulder, he said into her hair, "I know you would have wanted them. But we'll make such a full life that you'll be happy, Fiona."

"I'm already happy," she murmured.

"May I ask what is going on?" A voice, knife-sharp and full of indignation, came from the doorway. Fiona gasped and jumped back from Ambrose's arms.

"Mrs. Leighton!"

Her mistress still wore her gloves and hat, the ferret eyes narrowed into slits. "So, Miss O'Shea! Your 'superior' morals make exceptions for stealing your employer's time?"

Fiona could feel her heart pounding in her throat. Before she could respond, Ambrose grinned and sauntered over to the door with arm outstretched. "So very good to make your acquaintance, Mrs. Leighton," he drawled. "I'm—"

Mrs. Leighton jerked her hand away as if his had held a viper. "*You* are obviously riffraff and will leave my house immediately, or I shall send for the police!"

"Ah, well, you see, I can't do that just right away. Miss O'Shea will need a minute to collect her belongings." Turning to Fiona, who watched the exchange with held breath, he said, "Is there any reason we can't be married right away, dearest? Surely we can find a minister with some time on his hands."

"You mean, today?"

"I know you'd prefer to marry in Gresham, and so would I, but we can go back there after the honeymoon. Would somewhere like Switzerland please you? I must confess I'm not partial to Paris or Florence."

It seemed that Mrs. Leighton was on the verge of succumbing to vapors then, for her face flushed an even deeper crimson, and sputtering noises erupted from her lips.

Fiona looked back to Ambrose. It was outrageous, the idea of marriage after a nonexistent courtship, but then, so had been the idea of taking a boat to England at the age of eighteen. *And he's no stranger. I know what lies before me.* There would be times when he would be strong for her, and others when he would need to draw from her strength. *With God sustaining both of us.* Smiling across at him, she breathed, "Yes, Ambrose."

His bandage shifted a bit, meaning he had raised his eyebrows in his characteristic manner. "Yes?"

"Yes."

"Well, there, you see?" Ambrose said to the sputtering woman at the door. "I can't very well offer to excuse myself from the premises just yet, for I fear you'll use the opportunity to say unpleasant things to my very-soon-to-be wife."

"I'll go at once." Fiona hurried toward the door, but Mrs. Leighton stepped aside to block her with both hands on her hips.

"And so you'll just dance out of here without giving notice, yes?"

Fiona flinched at the wrath in the voice. She felt a hand on her shoulder.

"I'm afraid that's so, madam," Ambrose said from her side with a theatrical "tsk" for emphasis. "Sharper than a serpent's tooth is a thankless housekeeper. Isn't that how the saying goes?"

"I've had just about enough of you!" Mrs. Leighton hissed, turning on him. But then a strange thing happened. Color drained from her face, and the ferret eyes widened with shock. "*King Lear?*" she gasped.

"Well, I confess to taking some liberties with it, but—"

A hand flew up to her throat. "Why . . . I've seen you on stage. You're Ambrose Clay!"

———

Gresham, being the size it was, had no telegraph wire leading to the village. Messages of an urgent nature were wired to Shrewsbury and then sent via post to the surrounding villages. This resulted in a delay of one to two days, but was still more speedy than the regular post.

So it was late on a Saturday morning, March nineteenth, that Julia was handed a wired message delivered by Mr. Jones:

MARRIED YESTERDAY STOP. LETTER TO FOLLOW STOP. TELL PHILIP NOT TO WORRY STOP. AMBROSE CLAY

After reading the message several times until her mind could absorb the full meaning of the words, Julia looked at the date it was sent. March seventeenth. *One day after he left here.* Which meant he had gone to Fiona immediately upon arriving in London. *And then married on the same day!*

The recent turn of events in her own life had given Julia the conviction that engagements should be lengthy, allowing both the man and woman time to learn as much as possible about each other. But she could fault neither of them for their actions. Fiona was no naive seventeen-year-old. She knew Mr. Clay's faults as well as anyone did, and as for Mr. Clay knowing hers . . .

Julia had to think for a minute on that one. *I suppose burning bacon could be considered a fault.* But in the grand collection of faults, that one very likely occupied a minor place. The only regret Julia had, and she was aware that it was a selfish one, was that Fiona would likely never come back to live at the *Larkspur.* Nor Mr. Clay, and the absence of both dear people was already leaving a void she knew would be difficult, if not impossible, to fill.

Though she planned to share the news, she decided that Philip should be the only person to see the actual wire, since it contained a message to him, and because he'd been so torn up with regret after finding the misplaced letter. To her surprise, he frowned miserably.

"But they would have been able to marry earlier if I'd only brought her the letter."

"But you can't go back and undo that," she told him, touching his shoulder and marveling at how tall he was growing. In the year since they had moved to Gresham, Philip had caught up with her in height. "And perhaps it was good that Mr. Clay and Fiona had some time away from each other."

"But will they ever come back?"

That, Julia could not answer. Mr. Clay had just recently paid for three month's lodging in advance, but at the time he had been unaware that he was poised at the threshold of matrimony. "We'll just have to see what the letter says," she told him.

Aleda and Grace took the news with starry-eyed wonder and begged to be allowed to spread the news to the rest of the household. Julia gave them permission, with the exception of Mrs. Kingston, whom she felt she should tell herself. The older woman sobbed effusively for the joy of it, and, Julia suspected, also because she would miss having Mr. Clay to mother.

She was leaving Mrs. Kingston's bedchamber when another face materialized in her mind, that of Vicar Phelps. It would not be fitting for him to discover the news by happenstance. She was halfway finished writing a note in her office asking the vicar to call at his earliest convenience, when she realized that would simply not do. If she had learned anything about life in a small village, it was that news spread rapidly.

Regretting now that she had so hastily allowed her daughters to spread the news, she gathered light wraps and bonnets and asked Aleda and Grace to accompany her to the vicarage. She also invited Philip out of courtesy, but he mumbled something about going fishing.

They met Vicar Phelps and Laurel strolling arm in arm in their direction down Church Lane. When Julia was close enough to see the incredulous smile across the vicar's face, she thought, *Why, he already knows!*

"You received a wire too?" she asked before even offering a greeting.

"We were just coming to inquire the same of you. I assumed that you had, of course, but just in case . . ."

Finally etiquette was remembered and "good mornings" were exchanged. Laurel's brown eyes shone with excitement. "We were going to explore the ruins on the Anwyl after we spoke with you." Turning to her father, she said, "We're still going, aren't we, Papa?"

"Indeed we are," he replied, but there was a brief hesitation before he added, "Would you three care to join us?"

"Oh, may we?" Aleda exclaimed right away, hanging on to Julia's arm, with Grace doing the same on the other side.

Now no longer obliged to guilt over telling the household about the wire before thinking of the vicar, she dutifully shouldered another load, because almost a year had passed since she'd hiked the Anwyl with any of her children.

Still another guilt was beginning to gnaw at her for even considering the invitation. Would it only encourage the vicar to pursue something deeper than friendship—if indeed she hadn't imagined his feelings toward her? *Do other women spend so much time feeling guilty?* she wondered.

"We wouldn't want to intrude on your outing," Julia protested, but only mildly because of the hope in both her daughter's faces.

But the vicar smiled and shook his head, causing Julia to wonder if she'd imagined the earlier hesitation. "Not at all. We would be happy to have your company."

"Please, Mother?" Grace pleaded, her green eyes hopeful.

"Please?" Laurel Phelps asked as well.

In the face of such longing there was nothing to do but agree. "It does sound lovely, thank you."

"And why don't we stop by the *Larkspur* and invite Philip?" said the vicar. "Elizabeth's on her way to Alveley with Mr. Treves for a Ladies' Benevolent Society luncheon, or she would be along as well."

Julia noticed that Laurel Phelps's face did not alter at this invitation. But she also caught a relaxing of the girl's posture upon learning that Philip already had plans. *I hope he's not acting rude toward her again,* Julia thought, determining to talk with him and find out. She was well aware that competition for the trophy had intensified with the approaching end of the school year, but that didn't allow him an excuse to be rude to Laurel or anyone else.

The trick to catching minnows for bait, Philip discovered, was to lie on his stomach in a shady spot on the bank where his reflection couldn't be seen in the water and submerge his shallow net halfway, keeping it as motionless as possible. One or two curious little fish would ultimately decide to inspect the inside of the net, and then speed was required to snap them up inside, for they could dart away in a millisecond.

"Hey, I saw your mother and sisters heading for the Anwyl with the vicar and Laurel," Ben said, doing the same as Philip just a few feet away. Jeremiah would not be joining them today because relatives from Grinshill were visiting the Tofts. Actually, the decision had been made by Philip and Ben upon learning that if Jeremiah came along, he would have to bring not only his brothers but also two or three younger cousins.

"I know," Philip said listlessly, and just the subtle motion of his speaking caused a trio of minnows to scatter from the mouth of his net. "I saw them."

Frowning, Ben set his jar aside and sat back on his heels. "Why don't you like the vicar?"

"I like him just fine. I just don't like his daughter."

"But you can't blame her for trying her best in school." He shrugged. "*I'd* have a go at that trophy if I wanted it, and I'm your best friend."

Intrigued by his friend's last statement, and realizing that minnowing was futile as long as the conversation ensued, Philip took his net out of the water and wrapped both arms around his folded legs. "You would?"

"Of course. You're name ain't engraved on it yet, you know."

"Then, why haven't you? You're just as bright as I am."

Ben grinned and gave a shrug of his shoulders. The shade muted the fiery red of his hair to almost the same auburn as Philip's. "Lazy, I suppose. I just can't see spending so much time studying. Or writing papers over and over."

"But winning the trophy would make all of that worth it," Philip said, idly stripping one of the young river grasses in two.

"Well, fine. I'm just saying that you shouldn't blame Laurel Phelps for wanting the same thing you want."

It was the voice of reason, but coming from his friend, it seemed closer to disloyalty. Philip threw his pieces of grass in the water. *First my mother and sisters go off with her, and now Ben takes up for her!* It gave him reason to dislike her all the more, though he kept it to himself and flopped back on his stomach to catch more minnows.

————

The Roman garrison that was now ruins atop the Anwyl had been

404

a minor one compared with other sites across Britain. Covering only about six acres, it still had good stretches of well-finished masonry standing in places up to ten feet high on all sides except the north. Through the south gate there passed what must have served as a drainage channel, now filled with dirt and weeds, and the walls of two guard rooms still stood on either side of the west gate. Its various niches and crannies made it marvelous for exploring, and the toppled sandstone rocks that besotted the ground were convenient spots to stop and rest.

It was on two such rocks, about three feet apart, that Vicar Phelps and Julia collected their breath. Behind them, the girls continued to walk among the ruins after receiving a stern warning from the vicar not to climb any walls. And spread out before them was the village of Gresham. A stiff northeastern breeze seemed determined to snatch their hats from their heads. Julia had had to retie the ribbons under her neck twice, while the vicar, whose hat had no ribbons attached, had given up and tucked it under his arm.

"Can you picture the Roman soldiers who walked upon this very spot?" the vicar asked in a thoughtful tone. "We imagine them as hardy and robust, but some were terribly young. How many, do you think, looked out toward the southeast and longed for families back at home?"

Julia looked at him with a bit of awe, mixed with appreciation that he hadn't brought up the subject of Mr. Clay and Fiona. As happy as she was for them, she did not want to think about the fact that Fiona would probably never move back to Gresham. Perhaps he was feeling the same way about Mr. Clay. "Why, that never would have occurred to me, Vicar. But I'm sure homesickness is universal."

He smiled. "That's for certain. What was your very first impression of Gresham, may I ask?"

My village, she thought, staring out at the cottages and hedged pastures. Little over a year ago, she had pledged that Gresham would be home one day. What a blessing to have that actually come to pass. Now she could not imagine living anywhere else. "I found it charming and yet a little intimidating. I had never lived in the country before, you see."

"Nor I. So my reaction was the same as yours—charmed but yet intimidated."

A familiar gray slate roof with six chimneys caught Julia's eye. "And the *Larkspur* was the most intimidating sight of all."

"Yes?" He looked over his shoulder briefly to make sure the girls were not climbing on the crumbling walls, then turned back to her. "I can't imagine it ever looking unattractive."

"It sat abandoned for eight years before we arrived here." She described, then, the spider webs and moss-covered walls and overgrown garden. "The children wanted to turn back around and return to London. The thought occurred to me as well."

"And yet you had the tenacity to stay and persevere."

The compliment made her uncomfortable, because he was assuming she had some choice in the matter of leaving or staying. While she didn't care to bring up her husband's failings, it seemed dishonest to allow him to think it was sheer perseverance that caused her to turn the *Larkspur* into a home.

She cleared her throat. "Vicar, we had no choice but to stay. It was all we had."

"Truly?"

"That, and some money lent to me by my former butler."

"I'm sorry. I had no idea. Of course I took for granted that your husband's death had devastated your family, but I didn't realize it caused financial hardship as well."

Those past hurts had healed long ago, she'd thought. So why did the sympathy in his hazel eyes give her so much comfort? "God has provided, Vicar," she said simply. "More than I even deserve."

"You deserve . . ." he began, but then self-consciousness invaded his expression and he stopped himself. "I should see about the girls again. They're being a bit *too* quiet."

"I'll go with you," she said, allowing him to help her to her feet. They discovered the reason for the girls silence—they had apparently worn themselves out and were sprawled on their stomachs across the top of a flat boulder. But Laurel's energy was miraculously recovered at the sight of her father.

"Oh, please," she said, capturing his arm. "Play bear with us, Papa."

"Laurel . . ." He glanced at Julia quickly, but it was long enough for her to notice a certain pinkness above his blond beard.

"We haven't played it in *years and years*," the girl said dramatically.

"With good reason—you're too old." But his daughter persisted, and the vicar turned to Julia again with a resigned smile. "Mrs. Hollis, will you take charge of seeing that these little sprigs keep their eyes closed? Oh, and would you mind holding my hat?"

Julia took the bowler hat from him and smiled at the anticipation in all three young faces as Laurel explained the rules. "Is this similar to hide-and-seek?"

"Fairly similar. But at hide-and-seek, one doesn't get eaten by a bear." To the girls, he ordered, "Count to fifty now. And *slowly*."

While Julia watched the girls, Vicar Phelps made his way to the only archway still standing and stepped behind one of the posts. Soon the three girls finished counting, and first looking to Julia for permission, they began searching hesitantly behind rocks and walls. Eventually they happened upon the vicar, who raised up from his hiding place with a terrible roar and grabbed the first youngster in his path, who happened to be Grace. While she let out a mixture of squeals and giggles, the two others squealed and ran.

It didn't take long for Julia to grasp that the game was far too simple for even Grace's six years. There were no rules beyond hiding one's eyes and counting, and then came the search for the bear until someone was snatched. But they loved it and begged to play again and again until the vicar finally called a halt. *It's not the intricacies of the game they care about,* she realized. It was having Vicar Phelps pay them some attention.

If only my children had a father like him, she thought as they walked the gently sloping footpath down the hill, with the sun at its apex and the girls running a bit ahead of them. The notion occurred to her that it could happen. She didn't think she was mistaken about the vicar's affection for her. Perhaps one day he would ask . . .

Alarm snapped Julia out of her reverie, and she chided herself under her breath. *You would consider marrying a man you don't love just because he would make a fine father? Would that be fair to him? Why not draft up an advertisement and hire a husband as you would a gardener?*

"Mrs. Hollis?"

She looked at him, thankful that he could not hear her thoughts. "Yes, Vicar?"

"I know the game was a little silly. And not at all challenging to children their ages. I was surprised that Laurel wanted to play it after so many years."

"It was easy to see that they loved it," Julia said, smiling. "And I don't believe the simplicity of it really mattered. You made them laugh."

"Thank you for saying that, Mrs. Hollis," he said with an appreciative smile. "And for joining us today. You and your daughters made the outing much more pleasant."

Julia felt a subtle relaxing of her shoulders. She had not realized they were tensed. "We did?"

"Careful of that hole," he said, guiding her by the elbow around a deep rut in the path. He turned his face to her with puzzlement knitting his forehead. "Why did you sound so relieved just now, may I ask?"

"It's just that I noticed . . ." *Noticed what?* she asked herself. "Nothing, really. And we enjoyed the outing as well."

"Please tell me."

After a moment's hesitation, she said, "Perhaps I imagined it, but there seemed to be some reluctance on your part to invite us, Vicar. No doubt you felt obligated, having just announced that you and Laurel intended to—"

"Mrs. Hollis," the vicar cut in, and she felt a light touch on her sleeve.

"Yes?"

He gave her an affectionate smile. "Hush."

———

You weren't honest with her, Andrew's thoughts accused him later as Laurel and he sat down to a lunch of spiced beef and dumplings. Even though he hadn't overtly denied the hesitancy he'd felt about extending the invitation, he had allowed Mrs. Hollis to believe it was all in her imagination.

"That was great fun this morning, wasn't it?" Laurel asked while spreading butter on a slice of dark bread.

He smiled back at her. "Great fun."

Why don't you just come out and confess to her how you feel? he asked himself. Then he wouldn't have to be so anxious every minute he spent in her company. She would either reject his declaration of affection or accept it. Either way, he could give up the struggle to keep his feelings from showing in his face and in the tone of his voice.

But with second thoughts came reason. While he no longer believed that she would reject him because he wasn't an Adonis—for he had come to appreciate that she wasn't the shallow sort of person who focused on outward appearance—there was still the newness of her widowhood, the love she surely still felt for her late husband, to consider. She certainly didn't need another man's attentions at present. *Why do I have to keep reminding myself of that fact?* he chided himself.

––––––––

That evening, after Julia had tucked the children into their beds and had slipped into a nightgown, she sat at her dressing table in the lamplight and idly arranged the combs, lotions, and hairpins. *Why can't I love someone like Vicar Phelps, Father?* she prayed. *Am I only capable of loving men who are bad for me?* As she unnecessarily turned each hairpin so that the ends pointed in the same direction, she narrowed her prayer from "someone *like* Vicar Phelps" to "Why can't I feel any love for him? He's such a dear soul. There is plenty of affection, but . . ."

*S*even days later when the promised letter arrived—actually two letters counting the brief note included from Mr. Clay—Julia immediately carried them to the privacy of her room. She settled into her chair and picked up the first page of Fiona's precise handwriting:

My dear Mrs. Hollis,

Julia considered the greeting with a bemused smile. The "Mrs. Hollis" had become more and more unnatural to her ears as her relationship with Fiona grew deeper. But customs regarding servants and employers were set in stone, and so it would have seemed too radical for either of them to consider that it should be any other way. Now, however, it was time to put away the formalities. *If only I'm given the chance to tell her so,* Julia thought before turning her attention to the text of the letter.

> *As you can imagine, so much has occurred since my last letter. Ambrose and I were married at Saint Patrick's on the sixteenth, the day he arrived in London. No doubt your affection for both of us has caused you some misgivings over the haste of our actions, but you must put your fears to rest, my dear friend. I could not have imagined so much joy could be contained on this earth, and I pray daily that you will be blessed with the same happiness.*

"But I *am* happy, Fiona," Julia said, as if her friend were standing there before her, but then had to admit, *Just a little lonely.*

> *We had planned to honeymoon in Switzerland. Three days into our marriage, however, we were out making travel ar-*

rangements and purchasing extra clothing, and stopped for lunch at a French restaurant near Regent's Park, Montague's. As the hand of God would have it, we happened upon some acquaintances of Ambrose, a Mr. and Mrs. Bancroft, who manage the Prince of Wales theatre. They were in the process of assembling a cast for what they termed a "cup and saucer" comedy written by a Mr. T. W. Robertson, titled The Barrister. Three of Mr. Robertson's plays have been produced at the same theatre; in fact, School, which is now playing there, is enjoying tremendous success.

The Bancrofts were delighted to see Ambrose and invited us to share their table. Before the dessert course was served, Ambrose was offered the lead role in The Barrister! He turned them down politely, saying that we had plans for Switzerland, but I asked him to give their offer some prayerful consideration for a day or two. There was an unmistakable light in his eyes when the offer was made, Mrs. Hollis, and I could see that he longed to be upon the stage again. As for Switzerland, I assured him later that I would much rather see the Anwyl than the Alps.

We both took the matter in prayer, and Ambrose informed the Bancrofts yesterday that he would accept the role.

Though she was happy for her friends, Julia couldn't fight the melancholia that worked its way through her. *They'll have to live in London permanently,* she thought.

Rehearsals begin in three weeks, so we must busy ourselves with locating and furnishing a flat. Ambrose is determined I should perform no domestic chores whatsoever, but I have convinced him that I should feel like a visitor in our home if it is overrun with servants. We have agreed upon a cook and parlormaid, and must conduct interviews for both, as well. How strange it is, the thought of a former servant having servants to attend her!

"And if I know you at all, Fiona," Julia mumbled, "You'll treat them like gold."

The Barrister is scheduled to begin its run in early August, but there will be a two-week interlude between the end of rehearsals and the first performance. The Bancrofts feel that it revives an actor's enthusiasm for his role if he is able to slip

411

*away from it for a space of time. And, my dear Mrs. Hollis,
we would like to spend that time in Gresham.*

Thank you, Father! Julia prayed silently.

The remainder of Fiona's letter contained greetings to the children, lodgers, and servants. After reading it with much lifted spirits, Julia went on to Mr. Clay's letter. His began with the same greetings, as well as his appreciation to her for having sent him to London. *But I didn't send you; in fact, I tried to talk you out of going!* Julia thought with a smile and shake of the head. She read on:

> *I am to be involved in the theatre again, thanks to the thoughtfulness of my dear wife. Although I realize it will be a struggle during the times of despondency, I cannot help but feel the burden will be lighter with Fiona at my side and Christ in my heart. And I have a plan, my dear Mrs. Hollis, that will hopefully give us a life more normal than was my parents'.*
>
> *I am interested in the set of rooms over your stables. Would it be possible to have them refurbished, at my expense of course, as a second home for us? We will pay whatever board you ask, for knowing that a peaceful place of escape is available to us will lessen dramatically the pressures of living in London. Fiona and I have prayed over the matter and feel that I should take a recess for several months every time a role is finished, before taking on a new one.*

He went on to apologize for abandoning his room without notice, giving her permission to find a new lodger to take his place.

> *If the apartment above the stables is incomplete by late July, we'll rent a room at the Bow and Fiddle for our first visit,* he wrote. *So please do not feel pressured to hurry, my friend.*

Oh, it'll be ready, Julia thought on her way out of her room to find Karl Herrick.

One week into April, Gresham was a tapestry woven from the fresh green of new grasses and leaves, the yellow of wild daffodils, the begonia's fiery red, pink and white anemones, blue lungwort, and lavender ladies' smocks.

For the first time since he could recall, Philip actually paid attention to his surroundings as he walked to school with his sisters. Why not appreciate such a beautiful day, when in his hands he carried the most meticulously detailed diorama that would ever be seen in Captain Powell's classroom. He couldn't believe he had ever grumbled last week when the headmaster assigned the project to the sixth standard students—it had actually turned out to be fun.

He had crafted the shadow box, with Mr. Herrick's guidance, from scraps of oak provided by Mr. Jack Preston and Garland Worthy, the two carpenters working on the apartment above the stables. Settling on a theme had been his hardest chore, for he was allowed to illustrate any scene from a favorite book. It was Mr. Durwin who had brought up *Moby Dick*. At first Philip had politely rejected the suggestion, figuring a water scene and white whale too ambitious a concept. But then the idea grew upon him—the more difficult the project, the less likely anyone else in the sixth standard would create a similar one.

For at least the tenth time since setting out from the *Larkspur*, he gazed admiringly down at the box in his hands. To make sure he didn't drop it, he'd asked Grace to carry his lunch pail, and Aleda his books. If one squinted one's eyes, the fine blue netting from *Trumbles* looked just like a churning sea. He had carved the white whale from a bar of soap, pasted together match sticks to make a ship, and the sails were quilting squares Mrs. Beemish had provided. Captain Ahab was the most difficult task, but Mrs. Herrick had shown him how to mold and dry bread dough heavily mixed with salt, then clothe him with scraps of cloth. A sewing needle made a particularly lethal-looking harpoon. Mrs. Dearing had warned him that red paint would not adhere to the soap whale for blood, so tiny droplets of red felt were attached with pins.

"I wish I could have made one," Grace said from his side. Philip turned his face to her and smiled.

"You will when you're my age."

"But that's so long to wait."

"Then I'll help you make one this summer." The way her eyes lit up added to his feeling of well-being, and he found himself asking Aleda if she would like to join them on the project. "It could be even larger than this one. Perhaps we could divide it into four sections and make scenes from a fairy tale, like Jack and the beanstalk."

"Perhaps," Aleda said with just a little less enthusiasm, but still she smiled back at him. "Don't forget I'll be assigned one next year."

"Well, there, you see? If you begin it this summer, you'll have all year to make it as good as possible. Why, even better than this one, and that's saying a lot."

"I wonder what Laurel's will be like?" his sister remarked.

There was no maliciousness in her words, but they seemed to carry an unspoken implication—*we won't truly know if yours is the best until we see hers.* And he wouldn't put it past her to have portrayed something like the guillotine scene from *A Tale of Two Cities,* complete with a screaming mob. Tightening his lips, Philip thought, *I wish I could go to school one day without having to see that face!*

Helen Johnson met them at the side of the schoolyard. Philip held his shadow box tighter in anticipation of the cuff she would give him before running away squealing. But it was to Aleda that the baker's daughter gave her attention. "Have you heard about Laurel Phelps?" she asked in a breathless voice.

———

A broken leg! Philip thought miserably, all euphoria about his diorama crumbled to dust. As the news had been on everyone's lips in the school yard that morning, it had not taken long for him to hear the whole story. Last night she had gone into the cellar of the vicarage to look for some linseed oil to rub on the outer wood of her shadow box, and on her way back up the stairs, the tin had slipped from her hand, causing her to lose her balance.

I didn't mean I wanted something bad to happen to her! he thought over and over during morning prayer and Scripture recital. And when Captain Powell asked for a volunteer to deliver Laurel Phelps school assignments to her, he slipped up a hand.

———

After asking his sisters to tell his mother he would be late, Philip accompanied the five chattering Burrell children to the vicarage; Mark, Jacob, and Anna from the upper standards, and Nora and Peter from Miss Hillock's classroom. He had expected Ben and Jeremiah to rib him after school for the errand he had taken on, but they had been strangely silent about the matter, which made Philip feel worse. Had the words he'd spouted concerning Laurel Phelps been so hateful that everyone expected penance from him now?

I didn't mean any of it, he told himself and God one more time while shifting Laurel's books to his other arm. Perhaps if he thought it long and hard enough, both would believe him.

Dora Healy, a housemaid Philip recognized from church, let everyone in the vestibule as if she had been expecting them, which of course was true concerning the Burrell children. There was a bustle of activity as Miss Phelps brought the two smallest children out to them, handed them over, and passed out raisin biscuits. When they were gone and he still stood in the vestibule, the vicar's older daughter seemed to notice him for the first time.

"Why, Philip Hollis, good afternoon."

"Good afternoon, Miss Phelps." He nodded down to the books in his arms. "I brought Laurel's assignment. How is she?"

"She'll be fine. But why don't you come see for yourself?"

Philip felt a bit of panic. He had halfway hoped to hand the books over to whoever would happen to answer the door. But there was the matter of relaying the assignments, and he *had* raised his hand.

He had assumed that Laurel would be upstairs in bed, but he was led to the parlor, where she sat propped sideways on a sofa. Her dress covered both legs, but he could see part of a splint above her right foot, which was encased in a felt slipper. The vicar sat nearby, and both looked up from books when he entered the room.

"Laurel, Papa, Philip Hollis brought over some books from school," Miss Phelps said with a hand on his shoulder. Philip stretched his lips into what he hoped to be a smile and waited for the admonitions that were sure to come, but the vicar got up from his chair and approached him with an outstretched hand. "Good day to you, Mr. Hollis. How thoughtful of you!"

"Thank you, sir." In the face of such a welcome, it seemed easier to stand there and talk with the vicar than to think of approaching Laurel with humble pie, so while his hand was being pumped he added, "Captain Powell says there's no hurry to finish these assignments. And he and Mrs. Powell would like to call this evening after supper."

"Very good."

There seemed nothing more to say except good afternoon, but then he remembered his manners. "Uh, and how is Laurel feeling?"

His ears grew hot when he noticed the amused glance the vicar and Miss Phelps exchanged. "Why don't you have a seat and you can ask her yourself?" the vicar said.

"Oh . . . thank you, sir." He dared a glance over to Laurel's face

415

again as he was led to a chair. While she studied him curiously, he could detect no trace of hostility in her expression.

"How are you?" he managed.

Laurel frowned, but at her leg, not at him. "I'm already tired of having to sit. And Dr. Rhodes says it's going to be six weeks!"

Philip grimaced. "Does it hurt?"

"Only a little." She looked up at him again. "Have you ever broken a bone?"

"No, never." That sounded a little like one-upmanship to his ears, so he softened the denial with, "But I shouldn't be surprised if I did. Living in Gresham is rough on bones."

The vicar gave a short chuckle in the chair across from him. "It is at that, isn't it?" Though he hadn't meant his statement to be humorous, Philip found himself joining in the smile. Dora came back into the room then and served glasses of lemonade, and the vicar read a short article to them from a periodical called *Nature, the Weekly Illustrated Journal of Science*, about the massive destruction of fruit orchards in New England by gypsy moths, which had been accidentally introduced into the United States. Later, he was admiring Laurel's shadow box—the Ghost of Christmas Past approaching a bed curtain; admirable, but not nearly as nice as his—when the chiming of a cabinet clock informed him that he had been there a whole hour.

He was surprised when, after he had bade them farewell, Vicar Phelps rose from his chair and accompanied him to the front gate.

"How are your mother and sisters?" he asked casually.

"Fine, sir." It struck Philip, then, that aside from a couple of brief visits in the hall with the lodgers, the vicar hadn't been spending time at the *Larkspur* and hadn't accompanied his mother anywhere since their outing on the Anwyl. Perhaps he was busy or had even lost interest in Mother. The thought should have brought him comfort, but he found that it made him feel a little sad.

The next afternoon he determined he would stay only long enough to give Laurel the day's assignment, wish everyone good-day, and leave. He had gone the second and even third mile yesterday—probably more than enough to make up for the harsh things he'd said and thought about her. Any more visits like yesterday, and she would assume they were friends, and that just couldn't be.

But he didn't count on the Phelps having a table set up in the parlor, waiting for him to join them in a game of *Whist*. "I'm staying home to be with Laurel every afternoon this week," the vicar said, as

416

if he felt a need to explain why he wasn't out making calls.

Just half an hour, Philip told himself while listening to Miss Phelps explain the rules of the game. *Not a minute longer.* But that was before he realized four people were absolutely necessary to play. It seemed rather rude to call a halt to everyone's fun by leaving early. And afterward, Laurel asked him to describe his shadow box. He was a guest in her home, and there she was with a broken leg. What could he do but oblige her?

The vicar resumed his calls the second week and there were no more games of *Whist.* It occurred to Philip, then, that he was explaining Laurel Phelps's daily assignments to her, then going home and working on his own. Wouldn't it be a more efficient use of time for them to study together? Not for one second had he given up his intent to win the top student trophy, but he wanted to win it fairly and not have to wonder if it was because she was unable to compete at school.

"This is very kind of you," Laurel told him one day during the third week after they had checked each other's answers for a mathematics assignment. "I'm sure you'd rather be with your friends."

Philip shrugged but found her gratitude rather touching. He almost liked her then. "We still get to do things on Saturdays. Fish and play cricket and such."

"You do?" Her brown eyes brightened, and the dimples appeared in her cheeks. "I caught two bream in early April. I even baited my own hook."

"You like to fish?"

"I always wanted to in Cambridge, but my grandmother said it wasn't a proper activity for a young lady. Papa says we'll fish again when my leg is healed." She gave him a conspiratorial grin. "We didn't mention the bream when we wrote to Grandmother, though."

He was almost sorry, six weeks later, when the splints were removed. Not sorry that she could *walk,* he had to remind himself. But sorry they would have to go back to being enemies during the three remaining weeks of school.

Yet when she smiled at him from across the schoolroom her first day back, he found himself smiling back. Having an enemy hadn't been all that fun, after all.

*M*r. Randall Ellis arrived at the *Larkspur* in late May to take Mr. Clay's old room. He was a courtly looking older gentleman with the tall, slightly stooped frame and graying beard that one would naturally assume someone in his field of study to possess. Commissioned by the British Archaeological Association to conduct some excavations amidst the ruins on the *Anwyl,* he would be staying in Gresham for at least two years.

"Would you possibly have room for my assistant, Mr. Pitney?" he asked Julia over cups of tea in the library. "I would like to send for him as soon as possible."

"I'm sorry," she had to tell him. "But I won't have another room free until two of my lodgers marry in September." Mr. Durwin and Mrs. Hyatt had decided they would like to stay on at the *Larkspur* after a honeymoon trip to Scotland. "Perhaps Mr. Pitney could room at the *Bow and Fiddle* until then?"

"Yes, I'm sure that will do," the man smiled. "It's just so much more convenient to stay in the same place so we can record our notes together in the evenings. You won't mind his coming over to do that, will you?"

"Of course not." An idea occurred to Julia then. *Jensen's room?* While the butler's last letter had stated a desire to move to Gresham upon his retirement, Julia knew that he still had a few years to go. After thinking the matter over while refilling Mr. Ellis's cup, she said, "You know, I'm saving a room for a friend. But I doubt very much if he'll come to claim it any time before September."

"Are you offering it to Mr. Pitney?" the man asked with a hopeful lift of the brow.

"With the understanding that should my friend appear, Mr. Pitney would have to move to the *Bow and Fiddle* until the other room is free in September."

Mr. Ellis nodded, clearly relieved. "Thank you, Mrs. Hollis. I shall write to him at once."

Out of idle curiosity, she asked, "What is his given name?"

"It's Jacob."

"Jacob Pitney?" Julia wondered why the name sounded so familiar. She knew very little about archaeology and couldn't recall ever meeting an archaeologist before Mr. Ellis's arrival today. And then it occurred to her. To the man across from her, she said, "Would you happen to know if Mr. Pitney is ever called Jake?"

Mr. Ellis tilted his head thoughtfully. "Why, I believe I've heard his sister address him as such. You know how young people are about pet names."

"Yes." Julia smiled. "And I've no doubt Mr. Pitney will feel right at home here."

"Life is full of changes, all right," Mrs. Kingston said to Philip, who had his arms draped over the front gate and was watching her prune an azalea bush. The hammering and sawing noises had finally ceased over the stables, but the mid-June day had its own sounds. Mrs. Kingston's pruning shears clicked to an irregular cadence, a baker's dozen of birds trilled and sang in a nearby elm, children made playtime noises on the green, and from across the Bryce came the sounds of approaching carriage wheels and hoofbeats.

"Even when you're old like me," she went on with another snap of the shears. "I used to fear change, but now I've learned it can be rather exciting."

"Like your winning the blue ribbon?"

She stopped and smiled, absently scratching her chin with the tip of her shears. "Exactly like winning that blue ribbon. And of course you should know how that felt."

Philip knew she was referring to his "top student" trophy. While he had been very happy to be presented with the award in the town hall last week, his joy was mingled with sympathy for Laurel Phelps, who had desired the trophy just as much. She had been quite decent about congratulating him after the ceremony. He doubted if he would have been able to show such good sportsmanship had *she* won, and his opinion of her went up another notch.

Now Mrs. Kingston had moved over to her prized *Rosa Allea,* and she leaned down to drink in the fragrance of one of the flowers. *She'd* had no misgivings about accepting her award. Framed with oak and matted with ivory satin, the blue ribbon now occupied a place of honor on a wall in the hall, next to Mrs. Hyatt's and Mrs. Dearing's *Noah's Ark* needlepoint.

The sound of carriage wheels grew much louder, and Philip turned to see the squire's barouche approaching, pulled by two black horses. His attention was drawn to the elderly passenger, who was glaring at him with so much venom that Philip could only stare back open-mouthed. His eyes grew almost as wide as his mouth when Squire Bartley called out to his driver. "Stop at once, Charles!"

"Will you be gettin' out here, sir?" the servant asked after the carriage had come to a halt. But the squire ignored him.

"You, there!" he shouted to Philip.

Fighting the urge to turn and flee, Philip took three hesitant steps toward the barouche. "Sir?"

"Have you no respect for your betters?" the man snapped, leaning over the side of his carriage.

"Sir?" Philip repeated.

"Your cap, young man! It would seem that simple courtesy would—"

Suddenly the gate swung open and Mrs. Kingston stalked toward the barouche with blue eyes blazing and the pair of pruning shears clasped at her side like a saber. "It's not enough that half the village is terrified of you!" she said in a scathing tone. "But you now feel compelled to vent your spleen at a little boy?"

"I'm fourteen," Philip reminded her, but she would not release the squire long enough from her steel gaze to correct herself.

"If you are any kind of gentleman," she went on, "you will apologize to him this very minute!"

"Now see here—" the squire began indignantly, but she silenced him with a look, stepping so close to the carriage that their faces were only inches apart.

"I don't know how someone like you manages to sleep at night. But I pity your miserable old soul."

His face crimson, Squire Bartley opened and closed his mouth several times, like a trout on land. When he finally did speak, it was to mumble, "I beg your pardon."

Philip could not have been more surprised had one of the horses turned its head to speak the same words.

But the apology did not satisfy Mrs. Kingston, for she snapped, "It's the young man you've offended, not me."

Philip held his breath as the squire looked at him again and cleared his throat. "I beg your pardon."

"Yes, sir . . . thank you, sir," Philip responded awkwardly, undecided now between excusing himself or waiting to see if Mrs. Kingston would lecture him further. He opted to stay, just in case he should miss something. It would be great fun repeating the whole scene to Ben and Jeremiah. But instead of lecturing, Mrs. Kingston looked up at the squire with an expression bordering on admiration.

"Why, that took some courage, Squire. I take back everything I said about you."

"That's quite all right," the elderly man sighed. "It *was* wrong of me to scold the lad."

"Well, now. Everyone has a bad day. I've been known to burn a few ears myself."

The squire didn't seem surprised at this. His bushy eyebrows raised. "Mrs. . . . *Kingston*, is it?"

"Octavia Kingston. And I suppose you've another name besides squire?"

"Thurmond." He shrugged a little self-consciously. "Passed down from my great-grandfather."

"It's a good strong name."

"Why, thank you." Squire Bartley looked out toward the *Larkspur*'s garden, then back at the Mrs. Kingston's stalwart face. After some hesitation he said, "I wonder if I might . . ."

"You wish to see the rose bush, Squire?"

"Please, if I may. And then, perhaps you would care to tour the garden at the manor?"

Mrs. Kingston lifted the pruning shears still in her hand and seemed to consider them thoughtfully. "I've still quite a bit to do." Then a mischievous glint came into her blue eyes. "But I've a whole year, haven't I?"

I tell you, Mrs. Hollis, it just ain't fair," Mr. Trumble said to Julia while gathering merchandise to fill her order on the last day of June. "Those archaeology fellows bein' allowed to dig up the ground up there. Why, my marble collection will be worthless!"

"Perhaps Mr. Ellis and Mr. Pitney would be interested in seeing them," Julia suggested. "Most of what they find will be displayed in the British Museum."

"Yes?" After considering that for a second or two, the shopkeeper smiled behind his long mustache. "I wouldn't even mind given' them to 'em if they would agree to put my name on a little card. Then my family could go and look at it sometimes. For posterior, you know."

Posterity, Julia corrected silently. "I don't know why they should mind putting your name on a card, Mr. Trumble. I've seen donor cards in the museum."

The bell to the door tingled, and Philip, Jeremiah, and Ben walked through it. "Oh, hello, Mother," Philip said. "Hello, Mr. Trumble." His two companions gave greetings as well.

"Hello, boys," Julia returned. "Did you catch any fish?"

"We haven't gone yet, Mrs. Hollis," Ben replied. "We've been playing marbles."

"We decided to save the fishing for after lunch," Philip added.

"Ah . . . fishing," Mr. Trumble said dreamily. He leaned his elbows on the counter. "You'd best not say that too loud. I can just see all the bream and perch in the Bryce quacking with fear."

Julia dared not meet Philip's eyes, for she was having difficulty restraining her own smile over the idea of fish carrying on like ducks. Deciding a change of subject was in order, she said to the boys, "Mr. Trumble was just considering donating his collection of marbles to the British Museum."

"You mean you aren't going to sell them?" Jeremiah asked, voicing the surprise written across all three young faces.

"Not if they'll allow my name on a card."

"Speaking of marbles . . ." Philip dug something from his trousers' pocket. Opening his palm, he proudly displayed a large marble, called a *taw*, of polished white agate. "I won it off Nate Casper today."

Julia felt a sudden increase in the temperature inside the shop as a lump as big as the marble centered itself in her chest. "You . . . *won* it?"

"Why, yes, Mother." He seemed not to notice anything amiss in her expression. "It took some doing. Nate's about the best, even if he's only in fourth standard."

There was a chorus of agreement from Ben and Jeremiah, and words of congratulations from Mr. Trumble, but Julia paid them no mind. Watching her son standing there holding out a marble, she imagined a taller, older figure holding out a note-of-hand. And that was when the horror on her face must have shown, for the boys and Mr. Trumble became suddenly quiet.

"Mother?" Philip said, his blue eyes uncertain.

She forced calm into a voice that was on the verge of screeching like a fishwife. "I'm so disappointed in you, Philip. You will return it to Nate Casper today. And I never want to hear of your gambling again. Ever."

He blinked at her. "*Gambling?*"

"You did not buy that marble, and the boy didn't give it to you of his own free will."

"But everyone does it. And he could have won one from me just as—"

"Right away, Philip!" she cut in, then turned on her heel and left them gaping behind her. *I embarrassed him*, she thought as she walked home, but that was the least of her worries. *Maybe this was how his father got started. Marbles one day, money the next!*

As she neared the *Larkspur*, pulse still pounding in her throat, she was faced with two dilemmas. Mrs. Kingston was in the front garden, as usual. And at the back, there were the Worthy sisters to consider. Her heart sank. As dear as all three women were to her, she was in no mood to carry on polite conversation.

And yet she felt a great need to talk over what had just happened with someone who would listen and could help her see what she should do next. *Oh, Father . . . if only Fiona were here,* she prayed silently. But it was not Fiona's face that came into her mind next.

Julia paused at the crossroads and looked off to the east, down Church Lane. *I've practically ignored him lately. How can I go crying on his shoulder now?* But she could think of no other person in Gresham who could provide the comfort she so desperately needed at the moment.

She was barely able to keep her voice from shaking as she greeted the Burrell children coming from the opposite direction, the two oldest carrying little Molly and David on their shoulders. *Will some of them turn out like their father?* she wondered sadly. *Is weakness of character an inherited trait? And has Philip passed down the same to his son?*

Dora answered the vicarage door. "I'm sorry, ma'am, but the vicar ain't back just yet. Would you care to come inside?"

"Yes . . . no." Julia blew out a long breath. "I'm sorry, Dora. May I wait in the garden?"

"Why, of course, Mrs. Hollis."

She had just settled herself in one of the wicker chairs when Elizabeth came rushing out of the house. "Mrs. Hollis, what's wrong?"

The concern in her young face was almost enough to cause Julia to lose the rest of her composure. Still, she managed a weak smile. "I just need to speak with your father."

"Certainly. But I don't think you want to sit out here alone." Before Julia could protest, Elizabeth seated herself in another chair. Thankfully, she seemed to understand that Julia was in no mood for small talk. Laurel stuck her head out of the door just long enough to receive a shake of the head from her sister. Dora brought tea soon after that and then left them alone.

Presently the gate squeaked and there was the vicar. The tea and Elizabeth's company had calmed Julia down enough to exchange greetings. If he was surprised to see her, he didn't show it, but his brow furrowed thoughtfully when his daughter excused herself right away and went into the house.

"Mrs. Hollis?" His hazel eyes studied her face as he took her hand. "I gather this isn't a social call."

Julia shook her head. "I'm in need of some counsel, Vicar. Have you time?"

"But of course. Why don't we go to my study?"

She looked around and saw Luke Smith unharnessing the trap

from the horse, Mr. Sykes picking up fallen limbs in the churchyard, and to the north, Mr. Durwin and Mrs. Hyatt ambling along the riverbank. Sitting out in a front garden was an open invitation for interruptions, and besides, she didn't think she could speak of the things that were burdening her in so public a place. "Yes, please."

The study Vicar Phelps led her to seemed to fit his personality exactly, from the shelves filled with books to the rowing paddle attached to a wall. He took the chair from behind his desk and put it near the one in which she was seated. "Now," he said, giving her a reassuring smile as he took his seat. "Why don't you tell me how I can help you?"

She sighed. "It's Philip. He won a marble during a match with another boy, and it appears that this wasn't the first time."

"Yes?" The vicar nodded thoughtfully. "Did you speak with him about it?"

The scene at *Trumbles* restaged itself in her mind. "I'm afraid I humiliated him in front of his friends. But I was so frightened and angry that I just didn't think. And I ordered him to return the marble—I suppose he's done that by now."

"I'm sure he has. He's a fine lad, you know."

"Yes, he is," Julia agreed, grateful to him for reminding her. "And so protective of his sisters and me. I accused him of gambling, but now that I've had time to think about it, I doubt if he realized that's what he was doing."

"That's very likely the case. You know, I played marbles for keeps when I was his age as well."

"You did? You mean, you don't believe it's wrong?"

Now a smile curved under his hazel eyes. "Ministers are accused of believing everything is sinful. Everything enjoyable, that is. But actually, I don't approve of it, because it's still a simple form of gambling. And if a child becomes accustomed to winning something for nothing, it could lead to gambling with money when he's older."

Now the tears that Julia had held in rein for the past hour clouded her eyes, causing Vicar Phelps to get to his feet and begin a panicked search through his pockets for a handkerchief. He finally located one in his coat. "Now, now," he said, awkwardly patting her shoulder as he stood beside her. "It seems to me that if you'll just apologize for embarrassing him in front of his friends, and tell him not to play for keeps anymore—"

"Oh, Vicar," she sniffed into the handkerchief. "There's so much more to it than that!"

"There is?" He allowed her to weep for several minutes, still patting her shoulder. When she had finally regained her composure, she wiped her eyes again and looked up at him.

"I'm all right now."

"Are you quite sure?" He nodded toward the door. "Shall I get another handkerchief?"

"No, thank you."

"Would you care to tell me the rest, Mrs. Hollis?" he asked gently, taking his chair again.

Julia needed no further prompting. She had admitted her husband's underhanded behavior to only one other person, Fiona, over a year ago. But as she poured out her heart to the vicar, the humiliation of having to reveal this dark family secret gave way to relief, the relief of allowing someone who obviously cared about her to help shoulder the burden. When she was finished, Vicar Phelps immediately nodded understanding.

"You're afraid Philip will follow in his father's footsteps?"

She closed her eyes. "Yes."

There was a long silence, and when Julia opened her eyes again he was studying the fingers he had steepled over his crossed knee. She appreciated that he had not jumped in with an answer right away. When he raised his eyes and saw that she was looking at him, he smiled. "Tell me . . . was your late husband's father a gambler, Mrs. Hollis?"

"He passed away when my husband was an infant. But no, from what his uncle George said from time to time, Mr. Hollis was a decent man."

"What about his grandfather?"

"No."

"I see." He was quiet again for several seconds. "And are your children aware that their father gambled?"

"Not at all. *I* wasn't even aware of it until three weeks after his death."

Vicar Phelps leaned forward, resting his elbows on his knees. "I'm not a prophet, Mrs. Hollis. But I don't believe you have to worry about Philip. He strikes me as having a strong conscience."

She recalled how grieved he'd felt after opening Fiona's letter, and even the relief he'd displayed when finally confronted about his part in the ghost prank. And then his being so solicitous of Laurel Phelps after she broke her leg. "He has a good heart, Vicar. He forgets it sometimes."

"They all forget sometimes. Even we do. But as we discussed a minute ago, this wasn't an act of willful disobedience on his part. Don't you think he would obey you if you forbade his playing for keeps from now on? Explaining the reason why, of course."

"I believe he would." Anxiety quickened Julia's heartbeat. "You aren't advising that I tell him the truth about his father, are you?"

"Why, not at all, Mrs. Hollis," he replied right away, then shook his head for emphasis. "Perhaps you'll have to do so one day when he's grown, but for now, allow the boy to keep his illusions."

"I'm afraid the illusions are few, Vicar. My husband had little time for his children."

"Then it's all the more important that they aren't destroyed," he said gently.

"Yes." They sat wrapped in silence for a while longer, and then Julia became conscious of the time. Ten past five, according to the clock on the wall. She rose to her feet, and he did the same. "They'll wonder where I am."

"Won't you stay for supper? I could ask Luke to deliver a note to the *Larkspur*."

"Thank you, but I should go speak with Philip now."

"Yes, of course," he nodded, then offered his elbow. "But I do insist upon driving you home, Mrs. Hollis."

"Thank you." Finally Julia could muster a genuine smile. "For everything, Vicar. You're a good friend."

His kind eyes crinkled at the corners. "And so are you, Mrs. Hollis."

————

Philip was in his room when Julia arrived back at the *Larkspur*. He sat at his study table, idly moving a knight from square to square on his chessboard, and looked up at her with a masked expression. It was the trembling of his bottom lip that gave him away. She went over to him, leaned down, and wrapped her arms around his shoulders. "I'm so sorry, Philip. It was wrong of me to humiliate you that way. Please let me tell you how proud I am that you're my son."

————

Much later, after she had said her personal prayers and had turned

427

in for the night, she thought about how sweet was the restored fellowship with her son. While she was at the vicar's, he had not only returned the taw to the Casper boy, but returned to another boy marbles he'd won from him. *Just like Zaccheus,* she thought, smiling to herself in the darkness. *Thank you, Father,* she prayed again. *And thank you for Vicar Phelps's wise counsel.*

"He is such a dear man," she said aloud. *Did I remember to thank him?*

And then a question cropped up into her mind from seemingly nowhere. Was love something that suddenly swooped down upon a person, like a cold? She mulled that over for a moment. *It did in my case with Philip. But I know now that was only infatuation.*

What if love wasn't a mysterious "thing" that capriciously attached itself to whomever it willed? Could it be instead a deliberate choice of action? Jesus had commanded His followers to "love one another." Would He give such a commandment if people had no control over their ability to love?

And does that mean that romantic love between a man and woman can be cultivated, just as Mrs. Kingston cultivates her roses?

She recalled standing at a window facing the Anwyl and determining that, like Saint Paul, she would learn contentment. If contentment could be achieved through an act of will, then why couldn't love? And it would seem that a love purposely cultivated for a man because of his kind nature and comforting ways would eventually grow stronger and deeper than one based on mere physical attraction.

Julia pondered those questions and notions deep into the night. When she awoke the next morning, she expected her mind to be muddled from lack of sleep. Instead, she found that a strange clarity had sharpened her thoughts. She felt like a schoolgirl—one who has finally comprehended long division. Her steps were light all the way down the hall toward the kitchen as a joyful giddiness, a feeling she'd been convinced would never be felt again, surged through her.

———

Vicar Phelps called that afternoon just after lunch, when Philip and his friends were off accompanying Mr. Ellis on a look-see atop the Anwyl, and Aleda and Grace played in the stables with Buff's now grown kittens. Julia had somehow known since waking that the vicar would come sometime today. That was not the reason, she told herself as she walked up the corridor to greet him in the hall, that she was wearing her most flattering gown, a sea green silk with a ruffled bodice. Nor was it why she styled her hair in the latest American fashion that had looked so becoming on Elizabeth, clasping the sides at the crown of her head with a comb while the rest hung behind her back.

And the knowing smiles of Mrs. Beemish, Mrs. Dearing, and Miss Rawlins had nothing to do with his asking to speak with her privately after he had exchanged pleasantries with the three. Still, Julia avoided their eyes as she turned to lead him to the library.

When the door closed behind them and they had seated themselves in adjacent chairs, he spoke as she knew he would. While his face seemed tranquil enough, there was unmistakable tension in his voice. "How is Philip?" he asked first.

"Fine," she replied. "I do so appreciate your counsel. We had a long talk last night."

"I'm so glad."

Julia noticed then that he was knotting his fingers together, as Elizabeth was prone to do when nervous. *After all he's done for you, at least you could put him at ease,* she told herself. "Vicar?"

"Yes?" he said, straightening in his chair.

She smiled. "I shan't bite, you know."

The same stunned look he'd worn the time she told him to hush flashed across his face, followed by a smile and the easing of his posture. "Thank you, Mrs. Hollis."

"You're welcome, Vicar."

"I wonder if I might speak with you of a personal matter?"

"Yes, of course."

She could hear him draw in a long breath. "I believe you're aware of the deep affection I have for you, Mrs. Hollis."

"Yes, I am."

"If I may be so bold to ask . . . how do you feel about me?"

Measuring her words with care, Julia replied, "Next to my children, you're the dearest person in Gresham to me."

"I am?" There was an incongruous mixture of disappointment and hope across his kind face as he took another breath. "Mrs. Hollis . . . I'm well aware that I'm not every woman's idea of a perfect man. But do you think you might possibly *learn* to love me one day?"

"I have already begun to love you," she said quietly, firmly. She could not have imagined, even yesterday, that her feelings for him could deepen in so short an amount of time, but she was learning that once a decision is planted firmly in the mind, all the steps fall into place quite rapidly.

He stared at her, seemingly unable to believe his ears. "Does that mean—" he cleared his throat and shifted in his chair—"that you would consider being my wife, Mrs. Hollis?"

"I have already considered it, Vicar. In fact, I thought of little else last night."

The astonishment in his expression deepened. "Truly?"

"I would be honored to be your wife."

"Why, yes, that's . . ." Suddenly a smile spread across his bearded face. "You cannot imagine how amazed I am. And how delighted." Leaning forward, he took one of her hands gently in his own. "I will treat your children as my own, Mrs. Hollis, just as I know you will mother my daughters. And you . . . I will cherish. And I'll never allow a day to pass without thanking God for you."

His image became a little blurred as his words found their way into her heart. *I don't deserve such adoration, but I thank you for it, Father.* "I know that, Vicar." But then she held up her other hand, lest he get carried away and start making arrangements for the ceremony.

"I only have one request." She thought for a second. "Two, actually."

"Anything!" he grinned. "You've made me the happiest man alive."

"The engagement should be long. Several months, at least . . . perhaps even a year."

"*That* long?"

"We have daughters, Vicar. And I don't know how yours reacted to our dear friends', the Clays, rush into marriage, but mine consider it to be much more romantic than any fairy tale. I believe we should set an example for their sakes."

His broad shoulders sagged a little with disappointment, but then he gave a reluctant nod. "You're right, of course. I wouldn't want Elizabeth getting caught up in the excitement and deciding to marry her curate, when I'm not totally sure of her commitment to him."

"Thank you for understanding."

"Oh, well," he sighed. "Reason must prevail. I believe you said you have two requests."

"Yes. It would also seem reasonable, since you're going to begin courting me, that you should kiss me now."

Complete surprise altered his face. "Why . . . you're an astonishing woman, Mrs. Hollis!"

"Does that mean you'd rather not kiss me?"

"It most certainly does not mean that!" He grinned and got to his feet, then took both of her hands and helped her to stand. His kiss was slow, thoughtful, and left her feeling just a bit light-headed as she took a step back with her hands still in his.

"That was rather nice," she smiled. *And it's been a long time.*

His eyes crinkled at the corners. "Why not another, Mrs. Hollis?"

"Now, Vicar Phelps," she teased. "We've a whole year."

"A whole year," he sighed again.

They sat for a while longer—Julia in her chair and the vicar seated on its arm—perfectly content in each other's presence. They conversed quietly about many things—their children, the future, and anything else that came to mind.

"You know," he said after a period of comfortable silence had lapsed, "Napoleon Bonaparte once offered Madame Merieult a castle in exchange for her long red hair. He wanted to have it made into a wig to present to a Turkish sultan."

Turning her head to look at him, Julia asked, "Well, did she?"

He touched a loose strand of her auburn hair. "Would you?"

"If my family were desperate, I suppose I would have no other choice."

"Well, Madame Merieult was wealthy. So, in fact, she turned down the emperor's request."

Julia found herself a little relieved. "How do you know this?"

"It's just something I read from a history book recently. I thought of you right away and was glad to learn that she kept her beautiful hair."

"Why, Vicar," Julia said, smiling. "You're quite the romantic soul, aren't you?"

He appeared to blush a little above his beard but returned her smile tenderly. "I'm afraid so. Do you mind?"

"Not at all. And I suppose that means you wish to kiss me again."

His eyes sparkled as he leaned toward her. "I'm not the only romantic soul in this room, Mrs. Hollis." When they had kissed, a little longer this time, he said, "You know, Christmas weddings are quite lovely. Wouldn't seven months be enough time, considering the fact that I've been practically courting you since we first met?"

Suddenly a year *did* seem like a long time to Julia. "Very well," she replied.

Raising an eyebrow, he said, "Truly?"

"Truly."

"Do you think we could go find the children and tell them?"

It was so typically *him* to think of such a thing. As they walked together through the courtyard and toward the stables, Julia recalled how bleak her future and that of her children had seemed such a short time ago. *But you brought us through that valley, Father*. There would be other valleys, she knew instinctively, for life was not lived on a continuous plateau. And perhaps it was better that way—in spite of the pain they'd endured—for the mountaintop now seemed all the sweeter.